PRAISE FOR *THE END OF OCTOBER*:

'A page-turner that has the earmarks of an instant bestseller'
New York Post

'This timely literary page-turner shows Wright is on a par
with the best writers in the genre' *Publishers Weekly*

'A maniacal page-turner. [A] sweeping, authoritative,
and genuinely intelligent thriller' *New York Times*

WHAT READERS ARE SAYING:

'If you have a desire to really understand what is
going on in the world right now, this is a novel that
you cannot afford to miss!'

'Well-written and fast-paced. Most of all utterly,
scarily, believable'

'I HAVE LEARNED SO MUCH, and actually much of
what I learned has informed my understanding of our
current coronavirus pandemic'

'Very well written and researched, and an all-round
fascinating story'

'Almost a prophecy of what was to come! The writer must
be a time traveller. A thrilling and fascinating read'

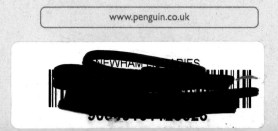

Lawrence Wright is a staff writer for *The New Yorker* and the author of ten books of nonfiction, including *In the New World*, *Remembering Satan*, *The Looming Tower*, *Going Clear*, *Thirteen Days in September*, *The Terror Years*, and *God Save Texas*, and one previous novel, *God's Favorite*. His books have received many prizes and honors, including a Pulitzer Prize for *The Looming Tower*. He is also a playwright and screenwriter, and he plays keyboard in the Austin-based blues band WhoDo. He and his wife are longtime residents of Austin, Texas.

THE END
OF
OCTOBER

Lawrence Wright

BLACK SWAN

TRANSWORLD PUBLISHERS
Penguin Random House, One Embassy Gardens,
8 Viaduct Gardens, London SW11 7BW
www.penguin.co.uk

Transworld is part of the Penguin Random House group of companies
whose addresses can be found at global.penguinrandomhouse.com

Originally published in the United States in 2020 by Alfred A. Knopf, a
division of Penguin Random House LLC
First published in Great Britain in 2020 by Bantam Press
an imprint of Transworld Publishers
Black Swan edition published 2020

A CIP catalogue record for this book
is available from the British Library.

ISBN
9781784165741

Designed by Cassandra J. Pappas
Typeset in 10.75/13.5 pt Sabon by Scribe, Philadelphia, Pennsylvania.
Printed and bound in Great Britain by Clays Ltd, Elcograf S.p.A.

*This book is offered as a tribute
to the courage and ingenuity of the men and women
who have dedicated their lives to the service
of public health.*

The contagion despised all medicine; death raged in every corner; and had it gone on as it did then, a few weeks more would have cleared the town of all, and everything that had a soul. Men everywhere began to despair; every heart failed them for fear; people were made desperate through the anguish of their souls, and the terrors of death sat in the very faces and countenances of the people.
– Daniel Defoe, *A Journal of the Plague Year*

'But what does it mean, the plague? It's life, that's all.'
– Albert Camus, *The Plague*

Contents

I. KONGOLI

1 Geneva   3
2 The Blue Lady   13
3 Fernbank   29
4 The West Wing   41
5 Quarantine   48
6 Henry Takes Charge   57
7 The Pilgrim   70
8 Salvador   75
9 Comet Ping Pong   80
10 Stoning the Devil   91
11 What Do We Have Here?   101
12 Jürgen   105
13 Something Big   114
14 Jesus Fucking Christ   128
15 In the Royal Court   135
16 The Question of Martyrs   144

II. PANDEMIC

17 The People Will Not Forgive   157
18 The Birds   165

ix

Contents

19 It's Not a Vaccine 179
20 We Treat Each Other 185
21 The Foaming 195
22 Queen Margaret 200
23 Lambaréné 209
24 Triple Play 214
25 Preserving the Leadership 224
26 The Human Trial 228
27 The Philadelphia Antiserum 233
28 Ice Cream 235
29 Grandma's Biscuits 246
30 What Would You Advise? 254

III. IN THE DEEP

31 Idaho 261
32 Something to Remember Me By 279
33 The War Zone 292
34 Snapdragons 301
35 All Life is Precious 309
36 Captain Dixon 315
37 Dolly Parton and John Wayne 324
38 Mrs Hernández 330
39 Satan is Loose in the World 334
40 Suez 340
41 The Finches 351
42 Into the Jungle 358
43 $34.27 364
44 Let Her Talk 370
45 Driving Lesson 375

Contents

46 Schubert   380
47 The Party Begins   387

IV. OCTOBER

48 Dolphins   395
49 The Graves   402
50 The Cosmos Club   413
51 A Farewell Kiss   417
52 Now It's in Us   424
53 The Ustinov Strain   431
54 Eden   443
55 October Revolution Island   452

    Acknowledgments   459

I

Kongoli

1

Geneva

IN A LARGE AUDITORIUM IN GENEVA, A PARLIAMENT OF HEALTH officials gathered for the final afternoon session on emergency infectious diseases. The audience was restless, worn out by the day-long meetings and worried about catching their flights. The terrorist attack in Rome had everyone on edge.

'An unusual cluster of adolescent fatalities in a refugee camp in Indonesia,' the next-to-last speaker of the conference was saying. Hans Somebody. Dutch. Tall, arrogant, well fed. An untrimmed fringe of gray-blond hair spilled over his collar, the lint on his shoulders sparkling in the projected light of the PowerPoint.

A map of Indonesia flashed on the screen. 'Forty-seven death certificates were issued in the first week of March at the Kongoli Number Two Camp in West Java.' Hans indicated the spot with his laser pointer, followed by slides of destitute refugees in horrible squalor. The world was awash in displaced people, millions pressed into hastily assembled camps and fenced off like prisoners, with inadequate rations and scarce medical facilities. Nothing surprising about an epidemic spilling out of such places. Cholera, diphtheria, dengue – the tropics were always cooking up something.

'High fever, bloody discharges, rapid transmission, extreme lethality. But what really distinguishes this cluster,' Hans said, as he posted a graph, 'is the median age of the victims. Usually, infections randomly span the generations, but here the fatalities spike in the age group expected to be the most vigorous portion of the population.'

In the large auditorium in Geneva, the parliament of health officials leaned forward to study the curious slide. Most mortal diseases kill off the very young and the very old, but instead of the usual U-shaped graph, this one resembled a crude W, with an average age of death of twenty-nine. 'Based on sketchy reports from the initial outbreak, we estimate the overall lethality at 70 percent,' Hans said.

'Pediatric or natal . . .?' Maria Savona, director of epidemiology at the World Health Organization, interrupted the puzzled silence.

'Largely accounted for in the reported cohort,' Hans replied.

'Possible sexual transmission?' a Japanese doctor asked.

'Unlikely,' said Hans. He was enjoying himself. Now his face drifted into the projection, casting a bulky shadow over the next slide. 'Reportable deaths stay consistent for the following weeks, but the overall total drops significantly.'

'A one-time event, in that case,' the Japanese woman concluded.

'With forty-seven bodies?' Hans said. 'Quite an orgy!'

The Japanese doctor blushed and covered her mouth as she giggled.

'Okay, Hans, you've kept us guessing long enough,' Maria said impatiently.

Hans looked around the room triumphantly. 'Shigella,' he said, to groans of disbelief. 'You would have got it but for the inverted mortality vector. That puzzled us as well. This is a common bacteria in poorer countries, the cause of innumerable cases of food poisoning. We queried the health authorities in Jakarta, and they concluded that, in a starving environment, the only people robust enough to seize the limited food resources are the young. In this case, strength proved to be their undoing. Our team deduced that the probable source of the pathogen was raw milk. We offer this as a cautionary tale about how demographic stereotypes can blind us to facts that would otherwise be obvious.'

Hans stepped down to perfunctory applause as Maria called the last presenter to the podium. 'Campylobacter in Wisconsin—' the man began.

Suddenly, a commanding voice interrupted. 'A raging hemorrhagic fever kills forty-seven people in a week and disappears without a trace?'

Two hundred heads turned to locate the source of that booming baritone. From the voice, you would have thought Henry Parsons was a big man. No. He was short and slight, bent by a childhood case of rickets that left him slightly deformed. His facial features and professorial voice seemed peculiarly outsized in such a modest figure, but he carried himself with the weight of a man who understood his value, despite his diminished appearance. Those who knew his legend spoke of him with a kind of amused awe, calling him *Herr Doktor* behind his back, or 'the little martinet'. He was capable of reducing interns to tears if they failed to prepare a sample correctly or missed a symptom that was, in fact, meaningful only to him, but it was Henry Parsons who led an international team in the Ebola virus disease outbreak in West Africa in 2014. He tracked down the first documented patient of the disease – the so-called index case – an eighteen-month-old boy from Guinea who had been infected by fruit bats. There were many such stories about him, and many more that could have been told, had he sought the credit. In the never-ending war on emerging diseases, Henry Parsons was not a small man; he was a giant.

Hans Somebody squinted and located Henry in the gloom of the upper tiers. 'Not so unusual, Dr Parsons, if you consider the environmental causation.'

'You used the word "transmission".'

Hans smiled, happy to resume the game. 'The Indonesian authorities at first suspected a viral agent.'

'What changed their minds?' Henry asked.

Maria had become intrigued. 'You are thinking Ebola?'

'In which case we'd see likely migration to urban centers,' Hans said. 'Not shown. All it took was to eliminate the source of contamination and the infection disappeared.'

'Did you actually go to the camp yourself?' Henry asked. 'Take samples?'

'The Indonesian authorities have been fully cooperative,' Hans said dismissively. 'There is a team from Médecins Sans Frontières in place now, and we will receive confirmation shortly. Don't expect surprises.'

Hans waited a moment, but Henry sat back, thoughtfully tapping a finger on his lips. The next presenter resumed. 'A slaughterhouse in Milwaukee,' he said, as a few conferees with an eye on the time ducked toward the exits. There was bound to be increased security at the airport.

———

'I hate when you do that,' Maria said, when they got to her office. It was glassy and stylish, with a fine view of Mont Blanc. A flock of storks, having hurdled the alpine barrier, circled for a landing beside Lake Geneva, their first stop on the spring migration from the Nile Valley.

'Do what?'

Maria leaned back and tapped her finger on her lips, imitating Henry's gesture.

'Is that a habit of mine?' he asked, leaning his cane against her desk.

'When I see you do it, I know I should be worried. What makes you doubt Hans's study?'

'Acute hemorrhagic fever. Very likely viral. Weird mortality distribution, totally inappropriate for shigella. And why did it suddenly—'

'Just stop? I don't know, Henry, you tell me. Indonesia again?'

'They hid the ball before.'

'It doesn't look like another meningitis outbreak.'

'Certainly not.' Despite himself, Henry involuntarily began tapping his lips again. Maria waited. 'I shouldn't tell you what to do,' he finally said. 'Maybe Hans is right.'

'But . . .?'

'The lethality. Stunning. The downside if he's wrong.'

Maria went to the window. Clouds were settling in, masking the majestic peak. She was about to speak when Henry interrupted her thought. 'I've got to go.'

'That's exactly what I was thinking.'

'I mean home.'

Maria nodded in that way that meant she had heard him, but the worried expression in her Italian eyes sent a different message. 'Give me two days. I know how much I'm asking. I should send a whole team, but I don't have anybody I can trust. Hans says MSF is there, so they can help. Just get slides and samples. In and out and on your way back to Atlanta.'

'Maria . . .'

'Please, Henry.'

In the manner of friends who have known each other a long time, Henry saw a flash of the worried young epidemiologist studying the African swine fever outbreak in Haiti. Maria had been part of the team that advocated the eradication of the indigenous pig that carried the disease. Nearly every family in Haiti kept pigs; in addition to being a major source of food, they functioned as currency, a bank for the peasantry. Within a year, thanks to the efforts of the international community and the dictator 'Baby Doc' Duvalier, the entire population of Creole pigs was extinct, a great success, almost unprecedented. The eradication stopped an incurable disease. But the peasants, already poor, were reduced to famine. The corrupt elite appropriated most of the replacement pigs the Americans provided, which were in any case too delicate for the environment and too expensive to feed. With no other resources, people turned to making charcoal, which denuded the forests. Haiti never recovered. It's debatable whether the hogs should have been slaughtered in the first place. We were such confident idealists back then, Henry thought.

'Two days, maximum,' he said. 'I promised Jill I'd be home for Teddy's birthday.'

'I'll have Rinaldo book you on the red-eye to Jakarta.' Maria assured him that she would call the Centers for

Disease Control and Prevention, in Atlanta, where Henry was deputy director for infectious diseases, and beg forgiveness; it was an emergency request on her part.

'By the way,' he said as he was leaving, 'any word from Rome? Your family is safe?'

'We don't know,' Maria said despairingly.

The Rome attack had been planned for Carnevale, the eight-day festival that takes place all over Italy before Lent. The Piazza del Popolo was packed for the costume parade and the famous dancing horses. The news that morning was filled with images of the torn carcasses of the beautiful animals, strewn among the dead celebrants and the rubble of the twin churches. 'Hundreds dead in Rome, the counting still going on,' the Fox host was saying. 'What's Italy's response going to be?'

The youthful prime minister was a nationalist, with his hair closely trimmed on the sides and long on top, the fashion for the neofascists taking over Europe. Predictably, he proposed mass expulsions of Muslims.

Jill Parsons switched off the TV when she heard the kids thundering downstairs, an argument already under way. They were bickering over whether Helen would be allowed to go to Legoland with Teddy and his friends. Helen wasn't even interested in Legos.

'Who wants waffles?' Jill asked cheerily. Neither child responded; they were still captivated by their pointless argument. Peepers, a rescue dog of mixed heritage, with black patches around his eyes like a panda, stirred from his corner and shambled over to referee the quarrel.

'It's *my* birthday,' Teddy said indignantly.

9

'I let you come to Six Flags on mine,' Helen replied.

'Mom, she stole my waffle!' Teddy wailed.

'I just took a bite.'

'You *touched* it!'

'Helen, eat your cereal,' Jill said mechanically.

'It's soggy.'

Helen coolly took another bite of Teddy's waffle. He shouted in outrage. Peepers barked in support. Jill sighed. The household always took a turn toward chaos when Henry was out of town. But just as she was rebuking him in her mind, her iPad buzzed, and there was Henry, calling on FaceTime.

'Did you read my mind?' she asked. 'I was telepathically summoning you.'

'I can't imagine why,' Henry said, hearing the argument and the barking in the background.

'I was going to cuss you out for not being here.'

'Let me talk to them.'

Immediately Teddy and Helen subsided into adorableness. It was a kind of magic trick, Jill thought, a spell that Henry cast over them. Peepers wagged his tail in adoration.

'Daddy, when are you coming home?' Teddy demanded.

'Tuesday night, very late,' Henry said.

'Mom said you'd be here tomorrow.'

'I thought I would, but my plans suddenly changed. But don't worry. I'll be back in time for your birthday.'

Teddy cheered, and Helen clapped her hands. It was impressive. Jill could never calm the waters like Henry. Maybe I'm too ironic, she thought. It must be Henry's total sincerity when he speaks to the children that subdues them. Somehow, they know they are safe. Jill felt that way, too.

'I made a robot,' Teddy reported, holding up the iPad to

display the conglomeration of plastic parts, electrical circuitry, and an old cell phone that he had put together for the science fair. The skeletal face had a pair of camera lenses for eyes. Jill thought it looked like a Day of the Dead doll.

'You did this by yourself?' said Henry.

Teddy nodded, his face radiant with pride.

'What do you call him?'

Teddy turned to the robot. 'Robot, what is your name?'

The robot's head tilted slightly. 'Master, my name is Albert,' he said. 'I belong to Teddy.'

'Holy smoke! That's amazing!' Henry said. 'He calls you "Master"?'

Teddy giggled and tucked his chin the way he did when he was really happy.

'My turn!' Helen said, grabbing the iPad.

'Hello, my beautiful girl,' said Henry. 'You must have a game today.'

Helen was on the sixth-grade girls' soccer team. 'They want me to play goalie,' she said.

'That's great, right?'

'It's boring. You just stand there. They only want me to do it because I'm tall.'

'But you get to be the hero every time you save a goal.'

'They all hate me if I don't.'

This was typical Helen, Jill thought. Where Teddy was sunny, Helen was dark. Pessimism oozed out of her, giving her an odd kind of power. Jill had observed that her classmates were a little fearful of her judgment. That quality, along with her fine features, made her an object of adoration among the girls and a troubling beacon to the pubescent boys.

'I heard the part about not coming home,' Jill said, when she had the chance to talk again. Henry looked tired. In the chiaroscuro of the iPad, he resembled a portrait of a nineteenth-century Austrian nobleman, with his penetrating gaze behind round spectacles. In the background she could hear flights being called.

'It's probably nothing, but it's one of those things,' Henry said.

'Where this time?'

'Indonesia.'

'Oh, Lord,' Jill said, letting the worry get ahead of her. 'Kids, finish up, the bus is coming.' Then to Henry: 'You haven't been sleeping, have you? I wish you would take some Ambien and just conk out properly for a night. Have you got some? You should take it as soon as you get on the plane.' She was annoyed that, for a doctor, Henry was so resistant to taking medications.

'I will sleep again when I feel you next to me,' he said, in one of those maddening endearments that would ring in her ears until he came home.

'Don't take chances,' Jill said pointlessly.

'I never do.'

2
The Blue Lady

FROM THE AIR, HENRY COULD SEE BLAZES IN SUMATRA. THE native forests and peatland were being torched to make way for more palm plantations. They supplied the oil used in about half the packaged products found in supermarkets, from peanut butter to lipstick. Each year, smog from the fires blanketed Southeast Asia, killing as many as a hundred thousand people in some seasons, and pushing global warming to a tipping point. As soon as Henry stepped outside the Jakarta airport and stood in the taxi queue, the heavy air scorched his nostrils. He looked at the masses of travelers coming and going and thought: Asthma, lung cancer, pulmonary disease, each inflicting its own cruel method of death. He had a professional habit of seeing pathology wherever he turned.

The monsoon season was under way. Black clouds were pregnant with rain, and the streets were swamped from the last downpour. Jakarta was a city of shantytowns, but also of skyscrapers sinking slowly into the earth. The booming population kept sucking water from the aquifer beneath their feet, causing the ground they lived on to collapse as the sea around them continually rose. It's a form of civic suicide, Henry thought.

'First time in Jakarta?' the driver asked.

Henry's mind was a long way off. The rain had begun again, and traffic had halted in a cacophony of frustration. A boy on a donkey cart piled ten feet high with chicken cages passed them on the sidewalk.

'I've been many times,' said Henry. Indonesia was a hot-house of diseases, a wonderful place for epidemiologists to practice their craft. The politics didn't help. At this very moment there was a measles outbreak, brought on in part by a fatwa against the vaccine. HIV was spreading more rap-idly here than in any other part of the world, which the government used to justify its persecution of homosexuals and transgender people.

The driver was portly and cheerful, sporting one of those round, brimless hats that Indonesian Muslims favor. A sprig of jasmine hung on the rearview mirror, its fragrance suf-fusing the stifling cab. Henry caught sight of the driver's reflection. He was wearing sunglasses, despite the rain, which was now pelting the windshield like bullets.

'You want a tour of old Java, boss?'

'I'm just here for the day.'

Traffic thinned a bit as they neared the Indonesian Min-istry of Health, but the rain did not relent. Henry saw clearly that he was going to be soaked before he got to the canopied entrance.

'Wait, boss, I help.' The driver opened the trunk and retrieved Henry's suitcase, then held an umbrella as he escorted Henry to the door. 'You come many times to Jakarta but you don't bring an umbrella in the monsoon,' the driver chided.

'I've learned my lesson this time.'

'You want me to wait?'

14

'I don't know how long this will take,' Henry said. 'Maybe an hour.'

'I am here for you, boss,' the driver said, handing Henry his card: 'Bambang Idris At Your Service.'

'*Terima kasih*, Bambang,' Henry said, exhausting his Indonesian vocabulary.

Three hours later, Henry was still seated in the ministry's antechamber with a dozen other somnolent petitioners. The tea boy looked at him expectantly, but Henry was fully caffeinated and his patience was at an end. Getting home was the only thing that mattered. He checked his reservation on his phone again. Still time to get to the camp and pick up the slides and then race to the airport. Just. Boarding for the midnight flight to Tokyo was in eight hours. If he missed that, he would miss Teddy's birthday. All because of some pointless bureaucratic one-upmanship.

The last time Henry had cooled his heels in this room was in 2006. There was a different health minister then, Siti Fadilah Supari, who refused to share samples for H5N1, an avian influenza virus with deadly potential. More than half of the six hundred humans infected from the birds, most of them in Indonesia, had died of the disease. If H5N1 had become transmissible across the human population, it could have swept the globe in a matter of weeks, with calamitous consequences. Epidemiologists across the world were on the edge of their seats, and yet Indonesia jealously clung to the microbes, arguing that the disease was a national resource, like gold or oil. Minister Siti called her new policy 'viral sovereignty.' Other countries, such as India, quickly latched on to the concept of owning patents on indigenous diseases.

Henry had been very much involved in the controversy. Withholding data was insane, he argued. Science knows no borders, nor does disease – especially a disease that can literally fly across international boundaries on the wings of a dove. Without the samples, the world community would be helpless to defend against a novel virus. The entire foundation of global health could be undermined. Indonesia made the case that other countries would exploit the virus to formulate vaccines that Indonesia could not afford. Henry worked out an agreement that would give Indonesia a 'shared benefit' from the scientific exploitation of the virus, although the pact stopped short of bowing to Indonesia's demand for unlimited access to the vaccines derived from the samples.

As soon as that deal was concluded, the argument became far more complicated. Ron Fouchier, at the Erasmus Medical Center in Rotterdam, modified the Indonesian virus in the laboratory, awarding it new functions, including the abilities to be airborne and transmissible among mammals. Yoshi-hiro Kawaoka, at the University of Wisconsin, did something similar with a Vietnamese strain of the same virus. The two men did this to create a template for a vaccine in case of a future pandemic, but as they were about to publish their findings, including their methodology, *The New York Times* scolded the scientists for undertaking such a 'doomsday' experiment. Such a virus 'could kill tens or hundreds of millions of people if it escaped confinement or was stolen by terrorists.' The U.S. National Science Advisory for Biosecurity put a stop to the experiment, but not before new questions had arisen about who 'owned' the newly created virus. The American and Dutch governments were repeating the same arguments that the Indonesians had previously made. Henry chaired a meeting of international health officials at WHO in 2012, in which they resolved that the Fouchier and Kawaoka papers be published without redactions, which they were. Knowledge was dangerous, Henry reasoned, but ignorance was far worse. The Indonesians accused Henry of deceiving them. The bad blood evidently remained.

Once again, the receptionist made her way to Henry, this time with a tight, condescending smile. 'Minister Annisa regrets that she cannot see you today,' she said under her breath, so that he might not be embarrassed in front of the remaining supplicants. 'She promises that tomorrow—'

'Too bad,' Henry said.

'Yes,' the receptionist said, caught off guard by the volume of Henry's voice, 'she feels very bad.'

'Too bad that I will have to implement an order of non-compliance. She can see me now, or she can deal with the international monitors tomorrow. It's entirely up to her. She's got till three p.m. to decide.'

The receptionist glanced at the clock. Three p.m. was forty-five seconds away. She hesitated, then rushed into the minister's office. Just as the second hand swept the top of the dial, the door opened again.

Minister Annisa Novanto was a cold-eyed apparatchik whose smile scarcely concealed the anxiety inside. Henry had first met her when she was a health officer in Bali, during a rabies epidemic. Her main interest then was in controlling the media rather than the disease. She did such an effective job that when Minister Siti was shuffled off to prison for accepting bribes, Annisa was appointed to take her post. She had recently taken the hijab, an indication of how far the country was drifting toward religious conservatism. She appeared to be just another compliant Wahhabi bureaucrat.

'Ah, Henry, you always surprise me,' the minister said. 'You might have given me more notice. We are very busy getting the pilgrims health certificates for the hajj. No need to summon the gendarmes.'

'This won't take long, Minister. I'm only here to inform you of my presence, as per protocol, and gather samples from this refugee camp in Kongoli. Then I'll be on my way.'

'Henry, really, this is such a minor matter. I'm stunned that Your Eminence would feel the need to come so far, at such expense—'

'I don't make policy, I just collect the data.'

'Already we gave slides to the Dutch. They made their conclusions. So we wonder why you come. We have no more problems in Kongoli.'

'That will be easy to determine. The isolates will tell us.'

'Isolates. Ah. Not necessary.'

The minister picked up a remote control and turned on the television. There was a Mexican soap opera, translated into Malay, but she wasn't paying attention. She turned up the volume until Henry could scarcely hear her voice. She indicated where listening devices were planted about the room. 'You put me in a difficult place,' she said. 'I must tell you something in confidence, so you will not need to pursue this.'

'I'm not going home without slides.'

The minister laughed soundlessly. 'It's funny, you see. They weren't at all ill.'

'They're dead.'

'Because we rounded them up and shot them!' she exclaimed. 'Revolutionaries. Insurgents. Undesirables. The camps are full of them. You Westerners have no understanding of what we have to deal with in this place. Of course we don't report such actions exactly. We offer other reasons. The coroner, maybe he makes a story. So, I am sorry you come such a long way to learn our little secret. Please, do me the favor of keeping it to yourself. You will place me in great jeopardy.'

If the minister was telling the truth about the cause of death among the detainees, it was doubtless true that she was placing herself in danger by confiding in Henry. Disloyalty was harshly punished. And yet.

'I still need to tour the camp,' he said.

Minister Annisa abruptly stood, her eyes afire. 'Out of the question! It's a security risk. The camp is run by armed gangs. They make a living on kidnapping. You cannot go in. Out of the question!'

'I'll take my chances.'

'It's not your decision!' she said. There was an edge of hysteria in her voice. 'Look, supposing the place is a pest-hole, what can we do with our meager resources? You make us a pariah. Tourists will not come. Why do we have to suffer for this?'

'Thank you, Minister, I will give you my report.'

'I forbid this!' she shouted, as Henry departed.

Bambang answered his cell right away. 'Yes, boss, I am here, still waiting. One minute, I am there.'

Henry stood under the awning. The rain had slacked off to a mild drizzle. Soon a three-wheeled motorcycle rickshaw puttered up. Bambang stepped out with his umbrella and a sheepish smile. The little vehicle was painted in exuberant colors that Henry might have described as cheerful, had it been less unwelcome.

'What happened to the Toyota?'

'My brother-in-law, he demand it back.' Bambang set Henry's bag in the tiny cabin. 'Much faster in traffic,' he said, a clenching argument.

Henry could feel his teeth grinding. It was going to be a very close thing. He hoped the French doctors were brisk and efficient and had the isolates already prepared. He had gotten the coordinates for the Kongoli camp from a satellite image, but Bambang already knew the location. 'It's for the gays,' he said.

'What do you mean?'

'The gay people, they put them there. Better for them, the authorities say. Otherwise, they are flogged, maybe they are hanged, some they drop from buildings. The extremists do this. So, the government hides them in these camps.'

'But everyone knows where they are?'

'Of course,' he said cheerfully.

They rode past flooded rice fields. The monsoon and the rising seas were drowning the country, water meeting from above and below, like a toilet flushing the land away. Five years from now, ten, twenty at best, the coastal areas would be submerged. This was normal now. Everybody accepted that disaster awaited.

Potholes. Buzzards on fence posts. A herd of water buffalo blocking the road, Bambang honking until the beasts laconically moved aside, an unmarked road, a gate, a guardhouse, Bambang turning into the road, a soldier hustling out, angrily shooing him away.

'They say no,' Bambang informed Henry.

Henry summoned as much authority as a man might when stepping out of a pink and green rickshaw with Hello Kitty emblems on the sides. He waved his credentials and an official letter from Maria. 'Health officer!' he said in his most imposing voice. 'See? World Health Organization. UN! UN!'

The guard retreated to his booth and made a phone call. Henry overheard puzzled shouts, and, in a moment, the guard stepped out and opened the gate.

The rickshaw passed tanks and military trucks and a small military cantonment arrayed around a water tower. Presently, it came to a high fence capped with coiled razor wire. Henry could see hundreds of people inside. In front of the impoundment was an overgrown parade ground. On the porch of a small cottage stood a slender officer with his hands on his hips. The man in charge.

'Sir, turn around,' the officer said. 'Off-limits here.'

'You don't understand,' Henry said reasonably. 'I am authorized to enter anywhere there is a health situation—'

'No your business. You turn around.'

Henry tried to hand the officer his credentials, along with Maria's letter, which had seemed so effective at the previous gate, but the officer turned around smartly and returned to the house.

Henry stood there, wondering what his next step should be. Only a few yards away, the detainees stared back at him, their faces filled with desperation and puzzlement as they awaited Henry's decision. It had begun to rain again, but nobody moved. He started to walk toward the encampment, but then he heard the sound of a bullet being chambered. A guard in a jeep nearby gestured with his gun to get back into the rickshaw.

A muezzin's cry announced the call to prayer, and at once the guards retreated and the detainees returned to the sprawling assemblage of tents and shacks and lean-tos, seeking a dry place to pray. Bambang got his prayer rug from under his seat and was about to spread it on the muddy parade ground when the slender officer appeared again on the porch and motioned him inside.

Henry sat in the rickshaw, confounded. There was nothing he could do. He had failed. Everyone else was praying. Maybe that's the last resort, he thought.

Presently, prayers were finished, and Bambang rushed back through the rain.

'Let's go to the airport,' Henry said. 'There's no reason to stay.'

'No, boss, is okay. We make a deal,' Bambang said, pointing at the officer on the porch.

'You gave him a bribe?'

'Not me. You.'

Henry silently cursed himself. It had never occurred to him that money alone might solve his problem. Bambang raced a wad of dollars to the officer, who took it inside, counted it, then emerged and nodded at the soldier in the jeep.

Bambang insisted on carrying the umbrella, saying it was part of the deal.

'Too dangerous,' Henry said.

'You are my responsibility!' Bambang replied proudly.

Henry had brought only one protective gown, but he gave Bambang two pairs of latex gloves (Henry insisted on

22

double-gloving) and a disposable mask to cover his mouth and nose, along with a warning not to touch anybody. The gate clanged shut behind them.

Danger is invariably present in the investigation of an unknown pathogen. Diseases may arise from many sources, including viruses, parasites, bacteria, fungi, amoebas, toxins, protozoa, and prions, and each has a strategy for survival. In addition to the multiple ways infection can spread, serious diseases can masquerade as something common and relatively harmless. Headaches may be a symptom of a sinus infection or a sign of an impending stroke. Fever, fatigue, and muscle aches can signal a cold or the onset of meningitis. Going into the field, alone, in an alien environment, with minimal resources, was the most perilous mission a disease detective such as Henry could undertake. On the other hand, the danger of an outbreak of virulent disease was great enough that Henry was willing to take the risk. He had long since recognized that luck was an unreliable but indispensable companion on such an adventure.

Henry and his driver were met by a delegation of young men, mostly in their twenties and thirties, with several teenagers among them. They were gaunt but not malnourished, and they had made an attempt to groom themselves despite their tattered clothes. Henry sensed a certain solidarity among them. Perhaps, having lived in the shadows for most of their lives, they had instinctively re-created their underground community.

One man approached Henry carrying a machete like a scepter. He had a gold stud in his nose and his hair was down to his shoulders. It had been dyed blond but it was growing out black. Henry did a quick calculation: three inches of

hair growth would equal approximately six months of in-
carceration.

'He wants to know if you are human rights,' Bambang
said, translating the man's remarks. 'He says they have been
demanding this but the authorities refuse to accept their
petition.'

'No, tell them I'm sorry. I'm just a doctor and—'

But the word caught fire as soon as it was out of his mouth.
'Doctor! Doctor!' the men cried. Some of them began to
weep and fall on their knees. It was clear from the clammy
faces and the dilated eyes that many were feverish.

'You are the first outsider in a long time,' Bambang said.

'Don't they have any medical assistance?'

Bambang asked the young man with the machete.

'French people, he says. They was here, but now all dead.'

'How many dead in the camp?'

'Many. No one buries them anymore. Everyone is too
frightened.'

One of the young men whispered something urgent to
Bambang.

'He says they have prayed for you, boss. They sees you at
the gate and they pray to Allah that you are a doctor who
come to save them. They says you answer their prayer.'

Henry knew how little he could do for them now. They
were inside a hot zone and everyone was contaminated.
He noticed a small backhoe in the back of the camp, apparently the only concession the authorities had made to the
epidemic – a way to swiftly dig trenches for mass graves.
Henry wondered where the gravedigger was.

The machete man led him through the muddy pathways,
Henry using his cane to steady his footing. Bambang walked

behind, holding the umbrella to little effect. The squalid camp had been thrown together whimsically, using cardboard and plastic bags and strips of canvas as building materials. Some of the roofs were tiled with crushed soda cans. A duck on a leash floated in a puddle beside a hut. Set apart from the hovels was a blue Médecins Sans Frontières tent, with the MSF symbol emblazoned on the side.

Henry cautiously pulled back the rain flap. The stench of death was nauseating.

'You go now,' Henry said.

Bambang's eyes were filled with horror by what he had seen, but he gamely stammered, 'I protect you.'

'No. I'm fine. But listen to me. Don't touch anything. Wash yourself, you understand? It will take some time for me to do my work. Wait for me outside.' He asked again, 'Do you understand? Don't touch anything!'

Bambang froze for a moment. Henry could see how frightened he was, and yet he offered the umbrella to Henry. 'You take it,' Henry ordered. 'Now go.'

Henry looked sternly at the men surrounding the tent, and they respectfully backed away, disappearing in the veil of rain.

Henry had long since grown accustomed to the perfume of decay. Most of the dozen beds in the infirmary were occupied by corpses. One patient tracked Henry with his eyes, too weak to do more. Henry glanced at the chart at the foot of his bed, and then put a fresh bag of glucose in the IV drip, the only useful thing he could do. The death rattle in his throat indicated that the patient would soon be quiet.

Three dead doctors lay in oddly contorted positions in the small clinic. They were like so many of the MSF people

Henry had met around the world – young, not long out of residency. Henry understood the courage it took to face an invisible enemy. Brave men and women who rushed into battle would flee from the onset of disease. Disease was more powerful than armies. Disease was more arbitrary than terrorism. Disease was crueler than human imagination. And yet young people like these doctors were willing to stand in the way of the most fatal force that nature has to offer.

But now they, too, were dead.

Henry lit a kerosene lantern, illuminating the face of a female doctor whose head was resting in a pool of dried blood on the examining table. Henry surmised that she was African or Haitian; many black doctors were enlisting in the medical corps. But then he realized that her face wasn't black. It was blue.

Henry had seen cyanosis before. It was normally caused by low oxygenation of the blood. Usually it manifested either in the lips and tongue or the fingers and toes. He had never seen anyone so completely blue. Cholera, he thought, the blue death. It made sense. Poor sanitation in the camp, God knows where the water came from. But anyone in the field knew how to treat cholera, and surely the doctors had been vaccinated. He glanced into a field cabinet, which contained a handful of elementary diagnostic equipment: a stethoscope, digital thermometers, bandages, a blood pressure cuff, a speculum, an otoscope set – the ready-to-go setup for a small nonsurgical team treating a localized infection for a week or so. The medicines were locked in a heavy box with a thick plexiglass door. Insulin, heparin, Lasix, albuterol, Cipro, Z-Paks, but mainly what Henry saw were antiretrovirals.

They were doctors, obviously, not laboratorians. They

had nothing to work with in the way of analytic equipment. Instead, there were posters and brochures about safe sexual practices. Apparently the team had intended to do a quick survey of the outbreak, treat as many HIV patients as possible with the antiretrovirals, and educate the detainees. They certainly hadn't packed for a long trip. There was a small pantry with cereal and a desiccated croissant. He glanced in the garbage, which had a number of discarded bottles of tetracycline. The doctors must have had the same thought, that it was cholera.

In a laptop on a bench behind him he found a folder of case histories by Dr Françoise Champey, presumably the young woman lying dead before him. Henry saw that she kept scrupulous patient records. There was also a lengthy unsent email, addressed to Luc Barré, chief of MSF in Paris. Henry's French was good enough to make it out. 'Luc, Luc, we need your help!' she began.

We are in a hot zone like you've never seen before! Already in one week we have dozens of infections in this pesthole. I sent you samples through the locals. Did you receive them? What are we dealing with here, we have no idea!

The lethality is extreme. We need equipment! We need pathologists! We cannot fight this, just three of us. Luc, I am frightened.

Below that, she wrote:

SHIT! Why can't this send? There is no internet, no phone, and I think they have made us prisoners.

After that, she must have kept the email open as an ongoing testament, ready to send at the first opportunity. Henry scrolled down to the last entry:

19 March, entering our third week. Pablo died yesterday.

My heart is breaking for his family, and when will they know that they lost him? Dear man. Antoine and I are both ill. We lie here beside our dead comrade. I feel so close to them. I have never loved anyone so much as these dead and dying men. I am thankful for this feeling, this intimacy. But I am also angry. We have been defeated by this monster, as I think of her. Yes, a monster. A creature we cannot see because we don't have the tools to peer into the cells, so she hides from us, laughing at us, and now killing us. Why did

The email ended there, its question unfinished, unsent, and unanswered.

3

Fernbank

EACH SPRING, WHEN SHE TAUGHT HER UNIT ON DINOSAURS, Jill took her kindergarten class on a field trip to Fernbank, Atlanta's natural history museum. The children were always wound up when they got off the bus, but the sight of an *Argentinosaurus,* the largest dinosaur ever classified, quickly subdued them. The five-year-olds looked like mice in comparison.

'He weighed over a hundred tons and measures more than a hundred and twenty feet long,' Jill explained. 'Can anybody guess how many school buses long that would be?'

'A hundred!' one of the boys shouted.

'Seventy-six!' another said.

'Three,' K'Neisha guessed, in little more than a whisper.

Jill cast an amused glance at K'Neisha's mother, Vicky, who was helping out on the field trip, one of the few parents she could count on when she needed extra hands. 'How did you know that?'

'I just figured that a bus is about forty feet long,' K'Neisha said.

K'Neisha wore a blue skirt, penny loafers, and a *Frozen* T-shirt. All of Jill's students were on free or reduced-price lunch, but it was easy to tell which ones, like K'Neisha, had family support. Jill tried not to have special pets, but she loved K'Neisha's smile and her shy intelligence. She was one of those children Jill wanted to know for the rest of her life, to see how she turned out.

'Look at *T. rex*!' a boy named Roberto said, pointing to the dinosaur skeleton just behind the *Argentinosaurus*. 'He's gonna eat the other one!'

'Actually, that's a *Giganotosaurus*,' Jill said. 'He's even bigger than a tyrannosaur.'

'*Giganotosaurus!*' the children exclaimed, loving the name. Some of them hopped in excitement as they stared up at the mysterious, fleshless creature. The empty eye sockets were both menacing and amusing, like jack-o'-lanterns.

'Everybody thinks it was just the dinosaurs, but five times in the history of the earth most of its living creatures were made extinct,' Jill said. 'Darren, keep your hands to yourself.'

Jill had conducted this trip many times, but she still loved seeing the enchantment of the children, the wonder in their eyes. When they got back to class they would make clay dinosaur models and bake them in the oven. Dinosaurs were her favorite fail-safe unit.

They entered another room with a visiting exhibition titled 'Mammoths – Giants of the Ice Age'. A model of the great beast stood in the center of the room, its tusks stretching out four feet in front of its trunk and curving upward like scimitars.

'This is what a fully grown woolly mammoth looked like,' Jill said. 'Can anybody tell me what animal it's related to that is living today?'

'Elephants,' the children shouted.

'Right. And they are about the size of African elephants. Do you know why they have all that fur?'

'Because it was real cold?' a girl named Teresa said.

'Exactly. They lived during the last ice age, starting about 400,000 years ago, and they survived up until fairly recently, by geological standards. The last ones died on an island near Siberia about four thousand years ago.'

'Why did they die?' K'Neisha asked.

'That's a good question. The answer is we really don't know. There were humans around then, and they hunted mammoths, so that was part of it. But it's not like the dinosaurs, where we can point to some big event like a comet striking the earth. The changing climate probably had a lot to do with it. The planet got warmer more quickly than they could adapt.'

In the center of the room was a baby mammoth. 'Ohh!' K'Neisha cried. 'It's so cute!'

'She's real, not a model,' said Jill. 'The sign says she's on loan from Russia. Her name is Lyuba.'

'Hello, Lyuba,' K'Neisha said.

The baby mammoth was too young to have grown fur, so every wrinkle in her skin was clearly delineated, making her look all the more like a baby elephant. Even her eyelashes were preserved. 'It says Lyuba was born about 42,000 years ago, in Siberia, and lived for about thirty-five days,' Jill said. 'It says she fell into a mud hole. She must have frozen very quickly to be so perfectly preserved. It's because of her and other mammoth remains that scientists are considering actually cloning a mammoth and bringing it back to life. Can you imagine what that would be like, to have mammoths roaming the earth again?'

The children nodded eagerly at this thrilling thought, then the boys raced back to the dinosaur exhibit.

'Maria, can you see the body?' Henry asked. Henry had taped Dr Champey's laptop to an IV stand and hooked it up to his satellite phone. The young doctor's naked corpse now lay on the examining bench, one arm bent above her head, the other reaching out as if to shake hands. Her knees were in the air, with her torso slightly thrust forward by a medical book Henry had placed between her shoulder blades. Her unblinking eyes stared at the light bulb above her. The blue lady.

Henry allowed himself a moment of pity for this last indignity, but such was medicine, and he knew this young doctor would have been willing to make the sacrifice. He wished he could have met her in life, to have felt the warmth of her offered hand. He was always taken aback by how cold the dead were.

'Yes, Henry, we have a good signal.'

In Geneva, Henry's broadcast was displayed on a screen in the same auditorium he had been in only a day before.

'Unfortunately, we do not have even rudimentary equipment here to perform a proper autopsy,' Henry said. 'But we must have tissue from the organs. So I will do what I can.'

He stood back for a moment and looked at the corpse with a dispassionate, analytical eye. 'She appears to be in her late twenties or early thirties. Well-developed musculature, perhaps an athlete or a runner. As you see, the cyanosis is entirely encompassing, indicating lack of oxygen, with pronounced emphasis in the upper torso. She is approximately 165 centimeters in height, difficult to say because of the contortion caused by the rigor mortis. We have no scale on this table, but I estimate the weight at fifty-four kilos.' He examined the crusted blood on the dead doctor's eyes and nose, and the frothy sputum around the mouth. 'Epistaxis,' he said. 'Probable heavy internal bleeding.'

Cholera didn't bleed.

He lifted her lip. Her teeth were white, well maintained. No evidence of jaundice.

'Dr Parsons, any lesions on the surface?' one of the doctors in the auditorium asked.

Henry noted a small scar on the woman's chin, and the mark of a smallpox vaccination on her left shoulder. Otherwise, she was flawless, he thought sadly. He could barely make out a tattoo on her wrist – what looked like a horseshoe.

There were no autopsy tools, so Henry had to improvise, using the only implements available. Instead of a scalpel, he found a pocketknife in a drawer. This will be messy, he thought as he tested the blade. He would like to provide what dignity he could.

'I am opening the chest cavity now,' he said.

He made the initial incision, tracing an arc from the right shoulder to under her breast, and then a parallel cut on the opposite side. The knife chewed through the flesh, resisting the task Henry was forcing it to perform. A trickle of blood seeped through the incision like melting ice. He then opened the belly down to the pelvic bone, peeled back the chest flap, draping it over the young woman's face. He scooped a portion of coagulated blood into a sandwich bag he found in the pantry.

There was a thin layer of yellow fat, which Henry scraped away to reveal the breastplate.

'At this point, I apologize,' Henry said. 'I have no saw available here. I must improvise.' Pathologists often used pruning shears to cut through the rib cage; all Henry could find was a pair of scissors used for cutting bandages. The blades fecklessly gnawed at the bone. 'I'm going to try to crack through the breastplate,' Henry said. 'Unless someone has a better plan.'

There was silence in Geneva.

Henry lifted the scissors high over his head, then plunged them into the bone with all his force.

Something happened. The doctors in the auditorium gasped. Henry wasn't sure at first what had occurred, then he saw that his gown was coated in a frothy pink liquid.

The breastbone had only a small fracture. Henry struck again and again. Liquid was streaming off his gown. It was in his hair and his ears. His glasses were so coated that he could scarcely see. He struck again. He could not hear Maria's cries. His entire focus was on breaking open the rib cage and uncovering the mystery inside. When it finally came apart, the disaster was apparent. Where there had been lungs, there was a kind of spumy swamp. 'Pulpy, bloody froth,' Henry said breathlessly, 'extensive hemorrhagic and edematous process. It appears that the cause of death—' Henry's voice suddenly caught, and he had to compose himself. 'The cause of death of this brave young doctor is obvious,' he said. 'She drowned in her own fluids.'

There was silence in Geneva until Maria spoke up. 'Henry, I'm ordering a complete quarantine. There'll be a team there by morning. But God, Henry, stop what you're doing. Scrub yourself immediately. We'll take it from here.'

Henry had one last task. He sent Dr Champey's email to

Luc Barré through his satellite phone. Then he walked out of the tent and slogged through the muddy camp. It was dark. The monsoon was at full force. From the narrow openings of their tents the detainees watched him pass with dread in their eyes. He was a specter, the ghost of their own futures. When he came to the gate, it opened and closed behind him. He noticed his roller bag sitting on the porch of the officer's house. Bambang and his rickshaw were nowhere to be seen.

He was nearly certain that the disease in Kongoli was not bacterial. This was something new. It could be a coronavirus like SARS or MERS, or a paramyxovirus like Nipah, but Henry could not stop thinking about the W-shaped mortality curve, which was famously characteristic of the Spanish flu pandemic in 1918. These thoughts were going through his mind as he stood in the downpour and stripped off his clothes, washing his hair and body in the rain in full view of the detainees and the commanding officer. He was as naked as the young doctor whose body he had just broken into with such violence.

All his professional life, Henry had imagined that he would rendezvous with a disease that was more clever than he, more relentless, more pitiless. There was a game to it, a match. Every disease had its vulnerabilities, and Henry had made a career out of being the best at understanding the strategy of an alien infection, figuring out its next move, imagining the brilliant counter. Eventually, he would win, if he had time. Some diseases didn't give you time, and then you relied on luck. He had been lucky, until now.

In this case, however, he had the feeling that luck and time were not on his side.

———

Jill was back in the classroom taking the clay dinosaurs out of the oven when the call came over the PA system for her to report to the principal's office. She had never been summoned in this manner before, so she knew something was wrong. Thoughts of her own children immediately jumped into her mind. She tried to push them aside as she left Vicky in charge and walked past the other classrooms, where life was still undisturbed. Her heart was beating in double time.

'It's a telephone call for you,' the office assistant said. 'They told me it was urgent.'

'It's about Henry,' Maria Savona said when Jill picked up.

Jill had been expecting a call like this for years.

'He's okay. But he was exposed to something, we don't know what. We've got a team in the air right now.'

'Where is he?'

'Still in Indonesia, in isolation. We will keep him there a few days to see if he manifests symptoms. Try not to drive yourself crazy with worry. We don't know the means of transmission of this organism, or even if it's contagious. It might be poison, it might be a parasite. Even if it's airborne, he's probably safe, he had a mask on. We'll know more soon.'

Jill knew from Henry that the mask was not much protection. He would have needed a full-face respirator and a Tyvek suit if he was working in a hot zone. Why hadn't he thought of that?

'I want to be candid with you, Jill. It's my fault. I'm the one who sent him. He did this as a favor to me. If anything happens to him, I'll never forgive myself.'

It wasn't Maria's fault. Henry would have gone, no matter what.

36

On the way home, Jill stopped at the bakery in Little Five Points to pick up Teddy's birthday cake for the party the next day. She was determined to behave as if everything was fine. Henry knew how to take care of himself. She would tell the children . . . something.

'Teddy, the birthday boy!' the gray-haired woman in a candy-striped apron exclaimed. The display counter was filled with cookies and cupcakes and fresh loaves of honeyed bread, a million beautiful calories begging for a home. The aroma itself was fattening, Jill thought. But rituals had to be observed.

Inside the baker's box was a red-velvet cake with white frosting and three Minions on top. Teddy grinned, showing a missing incisor. He loved Minions.

'Edna, you've hit another home run,' Jill said.

'Oh, I know my audience,' she replied. 'What about you, Helen? Why don't you pick yourself out a cookie? The oatmeal raisins are just out of the oven.'

Jill pulled into their drive. They lived on Ralph McGill Boulevard, near the Carter Presidential Library, in a 1920s two-story redbrick house that they bought during the recession. It was built by the people who had owned the brickyard, so it was solid – the one the wolf couldn't blow down, Henry said. They didn't have children at the time, or money, so they had set about remodeling it, just the two of them. Henry was adept with his hands. He built a workshop in the basement and trimmed the molding for the ten-foot ceilings, while Jill painted the living and dining rooms. One day Henry took a sledgehammer and knocked down the shiplap walls of the utility room behind the kitchen, then remade the space into a screen porch. That's where they ate most of their meals. Jill and Henry would sit there in the evening with a glass of wine, looking out on the zinnias and tomatoes in the garden. They talked about everything. Normal happiness. Something that the two of them had made together.

The house had good bones. An ample living room, with lots of light, looked out on the big tiled veranda that spanned the width of the house. The kids loved to play out there. There was an Amish porch swing they had bought online, and behind that, a trellis supporting a pomegranate that Henry had espaliered.

The upstairs they rented out to Mrs Hernández. She was a solitary older lady who said she had only one cat, but there were always more. When the smell of the litter became oppressive, Jill would have a word with her. Jill really wanted to boot her out and take over the whole house. They could afford it now. The kids would have so much more room to spread out, and Jill and Henry would have the master bedroom upstairs. This was an ongoing marital spat. Henry was frugal. There were three bedrooms downstairs, he pointed out, more than enough to accommodate their family, and the rent covered most of the mortgage. Jill suspected he was too softhearted to ask Mrs Hernández to leave.

Jill set the baker's box on the butcher block island in her kitchen. Teddy had invited three friends for cake. He was never one for big parties – not like Helen. They were such different children. After all the problems Jill had had getting pregnant, she called Helen her miracle baby. She never expected to have another child. Teddy – Theodore Roosevelt Parsons – was named after the president who had gone on a nearly fatal expedition in the remote headwaters of the Amazon. Henry had traveled to the same region in western

Brazil, a rainforest near the Bolivian border, on one of his epidemiological trips. A tribe of Cinta Larga Indians, who operated a diamond mine, were dying mysteriously. When Henry arrived, only a few members of the tribe remained alive. He tracked down the source of the illness – Jill seemed to remember that their supply of sugar had been poisoned by narcoterrorists intent on taking over the mine, or something like that. One dying woman was heavily pregnant. Henry performed an emergency delivery and found that the baby was still alive. Henry brought him home. Miracle Baby No. 2, Henry called him.

From the start, Teddy was solemn and withdrawn. Jill worried about him, wondering if the poison had affected his personality. Even as a baby, he seemed to her eerily digni-fied, like some fairy-tale prince who had been kidnapped and would one day reclaim his kingdom. Teddy was small but sturdily built and immensely curious. His dark eyes shone like polished onyx. He never sought popularity, but other kids were drawn to his aura of self-containment – he was like Henry in that way – friendly but not needing to impress anyone, radiating a kind of confidence that few children possess.

The problem was Helen. She had never really accommo-dated to having another member of the family, four years younger, and her opposite in so many ways. She was a lanky redhead, with a beguiling cascade of freckles. Life naturally bent in her direction: adored by teachers, envied by girls and pursued by boys, sought after by teams and clubs. Her life was destined to unfold in ways that Jill could only imagine. Sometimes, she would catch herself looking at Helen in a bathing suit, or when she was getting ready for bed, and would marvel at having produced such a lovely human specimen.

And yet, Jill worried about her. Helen was like a crystal, perfect but brittle. She was petulant and demanding. In her world Teddy was the only real competitor for affection and praise, and because he didn't seek it, his modesty was constantly rewarded by people who admired his intelligence and poise.

Before Teddy's guests arrived, Jill turned on the news. On Fox, Bret Baier was talking about the terrorist attack in Rome. She switched to CNN. Wolf Blitzer was speaking to a reporter standing outside WHO headquarters, in front of an avenue of national flags. 'Indonesia has agreed to allow international monitors to oversee the country's ports and transport facilities,' the reporter said. 'Meanwhile, the Kongoli camp has been cordoned off, and authorities say they have the situation fully under control.' Oh, Henry, Jill thought, when will you ever be home?

4
The West Wing

SOMEHOW EVERYONE MADE IT IN THROUGH THE SPRING blizzard. Washington traffic was a mess any day of the week, but in the snow the city became nearly impassable. Now the blinding sun was out, reflecting off the white blanket of snowfall that covered the Rose Garden and melting the icicles on the colonnade, but the Situation Room, in the basement of the West Wing, was in eternal night, a high-tech dungeon. It was where the president and his advisers exercised command and control of U.S. forces around the world and dealt with domestic crises. Flat-panel displays for highly secure video-conferencing lined the mahogany walls, regiments of black leather chairs surrounded the long oval table, and the ceiling was studded with sensors to detect eavesdropping equipment and unauthorized cellular signals.

The members of the Deputies Committee of the National Security Council – in addition to the CIA, they included State, the Office of Management and Budget, Treasury, Justice, Joint Chiefs, and Homeland Security – leafed through the morning packet, searching for something new or useful. Their job was to narrow the issues for their busy bosses and frame them in a way they could understand. Normally, the

Deputies Committee was chaired by the National Security Council's number two, but she had fractured her leg in a skiing accident in Jackson Hole, so it was left to Matilda Nichinsky to shoulder through the agenda.

Like a soap bubble, Tildy had floated inconspicuously through the layers of Washington bureaucracy, rising to the deputy secretary for homeland security without anyone really noticing. She was a gray insider, a keeper of secrets, trusted by one and all to facilitate decisions made by her superiors, as she had done for the last twenty-seven years. Life was lonely but affordable. She had excellent benefits. Within the tightly enclosed world she inhabited, Tildy was important, but not as important as she deserved to be. No one really understood the clandestine battles she had waged, the quiet victories, the enemies she had left lying in the road behind her. She had a singular talent for being underestimated.

'What is this group that claims credit for the Rome attack?' Tildy asked.

'They call themselves the 313 Brigade,' the agency man said. 'They're the ones who planned the Mumbai attacks in 2008. It's named after the 313 fighters who joined the Prophet Muhammad in his first military campaign. We took out their leader in 2011, just a month after we got bin Laden. Like all AQ groups they just want to kill as many people as possible. We think they're dangerous as hell.'

Defense asked if there was any information about future attacks. There was none.

The other deputies nodded, unsurprised. It was a typical agency debriefing. Lots of alarm bells coupled with no actionable intel. They didn't know the attack was coming, they didn't know where it was planned, all they knew was that the group was dangerous as hell. The agency was like a fire truck with no driver, racing nowhere in particular, sirens screaming, no water in its hoses.

'There's something else about the Rome attack,' the agency man said. 'There was a group of German tourists who had been at a café near the piazza. They survived the bombing, but two days later, when they returned to Stuttgart, four of them fell ill, and one died. Looks like the others might die, too. The Germans determined that they had been poisoned.'

'What poison?' Tildy asked.

'Botulism. The lab guys tell us that botulism is the most potent poison there is. A single gram can kill a million people. Fortunately for us, the heat of the explosion would have destroyed most of the bacteria.'

State discussed new tensions between Iran and Saudi Arabia caused by an Arab separatist group in Ahvaz, in southwest Iran, on the border with Iraq. 'Houthi rebels in Yemen have acquired more precise missiles from Tehran, with Riyadh in easy reach,' State reported. 'One direct hit could ignite an open war with Iran.'

Tildy turned to Defense. 'Do we have sufficient resources in the Gulf?'

'For what?' Defense asked. 'If you're asking can we keep low-level conflict from escalating, probably so. The Islamic civil war is being fought with pawns until now, but the big pieces are on the board. We'll have to decide how much we want to risk in a region that seems bent on mutual destruction.'

State chimed in: 'The Saudis want to dominate the entire Gulf, and then all of Islam. The only way they can do that is by annihilating Iran.'

Tildy asked Energy for an estimate of the time required for Iran to get back to full-scale production of nuclear fuel.

'They've built a new plant that can turn out sixty advanced centrifuges a day. We assess that they can produce enough highly enriched uranium to make a bomb every six weeks, if they choose to. Probably they've already made that choice.'

We think. We believe. We suspect. Maybe this, probably that.

Tildy had been in government long enough to know that intelligence was almost always vague and imperfect, which was why it was so easy to manipulate. Everybody had a piece of this geopolitical puzzle – or thought they did – but nobody had a clear idea of what was actually happening. Were the Saudis behind the insurgency in Iran? Was the U.S. supporting it? Were the Saudis and the Iranians arming themselves for Armageddon, or were those just rumors? A bluff? Partial facts were summoned to support poorly considered actions in parts of the world where America had few friends and no crucial national interests. That's how we got into Vietnam, she thought. That's how we got into Iraq. Libya. You name it. Half-assed intel coupled with ideological bravado. Trillions of dollars wasted. Meantime, government itself was under assault. Everyone in this room, except Defense, represented an agency that was in retreat, all because of misadventures prompted by ill-informed speculation. America didn't have the money to be America anymore. Or the guts.

Once again, Tildy noticed, Russia wasn't on the agenda. The old Russia hands in the intel community and at State had been largely washed out in what appeared to be an institutional memory cleansing. Everybody knows what's going on, she thought, but nobody knows where it's headed. And soon nobody will remember what the point was.

Tildy had spent three years in the Foreign Service when she was young, stationed in St Petersburg as a political officer. It was an intoxicating time in history, just after the Berlin Wall came down. Gorbachev won the Nobel Peace Prize. The Soviet Union, that monstrous instrument of oppression, finally succumbed – *poof!* – to its internal contradictions. It was possible to believe that history really had come to an end, that democratic capitalism was the inevitable destiny of humanity. Peace and harmony were the order of the day. America ruled the world, no rivals in sight.

Vladimir Putin was a young officer in the mayor's office in St Petersburg at the time, so Tildy saw him regularly. As an ex-spy, he naturally regarded her as a spy as well. He made no secret of his background – why bother? – and he treated her as a kind of trainee, giving her little tips. 'It's good you come to this,' he would say at the farm machinery expo or a cocktail party at the lovely Swedish consulate on Malaya Konyushennaya Ulitsa. He would point out her new 'counterpart,' as he would have it, just arrived from Paris or Bonn. Once he mischievously grabbed her elbow and piloted her across the ballroom to meet a stately woman in a black silk blazer. 'MI6,' he whispered. If Tildy tried to deny that she was anything other than a lowly political officer, Putin would smile and look knowingly into the distance.

You couldn't tell it now, but back then Tildy had a nice figure, not yet spoiled by the consolation of canapes and chocolates and maybe too much wine at dinner. She wasn't sure what Putin's intentions were, but she reported every encounter just to keep the record clear. He was a profiteer, to put it politely. Russia was broke and broken and had to sell off natural resources – timber, oil, precious metals, and such – in exchange for imported foodstuffs. In St Petersburg, the deals went through Putin, who was head of the office for international trade and investment. Much of the food was never delivered; instead, it was transformed into cash kickbacks. Tildy held Putin responsible for the tens of millions of dollars that passed through his sticky fingers while people starved. He was investigated, but it never went anywhere. He was already untouchable.

His expression was seldom unguarded, but there were moments when his face lost its careful composition and Tildy got a glimpse of his predatory eyes and that flat brutal mouth. Then he would suddenly brighten as if he had awakened from a nap, and shake his head. A smile would come over him, and he would be charming again. He professed to be enchanted by American culture. One memorable occasion during a White Nights barge trip around the canals, he picked out a little Fats Domino tune on the band's keyboard. The Americans in the crowd loved it. But Tildy had seen the mask fall, and recognized the killer underneath. In the chaos of depravity that followed the fall of the empire, this singular individual had the advantage of knowing what he wanted. He wanted revenge.

He had taken aim at the very heart of America – democracy – and his shot was true. As Tildy sat in the Situation Room with some of the most powerful leaders of government, not one of them would say that Putin had pulled the trigger and damn if he hadn't gotten away with it.

———

The last item was an outbreak of a mysterious disease in Indonesia. 'I suppose I'll take this one, since we have no actual health officials here,' said Tildy. As she did, the agency man stood up to leave. 'Meeting across the river,' he mouthed.

'Not yet,' said Tildy, summoning a cross old-lady tone that would be too much trouble to argue with. 'I've got some questions about this one.'

The agency man reluctantly took his seat.

'This seems to be a totally new disease,' Tildy said. 'Could it be a biological weapon?'

'Possibly,' said the agency man unhelpfully.

'Or something that walked out of a lab?' she asked.

'We don't have any information,' the agency man said.

Tildy was not surprised. 'That'll be all for today,' she said finally, releasing the deputies back into a world that was growing much colder.

5

Quarantine

'I'M FINE' WERE THE FIRST WORDS OUT OF HENRY'S MOUTH. Jill immediately teared up when she heard his voice, even though it was five in the morning in Atlanta. 'They just now gave me my satellite phone or I would have called you sooner.'

'Where are you?'

'I'm in a tent by myself. There are medical teams arriving from all over the place. They'll be up and running in a matter of hours.'

'How long do you have to stay in quarantine?'

'Fourteen days, as long as there are no symptoms.'

'Well, are there any?'

'No, and don't worry.'

'You must be going crazy.'

'I'm berserk. I should be leading the team, but instead I'm in this little tent with a cot and a camp chair.'

Jill laughed at the image, only because she was so relieved, but the thought of Henry having to hold still, alone, in the middle of a major health crisis was wrenching. 'If it weren't for you, they wouldn't be there at all,' she reminded him.

'Tell the kids how much I love them,' he said. 'And that I'll be home as soon as I can.'

He called Maria and dictated the team he wanted her to assemble. 'I need Marco to head it,' he said, referring to Marco Perella, who had been with him through many disease campaigns. Smart, ironic, reliable, he had started as an officer in the Epidemic Intelligence Service in Henry's lab at the CDC and was now his number two.

'He's already in the air,' she said.

'And we'll need something more than a basic field lab.'

'I've taken care of that,' she said.

'You're working fast,' Henry said appreciatively.

'I just made a list all the things I knew you were going to demand and started checking them off.'

'You know me too well,' he said. 'Listen, Maria, the Indonesian authorities have to be made to see the seriousness of this event. It's unlikely we'll be able to confine this outbreak to the camp. We need to run down everyone who has been in or out of this place in the last month. Food services, military, medical personnel – every single person.'

'Henry! I'm on it!' Maria exclaimed.

'I'm sorry, I know you are. There's nobody better. I'm just frustrated at being sidelined.'

'You're not sidelined. We're depending on you. I'll be in touch every day.'

Before he rang off, Henry said how sorry he was that Maria had lost a friend in the Rome attack.

'Ah, yes, thanks, Henry. We grew up together. She was my best friend from childhood. It's terrible for her family.'

'I'm sure it's hard for you as well.'

'You know what is really hard,' Maria said, her voice cracking. 'The hatred I feel for the people who did this. They don't care how precious are the lives they take. They only want to kill and draw attention to their own grievances. Maybe unconsciously they just want us to feel the way they do. And now I do. I've worked my whole life for health and for peace and now I'm full of rage. I can't stand what they did to my friend – and I despise the person they have made me become.'

Marco called moments later, from the plane. He was bringing a dozen top researchers from Atlanta. They would join with the WHO team and others who were already on the ground. Marco and Henry went through a familiar process of eliminating possible pathogens to concentrate on the most likely causes of an illness but, at the same time, making sure that they weren't ignoring less obvious candidates.

'Cyanosis,' Marco said, pointing to the most distinctive symptom. 'Do you think poison?'

Henry considered. There were cases of women dying after swallowing nitrobenzene to induce an abortion. They turned blue. Printers had been known to commit suicide by drinking India ink. Some heavy metals, such as cadmium, caused cyanosis, but the level of exposure would have to be extraordinary.

'What about rat poison?' Marco said. 'That could account for the bleeding.'

The camp was beset with rodents. Most such poisons were blood thinners, however, and the blood sample that Henry had extracted from the doctor's corpse was densely coagulated. If rats were carrying the disease, it could be spread by their ticks or fleas, like bubonic plague. If the plague bacterium, *Yersinia pestis*, got into the lungs, it became transmissible between humans, highly contagious, and almost impossible to treat. Lethality was nearly 100 percent.

Henry's mind was always stalked by the fear that some form of the plague would recur. At Hopkins, he had taken a course in the history of medicine and was fascinated by the plague bacterium. His professor drew a graph on the chalk board of the estimated human population over time. The chart showed steady growth until the sixth century, during the reign of the Roman emperor Justinian, when fifty million people died – about a quarter of the entire world population. The next plague pandemic was the deadliest outbreak in human history. Known as 'the Black Death' because of the gangrene that appeared on the extremities of the infected person, it began in China in 1334 and followed the trade routes through Central Asia and Europe, killing as many as 200 million people before subsiding in 1353. The last plague pandemic also began in China, in the mid-nineteenth century, and, thanks to steamships, quickly spread around the world. India alone lost 20 million people, and nearly 80 percent of those who contracted the disease died of it. There was still no effective vaccine for pneumonic plague.

Henry had already gotten several flea bites in his quarantine tent. He had not seen the characteristic swollen lesions of plague on the bodies in Kongoli, however. 'It's still possible that it is spread by rats,' said Henry, 'although according to Dr Champey's notes, the disease spread slowly at first, then went rapaciously through the camp, following the pattern of an infectious disease.'

'Have you got a median age of death?' Marco asked.

'They're working on the latest count,' said Henry. 'Most of the mortality is among young men, but of course the population of the camp is entirely male and skews young. Another thing to consider is that the reason the MSF doctors came in the first place was to treat the HIV infection, so presumably a significant percentage of the detainee population have compromised immune systems. That could make the disease somewhat less fearsome if it escapes into the general population.'

'But one assumes that the doctors themselves did not have HIV, and they also died,' said Marco.

'Yes, and rather quickly,' Henry agreed. 'We could be dealing with a disease that is not normally found in humans, but because of the lowered immune response the disease took hold and adapted to the human host.'

'Means of transmission?' asked Marco. 'Mosquitos, possibly? A bacterium in the water?'

'It moves too quickly for mosquitos,' said Henry. 'We'll see if the spread halts when your team takes control of the food and water sources, but it doesn't have the characteristics of any bacterium I know of. I put my money on a virus.'

'Ebola?'

'The suddenness of the onset does suggest that. The high lethality, the rapid spread, the hemorrhagic fever – yes, it could be Ebola. But the only strain of the Ebola virus known to be in Asia is Reston virus, and that's not been known to be pathogenic in humans.'

'What about Lassa fever or Marburg?'

'The carriers for those diseases are African mice and Egyptian fruit bats. Not found in Indonesia.'

'So, it's a puzzle,' said Marco.

'A considerable puzzle,' Henry agreed.

'Stay well, Henry,' Marco said as he signed off. 'We're going to need you on this one.'

———

Henry had come to virology late in his career. His early work was in highly pathogenic bacteria, the source of many formidable diseases. Pneumonia, history's great killer. Plague, the word itself evoking terror. Tuberculosis, still the number one cause of death from infectious disease. Yes, Henry respected bacteria. He thought he understood the clever mechanisms of contagion. Then Ebola had taken him to school. Among diseases, it was a diva – dramatic, sudden, and vicious. Bleeding was the most obvious symptom, out of every pore, eyes, ears, nose, anus, even the nipples, the fluid being a pathway for the virus to escape the body and search out new victims. At first, doctors mistook Ebola for Lassa fever, but one of the defining symptoms of Ebola was hiccups. No one knew why. Like influenza and the common cold, Ebola's genetic material was composed of ribonucleic acid, or RNA. Other viruses, such as smallpox and herpes, were formed from DNA, deoxyribonucleic acid. The singular character of RNA viruses was that they were constantly reinventing themselves over and over again in what was called a 'mutant swarm'.

Ebola was no more than a strand of RNA, coated in protein and wrapped in a lipid envelope. It sometimes developed branching arms or tied itself into a loose knot, like an ampersand or a treble clef. It was transmissible to humans from certain animals in the wild, especially bats and monkeys. It spent as much as three weeks in the body before symptoms showed up, so a full-blown epidemic could be undetectable until it suddenly fell like a guillotine blade. If the virus was left untreated, the mortality rate approached 90 percent, although intensive palliative care could cut that figure in half. Unlike influenza or measles, Ebola was not airborne. It only spread through contact with bodily fluids – sex, kissing, touching, and, especially, caring for the sick and the dead. It was a disease that specifically targeted love and compassion.

The singular figure who shaped Henry's approach to epidemiology was his first boss at the CDC, Dr Pierre Rollin, a Frenchman with merry eyes, who was chief of the Viral Special Pathogens Branch. Henry watched him give what Pierre called Ebola 101 in a mosque in Guinea during the 2014 outbreak. Imams from all over the country came. Ebola was a terrifying new phenomenon, but Pierre's clarity and easy manner did much to calm the panic, which can be more contagious than the disease. Once, in a distant field hospital, Pierre and his team were trying to help a deeply suspicious community contain the outbreak. Family members felt obligated to wash the bodies of their loved ones, although the corpses were still shedding the virus. After a young boy passed away, his parents demanded his body, which would almost certainly kill them and many others. Tensions were at a flash point when Pierre, then in his sixties, took a shovel and dug the grave himself. This show of humanity and compassion was a model Henry aspired to emulate.

Once Henry decided to devote his career to the study of viruses, he was daunted by the volume and diversity of the viral world, and shocked by the absence of scientific understanding. Twenty years before, no one thought there were viruses in the oceans, but researchers had since shown that a single liter of seawater contained about 100 billion of them. Curtis Suttle, a marine virologist at the University of British Columbia, collected seawater from oceans all over the world and found that 90 percent of the viruses he examined were totally unknown to man. Yet every virus carried the genetic codes for proteins – meaning that each one had a mission. What that mission was remained a mystery.

In 2018, Suttle and other scientists looked on mountain peaks for evidence of viruses in the free troposphere, the concourse of jet travel just below the stratosphere. They were seeking an answer to a puzzle about the occurrence of nearly identical viruses in widely separated parts of the planet and vastly different environments. Was it possible that viruses – say, in dust or sea spray – could be swept into the atmosphere and transported from one continent to another? The scientists placed buckets on mountaintops in Spain's Sierra Nevada, nine thousand feet high, and waited to see if viruses would rain into them. They were stunned by what they found. According to their calculations, more than 800 million viruses were deposited every day on every single meter of the earth's surface. Most of these viruses preyed on bacteria, not humans. The total number of viruses on the planet was estimated to be a hundred million times more than the number of stars in the universe.

When a virus infected a cell, it inserted its own genes, and then used the energy of the cell for reproduction – in effect, turning the victimized cell into a virus factory. Once under the genetic command of the virus, the cell might be ordered to produce new viruses until it burst open and died, releasing sometimes thousands or even tens of thousands of new viral particles into the host organism to invade new cells. Alternatively, the virus and the cell might learn to coexist, as was the case with herpes, and the infection would last indefinitely.

For Henry, the most surprising feature of viruses was that they were a guiding force behind evolution. If the infected organism survived, it sometimes retained a portion of the viral material in its own genome. The legacy of ancient infections might be found in as much as 8 percent of the human genome, including the genes that controlled memory formation, the immune system, and cognitive development. We wouldn't be who we are without them.

6

Henry Takes Charge

FOURTEEN DAYS AFTER EXPOSURE, HENRY OPENED THE FLAP to his tent and stepped out onto the muddy field, his quarantine at an end. The sun made a brief appearance, turning the air into a tepid broth. He wore striped blue pants and a white dress shirt, the same clothes he had worn at the opening-night cocktail party in Geneva ten days before. His cane had been burned, along with his spare clothes, and Henry slogged barefoot across the soggy ground – having also sacrificed the only shoes he had brought on what was supposed to have been a three-day trip to Geneva.

Lights had been set up on stanchions around the camp perimeter so the crew could work around the clock. Two new MSF tents were staffed by colleagues of the dead doctors. Mercy Corps was here. The Red Crescent had a truck with a camper attached. Epidemic Intelligence Service officers, wearing yellow gowns, were attending patients in a large tented infirmary. A cell tower loomed over the camp, and the roofs of the WHO trailers were covered with solar panels. Every agency that could get a team together was either here or on its way. Nothing like a sexy little epidemic to flush them to the surface. It could be another bureaucratic shouting match, Henry realized, just like with Ebola.

Inside the WHO trailer was a stripped-down field lab, but at least it contained the essentials. There was a jerry-rigged field isolator – essentially, a plexiglass box with ports containing thick, black latex gloves, which allowed the lab technician to manipulate the virus samples inside without fear of contamination. Live virus was dabbed into plastic well plates – trays with small, evenly spaced indentations – containing human cells in a liquid medium. Once infected, the cells began growing the virus. Other technicians were attempting to amplify sequences using polymerase chain reaction. If the source of the infection was an unknown virus, it might require deep sequencing that would have to be done in Atlanta.

'You're back,' Marco dryly observed. Marco was an ideal EIS officer: courageous, intuitive, and unmarried. On his left forearm was a tattoo of a dancing girl, a memento of the rabies epidemic in Bali that he and Henry had worked together. Marco even spoke a bit of Malay, which would be useful.

'Who's in charge?' Henry asked.

'Everybody,' Marco said.

Exactly what Henry had feared.

'Is anybody checking the hospitals?' he asked. 'The clinics?'

'Terry is on that. Nothing so far.'

'The morgues?'

'Somebody is. I think the Red Crescent.'

'We should have daily updates,' Henry said. 'Any suspicious deaths have to be investigated.'

'Already happening,' Marco said. 'Don't you want to get an update on what we've found?'

'It's viral,' said Henry. 'And it's something new. Probably avian.'

'Jeez, Henry, how'd you know all that?'

'I want a meeting with every delegation in half an hour. We don't have time to have people bumping into each other. There's a lot of work to be done, and quickly.'

'I'll let them know,' said Marco.

'And let me look at the lab reports.'

'Sure, but first can I make a suggestion? You really, really need a shower.'

The truth of that statement was evident. Marco pointed to a large suitcase in the corner, which Henry recognized with a sudden start of delight. 'Jill sent you some fresh clothes,' Marco said.

Scrubbed and refreshed, Henry stood on the porch of the officer's house. The officer and the other guards who oversaw the detention camp were themselves now quarantined behind the fence with other exposed personnel.

Representatives of a dozen international health organizations were gathered in front of Henry. Standing around the trailers and tents were another fifty or so medical workers from various countries. Some of the faces were familiar from previous epidemics or conferences. They were mostly young people, average age early thirties – the same population represented by the spike on the disease mortality graph. Over the years, Henry had noticed a strong slant toward women in these crises. When he was younger, almost all the EIS officers had been men. Now men were a minority, even in the

Red Crescent. Some of the medics were wearing Tyvek coveralls, and others were wrapped in garbage bags sealed with duct tape. Once again, Henry was stirred by the sheer nobility of talented young people placing themselves in the path of an unknown peril.

Among the faces in the crowd, Henry noticed, was the health minister, Annisa Novanto. She looked worried. Panicked, even. It was an unforgiving country she lived in.

For those gathered on the soggy parade ground who did not know him, Henry must have seemed an odd figure, small and slightly bent. Who was he to simply seize command of this impressive international array of medical talent? Some of the younger ones noticed the deference that the older heads in the crowd paid to him, but all were curious to see how this unprepossessing fellow would handle a discordant and highly competitive band of agencies, all bent on achieving medical glory.

Henry's attention was suddenly captured by something in the sky. An odd, distant honking. He stood gazing upward, quietly, patiently, until every face in the encampment had turned to see what he was looking at.

'Geese,' he said. 'Wonder where they're going? North, I suppose. China. Russia. It's interesting about migrating birds,' he mused, almost to himself, but with a voice that carried to the back of the camp. 'They fly in formation. Much more efficient, say the people who study such things. Gets them where they want to go a lot quicker. Not so much wasted energy. And every goose serves a purpose in that formation.' His voice suddenly hardened. 'Like we're going to do.'

The eyes in the camp returned to him. 'First thing, people all over the world are going to be worried about what's going on here. We need to be truthful, but we need to speak with one voice. And so any bit of information that we let out into the world goes through Minister Annisa, if that's agreeable to her.'

The shock and gratitude on Annisa's face was apparent. With a single stroke, Henry had enlisted his main antagonist into his command. By giving her what she most wanted, he also placed her and the Indonesian government under his direction. What had been granted could also be taken away. That was an authority he had just awarded himself.

Henry asked for reports on the progression of the disease. The team assessed that as many as half the detainees had symptoms, and of that group, lethality was over 60 percent. Without knowing the cause of the illness, doctors had little to offer those who were ill except Tylenol for the fevers and fluids to keep them from dehydrating. Beyond that there were comforting words and wild guesses. WHO and CDC had different counts on probable, suspected, and confirmed cases, but they agreed that fatalities were slightly declining, due to palliative care. There were no reports of disease outside the camp. So far the quarantine seemed to be holding.

Perhaps the disease was playing itself out, Henry thought. Many novel diseases came to an end as abruptly as they had appeared. Over eons, nature had hurled many threats in our direction, like meteors burning out in the atmosphere before they did any real damage. Then, of course, along came the big one, the one that wiped out the dinosaurs and most of life on earth. You never knew.

Marco complained that they were trying to send serum samples to the nearest Level 4 containment facility, in Australia, but dry ice for freezing tissue samples was hard to obtain, and commercial airlines were refusing to take the samples on board. Minister Annisa immediately pledged that the Indonesian army would devote special aircraft to transport samples whenever needed. One problem solved.

The EIS had been trying to track down Patient Zero – the person who first brought infection into a community. The interviews had been inconclusive; so many of the early cases had died. Such a person might offer a clue as to where the disease originated. Had it been seen before? Was it transmissible from human to human before it arrived in the camp? Or had Patient Zero contracted the disease by coming into contact with an animal – oftentimes, a pig, which shared so many genes with humans – and then become the unknowing laboratory in which the germ transformed itself into a human disease? Henry thought a pig was an unlikely source, since most of the internees were Muslims and didn't eat pork.

He also recognized that the identification of the first victims of the disease – gay Muslims with HIV – was likely to create a pandemic of its own – one of hysteria.

Diseases have a history of stirring up conspiracies. Jews were held responsible for the Black Plague in the fourteenth century, and they were massacred in hundreds of European cities, including two thousand Jews burned alive in Strasbourg, France, on Valentine's Day, 1349. When severe acute respiratory syndrome (SARS) first appeared, Sergei Kolesnikov, a member of the Russian Academy of Medical Sciences, charged that the new disease was a man-made synthetic virus that combined measles and mumps, although they are both paramyxoviruses and could not be the basis of a coronavirus. This fallible theory took root in China, which was loathe to assume responsibility for being the point of origin of the disease. A rumor spread like a contagion that only the United States was capable of genetically engineering such a disease, and that it had been deliberately seeded in China to retard its growth as a world superpower.

Henry regarded the battle against SARS as one of public health's great victories, but it came at a terrible cost. One of his dear friends was Dr Carlo Urbani, a specialist in parasitic diseases. Like Henry, Carlo wanted to stay in the field, not in some prominent office in the global medical bureaucracy. They had met at conferences in the past, but one night they were surprised to run into each other at a Bach concert in Milan. At the time, Carlo was head of the Italian section of MSF. That evening began a friendship based on more than professional regard. Carlo was an endearing contradiction: he was a bon vivant who loved good food and excellent wine, piloted ultralight planes, was an expert photographer, and played classical organ; at the same time, he was also a committed humanitarian, devoting his life to a singular mission of contracting the effects of parasitic flatworms on Vietnamese schoolchildren. In 1999, he was chosen to receive the Nobel Peace Prize on behalf of the MSF. He reminded Henry of one of his heroes, Albert Schweitzer, also a great organist and Nobel prizewinner in addition to his medical calling.

In February 2003, Carlo was working at a WHO outpost in Hanoi when he got an urgent plea from the Vietnam French Hospital. A patient who had recently arrived from Hong Kong was dangerously ill with what looked like severe bacterial pneumonia. Antibiotics had no effect. Doctors thought it might be a particularly aggressive influenza. Within days, as many as twenty healthcare workers had been infected. One after another, they began to die. Hanoi was engulfed in panic. Officials asked Carlo to take over the hospital.

Carlo's wife pleaded with him not to do it. They had three children. She told him he was being irresponsible. 'If I don't do this now, what am I doing here?' Carlo responded. 'Just answering emails and going to cocktail parties? I'm a doctor. I have to help.'

The index patient was a Chinese-American businessman, Johnny Chen. When Carlo examined him, he quickly realized this disease was not pneumonia or influenza, it was something new. There was no treatment. He notified WHO that an 'unknown contagious disease' had taken root in the hospital and was threatening to break out. He oversaw the quarantine and efforts to contain the infection within the hospital. He badgered reluctant local health officials into taking strict measures to contain the outbreak, and personally carried blood samples on his moped to a lab on the other side of Hanoi. There, the entire staff had fled, except for a single technician, a young mother, who isolated herself in the lab so she could help Carlo solve the puzzle of this new invader.

It was during this time, in early March, that Carlo called Henry. 'We're losing control of the hospital,' he said. Henry had heard similar stories from the Prince of Wales hospital in Hong Kong, and from Toronto, where half the SARS cases were healthcare workers. The world was on the verge of a major pandemic of terrible lethality. Henry and others pressed WHO to issue a travel advisory, one of the most draconian measures available to the organization. It had been a decade since its advisory about an outbreak of plague in

India. Making such a declaration was bound to trigger worldwide panic.

While the WHO officials were deliberating, a young doctor from Singapore boarded a 747 in New York, headed home. There were four hundred people on board, from fifteen different countries. Just before takeoff, the doctor fell ill. He called his colleagues in Singapore to report his SARS-like symptoms. That news sent a jolt through Geneva. They had to act fast – but act how? The flight made a scheduled refueling stop in Frankfurt. By the time it landed, the decision had been made: all four hundred passengers would be quarantined.

Now it was clear: a travel advisory was issued. WHO officials confronted China, which had hidden an epidemic of SARS in the south the year before and lied about the extent of a new outbreak in Beijing. There were reports that SARS patients were driven around in taxis to avoid detection by WHO officials who had arrived to inspect Chinese hospitals. Shaken by the severity of the epidemic and the worldwide outrage that accompanied the lack of transparency, Chinese officials turned about and imposed strict quarantines of hospital wards, enforced by armed guards and the threat of execution if anyone violated their procedures. Had the Chinese been more open about the disease when it first appeared, many people might have spared.

It was Henry's friend Carlo Urbani, the life-loving Italian doctor, who set up the rigorous protocol that prevented the disease from spreading more widely. Vietnam was one of the first countries to be declared free of the disease. But by then Carlo was also dead, a month and a day after being the first to identify the disease that would so quickly kill him. Thanks to his warning, and despite the absence of a vaccine, the SARS pandemic was contained within a hundred days and millions of lives were saved. Public health officials account it the most effective response to a pandemic in history. Henry considered Carlo a martyr.

Henry went through Dr Françoise Champey's case notes more carefully. They dated from the arrival of the MSF at the camp in the last week of January. There was indeed a full-on HIV epidemic in the camp, more than the doctors had been prepared for, so that early cases of the new virus were shunted aside as being ordinary influenza. The dozen patients who reported symptoms during the first ten days were treated with Tylenol and Tamiflu. They all recovered. Then everything changed.

Patient Luhut Indrawati presents with severe fever, 40.5C. Obstructed breathing. Was asymptomatic HIV-1 until 31/01, then rapid progression to high fever, acute lethargy. Perhaps Stage 3 HIV. Rapid onset difficult to explain. Copious hemorrhages from nose and ears.

She described the patient as a rice farmer from Sumatra. Two days later, Dr Champey tersely continued:

Patient Luhut died at 08:19. Cyanosis. Unknown cause. Five more cases.

She was working without laboratory equipment or even rudimentary diagnostics, but even if she had had them, she'd have been just as much in the dark as Henry was now. While the French doctors had been treating HIV, they had been exposing themselves to something new, something that was brewing and evolving. And what a perfect laboratory for the evolution of a newly transmissible human disease: a camp full of immune-suppressed individuals who couldn't defend themselves against a novel infection.

'*What did we do wrong?*' Dr Champey asked plaintively, a day before she died. She suspected that the disease might be a new strain of HIV. That made sense; there were many HIV subtypes, and the virus had a remarkable ability to recombine. But how did she and her coworkers get infected? They carefully followed the protocol. HIV was spread by sex or sharing syringes, not by washing, touching, or eating together. It was not spread by mosquitos. The transmission was too rapid to be anything other than an airborne disease, Henry had concluded, which ruled out HIV or any of its likely recombinations.

Henry got a call from Dr Champey's chief in Paris, Luc Barré, offering to send additional equipment or personnel. At the moment, there were more people in the camp than Henry could handle. 'The problem, of course, will come if there is a breakout,' Henry told him. He suggested that Barré prepare emergency responders at the first hint that the disease had slipped through the quarantine.

Before Henry signed off, he asked Barré to talk about Dr Champey. 'Her case histories have been very helpful,' Henry said. 'Meticulous, insightful. Obviously very well trained.'

Barré started to respond, but his voice caught, and he paused for a moment. 'Ah, Françoise, yes, she was one of the best,' he said thickly.

'I pictured her as an athlete,' said Henry.

'Indeed, horses, her passion. Jumping them, you know. Quite a dangerous sport. Any doctor sees the injuries from such people who ride. So she knows this but she loves it too much to give it up. She was a confident person. She demanded the most dangerous missions. To be frank, I did not imagine this was so much dangerous for her. We deal with HIV all the time. So I did not think that I was sending her to her death. She was my fiancée, you see.'

The slender officer who had pocketed Henry's bribe was shivering with fever. His body was covered with bruises, indicating internal bleeding. But he held steady as Henry questioned him about the nature of the disease.

'Chahaya,' Henry said, reading his name off his chart.

The officer smiled weakly. 'This is me. What remains.'

'What does it feel like?' Henry asked.

'Hard to breathe,' the officer said. 'Like a mountain on me.' He coughed, and frothy sputum ran down his chin. Henry wiped it away with a tissue, which would be incinerated.

Henry inquired about the other soldiers under his command. There were seven females confined in a separate enclosure. None of them reported symptoms. Officer Chahaya said they had been stationed on the outside of the camp perimeter. Several of the men were dead. Some seemed to be surviving the infection. Henry didn't expect Chahaya would be one of them.

When Henry came out of the infirmary, he found an Indonesian policeman waiting to make a report. Henry had instructed the Indonesian authorities to round up anyone who had had contact with the internees after the outbreak began. A food service had been contracted to deliver meals to the encampment. The drivers and even the kitchen workers had been placed under observation in a local hospital. Minister Annisa wanted to keep the panic down; rumors were already spreading about a gay disease infecting Jakarta.

Hospitals were beginning to fill up with the worried well, bringing their imagined complaints to the emergency room or demanding a vaccination for a disease that hadn't even been described.

'What about the gravedigger?' Henry asked.

'He dead, sir.'

Henry felt a numbing shock go through him. 'How long ago?' he asked.

'Five days, sir.'

Dead for five days, ill for possibly ten. Who knew how many people the man had infected during that time? A full-bore infection team would have to get to work immediately, interviewing family members and anyone they or the grave-digger had come into contact with outside the encampment. That might be thousands of people. If an epidemic was already under way in Jakarta, it would soon make itself known.

'And my driver, Mr Bambang Idris?'

'He gone, sir.'

'Gone where?'

'Mr Bambang, he go on hajj.'

7

The Pilgrim

BEFORE HE LEFT JAKARTA, BAMBANG IDRIS PAID HIS DEBTS, THE first step in making the pilgrimage. That meant settling up with his brother-in-law for the Toyota. Bambang's wives helped by preparing *ihram* – the white clothing that pilgrims must wear – and making Ramadan gift baskets. He begged their forgiveness for all the slights he had inflicted on them. He asked his children to pardon his discipline when he was too harsh or uncaring. He gave up smoking the clove cigarettes that he had been addicted to for decades. One must go to God with a clean soul and nothing more than one's good deeds.

The strangeness of his first trip on an airplane, being lifted into the air, looking down at the Indonesian archipelago – his homeland, splatters of seventeen thousand green islands that so quickly disappeared in the vast gray ocean – added to the sense of holiness that encompassed him. After his airplane meal, Bambang went to the restroom and changed into his pilgrim's garments, two seamless pieces of white material, made of terry cloth, one draped over his shoulder and the other wrapped around his waist. The garments were meant to resemble a death shroud. He could feel his nakedness underneath. He removed his socks and shoes and put on a pair of simple sandals. In such attire the rich and the poor were indistinguishable, as they should be in the eyes of God. Finally, Bambang reluctantly removed his hat, which he was otherwise never without, exposing his shiny bald head for all to see.

He felt guilty abandoning the little Western doctor, such a courageous man, going into a place of death like that! Bambang was troubled by the sense that he had betrayed a stranger, which was a severe violation of Islam. Was he really worthy of making a pilgrimage? If only he had not been so frightened. If only he had not rushed away in terror. But he was safe, and wasn't that something to be grateful for? Wouldn't God be pleased by his devotion?

Bambang had collected prayers from his family and friends for the day when he would climb Mount Arafat, where God was more likely to grant such requests. They were mainly prayers for health and prosperity. He would pray for a husband for his oldest unmarried daughter. He would pray for the release of his nephew from jail. He would pray to be a better man in the brief time he had left on earth.

He had to study up on some of the prayers. One was the prayer for the dead. With the immense crowds of believers on the hajj, so many of them elderly, people were bound to die. It was to be wished for. But there were catastrophes every year. Sudden stampedes caused by some whimsical panic would sweep through the crowds, sometimes killing thousands at a time. Bambang had heard about pilgrims being swallowed up in the sand as they slept. And, of course, diseases arrived from all parts of the globe, creating a vast international bazaar of infection. It was suggested that

Bambang purchase some small green lemons that would guarantee immunity.

Arrival in Jeddah was thrilling. Planes were coming from so many other countries, with Muslims dressed in identical white garments. Already Bambang felt that he was part of a great procession, stripped of race, class, nationality, ethnicity, any trace of individuality – a snowflake, perhaps, something he had never seen, but the blizzard of white garments conjured the image. His heart was singing. These were his brothers and sisters in the faith. They were all, he thought, like him, pure of soul, ready to meet Allah. Their faces – surely like his – were filled with excitement and expectation, even when they were herded into a vast holding pen and told to wait for the buses that would take them to Mecca.

Bambang waited. Night came. There was no food except for the predatory vendors selling dates and candy bars and bottled water for unconscionable sums. He lay on the concrete, exhausted, but also upset about dirtying his pristine garments. He was in a confused, suspended state – exhilarated and disappointed and angry and clinging to the hope that he would soon be spiritually transformed.

A wiry young man sat beside him, full of nervous energy. Bambang greeted him in his primitive Arabic.

'I don't speak that stuff,' the young man said. 'It's English or nothing.'

'You are British?' Bambang asked.

'Right you are,' he said. 'Manchester.'

His name was Tariq. They talked for a moment about football, because Bambang followed Manchester United.

Tariq reached into his suitcase and pulled out a pack of cigarettes, offering one to Bambang.

'It is forbidden,' Bambang said, although he wanted a cigarette more than he could say.

'Hey, mate, we're not in Mecca yet. Officially, we haven't really begun the journey, have we? We're just sitting on our bums going nowhere. I'll give up me Regals when I get to the mosque.'

The disrespect was as welcome as the cigarette. Bambang felt himself descending back into real life – scandalized, but also amused and grateful.

'What did you think about the brothers' action in Rome?' Tariq asked.

Bambang didn't follow the news.

'You didn't hear? They slaughtered six hundred disbelievers,' Tariq said. 'In Rome!'

From the young man's tone, Bambang sensed that Rome was a special place, uniquely hostile to Islam. Terrorism confused him. He considered Islam a religion of peace, but young Indonesians that he knew had been drawn to ISIS. His nephew had been caught in a dragnet of suspected cell members who were planning to attack election rallies. Many other families had similar stories. Bambang was shocked at the casual endorsement that Tariq offered for whatever it was that happened in Rome. Six hundred people – how do you kill six hundred people? And why?

'The press, you'd think the only ones killed was them bleeding horses! These trick horses,' the young man suddenly explained, remembering that Bambang didn't know what he was talking about. 'All dressed up in costumes, like. For some Christian ceremony, it being Rome.'

Bambang was quiet. It occurred to him that this young man might not be who he claimed to be. Perhaps he was an intelligence agent sent to trap Bambang in some careless remark. Perhaps he knew about his radical nephew. This was dangerous ground.

'It was a miracle,' Tariq was saying. 'It is only the beginning. Many more miracles to come. You will not believe them. All praise to Allah.'

Tariq ground the butt of his cigarette into the concrete and lay down. He fell instantly asleep.

Bambang was also asleep when the buses arrived just before sunrise. He awakened stiff and sore and cold from the pavement. He hung back a bit until Tariq boarded, and then chose another bus.

The highway to Mecca was crowded with pilgrims in buses, private cars, some in limousines, with practically no traffic in the opposite direction. Bambang had never seen a desert before. It was darkly orange, rumpled and treeless, but blue mountains were emerging with the dawn, casting long shadows across the sand, and a few stars lingered in the cloudless sky.

They passed under the Mecca Gate, the monumental arch that marks the entry to the holy region, where only Muslims were allowed to enter. Atop the gate was the representation of an open Qur'an, presenting itself to the heavens. The pilgrims embraced each other. Bambang did not even feel the tears streaming down his cheeks. His hajj had begun.

8
Salvador

SAUDI ARABIA, HENRY WAS SAYING ON THE PHONE. HIS DRIVER
had been with him in the camp; now he was on a religious
pilgrimage. He should never have been allowed to leave
Indonesia. Henry felt responsible.

'But how could you think that?' Jill asked. 'You warned
him how dangerous the situation was. You told him to wash
himself and burn his clothes.'

'Yes, but did he?'

'Didn't you say you told the police to find him? You can't
hold the world together all by yourself.' She might as well
have been standing in the closet addressing Henry's empty
suits. 'Really, Henry, you're driving yourself crazy over something that may not be a problem at all.'

'Nearly three million people from all parts of the world,'
he said. 'It's the worst scenario imaginable.'

'If he's actually ill.'

But Henry was not going to forgive himself. He was at the
airport. He would call when he got a chance.

The call rattled Jill. By nature, Henry avoided certain emotions, such as self-pity. He was steely, which was almost a

prerequisite for his line of work. Pain, suffering, death – these were common elements he witnessed all the time, but he put them away in some emotional filing cabinet. Jill could never do that. Emotion had far too much control of her life. Sometimes she admired Henry's reticence; other times she resented how closeted he could be about the things that had hurt him.

Perhaps because of his deformity he had long nursed the belief that no woman would ever be interested in him. He wasn't a virgin when they married, but at age thirty-six Henry was sexually inexperienced and intimidated by Jill's enthusiasm. He certainly didn't consider himself an appealing sexual partner, but he developed into a wonderfully attentive lover. He would do anything to please her, and Jill was happy to be his guide to the world of intimacy. There was still an unspoken pact between them that their sexual pleasure was a deep secret. It was an affair that stretched on and on.

Jill never felt she understood Henry completely. He held back so much. He rarely talked about his childhood, although as a teacher Jill could imagine how he would have been treated in school. She had many students who were impoverished, who lived without parents, who suffered infirmities. Life was a special challenge for them, and those who succeeded were ennobled by their effort. But few of them did succeed.

Henry had told her that his parents had been missionaries in South America, and that they perished in an air crash when he was four years old. She supposed that was why Henry had such strong opinions about the dangers of religion. Jill's own church experience, growing up in Wilmington, North Carolina, had been comforting but uninvolving, whereas religion seemed to be one of the few things Henry actually feared. Science was his way of protecting himself from the lure of belief.

'You're not open with me,' she had said on their first anniversary. It was supposed to have been a romantic date, but Henry's mind was somewhere she couldn't reach.

'I'm sorry, what do you want to know?' he said, genuinely puzzled. The restaurant was in a former church on Ponce de León, with exquisite stained-glass windows and waiters playfully dressed as monks and nuns. It was probably the only time Henry had been in a church as an adult. Jill had thought he would be amused.

'Something's bothering you.'

'Nothing's wrong,' Henry said. 'I'm enjoying being with you.'

'Tell me what you did today.'

'I was in the lab, as usual.'

'That's it?'

'I also went to Emory Hospital to assist with a patient.'

Jill had had too much wine. She was aggressive. She felt entitled to know why Henry wasn't fully present for their anniversary. And intuition was one of her strongest features.

'Who was the patient?'

'A nine-year-old boy.'

'What's his name?'

'Why do you want to know that?'

'Do you actually know who you're treating? Are they just patients or are they individuals?'

'His name was Salvador,' Henry said. 'Salvador Sánchez.'

'Was?'

'We couldn't save him.'

'God, Henry, no wonder you're so distant. What happened to this boy?'

'We shouldn't be talking about this, especially tonight,' Henry said, reaching for Jill's hand. But she wouldn't let him slip away. She wanted to know exactly what was going on inside him. 'Tell me,' she insisted.

'He had an unusual disease called necrotizing fasciitis.'

'What's that?'

'It's also called flesh-eating bacteria. It's very rare among children. The hospital asked me to attend.'

Jill recoiled, but she was driven to get inside Henry's mind. She thought that if she could just see the world as he saw it, even for one night, she would truly know the man she loved. 'What did it look like?'

'Don't do this, Jill.'

'Every detail.'

Henry sat back. He spoke in a tone similar to the one he had used to record his observations after the boy's death. He described a child that had been literally eaten alive. His body was swollen, filled with bloody abscesses and black patches of gangrene. The medical team had excised chunks of tissue and amputated one leg, but there was never much hope of saving him. A dozen family members were in the waiting room. Grandparents, siblings, cousins, and the hollow-eyed parents. Henry had spoken to them. He asked about how the boy had become infected – apparently, through a dog bite – and the family members told him stories about how special Salvador was, how great the loss was to the world. They could see that Henry was also desolate, and they tried to console him, as they did the children, by affirming again

78

and again that Salvador was in Heaven now, he was an angel, a star among the constellations.

By the time Henry finished telling about his afternoon, Jill was weeping so copiously that one of the waitress nuns came over to see if there was something she could do to help. 'Do you want me to call a doctor?' the nun had asked, and through her tears Jill had laughed.

That night, she truly began to understand Henry.

Jill had to tell the children something about where Henry was. She took them to Rosario's, a neighborhood Mexican restaurant in Little Five Points. Helen immediately jumped to the worst scenario. 'Dad's sick,' she said.

'No, no, he's fine,' said Jill. 'They had to isolate him for a week just to be sure, but he's totally fine. You know your dad, he never gets sick.' This wasn't true, Henry's immune system was nothing to brag about, but Jill used it as a defense against her own concerns. 'But he's got to go to Saudi Arabia because he's afraid the disease might spread.'

'Why does Dad have to go?' Teddy demanded.

'Teddy, I have asked myself that question a million times,' Jill said. 'I wish there were someone else who could do what your dad does, but he has a special talent, I guess. Think of him like a policeman. There are times when people have to be protected from danger, and that's what your father does, he protects us from disease. He protects all of us.'

Helen didn't say anything, but at that moment she decided she was going to be a doctor too.

9

Comet Ping Pong

AMONG TILDY NICHINSKY'S COMPLAINTS WAS THAT THERE IS no safe spot to talk in Washington, and yet people were leaking classified information all over the place. How did they get away with it? And where? There was the famous bar in the basement of the Hay-Adams, cheekily called Off the Record, where so many illicit conversations took place. The dining room of the Mandarin. A park bench on the Tidal Basin. When she considered them, they all seemed so clichéd.

Even from her high perch at Homeland Security, Tildy still could not see the intelligence community in its entirety. No one could. It was not just the sixteen official agencies that make up the IC, all of them formally and ineffectually overseen by yet another sprawling bureaucracy, the Office of the Director of National Intelligence. It was also the spin-offs, the private contractors, which were spread all over the city and the suburbs, some along the toll road to Dulles airport or in imposing glassy buildings in McLean, where the ex-CIA or Pentagon brass went to collect their golden rewards. Super-secret outposts were hidden in plain sight, such as in a strip mall in Crystal City, or on a forested hilltop in northern Virginia, called Liberty Crossing, where the

National Counterterrorism Center resided. Spyworld. Every day they poured out reports that buried the IC in excess information, so little of it useful or actionable. Fear was the growth hormone that had transformed America into a security state following 9/11. Now it was sustained by inertia and greed, and Washington was the capital of all that.

Yes, she had given much thought to where to meet in this spy-infested city. She was well aware of the administration's lynch mob, out to get anyone who spoke to the press. Tildy had once felt that way herself. It amused her in a dark way to think about how prissy she had been in the old days, when government secrets were sacrosanct and not traded about like baseball cards. Her reticence had been enforced by the stain on Russian Jews like herself, going back to Julius and Ethel Rosenberg, who betrayed the United States by handing over nuclear weapons designs to the Soviets. And not just the bomb. They also gave away the secrets to sonar, radar, and jet-propulsion engines – all the most important military secrets on which America still held a monopoly. For that they were sent to the electric chair. Ethel, less guilty than Julius, had to be shocked five times. Smoke rose from her head. The image was seared into Tildy's imagination: that's what happens to traitors – *especially Jewish ones*. And yet, from an early age, Tildy knew she too was capable of crossing the line. The difference between her and Ethel Rosenberg was that Ethel had harmed America, and Tildy wanted to save it.

Her ambition was her greatest secret. She was not the kind of Washington personality that people normally recognized. Nobody in this town turned their heads for the deputy secretary of homeland security. She was occasionally rolled out as a guest on CSPAN and the *PBS NewsHour*, and even a couple times on Fox. The unsexy policy bits. Infrastructure needs. New TSA requirements. Yawn. She suspected there were times when she was put in play simply because the department wanted its response to be ignored. At least she served a purpose. They would have a hard time finding someone else so authoritative and uninteresting. She was the nerdy bureaucrat that people steered away from at dinner parties, but also the one whose advice in a moment of pressure was the calmest and most reasoned. At those times, her superiors valued her because of her antiseptic reasoning and implacable sense of duty – qualities that, at other times, were her most annoying traits.

No one would ever suspect her.

She took a cab and paid with cash. She left off her glasses and wrapped a scarf around her head, very plausible with the late freeze. Gloves. Buried her face in a Brookings report on sustainable development. She could be anybody in this big stew of policy wonks, the least memorable person you almost never saw. Just being herself was a kind of disguise.

She went into Politics and Prose and pretended to browse – her cover for being in the neighborhood, in the remote possibility she was spotted. She purchased a book on gardening – although she lived in a condominium – then pulled her scarf over her head again and walked to the end of the block, to a green-fronted pizza parlor festooned with Christmas lights, Comet Ping Pong. A family spot. Kids playing foosball in the back room. Red-and-white-checkered tablecloths. Middle America, distilled innocence, the farcical opposite of a James Bond venue.

And yet Comet Ping Pong was a battlefield in the war over the future of the country. In December 2016, Edgar

Maddison Welch, a young family man from North Carolina, had come here. He might have brought his two daughters along had the family been on vacation. But Welch was on a mission. Like Tildy, he was trying to save America. 'I can't let you grow up in a world that's so corrupt by evil without at least standing up for you,' he explained in a cell phone video for his children as he drove up from Salisbury.

Welch had been fed a story. Shortly before the presidential election that year, the Twitterverse was consumed with a report that Hillary Clinton, the Democratic candidate, was part of a satanic cabal of pedophiles who were preying on children in the basement of the pizza parlor. Welch listened to Alex Jones and other conspiracists who propagated this bizarre smear. He took it upon himself to find out the truth one way or another. To protect his daughters. To save America.

It was a Putin gambit, Tildy suspected from the beginning. All the hallmarks. A preposterous notion arises on the dark web where the sociopaths manufacture their memes. It is picked up by the spiky-haired punks in Moscow. 'Fancy Bear,' they were called, although they were affiliated with military intelligence. They were pioneers of the Russian hacktivists, who would include Cozy Bear, Turla, Sandworm, and the criminal known as the Russian Business Network – all of them sponsored or condoned by the state and given the power not just to meddle but to wage a new kind of war. They disrupted the 2014 presidential election in Ukraine, a prelude to their far more sophisticated attack on American politics that began the following year. Gaining confidence, they moved on to disrupt the French elections and the German and Turkish parliaments. They had a simple goal: to destroy trust. Such a modern concept, almost like eliminating friendship, she thought. Could it be possible? In fact, it was surprisingly easy. All the virtues – loyalty, patriotism, courage, honesty, faith, compassion, you name it – are just social constructs, patches to cover the naked barbarism that is at our core. In the meantime, Sandworm turned its attention to destroying the Ukrainian infrastructure, attacking the networks that served the government, the railroads, the media, hospitals, banks, and the electrical power companies. In 2017, Sandworm planted a piece of malware called NotPetya on the computers of a small Ukrainian company, the Linkos Group, which managed the country's most popular tax accounting software. NotPetya was created in part on malware that had been stolen from America's own National Security Agency. The NotPetya launch would prove to be the most devastating cyberattack in history, quickly spreading around the world and causing an estimated $10 billion in losses.

Oh, yes, Tildy hated them. And it tore at her heart that Fancy Bear was so good at it. They were having such fun, ruining the world. Fancy Bear broke into the Clinton campaign emails and snatched the entire archive of John Podesta, the campaign chairman, and then gave Podesta's emails to Wikileaks and let the trolls on Reddit and 4chan pick them apart. It was a sport to conjure up the most absurd idea and see if people could be persuaded to believe it. Someone nominated 'cheese pizza' as a code word for child pornography. John Podesta was a regular customer of Comet Ping Pong. It all followed from there. Even Trump's national security adviser tweeted that John Podesta was drinking human blood in satanic rituals and Hillary Clinton was engaging in sex with children. All this in the basement of Comet Ping Pong.

Poor Edgar Welch. He was such a modern victim. Tildy imagined Edgar coming through the door right now, walking past the booths with children's birthday parties and the girls' volleyball team from GWU and men at the bar watching the Clippers play the Cavaliers. What would they be thinking when Edgar passed by, a small bearded man wearing jeans and a T-shirt, waving his AR-15, the school-shooting weapon of choice, and a .38 revolver in his belt?

Edgar fired three times. No one was hurt. One shot took off the lock of a cabinet door, which he thought would lead to a secret chamber in the basement. He was searching for the truth. The truth was that there was no secret chamber, no basement. The truth was that he was a fool. Poor man. Threw his life away in an effort to become a hero. Nobody had told him that the age of heroes was long gone. Quickly arrested, locked away. Now his daughters had no father, and Edgar the would-be savior sat in prison.

As Tildy might do. Such a fool I am as well.

It was not Edgar Welch coming through the door, it was Tony Garcia of the *Post*. A slight smile on his face, as if he were about to have a bit of sport. Early forties, she guessed, younger than she would have thought. Blue sport coat, gray wool slacks, old school. His reporter pad would be in his breast pocket. She would have to ask him for his phone.

Garcia looked around at the unfamiliar faces in the booths. Tildy raised her gardening book. He quickly slipped into the opposite bench and introduced himself.

'Do you know who I am?' Tildy asked.

'I could say no if you like,' Garcia responded. He had her pegged. Lifetime bureaucrat, probable cat lady, frowzy but intellectually vain, seeks to kvetch about her stupid boss.

All true, except for the cat.

'You cannot say anything about me. Not my name, my job, my age. Not male or female.'

Garcia agreed. He would renegotiate if the information was juicy enough. 'I brought my wife here on a date before we were married,' he said, a nice bit of opening chitchat, neutral but confiding. Also containing a question: Why here?

Tildy let this pass. 'You were in Russia,' she said flatly. It sounded like an accusation.

'Four years, Moscow bureau chief.'

'Now you cover culture, movies, books, pop things.'

'You make it sound like a comedown.'

'They kicked you off the career ladder, didn't they?' Tildy said in her prosecutor's voice. 'You were moving up, from general assignments to politics. They put you on the Romney campaign. You got a choice foreign posting, on track to be one of the top dogs. Then a little ghost from the past appears, some girl you probably forgot. But she didn't forget, did she?'

Garcia's face turned stony. 'What happened is supposed to be entirely confidential. If she's been parading her story around, there'll be consequences.' He looked uncertain and a little scared. Tildy had nailed her mark. 'And what's it to you?' Garcia suddenly demanded, on his high horse now. 'Is this the reason you dragged me out to Chevy Chase to a fucking pizza parlor?'

'You thought it was a secret, didn't you?' Tildy said. 'It's not easy to keep a secret in this town. You didn't do a very tidy job of keeping your own mouth shut. Sandra – that's her name, right? – didn't violate the NDA she signed. You got to keep your job – *a* job, anyway. Movie reviews. Restaurants.

Gave her a little money and she went away. But they never really leave, do they? Our little ghosts. And so every once in a while you'd talk about it, maybe to your locker-room friends, to a lawyer, to your therapist. The FBI comes for a background check on a possible government appointment, and you tell the truth. Good for you. But you carry your secret around in a bag full of holes. You're not very good at this, are you?'

Garcia's face gleamed with anxious sweat. 'What do you want from me?' he asked.

'I want you to do a service for your country. One that might even get you back on the career track, if you do it well. But if you screw it up it could destroy both of us.'

Just then, the waiter appeared, full of cheer and wearing a candy-striped shirt. 'We'll have the Yalie,' Tildy said, referring to the clam pizza, but also revealing another piece of Tony Garcia's background, 'and he'll have the DC Pilsner.'

Garcia blinked and was quiet. She even knew his preferred beer.

'I want you to have some information,' Tildy said. 'I cannot tell you directly, you'll have to figure it out yourself.' She had to communicate in a way that would still allow her to pass a polygraph. 'So we just talk naturally.'

'What should we talk about?'

'Russia.'

Garcia nodded obediently. 'Four strange years.'

Tildy spoke to him in Russian. 'They say that the women in St Petersburg are the most beautiful in the world. Was that your opinion?'

'Well, the women in St Petersburg certainly think so,' Garcia said. He answered fluently enough to satisfy her.

'It must have been hard for you to resist their overtures – or did you?'

'I assumed that any woman who approached me was a plant. So, yes, you know me well enough to know that I was not always successful. But I never betrayed a confidence. Never spoke about a source. Kept my notes and recordings locked away. I was careful. Very careful.'

'You wrote about the hackers. About Fancy Bear. One of the first to report this. I was impressed.'

'I impressed you?'

'Sometimes in the secret world you long for better reporters, so we get information to the public that we can't share ourselves. Fancy Bear was a terrible danger.'

'Still is,' said Garcia.

'It might be worth looking into what they're up to lately.'

'I cover movies, remember? Book reviews. Why don't you talk to Jarrell Curtis? He covers the IC, not me.'

'I don't control him,' Tildy said flatly.

Garcia drew back, his mouth turned into frown of humiliation.

'Oh, don't get your feelings hurt,' Tildy said. 'This is how it's done. I need to be protected. You're a liability, but you know the territory. You hurt me, I hurt you. So we're on even ground.'

'Why does this mean so much to you?' he asked.

'Do you remember the cyberattacks on the Saudi petrochemical plant in 2017?'

'There were many that year.'

'There was one that was special. All the attacks were designed to harass the Saudis, slow down production, maybe interfere with the plan to take Saudi Aramco private.

We expected that. They started in January with the attack on the National Industrialization Company. Privately owned. It went totally dark, hard drives wiped out. Typical Iranian frat-boy stuff. Other plants followed. They used a bug called the Shamoon virus. But in August there was another kind of attack. It was not just about turning off the lights. It was meant to kill. The intent was to blow up the plant using malware they placed in the safety controllers.'

'I thought those controllers were designed to be invulnerable. Triple fail-safe.'

'They are. That's what's so worrisome,' said Tildy. 'Triconex controllers are a lock-and-key system. You can't get into it remotely; there has to be physical contact.'

'So it was an inside job.'

'That's the problem. It wasn't. Somehow they infected the system from the outside. We don't know how. A magic trick. They were intending to blow the place up, but something went wrong, a tiny flaw in the implant, now probably repaired.'

'I didn't know the Iranians had that capacity.'

'They don't. It was Russia.'

Garcia looked perplexed. 'Why? I mean, I can see that Russia would look at the Saudis as oil competitors, but that's taking the game a little far.'

'We thought at first they were just doing it as a favor for the Iranians, or maybe for the money. Now we think it was a test. But here's the deal. Similar controllers are on tens of thousands of systems all over the world, especially in the U.S. They're in our nuclear plants, our power plants, our refineries, our water-treatment plants. Think what that means: oil spills, gas leaks, explosions, vital equipment tearing itself apart, and imagine what happens if a nuclear plant melts down. We knew they were targeting our infrastructure, but we thought we were ahead of them, or at least even, but we miscalculated. Terribly.'

'It's diabolical, but brilliant,' Garcia said. 'Find the one system that is supposed to be tamper proof, the very thing that is supposed to prevent a catastrophe, and turn it into a bomb.'

Tildy nodded. He got it.

'Is there more?'

'You'll have to find out.'

'By asking me here, you're saying there is.'

'I'm suggesting that you consider what might be possible under such circumstances.'

The pizza arrived. Garcia took a sip of the beer that Tildy had ordered for him and waited until the server departed. 'If they can get into one system, especially one that sophisticated and supposedly tamper proof, who's to say they haven't compromised others? I'm sure you've thought about that.'

Tildy stared at him.

'I'll take that as a yes,' Garcia said. 'I mean, it's obvious. And jeez, it's like a one-button operation, shut the fucking country down, right? Not just a headache but a mortal blow. Take years to recover.'

Tildy did not respond. She had come to the edge of her safety zone. She stood up and left Garcia with the pizza and the bill.

10

Stoning the Devil

HENRY GRIPPED THE HANDRAIL AS THE LITTLE BOEING HELI-copter bumped over a mountain peak. He had never liked helicopters. Nor was he happy about heights.

From the air, he could see the sun setting over the Red Sea, darkening the land below. Then Mecca appeared before him, a brilliant island of light. Skyscrapers ringed the Grand Mosque, which was lit up like Yankee Stadium. In the center, inside an arena of what appeared to be glaringly white beach sand, was a great black box, the Kaaba, the focus of Muslim prayers around the world. Suddenly the sand shifted like a great wave as three million worshippers rose from the sunset prayer.

'Can we get closer?' Henry said.

'Henry, have you become a Muslim? It is forbidden to nonbelievers.'

Henry looked over at Prince Majid at the controls. He was grinning. 'I can accept your conversion. It's very easy.' His voice came through surprisingly crisply on the headset.

'You know my position on religion,' Henry said.

'If you insist to remain an infidel, we will have to land at our police outpost, as I intended. There,' he said, pointing at a tented compound on a hillside overlooking the city. 'We have a good view from that point.'

Henry and Majid had known each other since 2013, when Majid had come to Geneva to report on an epidemic in Saudi Arabia the year before. Ron Fouchier, the great virologist at the Erasmus Medical Center in Rotterdam, was the first to describe the disease, a coronavirus called Middle East Respiratory Syndrome, or MERS. Forty-four people had fallen ill in the initial outbreak, and half of them died. The disease subsequently broke out in South Korea, affecting about 180 people. Researchers discovered that MERS was endemic in camels, although it wasn't clear whether the animals got the disease from people or vice versa. An odd feature was that 80 percent of the human victims were male. Why was that? It was Majid who discovered that the virus was ferried along by dust, and that women who wore veils were partially protected – a brilliant deduction that caught Henry's attention.

And it was while Majid was first in Geneva making his report that his uncle got fired and Majid was abruptly promoted to head the Health Ministry. He was immediately faced with the most serious decision a person in that position could make: whether to call off the hajj that year. Every Muslim is commanded to make the pilgrimage once in their lives if they are physically able to do so, and to shut the door on them would have spiritual consequences. Not to mention the financial shortfall. After oil, the hajj was the only real business Saudi Arabia had. With reported cases of MERS diminishing, Majid finally declared that only the elderly and those suffering from chronic diseases should avoid making the pilgrimage. It turned out to be the right call, although one Spanish woman was diagnosed with the disease after she returned to her country. It could have been otherwise, Majid knew. He was lucky.

Although they had kept up as colleagues over the years, Henry had never been in the kingdom before, and he had only stereotypical images of the place in his mind – sand, women in black, fantasy palaces. When he landed in Jeddah, he was escorted to the luxurious royal terminal. There were veiled women – princesses, he supposed – in the lounge, smoking hookahs and looking bored. They gave him a curious look. He was an intruder, neither Arab nor royal and clearly not a celebrity.

A group of men entered in long white thobes, like a flotilla of swans. They were big men, fit, handsome, a perfectly matched set, each of them with identically trimmed black beards and the traditional red-checkered headscarf. The cordon they formed enclosed another man, similarly dressed but wearing a black cloak embroidered with gold trim. It took Henry a moment to recognize his friend: he had never seen him in his native garb, but now Majid really did look the part of a prince. For the first time, Henry imagined that his friend could one day be king.

But now they were hovering over the hillside in the helicopter while one of the cops chased a goat away from the landing zone. Majid adroitly settled the copter on the improvised space between the police Land Cruisers and the encampment. It took Henry a moment to get his legs in working order.

'What happened to your cane?' Majid asked.

'Burned,' Henry said.

Majid looked at him queerly but did not pursue the matter.

Henry noticed a cell tower and a satellite dish. Fortunately, communication wasn't going to be a problem. In one of the tents he glimpsed an operations center, with closed-circuit video feeds from cameras inside the holy area. He followed Majid into the largest tent. A chandelier hung from the center point, illuminating the oriental rugs and the brilliantly colored quilted walls. There were no chairs, only banquettes against the sides of the tent, leaving a large empty space in the center – representing the desert, Henry supposed. It was chilly inside the tent, and he realized that it was air-conditioned.

Majid sat on the carpeted floor against the banquette, his movements lithe and natural. He motioned for Henry to do the same, then offered a hand when he saw the awkward way in which Henry descended, dropping to one knee and then falling backward onto his butt. Henry missed his steadying cane. He was going to have a hard time living without chairs.

A servant appeared with a long-snouted brass ewer and poured a dollop of hot liquid into a demitasse. 'Arab coffee,' Majid explained. 'Can you smell?'

Henry inhaled the steam from his cup. 'What's that spice?' he asked.

'Cardamom, cloves, and saffron,' Majid said. 'We are addicted to this concoction.' He spoke to the servant in Arabic, and the man rushed out of the tent. In a moment, he returned in the company of a policeman. Majid introduced him as Colonel Hasan al-Shehri – dark and broad-shouldered, with sharp features awarding him an air of a predatory bird. He was in charge of the early-warning surveillance system, which monitored symptoms that might lead to disease outbreaks. More than thirty thousand health workers were at their posts to support the massive number of pilgrims.

'At your service,' the colonel said, when the prince apprised him of Henry's eminence.

Henry asked whether he had detected epidemic disease among the pilgrims.

'Nothing more than the usual hajj flu,' the colonel said. 'There are fewer patients in the infirmary this year. Mostly pneumonia.'

'Deaths?'

'About two thousand so far.'

'They come here to die,' Majid explained. 'They see it as a blessing. We try to keep the contagious ones away, but many arrive in advanced stages of chronic illness. Of course, we have to bury them and do all the paperwork. It's quite a headache.'

'I need to locate this Indonesian man, Bambang Idris,' Henry said.

'When do you need him?' Colonel al-Shehri asked.

'As soon as possible.'

'It should be no problem,' the colonel said. 'But now is impossible. Tonight the pilgrims are scattered, sleeping under the stars. They awaken soon, before dawn, and return to their tents after prayer. We will bring him to you.'

'So, it's settled,' Majid said, as a servant unrolled a length of plastic. 'Tonight we take our dinner, and tomorrow we find your man.' Two other servants set a roasted lamb and a large bowl of saffron rice on the floor, along with bread and hummus and dates and dishes that Henry didn't recognize. Majid and the colonel sat cross-legged on the floor, but as Henry was about to join them, clumsily, someone brought him an old schoolroom chair with a folding tray arm. The servant made Henry a plate with too much food, and he followed the example of the other men, eating only with the fingers of his right hand.

They took tea at a camp table on a rocky promontory overlooking the city. By now night had fully occupied the sky, which was splattered with stars that seemed merely a few feet away.

'I can see why religions are born in the desert,' Henry said.

'Yes, we have this problem,' Majid said. 'God is always on top of us.'

Exhaustion suddenly overwhelmed Henry. He had not stopped since he left Jakarta. There was nothing else he could do tonight, he realized gratefully, as a servant directed him to his own tent, with an actual bed, which he fell into as soon as the flap was closed. He thought about Jill, missing her, longing for her. Odd images raced through his mind as his neurons discharged the anxiety that now followed him everywhere. His dreams were a battlefield.

Bambang couldn't sleep. He had spent the day praying on a rock on Mount Arafat. Pilgrims were scattered among the boulders like a flock of pigeons, and Bambang had been lucky to locate a spot where he could be alone with his thoughts. He made the prayers that his family and friends had urged upon him. Each would have the force of a hundred thousand prayers outside of Mecca. Sometimes Bambang's mind wandered, and he worried that – in this, the holiest spot on earth – his doubts would also be amplified thousands of times.

The sun had been brutal that afternoon. His skin was blistered and the ground was hard, but he accepted the pain and the ceaseless itching as a sacrifice, pushing his discomfort away to concentrate on his prayers. The counter he carried tallied 476 prayers that one day. He imagined how many that must be when multiplied by a hundred thousand. More than all the prayers of his lifetime. Of many lifetimes. He was certainly blessed.

He contemplated the experience of entering the Grand Mosque the day before. As he had walked through its towering arches into the octagonal courtyard he had felt himself an insignificant drop of consciousness in the great sea of humanity. There it was, the Kaaba, looming over the pilgrims, a great cube of rock draped in black and inscribed in gold. The pilgrims circled it, counterclockwise, seven times, and with each revolution Bambang edged closer, hoping to kiss the Black Stone, the mysterious relic embedded in the corner of the Kaaba, inside a silver portal. The pilgrims pointed to the stone with longing and reverence. People said that it was from the time of Adam and Eve, and that the Prophet himself had laid it in the cornerstone. In Bambang's last rotation, men were jostling fiercely to claim their prize, and amazingly Bambang had done it, he had added his kiss to the holy of holies. Afterward, he had prayed from one of the highest terraces of the mosque. He could see millions of believers before him, pressed shoulder to shoulder, as tightly as threads woven together in a single garment. Bambang felt transported and redeemed, as close to being a pure spirit as he could ever hope to achieve.

And now he lay on the plain of Muzdalifah, staring into the face of creation. The stars rotated slowly in universal progression. Such majesty. Bambang felt insignificant but also swollen with joy. Then he turned to one side and vomited.

No one seemed to notice. The other pilgrims were sleeping. Bambang shoved sand over the mess. He was embarrassed, but then he wondered if this was a good sign. He had prayed to expel the evil inside him. Perhaps this was how it happened. Suddenly. With shocking force. He had thrown off the burden of his misdeeds. He was surely purified.

But his strength had fled. He was dizzy. He tried to stand but only got to his knees before deciding to lie back down again and let the stars turn over him. Hours passed. Bambang did not know what to make of his condition. Was he being elevated to a higher state, in transition to whatever awaited him? Surely his prayers would take him to a new level, and this sensation must be a test.

The voice of the muezzin awakened the other hajjis. They unrolled their mats and recited the dawn prayer. Everyone was stiff from sleeping on the ground, so Bambang did not feel conspicuous. He was strong enough now to stand, but he did not feel inclined to take breakfast. Instead, he folded himself in with the first group that was walking to Jamarat, sunrise being the most blessed time to make the march. Pilgrims filled the road for miles, moving in a shuffle. Bambang could not see the beginning or the end of them. The sun climbed the sky. Sometimes the pilgrims passed under misters to cool them off. There were people lying on the rocks, exhausted and dehydrated, perhaps even dead; it was hard to determine. Lucky ones carried umbrellas advertising Egypt Air. Overhead news helicopters were circling.

The procession passed through lengthy tunnels under the blue hills. The pilgrims had been cautioned that this was the most dangerous portion of the hajj, because this was when panics arose. Someone faints. People stop to help. Those behind press ahead impatiently. Confusion sets in, along with anger. Then, almost like a bomb going off, a frenzy takes over. The crowd becomes a mob. People are trampled. Hundreds, even thousands, die all at once. It's over as quickly as it started, and no one knows why or exactly what happened.

Bambang had a plastic jar containing forty-nine pebbles that he had carefully selected from stones on Mount Arafat. The pebbles were for the stoning of the devil, represented by three large columns, each standing inside a walled arena at Jamarat. The pilgrims were reenacting the actions of Abraham, who resisted the temptation of Satan by throwing stones at him on this very spot. The road forked into different branches, each of them feeding into a vast structure resembling a multilevel parking garage. Bambang already felt light-headed and squeezed by the chanting crowd pressing against his sides, exhausting the oxygen in the air they all breathed at once. The noise inside the structure echoed off the concrete, building to a roar. A bolt of dangerous energy surged through the mob.

He had hoped to get to the rooftop of the stoning place, but he was shunted to a middle level. In the center of the structure was a portion of the Jamarat column, an imposing wall of granite rising from a concrete basin. When it became visible, the pilgrims pressed forward more insistently, trying to get to the edge of the basin where they could hurl their pebbles. Cursing Satan, some of them also threw sandals or umbrellas.

Bambang had his first pebble ready in his hand, but by now he had no control over his movements. He was roughly shoved ahead by the strength of the crowd, mashing him against the woman in front of him. Fear and ecstasy raced through him like an electrical current. Amid the din, he tried to pray, 'Here I am, O Lord, here I am! I am at your service. You have no partners, here I am.' Already poorly aimed pebbles were pelting him.

And then he was pressed against the edge of the basin itself, the stone column confronting him like Satan in the flesh. Pilgrims screamed in his ear. He raised his hand to throw the first pebble, but it fell short of the column. He was shocked. How had he become so weak? He reached into his jar for another pebble, but the jar fell out of his hand. He felt it strike his foot, but it was impossible to bend over to pick it up. He could feel his knees buckling but he couldn't fall, he was pinned upright.

Now he detected the circular motion of the crowd propelling him along the side of the basin amid a fusillade of stones. He thought he might be screaming, but the roar was too loud for him to hear his own voice. He was no longer touching the ground. The crush lifted him out of his sandals. He prayed to be saved. He prayed to be alone and untouched. There was no air anywhere; he prayed for breath. Then a gap opened in the crowd as they slipped past the edge of the basin and Bambang fell to the ground, thanking God for his deliverance as worshippers helplessly trod upon his body.

11

What Do We Have Here?

WHILE HENRY WAITED IN THE TENT OVERLOOKING MECCA for Majid and Colonel al-Shehri to return from the holy city, he joined a conference call with Maria Savona in Geneva, Catherine Lord, the chief medical officer at CDC in Atlanta, and Marco Perella, who was still in the Kongoli camp in Indonesia. Marco had good news: amazingly, other than the dead gravedigger, there were no reported cases in Jakarta.

Catherine Lord took over from there. 'It's something in the Orthomyxoviridae family. Probably influenza, but we've compared it against thousands of virus sequences in the database, and so far we haven't been able to find an identical match.'

Like so many dangerous things in nature, influenza viruses were beautiful, covered with protein spikes called hemagglutinin (H) and neuraminidase (N), which functioned like a pirate boarding party. The hemagglutinin fastened onto a cell like a grappling hook and plunged viral particles into the cell. Once inside, the virus used the cell's energy to replicate itself thousands of times. As the newly hatched viruses budded from the cell, the neuraminidase protein cut them loose. Within a few hours of exposure, the victim became infectious, releasing half a million virus particles into the air with every cough or sneeze. The particles floated into the lungs of people nearby, or landed on surfaces, where they could survive for hours at a time. Influenza had many strategies for propagation, but the most insidious was its ability to mutate, constantly reinventing itself, slipping past the body's attempts to create immunity and science's efforts to make effective vaccines.

Influenza viruses fell into four distinct groups. By far the most common and the most virulent in humans were influenzas A and B. In the Kongoli cases, influenza A was the most likely category, because it was typically more virulent than influenza B. There were eighteen hemagglutinin and eleven neuraminidase subtypes in influenza A viruses that had been discovered so far, but only H1, 2, and 3, and N1 and 2, typically caused seasonal human influenza. The highly infectious 1968 Hong Kong flu, for instance, was an H3N2 virus. Influenza B viruses were found only in humans, and could also be severe, but they did not cause pandemics like A viruses did. There were two other influenzas, C and D, which differed from A and B by not having the neuraminidase protein. Influenza C was common in humans, especially in infants, but rarely life-threatening. Influenza D was usually found in cattle, with occasional cases found in humans and domestic pigs.

'Also, we can't seem to get this damn Kongoli to grow,' Catherine continued. 'We've used chick embryo fibroblasts, MDCKs, Vero cells from African green monkeys, bats, and baby hamster kidneys, but none of the standard cell lines work with this stuff.'

'Where does it stand now?' Henry asked.

'We're just starting to test it in ferrets and chickens,' said Catherine. 'It's a mystery bug.'

'Maria, are there any other outbreaks that resemble Kongoli?' Henry asked.

'We've got seasonal influenzas circulating, both A and B, but they are historic strains, nothing novel. So far it's been a moderate year.'

The conversation was tense and urgent, but also puzzled and frustrating. Everyone understood the stakes. They were facing what could be the most catastrophic pandemic of their lifetime. It had to be contained, and, fortunately, with the exception of the gravedigger, it seemed to be. Unlike during the 2018 Ebola outbreak in the Democratic Republic of the Congo, where international health workers were murdered by armed militias, in Indonesia workers were protected by government forces. The Indonesian authorities were doing their job. If they could keep the disease bottled up in the Kongoli camp while researchers figured out exactly what it was, the NIH and pharmaceutical companies would work to develop a vaccine. With luck, humanity might slip past this mortal threat. The stray pilgrim in Mecca was worrisome, but he was an outlier. There was nothing to be done but to find him and put him in quarantine immediately.

'Have you produced an electron micrograph?' Henry asked Catherine.

'Yes, we have a negatively stained sample that revealed typical influenza particles, but it was weird.'

'Weird in what way?'

'There were no neuraminidase proteins.'

Henry suppressed a groan. This meant this was not influenza A, and the only flu treatment in widespread use – neuraminidase inhibitors, such as Tamiflu – would be useless. Until now, pandemic flu had always been of the A type. Now they had a new contender, with qualities that had never been combined before. It was a totally novel virus.

'Have you considered that it could be an influenza C?' Marco asked.

'Yes, of course, but when we put it through electrophoresis' – the process of separating charged molecules in a cell according to their size – 'we found that the virus has eight genomic segments.' That was a characteristic of influenza A, rather than C or D, which had seven RNA segments. 'We've never seen anything like it,' she concluded.

As the call was ending, Catherine pleaded, 'Henry, we need you back here. You've been gone for two weeks now. With you and Marco both in the field, we're shorthanded at the top.'

'I'll be back as soon as possible,' Henry said. 'I just want to make sure there's no contagion here in the kingdom. Give me another week.'

'A week!' Catherine said in dismay.

Maria weighed in, offering to send another team from WHO to oversee the hajj surveillance.

'How long would that take?' Catherine asked.

'I can get them to Jeddah in three days,' Maria said.

As soon as the conference was finished, Henry called Jill.

'I'll be home on Friday,' he said exultantly.

12
Jürgen

IN HENRY'S MIND LOOMED THE SPECTER OF THE 1918 INFLU-
ENZA, which had infected 500 million people and killed as
many as 20 percent of them. The victims were disproportionately young and vigorous adults. No one knew exactly
where it originated; it was termed the 'Spanish' flu because,
during the First World War, Spain was neutral, and the press
was free to report on the outbreak. Later investigations
suggested that the first cases had been in Haskell County,
Kansas, or in the Ford Motor plant in Detroit, or in China,
or Austria – no one really knew. But once it got into the
compressed quarters of the military camps and troop trans-
ports, it became a raging beast, leapfrogging efforts to contain
it, spreading through cities and even the smallest villages
around the globe, killing far more people than the war itself.
The bewildering disease – repeatedly misdiagnosed as cholera, dengue, meningitis, and typhoid – was a more dreadful
adversary than anything the contemporary medical establishment had ever encountered. Some infections took a week
to manifest symptoms, but some victims were fine at lunch
and dead by dinner. And like the Kongoli virus, the Spanish

flu was hemorrhagic. Sudden nosebleeds were common. Lungs dissolved into a bloody froth.

The idea that Kongoli would simply flame out was in all likelihood a wishful fantasy. Still, it had happened before. In February 1976, at Fort Dix, New Jersey, a young recruit named David Lewis collapsed and died after a five-mile march. After more than two hundred soldiers fell ill around the same time, doctors detected two strains of influenza A at the post. One of them, H3N2 – a variant of the earlier Hong Kong flu – was labeled A/Victoria. It was highly infectious, but of average virulence. The other strain, which had killed Private Lewis and infected perhaps one other person, was unknown, so the post doctors sent it to the CDC.

It was H1N1, with the same genetic architecture as the Spanish flu. This time it was called 'swine flu,' because pigs had been the reservoir for the disease. (In 1918, the transmission had likely been the other way around – from humans to pigs.) Pigs were often blamed for being virus factories because they were an almost perfect bridge between avian influenzas and human diseases. Once inside a pig, the virus adapted itself to mammals and, having breached the species barrier, was ready to conquer the world.

In 1976, alarmed by the situation at Fort Dix, President Ford called for an all-out effort to immunize the population against the swine flu as quickly as possible. Drugmakers were released from liability to speed the development of vaccines. Then another mysterious outbreak took place that August at an American Legion convention in Philadelphia, killing twenty-nine people. The initial diagnosis of swine flu was wrong – it turned out to be an atypical pneumonia that would later be called Legionnaires' Disease – but the press and the political establishment whipped up so much public alarm that any doubts about mass vaccination were tossed aside. In September, the first inoculations for swine flu began. A month later, people began to fall ill – not from the flu, but from the vaccine, which was implicated in causing a paralytic disease called Guillain-Barré Syndrome. In December, the vaccination program was halted. During this time, no one else got swine flu. It was a political disaster for Ford and a caution to future political leaders. In 1918, the H1N1 flu killed between fifty and a hundred million people. In 1976, it killed only one.

For Henry and his colleagues, desperate for answers, a maddening feature of the 1918 pandemic was that there was so little record of it. For decades, it had been weirdly forgotten – buried in human memory, along with its secrets. What had made the virus so virulent? Why had it feasted especially on the young and vigorous – those who should have been the least susceptible to its killing powers? In 1951, the Swedish pathologist Johan Hultin traveled to an Alaska outpost called Brevig Mission, where, in 1918, influenza killed seventy-two of the town's eighty residents. They had been buried in the permafrost, and Hultin gained permission to exhume several bodies and examine them. He was unable to isolate the virus, and the failure haunted him. Nearly fifty years later, in 1997, he learned of the work of Dr Jeffery Taubenberger at the Armed Forces Institute of Pathology near Washington, D.C. Dr Taubenberger had been attempting to reconstruct the 1918 influenza, using specimens preserved in wax from soldiers who had died during the pandemic. The then-elderly Hultin offered to return to Brevig Mission and look again. The only tool he took with him was his wife's garden clippers. This time he dug up the remains of a woman, approximately thirty years old at her death, whom he called Lucy. Her extreme obesity had kept her lungs from being entirely destroyed. Hultin cut out her lungs with the garden clippers and took them home to San Francisco. He might as well have been carrying a hydrogen bomb.

Hultin mailed the lungs to Dr Taubenberger. They were filled with viral material, enough to make a clone of the virus that killed Lucy. It was used to infect macaques, and within days their lungs were destroyed. Like Lucy, and like the French doctors in Kongoli, the monkeys drowned in their own fluids – a result of their overwhelming immune reaction.

Many people questioned the wisdom of bringing the Spanish flu virus back to life. No matter how carefully managed they might be, viruses sometimes escaped the confinement of the laboratory. Even at the CDC, one of the most carefully controlled labs in the world, eighty-four scientists – including Henry – had been accidentally exposed to a live strain of anthrax after it had supposedly been rendered inactive. Smallpox had escaped labs in England on multiple occasions, killing eighty people in total. Carelessness was an underestimated threat to civilization.

Before he came to the CDC, Henry had worked the other side of diseases: he had created them. Fifty miles northwest of Washington, there still stood an old farmhouse set among famous Civil War battlefields. The grounds of the former estate had been fenced off with the highest security available. Fort Detrick, as the facility was called, comprised a number of medical missions, including the National Cancer

Institute at Frederick, the National Interagency Confederation for Biological Research, and the U.S. Army Medical Research Institute of Infectious Diseases. It was here, in the middle of the Second World War, that the U.S. began its secret research into biological weapons.

There is a long history of enlisting pestilence in the waging of war, going back to the fourteenth century, when the Mongols catapulted the bodies of plague victims over the city walls of Kaffa, in the Crimean peninsula. The U.S. program tested anthrax and other dangerous diseases on human volunteers – mainly, conscientious objectors. After the Second World War, Nazi scientists who had experimented on prisoners of war and concentration camp victims were brought into the American research effort. They explored the use of insects, such as lice, ticks, and mosquitos, to spread yellow fever and other diseases. They studied the example of the Japanese in the war who had dropped plague-infested fleas into China, and poisoned more than a thousand wells with cholera and typhus, creating epidemics that lasted long after the war ended. In 1969, President Nixon outlawed the development of offensive biological weapons. Experiments with novel diseases continued, only now they were categorized as defensive measures.

Henry didn't dismiss the need for such research. It was vital for national defense, and intellectually thrilling. He had joined an obscure and clandestine world where his counterparts – in Russia, Iran, China, North Korea – knew each other only by reputation and rumor. They played a game in which one's cards were rarely shown. Terrorists were also actively cooking up diseases. Al-Qaeda attempted to cultivate anthrax. The apocalyptic Japanese science-fiction cult Aum Shinrikyo, with microbiologists on staff, also experimented with anthrax as well as botulism. These diseases, at least, were not contagious, but there was little reason to think that terrorists would stop short of that.

Henry was good at his job – more than good, in fact – but he was modest enough to recognize that the true genius in this dark endeavor was Jürgen Stark, his charismatic chief. While their counterparts in the realm of nuclear physics were creating bombs that could eliminate life on earth, Henry and the other young scientists in Jürgen's lab were doing much the same, tinkering with nature to learn how to destroy humanity.

Jürgen's team had been assembled at the National Biodefense Analysis and Countermeasures Center. The entire building was classified; no one else on the Fort Detrick campus knew what went on inside. The goal was to engineer biological pathogens that might be created by terrorists or malign states. In 1972, the United States had joined more than 181 countries in signing the Biological Weapons Convention, which banned the development, production, and stockpiling of toxins and biological weapons. The Soviets had also signed, but they saw the treaty as an opportunity to expand their production and create a biowarfare monopoly. Even now, Henry knew, the Russian biowarfare unit was expanding. Putin openly declared that Russia was developing 'genetic' weapons that would be 'comparable to nuclear weapons'. Hampered by the legal restraints, Henry and others secretly labored to keep up with Russia's bold advances in the darkest realm of science.

Jürgen was tall and slender with Nordic blue eyes that broadcast the self-confidence and brilliance that were his special gifts. He was vain about his looks and especially about his hair, which was platinum blond and almost as white as the lab coat that flapped behind him as he fluttered through the office. He wore his hair long enough that sometimes it caught in his eyebrows, and he would toss it about like a prideful schoolgirl when he wanted to make a particular point. Every moment in that lab was uneasy and exciting and charged with meaning, reflecting qualities at the core of Jürgen's mesmerizing appeal. He was one of the greatest scientists Henry had ever known – imaginative, technically brilliant, and willing to go to extremes.

As far as Henry knew, Jürgen had no romantic relationships. His sexual preference was the subject of endless speculation among the researchers. He rarely sought out colleagues for a drink or dinner, unless there was a professional objective in view, and on those occasions he could be irresistible. Henry knew that charm was a social mask that Jürgen put on, but even so, he marveled at Jürgen's ability to metamorphose.

Jürgen had a fetish for orderliness. Henry had never seen a lab as clean and tidy. A prank among the researchers was to cant the incubators and colony counters so that Jürgen would compulsively readjust them every time he passed by. He never seemed to catch on. Once Henry found the men's room closed off because Jürgen was having it repaired. 'The corners were out of line,' he said. After the repair, Henry couldn't tell the difference.

One day as Henry was leaving, Jürgen asked what he was doing that night. The question caught Henry off guard. 'I'm going to a movie,' he said.

'What are you going to see?'

'*Adaptation.*'

'What's that?'

'It's a comedy about a guy trying to write a movie. It's supposed to be funny.'

'Have you got a date?'

'No. You want to come?' That seemed to be the object of the inquiry.

Jürgen looked surprised, as if the thought hadn't occurred to him. 'Oh, no, I really don't like movies.'

That answer was a bit irritating, but Henry decided it was up to him to goad Jürgen into doing what he obviously wanted to do, which was to enjoy some human companionship. They wound up going out to dinner after the show. It was the first time Henry heard Jürgen laugh, a kind of tee-hee-hee laugh, which sounded experimental.

Jürgen rarely entered a lab when animals were on the table. There were awful scenes in those rooms sometimes, especially with the primates, which were childlike and helpless but also knowing and vengeful. There was a rule that no animal should be subjected to a procedure in front of the others. If the screams of a test animal reached the ears of those in cages waiting their turn, they would cry out in terror.

Jürgen couldn't stand it. More than once, Henry spotted him weeping. His repentance was evident in the canvas shoes, the vegan diet, and the quaver in his voice when he spoke of the need for additional animal trials. He was the most brilliant figure in a field he despised, like a great warrior who hated killing but also saw the cost of failure. He believed – and Henry came to believe as well – that the future of civilization, and perhaps of humanity, rested in the hands of the highly classified research that Jürgen and his team were conducting on the old Maryland farmstead that had become Fort Detrick. That future also demanded the euthanization of thousands and thousands of animals.

Henry could scarcely reflect on those years without obsessing over the weakness in his character that had led him to enter what he now regarded as a cult. It was a scientific cult, to be sure, not a pseudo religion, and yet it bore the hallmark of any powerful cult in that it presented itself as the extreme opposite of a prison of thought. Freedom was what Jürgen Stark was selling: the freedom to imagine, to experiment, and to create anything, no matter how dire or dangerous. Instead of threatening the future of humanity – they told themselves – we are saving it. If we turn away, who else will shoulder the task? Who else has the skill, the judgment, the insight, the moral courage to venture into the darkest chambers of the human mind? Who else would enter this closet of death, solely for the purpose of blocking the villains who would do us harm? Who else could hack the mind-set of the malevolent forces of the world so that when – not if – they discover the same virulent forces that we are manipulating into existence, we will be ready with the antidote? 'Only we can do it' – it was a refrain that Henry couldn't get out of his mind. They all believed it, and took comfort in each other's belief.

13

Something Big

PRINCE MAJID AND COLONEL AL-SHEHRI WALKED QUICKLY through the vast tent city of Mina, guided by a boy scout named Mamdouh, who dodged the strolling hajjis and darted through the dirty pathways like a little goat. Majid was breathless but amused by the boy's agility and thoughtlessness.

There was order imposed on this mass of humanity. A hundred thousand identical white tents, made of fire-resistant fiberglass, were formed into neighborhoods corresponding to countries of origin. The paths were color-coded and the tents numbered. Every pilgrim was obliged to carry a badge in the color of his country with the number of his tent. Theoretically, no one could get lost, but thousands of boy scouts like Mamdouh were on hand to serve as escorts for those who still managed to become disoriented.

Mamdouh took a turn into the yellow corridor and they arrived at the huge Indonesian encampment – a quarter-million people, an appropriate allotment for the world's most populous Muslim country. The scout consulted the GPS on his iPad and located the tent number corresponding to Bambang Idris's name. Inside were about fifty men with bare torsos sitting cross-legged and talking in low tones or sharing the photos on their phones.

'Bambang Idris?' Colonel al-Shehri shouted, awakening those who were napping on the floor mats.

One of the men responded that Mr Bambang had gotten separated from them on the march to Jamarat. Another pilgrim suggested that he might have gone to the slaughterhouse to sacrifice his animal, or perhaps he was having his head shaved. These rituals were to be performed after the pelting of the Devil. The men in the tent were just waiting for the crowds to subside to do the same.

All Majid had was a visa photo of Bambang. It was going to be difficult to pick him out of the mass of identically dressed humanity, even more so if the barber had done his work. The prince enlisted an English speaker who knew Bambang to join them – at once!

First they made their way through the massive slaughterhouse, which contained ten thousand butchers. They could hear the bawling sheep awaiting their turn with the knife. There was a registry in the office with phone numbers for pilgrims who had purchased their ritual animal and would be notified by text when the slaughter had been accomplished. Bambang's name was not on the list. Pilgrims could also elect to butcher the animal themselves, so Majid and the others walked the long suspended hallways above the slaughter pens searching for a slightly rotund Indonesian man in his sixties. There were only a handful of hajjis among the butchers, and none of them resembled the man they were looking for.

A thousand barbers were lined up in Mecca's streets and stalls, with a horde of customers awaiting them. Colonel al-Shehri commandeered a bullhorn from one of the hajj police and walked through the city calling out Bambang's name. Young boys danced along with the prince and the others, associating themselves with this inexplicable excitement. Among the children, Mamdouh, the scout, assumed a new air of authority, and he too called out Bambang's name. The children imitated him, and soon dozens of them were crying, 'Bambang Idris! Bambang Idris!' But no one answered.

Majid got a call on his cell phone from his assistant health minister. His staff had examined the records at the twenty-five hospitals and two hundred health centers established for the hajj. 'Your Excellency, I assure you, we do not have this man.'

Majid tried to suppress his mounting anxiety. It was evident in the faces of the other men as well. They were all sweating heavily from the heat and the exertion of their rapid march.

Majid finally asked Mamdouh if he knew the way to the morgue. The scout nodded and set off toward the Muaisem, just outside the holy district. When they arrived, Majid directed Mamdouh to return to his duties; he did not want the boy to see what might await them.

It was a comparatively small facility, given the industrial scale of everything else associated with the hajj. When the prince and his entourage entered, the reception area was empty. Prince Majid found himself staring at his own official portrait behind the desk. Colonel al-Shehri walked down a hallway and returned with a sheepish attendant, who had been smoking in another room. He snapped to attention when he recognized the prince.

Majid showed him Bambang's photo. The attendant

shrugged. He wasn't in charge of admissions, he said, and the director was away at the graveyard.

'Isn't there a record of those who have been admitted here?' Majid demanded.

'Of course.'

'Well, then, where is it?'

'It is on the director's computer, Your Excellency.'

'Then look there for this man.'

'I can't,' the miserable attendant responded. 'He does not give me the code. And he and his assistant, they are together.'

Majid demanded to see the room where the bodies were kept. The attendant escorted them down a dark hall with waxed stone floors, passing several gurneys, and then pushed open a double door to a refrigerated room that was completely empty.

'Where are the bodies?' Majid demanded.

'As I told you, Your Excellency. They are buried.'

'They don't even mark the graves?' Henry asked despairingly.

'It is our custom to bury the dead rapidly,' Majid explained. 'We believe the dead are all equal, and so even the king is buried anonymously.'

'Do you know how he died?'

'When we finally talked to the coroner, he said he had been trampled to death.'

Henry sank into his schoolboy chair, completely defeated.

'One other thing,' Majid said. 'I hesitate to say this. We have a report from three of our hospitals of a hemorrhagic fever among the pilgrims.'

The news was like an icy shower rousing Henry from his demoralized state. 'I have to examine them. Immediately.'

'Henry,' Majid said, 'this is a very delicate matter. I understand your urgency, but non-Muslims are barred from the holy precincts. And I fear that the patients are too ill to be moved.'

'I'm sure your deity would rather have his worshippers alive than sacrificed because of some disputed Wahhabi protocol.'

'We have excellent doctors already attending the situation,' Majid said, ignoring the barb. 'They can provide you any information you need. Tests, blood, we can even do Skype so you can participate.'

'Yes, we can look at the blood work, we can examine the scans, but we need a diagnosis at once. How much time do we have?'

'The pilgrimage ends tomorrow.'

'I am the only one who has actually witnessed this disease. I must examine these patients.'

'Henry!' Majid exclaimed. 'Having you in the country as an unbeliever is already a major transgression, according to many. But to go into the holy region, this is not possible.'

'So, okay, call me a Muslim,' Henry said curtly.

Majid turned to Colonel al-Shehri and asked him to leave the tent. When they were alone, Majid spoke quietly but passionately. 'Henry, my dear friend, I'm not asking for you to become a hypocrite. This for us is worse than being an infidel. We have faced such problems before. In 1979, when radicals took over the Grand Mosque and held hundreds hostage, we turned to our French friends for help. They were not Muslims, but they pretended to be. In this case, we required non-Muslims to do the bloody work because violence of any type is forbidden inside the holy areas. Not even a blade of grass can be cut! But these people had to be eliminated, and the French special forces did that for us.

'Now, we have a different situation. Entirely different! We have competent Muslims in our hospitals. They are not creating harm, they are trying to save lives. I recognize that you have a special gift. I can think of no one better than Henry Parsons to oversee this tragedy. But if you wish to go into our holiest city, you must do so with a pure spirit. I don't know how you became so bitter about religion, but I ask you to honor that Islam is who we are. If you disgrace our religion, it is as if you spit on our soul.'

Henry was moved by his friend's sincerity, but not by his argument. Religion of any sort aroused intense feelings in him that were difficult to categorize. He felt contempt. He felt fear. He felt curiosity. There were other emotions swirling around, but he considered that the fear and curiosity were similar to his aversion to heights. He didn't want to get close to the edge, but still he was drawn, and that inner compulsion frightened him. Therefore, he was prone to lash out.

'I have nothing but respect for you, Majid, I am sure you must know that,' Henry said. 'Nor do I think less of Islam than any other belief system. They are all the same to me. But tell me, how many people died in 1979, when you let the French soldiers inside?'

'Hundreds, maybe thousands,' Majid said. 'We speak about it only in whispers. Perhaps no one alive knows the truth of this even now.'

'You're a doctor. You have the responsibility for the health of your people,' Henry said. 'Tell me, doctor: How many might die if a novel epidemic takes hold inside the hajj?'

Majid was silent.

119

'I've seen what it does to people,' Henry continued in his unsparing indictment. 'Extreme fatality. Horrible deaths. They were also Muslims. But they were only a few hundred. Here you have millions. If you truly care about your religion, you must act.'

Majid closed his eyes. Henry realized he was praying. Another emotion that sometimes clouded his thinking where religion was concerned was envy. How pleasant to believe that a force outside of one's self cared about human events, a force that could influence the outcome of a dilemma such as this one – if only a person prayed hard enough and persuasively enough to capture the divinity's attention. The concept of holiness meant nothing to Henry, but he recognized that Majid lived partly in the supernatural, where the imaginary had the force of the real, and what felt morally weightless to Henry imposed an awful burden on the conscience of his friend.

Majid's eyes opened, and he abruptly summoned Colonel al-Shehri, who was standing just outside. They spoke in English, for Henry's benefit. 'I listened to God, and he told me that Henry is a true Muslim,' Majid said. Al-Shehri glanced at Henry with a scornful expression and then quickly turned back to his prince. Whatever doubt or animosity al-Shehri harbored would simply be pushed aside. There were really only two forces in Saudi Arabia – God and the family that owned the country – and one did not question either. The colonel called for a Land Cruiser and the three men drove down the hillside, across the ring road, and through a gate marking the entry into the holy quarter.

'Do me one favor, Henry,' Majid said under his breath. 'You are under my protection, so do not provoke anyone.

And since I don't have time to teach you to pray, we must be out of the city before sunset.'

Henry kept his eyes averted as they rode into Mecca, as if not seeing was a way of not actually being there. Still, he had the sense of an ancient place awkwardly retrofitted for the modern age, skyscrapers on narrow streets, a city that was partly quaint and partly posh. He could also feel Colonel al-Shehri's condemnation emanating from the front seat like a warning siren that only true believers could hear.

Once inside King Abdullah University Hospital, Henry felt less of a trespasser. Dr Iftikar Ahmed, a white-haired Pakistani, greeted them and walked them immediately to the scrub room, where they were fitted with gowns and gloves and masks. Dr Ahmed was in a state of high anxiety, his eyebrows reaching nearly to his hairline. There was a faint sheen of sweat on his brow, and he spoke rapidly in a high voice with a singsong Pakistani accent. 'We had four patients this morning, but now there are ten,' he said. 'Ten! Ten! And one of them is a nurse.'

Henry noted the sanitary hallways and the properly gowned hospital personnel. They took an elevator to the fifth-floor isolation unit, which was behind a double set of air-lock doors. It smelled reassuringly of formaldehyde. Henry allowed himself a small measure of relief.

Six patients were in the ward, two of them already intubated. Henry asked Dr Ahmed when the first case had appeared. 'Only two days ago, we had one from Indonesia, then yesterday three more. Today, six, including this man here,' He pointed to a thin young man under an oxygen tent.

'Where did he come from?'

'Manchester, England,' Dr Ahmed said.

Henry looked at the chart. The patient's name was Tariq Ismail. His fever was 40.2 degrees Celsius – over 104 degrees Fahrenheit. A heart monitor registered minimal electrical activity. There was a chest tube to drain off the fluid on his lungs.

'He came complaining of an earache, so we didn't take it so seriously,' Dr Ahmed continued. 'On examination, we discovered that the drum had ruptured. We did paracentesis to reduce the inflammation, but then the locus of pain moved behind the eye orbit. Now, he has lost his sight completely. The damage to his lungs is, I fear, beyond repair. And, as you can see, we have the onset of cyanosis.'

The young man's lips were vividly blue, as were his fingers.

'What about the blood work?'

'Extremely high concentrations of interferons.'

'A cytokine storm,' Henry said. An uncontrolled immune response. Fever and the aches that wracked the joints were evidence of white blood cells pumping out cytokines, the body's foot soldiers in the war against infection. A cytokine storm was triggered when the body felt itself to be under mortal attack, and every weapon at hand was put into play. It was total war. Henry had seen the results in the body of the young French doctor he autopsied in Indonesia. Her lungs had been liquefied by her own overwhelming immune reaction.

'Another odd thing,' Dr Ahmed said. 'Notice the swellings on the skin.' He indicated what looked like small hives along the neck and chest. 'Subcutaneous emphysema. Like little balloons. Apparently from the air being forced out of the lungs.'

'Is he conscious?' Henry asked.

'He was earlier,' said Dr Ahmed.

Henry leaned down toward the young man. They were separated by the oxygen tent and the respirator, so there was little chance of infection. And yet Henry knew that the air in the room was charged with the infectious particles of a nameless disease that no one yet understood.

'Tariq,' said Henry. 'Can you hear me?'

Tariq's eyes fluttered.

'Are you in pain?' Henry asked.

'Not pain,' he whispered. 'Something else. Big. A big feeling.'

Henry knew the feeling he was describing. It was death.

'Tariq, do you remember meeting a man from Indonesia? Perhaps when you first arrived.'

A long moment passed. Then Tariq managed to say, 'Can't.'

'Can't what?'

'Think.'

'This is important,' Henry urged. 'Please try to remember. His name was Bambang Idris. Do you hear me? Bambang Idris. Maybe sixty years old. Did you meet anybody by that description?'

But Tariq was silent. The heart monitor let out an alarm that sounded like a scream. Dr Ahmed looked at Henry, then switched off the monitor. Both Prince Majid and Dr Ahmed said a quick prayer.

'Shit!' said Henry, forgetting where he was.

Dr Ahmed and a nurse looked at him curiously. 'Dr Parsons is new to our religion,' Majid explained. 'I am his guide.'

The others in the room broke into broad smiles. *'Mashallah,'* Dr Ahmed said. 'Allah be praised.'

'The purpose of our prayer is to prepare the believer for his journey into death,' Majid said, as if Henry were under his instruction. 'We ask God to lift his burdens and make the place he is going better than the world he departs. I will teach it to you when we have a moment.'

Henry nodded like an interested student, but his face burned with shame. He, who hated deception of any sort, was now a deceiver. He cared about Majid, and now he had compromised him, perhaps even endangered him. He shrank from the welcoming smiles of the Muslims in the room, who felt joy for the salvation they believed Henry had earned. But Henry knew that salvation would never be his.

Dr Ahmed was looking at him expectantly, obviously awaiting some acknowledgment about his conversion. Instead, Henry's tone grew sharp. 'You said there were ten patients. Here there are only six.'

The expression on Dr Ahmed's face immediately changed. 'We have no more room for isolation,' he said apologetically. 'We are always crowded during hajj, and this season we are at capacity. Even more than that.'

'So where are the others?'

Dr Ahmed spoke to the nurse, then said, 'Three are in the ward on Level Two, and one' – here he broke off and confirmed the news with the nurse – 'one left the hospital. We think she returned to her delegation.'

In the appalled silence that followed, Dr Ahmed hastened to explain. 'We didn't know what we were dealing with. We still don't! You tell me, what is this, some kind of plague?'

'It's influenza, but of an unknown type,' Henry said. 'Three labs are already testing the antibodies of survivors in Indonesia to see if they match any known strains.'

'This man' – Dr Ahmed indicated the dead man beside them – 'we gave him antivirals. Is there a preferred course of treatment?'

'There's little else to offer, aside from fluids and Tylenol,' Henry said. 'Some will recover. In Indonesia, despite the palliative care, the lethality is 45 percent.'

'But this is like the Middle Ages,' Dr Ahmed said. 'We have nothing else to offer them?'

Just then, Dr Ahmed received a call. Henry cast a sober and apologetic look at Majid. Weighing on his mind was another demand, the gravest he had ever considered.

'Bad news,' Dr Ahmed said as he got off the phone. 'Very bad news. We have new patients reporting hemorrhagic fevers.'

'How many?' Majid asked.

'Seventeen in the last hour,' Dr Ahmed said. 'This call concerned a request from Saudi National Hospital. They are overrun with pilgrims with similar symptoms. They wish to send them here. But we are beyond capacity already! There is no place to put them. To speak of isolation for so many is impossible. And another has died, the nurse I told you about.' He took a deep breath. 'Nour was her name. She was one of our best.'

Henry steeled himself to speak, but Majid said the word before it came out of Henry's mouth: 'Quarantine. We will have to lock down the hospital. No one leaves. I fear all the hospitals will suffer the same consequence.'

Henry could see the fear in Dr Ahmed's eyes. To be locked inside with a ravaging disease was terrifying, even for professionals. Sanitation was already compromised. No doubt the hallways were swarming with virus from the influx of new patients. The nurse was only the first staff member to be sacrificed; more would certainly follow.

'You will be supplied with all the food and medicines you require,' Majid said encouragingly. 'Additional medical personnel as well. This is a national emergency. We will do whatever is needed to assist the hospitals, and, of course, you will be recognized for your courage and steadfastness. As doctors, we sometimes have to place ourselves in a position no one would ever wish to be in. But this is our honor.'

'Not just the hospitals,' Henry said.

'Yes, Henry? We will require a list of key locations. It is good that you are here to advise us.'

'Mecca,' said Henry. 'The entire city must be shut off. No access either direction.'

Majid looked at him as if he were insane. 'Do you know what you are saying? Three million people are here! We cannot demand that they remain and – and what? Die? It's not human, Henry! Also, I think, not possible.'

'Three million people,' Henry said. 'Tomorrow they begin to return to their homes – in Morocco, China, Canada, South America, even on the smallest islands in the Pacific and little villages in the middle of Africa. But they will not travel alone. They will bring this disease with them. And the whole world will be infected, instantly, with no warning, no time to prepare. The experience we are having right now, in this hospital, will be repeated again and again. Even another week or ten days could make a difference for scientists all over the world who are racing for a vaccine or a cure or anything that could diminish the power of the disease. We've got to buy time, that's all we can do.'

As he spoke, Henry could clearly envision the full catastrophe spreading out before him. 'I'm not just talking about containing a pandemic,' he said in a low, even voice. 'I'm talking about saving civilization.'

Another alarm went off, shattering the stunned silence. Dr Ahmed walked over and turned off the monitor on the latest dead patient.

14

Jesus Fucking Christ

MEMBERS OF THE DEPUTIES COMMITTEE WERE GRUMPY AT being roused so early on a Saturday morning. It was an hour before dawn. A young public health officer in Service Dress Blues was busy setting up her PowerPoint as they drifted in, grabbing coffee from the samovar that the White House mess had hastily sent up. The limos were lined up on Executive Alley, their exhaust curling in the chill night air.

'We have a situation,' Tildy said as the deputies found their chairs. 'Actually, two. A potential influenza pandemic in Saudi Arabia and a Russian defense agreement with Iran.'

Defense spoke up. 'Russia moved their latest air-defense system into Bandar Abbas, in support of the Iranian naval base in the Strait of Hormuz. It's a pinch point on the Persian Gulf, one of the most critical geographical points on the globe.'

'Why?' Tildy asked. 'And why now?'

'They are consolidating their hold on the Levant, giving them control of the oil lanes in the Gulf and the Med,' said State. 'They're doing it now because they watched the Saudis bulking up on our weapons and saw an opportunity to make a big sale to Iran.'

Even here in the Situation Room, Tildy had to be careful talking about Russia. People got fired for being too frank on the subject, but Defense was throwing caution aside. 'This is a big problem for our strategists,' he said. 'The new Russian air-defense system is the S-500. They call it "the Triumfator". It's designed to bring down the F-35, our most sophisticated stealth aircraft.'

'So we're compromised in the region,' Tildy said.

Defense nodded glumly.

'I'm sure you have plans for this contingency,' Tildy said to Joint Chiefs.

'We have gamed this from every conceivable angle. Broadly speaking, we've come up with two responses: the bloody kind and the other kind.'

'Let's hear the bloody one.'

'We take out Iranian air defenses right now, before they've got it all set up. We sink their warships in the harbors. We mine the Strait. We bomb the nuclear sites. We demand regime change or else.'

'It sounds like the prelude to a war with Russia,' Tildy said. The thought did not unsettle her. In her opinion, Russia was the main source of evil in the world. She had seen the war plans. She knew the dangers. But there was no other way of dealing with Putin. One had to be resolute and maybe even a little crazy.

'That brings up the other response,' said Joint Chiefs, 'which is that we live with it. This is not the Cuban missile crisis.'

'The Israelis won't sit still for it,' Defense said.

'Meaning that they will bomb Iran by themselves?' Tildy asked. 'Nobody believes that.'

'We can't fight everybody's war for them,' said State. 'There's only one real option, and that's diplomacy.'

'So we simply talk Putin into withdrawing his assets?' said Defense. 'I'd love to hear the argument you make.'

'You all think that Putin controls Russia,' the agency man said dismissively. 'A million bureaucrats really run the place, and they pay minimal attention to the Great Leader. It's a third-rate country masquerading as a superpower with an economy about the size of South Korea. We give it far more credit than it deserves. On this subject, we're in agreement with State.'

Buoyed by this, State continued: 'And then there's the Mad Prince. Saudi and Iran have been straining at the leash to go to war. Everybody knows that the Saudis are overmatched. The only card they hold is American power. They're totally convinced that if the Mad Prince lands the first punch, Sugar Daddy will be there to finish the fight.'

'May I just say something?' All eyes turned to the young woman in the back of the room.

'Remind me of your name,' Tildy asked.

'Lieutenant Commander Bartlett, ma'am. Public Health Service.' She was standing in for Health and Human Services.

'You're here to speak about the flu, I believe.'

'Yes, ma'am. The surgeon general asked me to brief the deputies. He's sorry he couldn't be here himself, he was—'

'We're not finished talking about war with Russia,' Tildy said sharply, taking her in. Bartlett was maybe thirty years old, two or three years out of med school, wearing one of those sexless blue naval uniforms with a white shirt and tie, her dirty-blond hair pulled back in a regulation bun. She looks a little like I did at her age, Tildy thought. Deep South, based on her accent.

'I'm so sorry to interrupt, I know it's against protocol. But this is about the situation in Saudi Arabia – and everything, really,' Lieutenant Commander Bartlett said, speaking quickly now, as if she were afraid of being sent out of the room. 'I don't want to downplay the war thing, but this could actually be a time when we don't want to be in the Persian Gulf.'

'This is your opinion?' Tildy asked. She was becoming very impatient with this young woman.

'Yes, ma'am, I suppose you could call it that. Based on what I know already. If you could just hear me out for a moment . . .?'

Tildy nodded, and the inevitable PowerPoint slide appeared. The first slide was a spiky round ball, tinted in red and green, looking like a Christmas ornament. 'When you say "flu," this is what we're dealing with,' Bartlett said.

'We don't really need a lesson on flu,' Tildy said.

'Yes, ma'am. The thing is, this one is novel. We've never seen it before. It doesn't correspond to any historic strain. And that's a real problem, because there is no built-up immunity in the general population.'

'So we're all going to get the flu?' the agency man asked.

'Very likely.'

'Have you got a vaccine?'

'No vaccine. We're working on it, but we still haven't figured out what we're dealing with.'

'How long will it take to develop the vaccine?' Tildy asked.

'With luck on our side, we could have an experimental

vaccine for small-scale testing in six months. We have initial sequences already, and we're analyzing the bug to find some new way to attack its defenses, which are pretty impressive. We have to do animal testing while we prepare the first lots for human trials. This all takes time, especially scaling up to millions of doses. But we don't have time.'

'What do you mean?' Tildy asked. 'How much time do we have?'

'I think till Monday,' Bartlett replied.

'What in the world are you talking about?'

Bartlett described the scene in Mecca. The latest reports counted fourteen deaths in Mecca hospitals; this was in the last several hours. 'We have no sure way of knowing how many people are infected,' she said. 'But WHO has been doing a study of the Indonesia outbreak. They calculated the attack rate as about 70 percent, meaning that seven out of ten people exposed in the Kongoli camp contracted the disease. It was an easy test because *everybody* was exposed. And most of them died. Now, in Mecca, you have a very similar situation on a huge scale. Let's say a thousand people are exposed right now. By the end of the day, each of them is likely to have spread the contagion to two or three people, and then those two or three infect another two or three. You see how quickly it multiplies. And I'm telling you, these are very conservative estimates. So by tomorrow there'll be at least two thousand carriers, and *they'll* be spreading it, as well. The point of all this is, tomorrow night they'll be getting on planes and flying back home. Three million people. I think the figure is that twenty-seven thousand of them are Americans. And while they're on the plane, they'll be infecting new people.' She put up a new slide. 'I made this up real quick based on Saudi statistics, so who knows. But this will give you an idea of what's going to happen on Monday.'

The slide displayed the probable destinations of twenty-seven thousand American Muslims. Nearly every American city was indicated by green dots. Some were densely impacted – New York, Los Angeles, Dearborn, Houston. 'And this is the rest of the world,' Bartlett continued, showing another slide that painted the globe in bright green splotches. 'An almost instant global pandemic of the most lethal influenza we've ever seen.'

'Jesus fucking Christ,' the agency man said.

Tildy found it hard to breathe. She immediately thought how poorly prepared the country was. And what to do about all those returning Americans? Why did they have to be Muslims? She could envision the likely political and social consequences, but she pushed those thoughts away. There were too many other things to consider. 'How long do you expect this pandemic to last?' Tildy finally asked.

'The normal flu season usually starts in late October and peaks in February, sometimes running till May. This just happens to hit us right at the time influenza should begin slacking off, but as I said, we don't know anything about this critter. Maybe shorter, maybe longer. And of course, influenza mutates like crazy. So it could become less virulent, or more.'

'You're going to scare the crap out of people when the news gets out,' the agency man observed.

'And that's a public health problem as well,' Bartlett said. 'There will be runs on the stores. Pharmaceuticals, groceries, batteries, gas, guns, you name it. Hospitals will be overwhelmed, not just with sick people but with the worried well. The course of infection varies, but given the speed of its advance in some of those stricken, we expect several deaths en route.'

'People dying on airplanes,' Commerce said.

'And in airports, train stations, yeah.'

'We're talking about a shutdown of the entire transportation system,' Commerce said accusingly.

'Exactly,' the tone-deaf Bartlett said, as if Commerce were proposing a wonderful idea. 'As much as possible, we need to urge people to shelter in place. It would be best to announce it this morning so that preparations can be made – the National Guard called up, police reinforced, borders closed, sports and entertainment facilities shuttered, nonemergency cases discharged from hospitals, schools closed, public meetings postponed, and the government shut down. In addition, any travelers need to get home at once, before the pandemic takes root in America.'

The deputies simply stared at her.

15

In the Royal Court

PRINCE MAJID PILOTED THE HELICOPTER OVER THE SARAWAT Range. Below them was the twisting road leading from Mecca up the steep escarpment – the road that Mohammed bin Laden, Osama's father, had built, the road that finally united the kingdom into a single entity, establishing the father as a hero and propelling the son toward his own fateful destiny. Atop the escarpment was the resort town of Taif, and beyond that, the endless desert, like a sea, flat and calm, broken only by long sepia waves of sand.

The shadow of the helicopter glided across the desert like a spider. 'You can't judge from above,' Majid said. 'Some places are quite beautiful and full of mystery. But it is also what it appears to be – a big nothing. Emptiness. This is the soul of Arabia. You have to understand that to really know who we are. We live always with the idea that the desert awaits our return. For centuries we lived with scarcity – a camel, a tent, dates, we even ate the insects! Like some primitive tribe that knows nothing of automobiles or kitchen stoves or markets or even running water. This was the life my grandfather led for most of his years on earth. And he was king!

'And then came oil, and we left the desert, but the desert didn't leave us. It is inside us, this emptiness. It waits for us, as we sit in our palaces in the cities. The desert knows that one day the Arabians will return to her. She is a patient mother. But also a kind of monster. Everything will be taken away from us. One returns to the desert with nothing.'

Majid steered toward a highway that sliced through the desert, its margins blurred by the ever-encroaching sand. The two friends felt themselves enclosed, not only in the capsule of the helicopter, but also by a kind of forbidden knowledge. The world outside the space they inhabited was dimly aware of the looming peril, but the dread the two men carried in their hearts would be shared and spread, and soon everyone would know the solemn contest that humanity was facing.

'Of course, illness is always present during hajj,' Majid said. 'People bring diseases from across the planet. Meningitis, typhoid, cholera – we have dealt with all of them. Last year, we congratulated ourselves: a pilgrimage with no epidemic at all. And yet, I always imagined such a disaster awaited us. This has been my greatest fear. It feels to me like a curse on Islam. This disease came from Muslims and now it infests our most holy place. We are the victims, but the world will blame us for this.'

Other roads became visible on the desert floor, and then Riyadh, the capital, a low-slung city with a handful of sky-scrapers, appeared on the horizon. Majid steered away from the main part of the city toward a complex of buildings housing the royal palace and the Shura Council, enclosed by a high, octagonal wall. Henry could see the dome of the royal mosque and a series of buildings and interior roads, all laid out in perfect symmetry, reflecting the Islamic devotion to geometry.

Majid pointed out a large dark hole in the sand not a hundred yards from the palace. 'This is where a Houthi missile landed a week ago. So much for those Patriot missiles you guys sold us.'

The helicopter pad was just inside the perimeter of the complex. As they were setting down, Henry noticed gun emplacements, as well as what he took to be the Patriot missile battery that Majid referred to. The conflict between the Saudis and the theocrats in Iran was boiling over, spurred on by Iran's continuing to supply the Houthi rebels in Yemen with more modern weaponry, including the missile that had only narrowly missed the royal palace.

A silver Rolls-Royce ferried them to the immense palace, which dwarfed the artifacts of royalty that Henry had seen in France and Russia. The sheen of the ornamental tiles in the grand hallway was blinding. He felt assaulted by the scale of the place. At one intersection, Henry could see fifty yards in either direction. The echo of their footsteps resounded like a battalion trailing behind them. In Henry's opinion, royalty was a form of tyranny, which justified itself in the name of God or national glory, and yet despite himself he was a little in awe of the majesty with which Prince Majid swept past the guards completely unchallenged. Seeing him in his familiar context opened Henry's eyes to the breadth of power his friend commanded.

A royal guard saluted and opened a massive door to the king's private salon, which was embellished with gold, like a medieval manuscript. Majid motioned Henry to follow him to one of the seats against the wall. Ministers and other officials were lined up on either side of the old king, who fingered prayer beads and stared at the pattern in the carpet. His son, the crown prince, sat next to him, whispering occasionally into the king's ear – presumably telling him the decisions he had just made in his father's name.

Henry studied the face of the crown prince. He was young and handsome and totally ruthless, a man who made a habit of imprisoning or killing his enemies and defying the condemnation of the world and his own family, which was cowed by his appetite for revenge.

'They are talking about Iran,' Majid said under his breath.

Henry waited, knowing there was no time for waiting.

If the ministers in the room were plotting war with their rival, they seemed strangely passive. The discussion proceeded in a lugubrious fashion, as the crown prince acknowledged first one and then another, treating each opinion offered with a ceremonial nod that suggested how weightless their views were to him. Military people were in the room, their uniforms bedecked with medals, and a blind cleric with a long white beard, and a dozen other members of the Shura Council. Even without speaking the language Henry could see that a decision had already been made, which everyone in the chamber knew. He could also read the anxiety in their faces. War was coming.

The crown prince finally addressed Majid, who responded respectfully, but urgently. It was clear that his remarks infuriated the crown prince. Henry heard his own name mentioned, and saw that the palace courtiers unanimously condemned him with their eyes. Once again he realized what a transgression his presence was, first in the sanctuary of their religion and now in the inner chamber of power.

'We can speak now in English,' Majid said to Henry. 'Many of them understand it. I've told them who you are and why you've come.'

The crown prince spoke first. 'My cousin says you are concerned about an outbreak of illness in the holy city. We face this problem every year, and we have always handled it without the guidance of strangers. We appreciate your interest, but we have no desire to prevent pilgrims from returning to their families. This is totally out of the question.' He smiled, as if that was the end of the matter.

'Your Highness, may I acquaint you with the situation before you make your ruling?' Henry asked. 'I realize you will be held responsible for the consequences of your decision, and I would not want you to be seen as being headstrong and careless by people who may not understand your dilemma. At least you can respond with the advantage of superior knowledge on your side.'

The crown prince's smile hardened into a grimace. The insult in Henry's remark was plain for everyone to understand, as well as the threat behind it. That it came from such a small man, who was neither rich nor royal, who was noticeably crooked in his stance, made Henry's remarks all the more galling. The king suddenly awakened from his trance and looked directly at Henry. The wrath in the old man's face was plain.

'The world is going to experience a major pandemic,' Henry continued. 'We can't stop it. As of now, we have been able to contain it in Indonesia. Mecca is different. No doubt many Saudis have already traveled to Mecca on their daily business, possibly carrying the disease into the rest of the kingdom. We will soon know. We can be certain that many of the three million pilgrims are infected, and they will take this disease back to their own countries. No one will be able to stop its advance. What I'm asking you for is time. By quarantining the pilgrims, you can slow the progress of the disease and perhaps give scientists a head start to find a vaccine, or even a cure. At least it would give governments a bit of time to prepare for what is about to happen.'

'How much time are you suggesting?'

'One month.'

The crown prince laughed. 'But this is the flu!' he said. 'We have the flu every year! We all get the flu, even the royal family!'

'This flu is more like a modern plague. The kingdom will be the first to feel the full force of this disease the moment you allow the pilgrims to leave the holy city. And as you say, even the royal family is not immune.'

For the first time, the crown prince looked at his advisers, apparently at a loss.

Then the blind cleric spoke, his milky eyes directed toward the king. He made some pronouncement that Majid had to translate. 'The grand mufti, he says that Iran has done this to us.'

'If someone did this, they are not attacking Saudi Arabia, they are attacking humanity,' Henry said.

'This is what you say,' one of the shura councilors said. 'But how can we know this is not a conspiracy of Iran to attack the kingdom? They want to strip us of our legitimacy. They accuse us of not being a proper custodian of the holy places. This is the agenda of the Shiite autocrats in Tehran. They are willing to destroy Islam to achieve their wicked goal. So when you tell us that a plague is among the pilgrims, we ask ourselves, "Who benefits from this?" And we know the answer.'

A different councilor added, 'The West would also like to destroy us.'

The mufti made another utterance.

'He says the proof is whether the Shiites are also affected by this disease,' Majid said. 'I told him we will check on this.' Seeing the look in Henry's eyes, he muttered, 'I'm sorry, but we have to deal with this.'

One of the military men, whom Majid identified as the head of the National Guard, General al-Homayed, asked Henry how he imagined such a quarantine would be enforced. 'There are many more pilgrims than we have police or soldiers,' he said. 'And it is not a walled city. People can walk out in any direction. Are we to surround our holy city with tanks and troops and shoot any Muslim who tries to escape?'

'Obviously, I'm not a military man,' Henry said. 'You can think of every person inside the city as being a suicide bomber. They don't know that their bodies have been turned into weapons. No doubt they're terrified. I wouldn't blame them for wanting to flee. But anyone who leaves the city takes death with them. It would be your job to protect the people outside Mecca from being exposed.'

'And just let everybody inside fall ill to this disease? In a strange land, without their families? How many people will die if we impose this quarantine?'

'Hundreds of thousands,' Henry said. 'Maybe as many as a million people.'

The princes and the courtiers and the king looked at Henry as if he were insane.

'A million *Muslims*,' the mufti impatiently burst out in English, as if his suspicions had been confirmed.

'A small number compared to those who will follow if this disease remains as virulent as it is now,' Henry said. 'I cannot exaggerate how dangerous this may be. We have no medicines to alleviate the symptoms, no vaccine to halt its progress. Such things are possible, perhaps, if we have time, but the only way we can gain even a bit of time is to prevent the pilgrims from returning to their homes and spreading the virus everywhere at once. Billions could die.'

'This is in God's hands, not ours,' the mufti said.

'Can we supply the needs of all these pilgrims until the disease is finished?' the crown prince asked one of the councilors.

'Your Highness, we can try,' the councilor said. 'But our resources are already stretched.'

'We cannot spare our troops for this,' the general warned. 'Otherwise, we leave ourselves open for attack.'

'We face a greater enemy,' Majid said urgently. 'He is already here. He has invaded our sanctuary. He is killing Muslims – right now!'

'We need time to consider this,' the crown prince said.

'We have no time, we must act immediately!' Majid declared.

'You interrupt our war council with this news,' the crown prince said. 'You tell us we have no choice. You frighten us with these theoretical outcomes and demand that we believe you. But we have many other important responsibilities. We cannot do everything at once. These claims must be investigated.'

'If we don't decide to do this at once, we will fail,' Majid said. 'Anything we do after today will be pointless. We must decide now.'

The eyes of the crown prince had turned to ice as he stared at Majid. Henry worried for his safety. Suddenly the king spoke. His tone was sharp and decisive. Abruptly, the crown prince and his advisers, along with the mufti, rose and left the room, leaving only the military men behind. The king motioned for Majid to come sit beside him. He put his hand on Majid's and said, 'Do what you can to stop this.'

As they left the palace, it occurred to Henry that sometimes it was better when only one voice matters after all.

16

The Question of Martyrs

WASHINGTON WAS FINALLY WARMING UP, AND TONY GARCIA decided to walk the several blocks from the *Post*'s offices to the stately Jefferson Hotel, on 16th and M. Even in the fading afternoon light he could feel the temperature rise as he crossed from shade to sun like a blush on his cheeks. The trees were budding in Franklin Square. Seeing young women in sleeveless dresses lifted his mood.

He had recovered from the humiliation inflicted by that woman, Tildy Nichinsky, whose name he wasn't supposed to know. But she had picked him out. She had done her research; she knew what he was capable of. That was why she gave him a scoop, a major story, which might get him – well, it was too early to start thinking about prizes. But he was definitely back in the game.

The Quill Bar in the Jefferson was a famous meeting spot for the power brokers in the capital, with its brass lamps, plush leather chairs, and mahogany-paneled walls adorned with portraits of the presidents. The place reeked of wealth, history, and power. One could feel important and consequential just by being in this room. Even the drinks were gleaming and beautiful, as if they were not just drinks but potions. Garcia walked toward the sound of the shaker as the bartender prepared a cocktail.

'I'm here to meet Richard Clarke,' Garcia said.

The bartender gestured toward a private room behind the bar. Garcia had never noticed it before. It was filled with books and nineteenth-century lithographs of Native Americans. Clarke was on his phone, giving clipped answers. He had receding white hair and freckles, signs of a former redhead. He wore glasses, a blue suit, and a menacing smile. He gestured toward a chair. Garcia obediently took a seat and placed his tape recorder on the glass coffee table between them. Clarke wagged his finger, and Garcia put the recorder away.

He had never met Dick Clarke, but he knew his reputation. He had served in the White House in three different administrations, notably as the counterterrorism czar under George W. Bush on 9/11. Now he ran a consultancy for corporate risk management and strategic intelligence. But what made him useful – and dangerous, in the eyes of his critics – was the endless list of his protégés strategically placed in various government offices. Clarke had his hands on the innards of the bureaucracy. Few in this grasping city had so carefully cultivated the people who actually made the government work. And they repaid him with information.

After several more yeps and nopes, Clarke set his phone aside. 'What's this about?'

'It starts with the cyberattack in Saudi Arabia in 2017,' Garcia said.

'Is that a question?'

'Do you agree it was the Russians who did it?'

'That's what people say.'

'How would people know?'

Clarke shrugged. Garcia realized that he was one of those people who titered out information in the smallest measurable units until he was offered something in return.

'I used to cover Fancy Bear,' Garcia said, by way of prodding.

'And now you cover movies.'

So it was going to be like that.

A waitress entered. Clarke ordered a Tito's Gibson. Garcia did the same.

'Look, I got a tip and I'm following up. From somebody in the administration. Pretty high up,' Garcia said hopefully. 'It's about Russian infiltration of American utilities.'

'Oh. Tildy's thing,' said Clarke. 'She's been hawking this story to any reporter who'll listen.'

'Well, I guess I'm the one who listened,' Garcia said lamely.

'I like Tildy,' Clarke said. 'She's smart. A little obsessed, but you need that in her job. So, what do you want to know?'

'Start with how we concluded it was the Russians who attacked the Saudi plant.'

Clarke offered one of his flat smiles. 'That's actually not a dumb question,' he said, as if he were bestowing a compliment. 'When it happened, I assumed it was Iran, like everybody else. They had already hit Aramco with a wiper attack, in retaliation for Stuxnet. Erased all their software. Thirty thousand workstations. The Saudis had to go around the world buying up hard drives. But nobody actually got hurt. With the new attack it looked like the Iranians were just upping their game, putting a little blood on the floor. That was before we tracked it to the Russians. We

146

now know the code used in the Saudi attack was written by the venerable Central Scientific Research Institute of Chemistry and Mechanics, an old Soviet department.'

'What was their motivation?'

'It could have been a trial run. The Russians did a lot of that in Ukraine, like Sandworm, just trying things out until they got serious and took down the electrical grid. Same with Fancy Bear. Before they got into manipulating American politics they put out a lot of fake news to perfect their technique. And then they sprung the trap.'

'I still don't see why the Russians would attack Saudi Arabia, even if they're using a false flag, pretending to be Iran.'

'Think about it this way,' Clarke said. 'How would Russian interests be served by a war between Saudi Arabia and Iran?'

'The price of oil would go through the roof. It would rescue the Russian economy.'

'Think deeper.'

'It would lead to war between Russia and the U.S.'

'I doubt it,' said Clarke. 'Putin is a tightrope walker. He wants to draw the U.S. deeper into the Middle East without actually going to real war.'

'Wouldn't the Iranians just take out the Arabian oil fields right away? Destroy the Saudi economy?'

'That's not their preferred goal,' said Clarke. 'Most of the Saudi oil is in the Eastern Province, which is largely Shiite. The Iranians want to annex that and take control of the Saudi resources. They've got lots of missiles and the coordinates for all the desalination and power plants in the kingdom. Without water and power, there won't be much left of Saudi Arabia.'

Garcia took mental notes of everything Clarke was saying, but it was going by pretty quickly. 'So how does this affect the U.S.?' he asked.

'We'd be dragged into another decades-long conflict. It would bleed the country dry. Meanwhile, Russia would pull the plug on our power grids, just like Tildy says.'

'So, we'd be without power for a while?'

'It would be a lot more serious than that. Do you remember the gas explosions north of Boston a couple years ago? Houses were blowing up. The fire departments were fighting eighty fires at once. All because some probably stoned technician accidentally over-pressurized the gas lines by a factor of three, forcing the gas to leak out. At the first spark, *boom*. So imagine the damage you could do if you controlled the valves and meters of utilities all over the country. The water plants, the nuclear facilities. Many of them are governed by those same Triconex systems, which were designed to keep the Saudi utilities safe. They'd be blowing up transformers and generators, knocking off power for months or even years. Russian subs sniff around the undersea cables. They could cut off the internet or compromise it to the point that it becomes unusable. Pretty much everything this country runs on could be brought to a halt.'

'Wouldn't that be true of Russia as well?'

'They've got much greater control over their infrastructure. It's very strictly regulated. Probably they have a program to isolate their systems controls from the internet. So they would have a considerable competitive advantage in a cyber-war where the target is the infrastructure that supports civilization.'

'Am I going to be able to quote you on all this?'

148

'I haven't decided,' said Clarke. 'I'll let you know when you're closer to publishing something.'

In the end, Clarke did allow his name to be used, but it made no difference. The article appeared on the front page of the *Post* and was applauded and then forgotten.

Marco Perella was back at the CDC in Atlanta when Henry Skyped in. 'You're growing a beard,' Marco observed.

Henry defensively covered his chin. 'I have so little time I thought I could economize on shaving,' he said. 'Do you think Jill will approve?'

'It's a pretty good beard,' Marco said. 'I think you should keep it.'

Henry smiled. 'I'll take it under advisement.'

'By the way, we've got Lieutenant Commander Bartlett on the call,' Marco said.

Henry recognized her immediately. 'Jane!' he exclaimed. 'I'm so relieved that you're a part of this.'

Bartlett flushed. Henry Parsons was one of her heroes. Like Marco and so many other young epidemiologists, she had interned for Henry and then made a career of public health.

'Are you still in Saudi?' Marco asked.

'I have to stay until we have the quarantine established,' Henry said. 'What are you finding?'

'Some surprises,' said Marco. 'You want to take a guess?'

'Earlier outbreaks,' said Henry.

'Crap, you're no fun to play with. How'd you know that?'

'That's what they found in 1918, as you know. There were precursors. Milder, of course. And older people did have some immunity, suggesting that there must have been a similar strain circulating in the nineteenth century. But then the virus mutated and turned itself into a killer.'

'In this case, it was China,' said Marco. 'Two outbreaks, one in Zhalong last October, and another in Poyang Lake a month later. We think there were seven fatalities, but the Chinese have still not published anything. WHO sent their vets up to check the water birds and, yes, they found Kongoli in the cranes. There is a rumor of a serious outbreak in North Korea. Something is going on in the tribal areas of Pakistan, and there may be a bird die-off in northern Iran, and what do these all have in common besides the maddening lack of confirmation?'

'Migratory flyways,' Henry said.

'Exactly. So it looks like the birds may have picked up something in Siberia and gone to Poyang Lake, which is the largest body of freshwater in China and the meeting place for millions of wild birds of all kinds. They winter over, exchange infections, maybe one bird gets infected with two different influenza viruses at the same time, they reassort, sharing gene segments, and presto, you have Kongoli, one of nature's deadliest creations.'

'But why have we never seen it before?' Bartlett asked. 'A totally new category of influenza. The hemagglutinin protein is completely unique and doesn't fit any of the known sub-types of influenza A or B. Without the neuraminidase protein, it's difficult for us to attack. Moreover, the PB1 gene is identical to 1918,' referring to the protein in Spanish flu that made it so pathogenic. 'It's highly virulent, and well defended, and it moves fast. One has to admire its perfection.'

'As if it were designed to inflict maximum death,' Henry observed.

'Really, Henry,' Bartlett asked, 'you think this was man-made?'

'Biowarfare has always been a part of the arsenals of the great powers. We shouldn't be surprised if this turns out to have been concocted in a laboratory. We know the Russians have tinkered with influenza. Good scientists. Maybe they wanted to see what could be done, if there was some way of collaborating with nature to build the ultimate weapon of war, one that can destroy the enemy without fingerprints.'

'It only makes sense if they have also developed a vaccine,' said Bartlett.

'Or if they don't care if they also die,' said Henry. 'If they think they will become martyrs.'

'This seems far too sophisticated for al-Qaeda,' Marco remarked.

'We know al-Qaeda has attempted to purchase bioweapons,' said Henry. 'And look at Aum Shinrikyo. They had microbiologists working with them, scientists who would have been capable of editing genes if they had had the technology we have today. We shouldn't underestimate the ability of any terrorist group to be able to manufacture novel viruses.'

'I just can't imagine a real scientist doing such a thing,' said Marco.

Henry said nothing. That was not a part of his life he cared to share.

An hour before dawn, on the last day of hajj, the sleepy pilgrims awakened to the roar of hundreds of helicopters filling the sky. Most of the pilgrims were packed and ready to leave later that morning. The hajj tour buses were waiting to take the travelers to the airport, but by the time the muezzin called for prayer, Mecca was surrounded by tanks and jeeps. Soldiers were stationed at roadblocks, erecting fences and unfurling curls of razor wire. The pilgrims had become prisoners.

While Majid and Colonel al-Shehri prayed on the promontory overlooking the city, Henry observed the encirclement of the city from their camp in the Mecca hills. Instead of praying, he reflected on all that he had done wrong. He was wrong to have gone into the Kongoli camp so poorly prepared, taking along the barest protection, thinking only of getting home as quickly as possible. He was wrong to have allowed the driver, poor Bambang Idris, to accompany him into the camp, not knowing what awaited them. He was wrong to have let Bambang out of his sight until he was certain that the man had not been infected. He was wrong not to insist that the driver be quarantined and forbidden to leave the country. All of these things weighed on Henry's conscience. He couldn't afford to waste mental energy castigating himself in this manner, but he couldn't forgive himself, either, and he knew he never would.

And now, at his urging, three million people were surrounded and held captive. Many would die. Eventually the disease would find its way out of the city. In any case, it was already seeded in the avian population and would soon appear wherever the birds touched down. At best, Henry had only slowed an inevitable history-shaping pandemic. Governments would fall. Economies would collapse. Wars would arise. Why did we think that our own modern era was immune to the assault of humanity's most cunning and relentless enemy, the microbe?

As the prayer ended, Majid entered the communications tent. He appeared physically burdened by the message he was about to deliver. 'Brothers and sisters, we have been chosen to make a great sacrifice,' he said into the microphone. As he spoke, his words were being translated into dozens of languages and broadcast from loudspeakers stationed throughout the holy region. He explained about the contagion that had spread through Mecca. 'It is our duty to prevent this thing, this terrible disease, from spreading. Remain calm. Your needs will be taken care of. Food will be supplied. Doctors and nurses will attend the ill. We will protect you. But you must not try to leave.'

Henry watched the pilgrims gather at the edge of the city, staring out at the troops in their vehicles and at the gun emplacements. Even as Majid was speaking, a young pilgrim began walking forward – defiantly, headed toward a space that had not yet been fenced. Nervous soldiers watched him approach.

'I repeat,' Majid said. 'Do not attempt to leave.'

Suddenly, the young pilgrim broke into a run. Behind him, other pilgrims surged forward. And then, Henry watched as the young man's body was ripped apart by machine gun fire. The horde of pilgrims came to an abrupt halt. The sound of their wailing carried all the way into the hills.

'May God forgive us,' Prince Majid said. 'May he accept our painful sacrifice.'

II

Pandemic

17

The People Will Not Forgive

JILL HADN'T HEARD FROM HENRY IN FORTY-EIGHT HOURS, which was unusual; he was almost always in touch every day, especially when he knew she was worried about him. Now she was beside herself with anxiety and still the phone hadn't rung. There was not even an email.

Finally, she sent a text: 'Ok?'

Eventually, the reply: 'Yes. Sorry. Later.'

That evening after the kids were in bed she found a report on MSNBC about the boy who was shot to death in Mecca. He turned out to be the nephew of an ayatollah in Qom. The outraged Iranian authorities were making threats and demanding justice, although what justice might be in this case was not clearly stated. On CNN, a reporter named Nadia al-Nabawi inside Mecca said that hospitals weren't giving out any information about the disease or the number of patients or even the fatalities. 'They tell us informally that they don't want to create panic, but the absence of reliable information has people wondering what's going on, and who to believe.'

Henry finally called a little after ten.

'Good Lord, what time is it there?' Jill asked.

'It's very late,' he said. 'I only just now got a chance to talk.'

'I know you wouldn't do this to me if you weren't really busy, but honestly, Henry, I've been worried sick. You look exhausted. And what's that on your face?'

'I've been growing a beard,' he said sheepishly. 'It helps me blend in here. I'll shave it if you don't like it.'

Jill studied the grainy image on the screen. 'We can postpone that decision until you get home. Which is when?'

'Honestly, Jill, I don't know. They need me here, but of course I'm wanted back in Atlanta. The main thing is that the quarantine is holding for the moment and, amazingly, no reports of influenza in the kingdom outside of Mecca.'

'I was watching some of the coverage,' Jill said. 'A lot of people are saying it's an overreaction.'

'Who is saying this?'

'The Iranian ambassador to the UN claims that it's just ordinary influenza, that nobody in his delegation is sick, and they all want to come home. They are demanding that they be set free and allowed to return immediately.'

'It's a lie,' said Henry. 'The Iranian pilgrims are suffering like everyone else. This is all about geopolitics, it has nothing to do with the health of their citizens.'

'I just want you to get out of there.'

'I want that more than anything, and I will get out, as soon as I can. But, listen, Jill. This disease isn't going to stay in Mecca. Even if we can keep the pilgrims locked up until this wave passes, the birds are carrying it. I don't know how much longer it will be before it hits the U.S. Maybe a week, maybe a month. I want you to take the kids and stay at your sister's farm. Take a couple month's worth of groceries.

Don't see anybody. Don't even touch the mail. Just hunker down and wait for me.'

'I know you're concerned about us, but really, Henry, there's a lot to be considered. I can't just drop everything and crash at Maggie's for however long.'

'Please, Jill, I know it looks safe for the time being. But this disease will move really fast. I'm pleading with you. Get out. Go someplace remote, as far from other people as you can find. Shelter with the kids until the contagion dies out.'

Henry had never sounded so scared.

Henry saw Majid standing by himself, looking at the lights of the imprisoned city. Seeing his friend there – agonizing over the fateful choice he had made – reawakened the guilt Henry was nursing over his own failure to stop the disease. The men stood together silently for a moment. 'What we have done, it will destroy us,' Majid said. 'This' – he gestured toward the city – 'the people will not forgive, no matter how it turns out.' He took a breath to clear his mind. 'Tell me, Henry, what are the prospects for a vaccine?'

'I talked to Dr Ahmed,' Henry said. 'He provided an isolate from a recent victim. The CDC compared it with the sample I took from Kongoli. There's been a change.'

'That could be good news.'

'Yes, it could be. Or it may be that the virus is becoming more infectious, more lethal. The problem is that we might be able to design a vaccine for the virus we have on hand, but we can only guess at where it's going.'

'We have to offer them some hope,' Majid said. 'Some reason to accept their suffering.'

'My team at the CDC isolated what they think is the

159

pathogen. If they're right, they might come up with a candidate vaccine for initial safety testing in two months.'

'Too late,' said Majid. He looked back at Mecca. The mosque glowed like a great ship on a dark sea. 'Truly, I don't know if I can trust my own troops. The idea of holding their brothers and sisters in the holy city, offering them like a sacrifice to this awful disease, many say it is a plot against Islam.'

There was something in Majid's voice that made Henry ask, 'What do *you* think?'

'I wait to see,' he said.

'It's complex and uncertain,' Marco explained on a Skype call with Henry the next morning. 'We're taking whole blood from survivors seven days after infection. At that precise moment there is a unique cell type, I'm sure you know—'

'The plasmablast,' said Henry, wondering why he hadn't thought of it.

'Right, it encodes the antibodies that react to the pathogen that is causing the infection.'

'And then you clone those genes to produce synthetic antibodies.'

'Exactly. We'll use them to simulate a natural immune response.'

'How long will that take?' Henry asked.

'A few weeks at least to find the best antibodies to block the virus, and several more to create a cell line, and then a month to begin large-scale production. It's not a real vaccine, obviously, but it might offer some passive immunity. Of course, it will be available only to rather small numbers of people. But if we don't do something to slow the progress of the disease, we don't stand a chance.'

Henry tapped his lips, sinking deep into his thoughts, searching for something no one else had come up with. 'There was this study,' he finally said. 'Something about transfusions in 1918.'

'Do you remember the authors? The journal?' Marco asked.

'All I remember is that there were doctors a hundred years ago in the same position we're in now. They tried something that I think may have worked.'

'I'll find it,' said Marco.

Majid came into the tent and waited patiently until Henry was finished. 'May we talk?' he asked. 'Something new has happened.'

The prince dropped heavily to the rug without his usual grace. He was clearly worn down by the last several days. Neither of them had slept more than a few hours during that time.

'This is not about the influenza, it's about what the crown prince and his councilors were talking about when we met,' Majid said. 'Just now I learned that one of our cousins was assassinated. Amira. She was vacationing in Sicily. Very beautiful, young, a free spirit, at least for Saudi Arabia. One of your magazines, *Vogue*, took some photos of her that were much discussed. Many people condemned her. Iran in particular spoke of her as a libertine and an example of the decadence of our family. So perhaps some offended Muslim decided to murder her. But our intelligence tells us that there was a team of killers from the Iranian Revolutionary Guards who followed her and trapped her at the private beach where she was swimming. They held her underwater until she drowned.'

'You think this is retaliation for the young man who was killed trying to escape the quarantine?'

'It seems likely. In any case, the crown prince and his councilors are seeking war with Iran. They are demanding an increased U.S. naval presence in the Gulf.'

Colonel al-Shehri suddenly interrupted their talk. Henry noticed a nervous tic in his right eye. His hands were trembling. The man was close to the edge. 'What is it, Hasan?' Majid said, dropping all formalities.

'We fear there will be a breakout,' he said. 'We have drone surveillance of four large groups forming at different spots. They do not belong to one delegation or another. It appears that some agitators are taking control of the mosque itself. The police inside are no help, they may even be with the insurgents.'

Majid absorbed the news with a deep, reflective sigh. 'We should not call them insurgents,' he said. 'They are prisoners, held without charge, and probably condemned to die. Tell me, Hasan, what would you do if you were in their place?'

'Majesty, I always remain loyal, but I believe my uncle is among them. He is a good man, my father's brother, many years in the National Guard, and now his own troops surround the city. This is not unusual. Many of our men have friends and relatives inside.'

Majid nodded. 'Hasan, I have not told you this, but my sister is also there, making her first pilgrimage, and now I have issued this order that may result in her death. Her children call me repeatedly. What can I tell them? This is personal for all of us. As a brother, I am outraged! But as the minister of health, I am their jailer. I cannot consult my conscience, because there is no clear answer for me.'

While they were talking, they heard the screech as someone from the mosque inexpertly turned on a microphone that broadcast through the minarets. It was not prayer time. 'Fellow Muslims!' a young man's reedy voice cried. 'Must we die like animals in a cage? We are millions. They cannot kill us all. But if we stay, everyone will die!'

Majid and the colonel walked out to the promontory to watch. Henry trailed respectfully behind. So much depends on what happens now, he thought. Everyone trapped inside the city longed for life, but many of them carried death inside them. Even if they managed to flee, there was no escape. Wherever they went, they would bring the disease, and they would give it to the people they cared most about – children, spouses, teachers, friends, coworkers. A kiss, a cough, a casual handshake, could kill. Some would survive the ordeal. Others, for reasons scientists still could not fathom, would be immune, untouched. But most of those who were infected would have another destiny.

'It is a conspiracy to murder Islam!' The young man's voice echoed into the hills. 'And those who keep us here are the servants of our enemies. They are killing our brothers and sisters! I say to them, Hell awaits you!'

Even at this distance, the men watching on the hilltop could hear a rumbling, like the approach of a great storm, as the pilgrims gathered their nerve and gave voice to their resolve.

'We must stop them,' Majid said to the colonel. 'Tell the commanders: no one gets through. Fire quickly to stop the surge. Kill the leaders first.'

163

The colonel rushed into the communications tent.

Henry wondered what the soldiers below, with their weapons ready, were thinking. Would they see the throng as fellow Muslims, besieged, defenseless, unjustly held, so many of them friends or family members longing for the safety of home? Or would they see death in their faces, the death that might await so many more if the afflicted managed to escape into the world?

'Arise, oh Muslims!' the young man cried.

A huge cheer went up, and a moment later tens of thousands of pilgrims gathered at the perimeter, chanting, 'God is great!' Soon there were hundreds of thousands. The chant turned into a roar as the vast mob lurched toward the fences. The faster ones reached first and began to climb, but then automatic weapons rang out, and bodies fell. Like a single organism the crowd slowed, but it didn't stop. Pressure from the rear pushed the entire mass forward, over the bodies of the dead leaders, as the guns continued to fire, but fewer of them now. The force of the crowd crushed those in front into the barriers, and then the fences themselves toppled, and the liberated pilgrims raced into the desert, past the soldiers, who no longer fired.

18
The Birds

JILL HEARD THE NEWS AS SHE WAS GETTING READY FOR BED. An international quarantine was imposed on Saudi Arabia. The airlines ceased service and borders were closed. Oil tankers turned around and abandoned the Saudi ports. Millions of pilgrims were stuck in the country.

Henry was stranded.

'It's a necessary precaution,' he told her when he finally called.

'But, Henry, you're needed here! Not just us, the country needs you! I'm getting calls from Catherine and Marco asking me to do *something* to get you home. So it's not just some desperate wife saying this. Your colleagues need you! I need you! Your children need you!'

'Jill, I want to come home, I really do! I've already spoken to someone in our embassy here. I thought they must have diplomatic flights or at least military ones.'

'And?'

'They don't. It's a total shutdown. It's that whole thing about the Muslim flu. It's just an excuse to keep them out of the country, but it also may help slow the progress of the disease.'

165

'Henry, you don't actually approve of this, do you?'

'Let's say they're doing the right thing for the wrong reason. We don't have many tools to fight this thing. Every time we try to bottle it up in a quarantine, the disease finds a way out. But we have bought some time, and maybe we can buy some more. But, of course, that doesn't get me home.'

All Jill could think about was that Henry was imprisoned in a country with the most devastating disease of their lifetimes.

Marco's face appeared on the screen. At first, Henry thought he might be ill. The fluorescent light underscored the exhaustion that was written in Marco's bleary eyes and on his haggard features. 'Are you okay?' Henry asked, trying to mask his concern.

'I'm fabulous,' Marco said, breaking into a grin. The old Marco. 'By the way, I dug up that study you mentioned,' he said. 'I don't know how you keep all these things in your head.'

The paper, from the *Annals of Internal Medicine* in 2006, was a meta-analysis of a novel treatment for the 1918 influenza. The authors examined eight studies conducted during the pandemic when no effective treatment had been found – just as now. In desperation, some doctors at the time resorted to the idea of transfusion, transferring the blood serum from survivors into symptomatic patients. 'These are terrible studies,' Marco said. 'No random trials. No dosages given, nothing standardized. They were done in wartime, under censorship, which may have prevented the publication of negative outcomes. The results are all over the place.'

Marco was sitting at his desk in the virology lab at the CDC, with his colleagues gathered around, where Henry longed to be. All of their faces, like Marco's, were studies in sleeplessness, but there was also a glint of hope in their eyes.

'But . . .?' Henry asked.

'But there was a measurable reduction in lethality.'

Transfusion had its own set of hazards, as everyone knew, including lung injuries that could be fatal. It was a last-ditch measure. For ordinary transfusions, both the donor and the recipient needed to be tested and the donor blood screened for infectious agents. The procedure had to be done in a highly sanitary environment. If successful, there would be many more potential recipients than donors, raising incendiary triage issues.

'I found something else, more recent,' Marco said. This was from *The New England Journal of Medicine*. In June 2006, a Chinese truck driver tested positive for H5N1 influenza A, which was pandemic in poultry and highly fatal in the few human cases that were reported. The driver had been sick for four days when he reported to a clinic in Shenzhen. He was treated with antivirals, which failed to stem the progress of the disease. In desperation, doctors obtained plasma from a convalescent patient who had recovered from the same infection several months before. The driver was given three 200-milliliter transfusions over two days. 'Within thirty-two hours, the viral load was undetectable,' Marco said.

'Get Jane Bartlett on the call,' Henry said.

Moments later, Lieutenant Commander Bartlett's face swam into view.

Marco explained the dilemma, which she was quick to grasp. Transfusions were different from monoclonal antibodies, which could be purified, tested, and mass produced. On the other hand, with transfusion, a single convalescent individual could supply sufficient plasma to treat several patients at once.

'You're talking about one confirmed patient in the last hundred years,' Bartlett observed of the studies mentioned. 'I don't see how we can make policy based on that. Is the CDC willing to recommend the treatment?'

Marco waited for Henry to answer. 'Not without human trials,' Henry conceded.

'So, another six months,' Bartlett observed. 'If we don't have Medicare and private insurers on board, who's going to pay for the treatment?'

'Can't you ask Health and Human Services to authorize it as a public health emergency?'

'Henry, of course I can, but that's not going to solve the insurance problem. This procedure is completely untested. The studies are unreliable and inadequate. The liability issues for physicians are formidable, maybe unmanageable.'

'But if you were treating a patient with Kongoli – fever spiking, viral load climbing, unresponsive to any treatment – what would you advise?' Henry asked. 'What would you do?'

'*Anything*,' Bartlett said, her voice breaking. Everyone immediately recognized the emotion. They had all lost someone. They knew what was coming.

Despite the panic, there was practically no evidence of Kongoli in the U.S. An outbreak in Minneapolis was mild and quickly contained. The index case was a traveler from the Middle East, which fed conspiracy theories about the Muslim disease. It turned out the traveler was an evangelical Christian who had been on a trip to the Holy Land. How he came down with Kongoli was a mystery.

At the same time, more than twelve hundred cases of seasonal influenza were diagnosed in Minneapolis, nearly all of them H1N1 influenza A, the great-grandchild of the 1918 pandemic – still considered a virulent strain, having killed eighty thousand Americans in 2017, and as many as half a million worldwide. But only four patients tested positive for Kongoli, including the traveler, and they all survived, lending hope to a theory that a competitive flu strain might provide some immunity against a new pandemic.

There was comparatively little influenza A in Little Rock, where the second outbreak occurred, and there Kongoli proved much more contagious. Still, the virulence was within the parameters of what people thought was an ordinary flu season. Within a week, grocery stores reopened, and other businesses quickly followed. Political pressure was building to open the borders and let the economy breathe. In places where the flu had not yet been reported, people told themselves that, for the moment, they were still safe.

And then came Philadelphia.

Of all the cities to suffer the heavy blow of contagion, Philadelphia was the one most informed by history to endure it. In 1918, Philadelphia, a city of about two million people, hobbled by corrupt and incompetent officials, had been crushed by the Spanish flu. Philadelphians died by the hundreds and then by the thousands – 4,597 in a single week in October 1918 alone – ten times the number of citizens who had died of all causes prior to the outbreak. Doctors and nurses worked heroically, but they suffered the highest death rates of all. Gravediggers either died or stopped working. The accumulation of corpses posed its own health problem, but more than anything else it broke the city's morale. Bodies remained for days in the homes where they died; cemeteries hiked up the price for burials and then forced family members to dig the graves themselves. Eventually, the city excavated mass graves with steam shovels, with priests giving committal prayers as the bodies were hurled into the trenches.

More than a century later, Kongoli crept into Philadelphia, seeding itself across the city with little notice. On Easter Sunday, hundreds of thousands of churchgoers attended services, and many of them were exposed to freshly infected parishioners. Within days, the city was brought to its knees.

The Penn Presbyterian Medical Center was as well equipped as any top-level big-city medical center to handle an epidemic, but not at all prepared for thousands of desperately ill citizens. The same was true in every hospital in the surrounding counties in Pennsylvania and New Jersey.

Philadelphia mayor Shirley Jackson had studied the history of pandemics. Her mother had been a nurse, so she had grown up around the medical profession. She had participated in a table-top exercise at Johns Hopkins concerning a hypothetical deadly disease outbreak. She knew the protocol. And she was decisive by nature. As soon as the disease was detected outside Saudi Arabia, she put into effect the Incident Command System, imposing coordination between local health officials, hospitals, emergency responders, and federal agencies. She got in touch with Lieutenant Commander Bartlett at the Public Health Service, who, in addition to her White House liaison duties, was coordinating urban health responses. Mayor Jackson demanded additional medical supplies from the nation's emergency storehouse. She called the heads of the three medical schools in the metropolitan area, instructing them to immediately train their students in emergency care. All first responders in the greater metropolitan area received infrared thermal cameras that attached to their smartphones so that they could instantly detect fever. Provisional hospital space was created in the Wells Fargo Center, where the 76ers played. No big-city leader did a better job of preparing for the contagion. She was lauded for her leadership on the front page of *The New York Times*.

What Mayor Jackson wasn't prepared for was the panic. There was a startling rise in suicides and homicides, as well as hate crimes, especially against the large Muslim community in the northern part of town. By now the origin of the disease – in an Indonesian detention camp for Muslim homosexuals – was well known, and the conspiracists were inflaming fears that Kongoli was a plot. According to one theory, Muslims had created the disease to destroy Christian civilization. Another theory posited that Muslims were being targeted for elimination by neo-Nazi scientists. A third theory postulated a worldwide war against homosexuals. These fantasies were promulgated in social media, led by Russian bots and amplified by internet rumor-mongers, stirring strife by remote control, urging people to take to the streets when they had been warned repeatedly to shelter at home. The imam of Philadelphia's main mosque urged his parishioners to ignore the conspiracy theories, but while he was speaking, two firebombs were thrown into the building.

Until now, Shirley Jackson had not been seen as one of the nation's great civic leaders. She had gone into politics after her husband, an Episcopal priest, died of cancer. Jackson had thrown herself into public service because it gave meaning to her own suffering. She instinctively knew how to talk to people who were frightened or grieving. 'Philadelphians are being tested,' she observed in one of the daily video council meetings she instituted. She was nakedly candid. 'Our hospitals are crippled, not just by the toll the influenza is taking on doctors and nurses but also by the loss of technical workers, medical assistants, therapists, pharmacists, and – critically – janitorial staff, which are so diminished in some facilities that bacterial infections are killing more patients than the influenza.' She went on to describe how illness and fear had ravaged the death industry. Private ambulances were essentially absent. She commandeered FedEx and UPS trucks to serve as death carts, which ferried the dead to the mass graves that were hastily dug in city parks. Countless bodies remained unclaimed or undiscovered. 'We in this city will not be divided by fear,' she said. 'Philadelphia is still and always will be the city of brotherly love. That is who we are. No matter what you read on the internet or who somebody wants to blame, our job is to love our brothers and sisters, to comfort them in this time of tribulation, to unite our community. Remain calm, open your hearts, aid the needy, and we will get through this together.' The mayor inspired Philadelphians to rise to the challenge by volunteering in local hospitals and helping with the grim task of disposing of the dead. She set an example by tending the homeless, who were disproportionately affected by the new plague.

Mayor Jackson's death from Kongoli flu, ten days into the epidemic, was a demoralizing blow from which the city never fully recovered. And the contagion spread.

———

A farmer in Arkansas died of Kongoli. Not much was made of his death at the time. He was a scoutmaster in a little mountain town, and he had taken his troop on a weekend trip to Little Rock, so it was thought that that was where he contracted the disease. But none of the scouts became ill. It was a week after his death that the CDC learned that what the farmer farmed were chickens. An alert went out to health officers around the country to be alert to infections in domestic fowl.

Mary Lou Shaughnessy was a field veterinarian with the regional U.S. Department of Agriculture office in St Paul, Minnesota. Her job was to ensure the health of exportable farm animals. An entire industry can go down in an instant. When mad cow disease was found in a single Holstein in Washington State in 2003, more than thirty countries immediately halted imports of American beef. Minnesota was especially sensitive to the issue of avian influenza, since the state was the leading producer of turkeys in the entire country – nearly fifty million birds in six hundred farms around the state. Minnesota also happened to be a major stopover for migrating birds on the Mississippi Flyway, which reached all the way from the tip of Canada, on the Arctic Ocean, to the Gulf Coast of Louisiana.

Mary Lou rode out on Route 23 with her partner, Emily Lankau, the state veterinarian. The two women had teamed up before, and they volunteered for this trip to spend more time together. They had both been in a cappella groups in college, and they loved to harmonize on road trips. They were headed to Kandiyohi County, the center of the turkey industry, where the highly pathogenic avian influenza H5N2 erupted in 2015. It was likely that the domestic fowl got the disease from migratory birds coming from Asia. More than 48 million turkeys died or were exterminated.

They drove past grain silos and railroad crossings. There wasn't much to see at this time of year. This part of Minnesota is flat, fertile land, but the fields were still fallow in March; it would be another month before corn and soybeans would go in the ground. 'We may as well do the Stevenson place first,' Emily said.

'Get it over with, you mean,' said Mary Lou.

Mr Stevenson – neither could remember his first name – was a tricky case. He was one of the largest farmers in the area, but he was also part of a militia group, known as the Minnesota 3 Percenters, a name drawn from the assertion that only 3 percent of American colonists took up arms against the British Empire during the American Revolution. The group was best known for bombing a mosque in Bloomington, although Stevenson was not indicted in that incident.

It was easy to spot the gate to his farm by the upside-down Stars and Stripes on the flagpole – a signal of distress that annoyed nearly everybody in the county. Stevenson made it clear he didn't care. He was a survivalist who homeschooled his children, so there was little interaction with the outside world in any case.

Mary Lou pulled up to the house in a white Ford Explorer with the USDA logo plainly emblazoned on the door. She and Emily got out of the truck wearing their cheeriest expressions. Stevenson was already standing behind the screen door.

'Mr Stevenson, how are you today!' Mary Lou said. She had been raised in the South and could affect an easy ebullience that stepped right over any sign of hostility.

174

'You're supposed to notify,' he said through the screen. 'I didn't get any notice. None whatsoever.'

'Yes, well, you don't have a phone. We talked about that last time.'

'I do accept mail.' By now, his brood of children had gathered around him.

'We are entitled to make spot visits, Mr Stevenson. And I certainly would have called, or mailed you a letter, but we're operating under emergency conditions.'

His face brightened. 'What emergency?'

'Gosh, Mr Stevenson, don't you follow the news? There's a terrible flu. Lots of people sick, just awful. There was a big outbreak in Philadelphia. Sure hope it doesn't come to Minnesota! The thing is, we have to check the birds, make sure they're okay.'

'My birds are fine.'

'I'm glad to hear it. We'll just have a look and then be on our way.'

They drove the truck to an empty patch of grass midway between the house and the barns. Emily stretched out a mat of heavy plastic, and the two women unloaded their gear – garbage bags, ice chest, swabs, a pump sprayer for the disinfectant, and their personal protective wear. The Stevenson kids were sitting on the grass or in a tree swing watching them put on their gear.

'Why do I feel like a stripper?' Emily muttered. 'This is, like, the opposite.'

'Maybe we should do a little dance,' Mary Lou said.

'I think not.'

First came the hooded Tyvek suit, then double plastic booties over their tennis shoes. A pair of plastic gloves, duct-taped onto the sleeve of the suit. A second pair of gloves. A hairnet and goggles. And, finally, the N95 respirator. They sprayed their garments with disinfectant, to eliminate any outside contamination. Perceptions get narrowed down in this outfit – your vision is constricted, and your hearing is muted. Walking is cumbersome. It's easy to feel claustrophobic and paranoid and a little ridiculous. The Stevenson kids followed them to the first barn.

This one was for the toms. The hens were in the other barn. There were twenty-seven thousand birds between the two. Emily slid open the door. It was a well-run operation, she had to admit – clean, brightly lit, plenty of air, fresh bedding. Still, it always struck her when she entered a poultry farm how much it resembled a prison. The birds were all white, circumnavigating the rows of feeders like inmates in the yard. They had pink wattled necks with bluish cheeks, looking nothing like their majestic, vividly feathered cousins in the wild. Their throats vibrated as they gobbled constantly in near unison. The smell was awful, as usual.

One of the Stevenson kids, a boy, had put on booties and coveralls and come into the barn. 'What's your name?' Mary Lou asked him.

'Charlie.'

'How old are the birds in here?'

'Seventeen weeks.'

'About ready for market, I suppose.'

'Yes, ma'am.'

As they walked through the mass of turkeys, the birds dispersed, making a wary circle around them. Emily took note of the birds behind them. Healthy birds are curious birds, and they will normally tag along, like the Stevenson kids. While Mary Lou and Charlie chatted, Emily began taking swabs. She grabbed one of the toms and pinched his cheeks until his bill opened, then ran a swab over the mucosa. She put the swab into a five-milliliter polypropylene tube and labeled it. She got Mary Lou to help turn the big tom upside down so she could rotate a swab inside the cloaca to collect the epithelial cells.

'What are you doing?'

Emily looked up to see a little barefoot girl in a dirty pinafore.

'Honey, you shouldn't be in here without your daddy. Didn't he tell you that?'

She nodded.

'Then go on back to him, he'll tell you what we're up to.'

When she balked, Charlie shouted at his sister to get out. She gave a sour look and walked as far as the door, not entirely out of the barn.

Emily finished the first bird by drawing blood from a vein under its wing. She continued taking samples from a dozen other birds selected more or less at random.

'Emily!'

She turned to see Mary Lou standing with Charlie at the other end of the barn.

'Look at them,' Mary Lou said, when Emily joined them. One turkey was sitting and refused to stand when prodded. Emily knelt down and peered in the bird's face. His head was drooping, and his eyelids were swollen.

'Charlie, have you had any birds die recently?'

Charlie didn't answer. He was staring at the barn door, where Mr Stevenson stood, backlit by the sun, his hands in

177

the pockets of his protective overalls, his shadow reaching across the floor of the barn. He abruptly turned and left.

When Emily and Mary Lou finished their sampling, they went back to the tarp beside their truck and reversed their procedure. They stood in a footbath, and then wrapped up their protective garments in a garbage bag, which they sprayed with disinfectant. They also sprayed the tires of their truck. They wiped their hands and face with Purell. And then they raced to the FedEx store in St Cloud to send their samples to the USDA lab in Ames, Iowa.

'I've got a bad feeling about this,' Mary Lou said.

19

It's Not a Vaccine

'DAY AFTER DAY WE GET THE SAME REPORT FROM YOU,' TILDY said, scolding Lieutenant Commander Bartlett, who had become an ominous fixture at the Deputies Committee meetings – like the Ghost of Christmas Future, with grim visions delivered in a laconic southern drawl. 'No vaccine,' Tildy recited, counting on each finger. 'No treatment. No cure. You have to tell us something positive! The American people are beside themselves with worry.'

Bartlett responded with a look that Tildy instantly recognized as pity. 'We have *plans,* ma'am. We've had *plans* for years, at the CDC and NIH and Johns Hopkins and Walter Reed, we've had lots of plans. We just haven't ever been given the resources and personnel to carry them out. Like ventilators. We figure that maybe 30 percent of hospital patients reporting severe influenza symptoms will need to be ventilated. Right now we can accommodate about 1 percent of patients who require them. Meantime, people are dying of other treatable diseases because we have no stockpile of essential medicines. They're all made in India or China, which are also suffering this pandemic. We're running out of syringes, diagnostic test kits, gloves, respirators, antiseptics, all the stuff we need to treat patients and protect ourselves.'

'Honey, I don't think you understand.' A deep voice suddenly broke in. The vice president was a former governor and radio host known for his tough demeanor. The president had made him the official point person for the pandemic, and recently he had begun attending the Deputies Committee meetings. Once he started coming, the room filled up with staffers and note-takers jammed against the walls. 'We need deliverables! And I mean today! The president wants action, and he wants it now!'

Bartlett stiffened. 'I know what you people want me to say, but that's not my job, is it? I am supposed to be giving you information. Real information. What you do with it is your job. Now, if you had been doing your job and providing us with the resources we asked for, maybe we wouldn't be sitting here sucking our thumbs while people are suffering and the economy is going to hell and the graveyards are filling up and all because people like you didn't care enough about public health to pay attention to our needs.'

The vice president looked like he'd been hit with a crowbar. For a moment, everyone was afraid to speak.

'Mainly, we have to give something to the president that will project a sense of calm,' Tildy said gently. 'Of hope. Of progress. Like that soon people will be able to get a shot and they'll be protected.'

Bartlett shook her head ever so slightly. The pity thing again. 'Even if we had a vaccine, the question is, who gets the shot? It takes months to ramp up production, and it won't even start unless the drug companies are protected against liability. I mean, we don't have time to do standard human safety testing. And let's say we get ten thousand doses the first week, and a hundred thousand the week after, and five hundred thousand the next week, and so on. It'll still take months to scale up to the point where we'll have enough material to create some kind of herd immunity. Even then, you may need two or three doses to be safe.'

While recovering his dignity, the vice president had put on reading glasses and busied himself by leafing through a briefing folder. 'What's this about antiserum?' he demanded.

'NIH is testing the serum of surviving victims to see if it can be used to provide passive immune therapy,' Bartlett said.

'Well, can it?'

'Some. Temporarily. In theory.'

'Can we have the president say that a vaccine is in development?'

'It's not exactly a vaccine.'

'What exactly is it?'

'It's a monoclonal antibody. It's something that the immune system makes by itself after an infection or vaccination, but we can make it synthetically. It might provide immunity for a few weeks.'

The vice president's impressive jaw clenched in frustration. 'Can he say that there is a promising treatment—'

'It's not a treatment. At best it offers a few weeks of—'

The vice president held up a cautioning hand, indicating his displeasure at Bartlett's interruption. '– and that *real progress* is being made. I think we'll leave it at that.' The vice president assembled the briefing papers and lifted them over his shoulder, knowing that an aide was there to snatch them out of his hand.

'We haven't tried it in humans yet,' Bartlett protested. 'We're running it through ferrets.'

'Tell me one thing,' the vice president said. 'Are the ferrets alive?'

'Most of them, but the experiment is still ongoing—'

'More than there would be if they hadn't taken this stuff?'

'That's impossible to say. We don't have the mortality data yet.'

'And you would have that when?'

'In about two weeks.'

The vice president pursed his lips. 'Why not human trials?' he asked. 'Why not now?'

'It will take several months to make a product suitable for human use, and even then a single monoclonal antibody might not be enough to prevent a rapidly changing virus from escaping. So it's high risk. Meantime, you should consider making a priority list saying who gets the antibody serum and in what order. It's going to be really scarce. Members of the government? First responders? Children? Military? Pregnant women? National Guard? A lottery? These are choices you'll have to make.'

'Agree that we need to do this. But no on the lottery or releasing the schedule. It'd be a political mess. We should keep the vaccine secret and—'

'It's not a vaccine, sir,' Bartlett reminded him. 'And remember, after several weeks people would need another dose unless we have a real vaccine by then.'

The vice president glared at Bartlett with all the force his telegenic blue eyes could summon. 'We'll keep *whatever* secret until we've secured the most vital elements of our society, so people aren't struggling over questions like how many children are going to die while the bosses are getting their booster shots.'

'We've got a raging epidemic in Philadelphia, only two hours away from here, so you can understand we're in kind of a hurry,' Tildy said, in her most courteous voice.

'We have influenza in Washington as well, ma'am.'

'Jesus,' the vice president said. 'When did this happen?'

'The reporting came in this morning from three hospitals in the city. A total of nineteen cases so far. If it develops as quickly as it did in Philadelphia, it will be a full-blown epidemic in three to five days.'

Tildy was silent. She looked around the table and saw the despair in the faces of the deputies, which she was sure was reflected in her own expression as well.

'The good news,' Bartlett said, and suddenly everyone leaned forward, 'the good news is that, if we're lucky, we could have an effective vaccine at scale in about six months, hopefully in time for the second wave.'

'The what?'

'Typically, with a pandemic, you have two or three big waves of contagion before it settles down and becomes the normal flu you get every year. That lasts until the next pandemic comes along. So, if this one is like the 1918 flu, the really big wave will hit in October. But of course we don't know what this one will do.'

The silence was broken by a loud sneeze. Everyone gasped.

'It's allergies,' the agency man said defensively.

'You say this is a completely novel disease,' Tildy said. 'What are the chances that it's man-made? Something the geniuses cooked up in a lab?'

'We haven't been able to determine whether it's an

engineered virus,' Bartlett responded. 'It doesn't have the usual sequence characteristics of a virus cooked up in a lab, but it's also not something we've ever seen in nature.'

'Who has the capacity to make such a thing?'

'That's not my area, ma'am.'

Tildy looked at the agency man. 'Russia is at the top of the list,' he said.

'The Russian people have been told that Kongoli is an American plot,' State said. 'They're hysterical over this.'

'Well, is it?' Tildy asked.

The question lay on the table before the vice president finally said, 'Don't be ridiculous.'

20

We Treat Each Other

ON A COMPUTER IN PRINCE MAJID'S JEDDAH PALACE, HENRY studied the concentration of Kongoli outbreaks on a world map. In the month since the Mecca outbreak, the disease had spread widely, despite the quarantine. Red in various hues indicated the presence of the disease. Saudi Arabia and Iraq were crimson. The infection spread from there. It was a lighter red in Iran, diminishing in intensity to a pale pink in Afghanistan and Turkey. Russia was curiously unaffected, except for a pink dot on Moscow. China was pale in the eastern portion and red in the west, where the largely Muslim Uighur population was concentrated. India was covered with pink dots in the cities, but Pakistan was barely touched. A large pink stain blanketed northern Europe. Red dots of different intensities were scattered across the U.S. but no sizable pink splotches; it was mainly in the cities. Canada had a single mild outbreak in Toronto. The Southern Hemisphere was virtually untouched. That would likely change as it moved into winter.

'We know the disease is in the avian population, so that could account for some of the randomness,' Henry said. 'But I've never seen an influenza map that looked exactly like this.'

Majid was standing behind him. 'Is it possible that the disease was seeded in some places?' he asked.

'I was thinking the same thing. If this is an engineered virus, it would make sense that the perpetrators would pick targets.'

Majid paused, then said, 'Funny about Russia.'

Henry nodded. 'Lots of disease all around it, but very little in Russia itself. They have an unorthodox vaccine for seasonal flu, which is different from the world standard. It's an attenuated live virus, which has advantages. It's inhaled, rather than injected. It's cheaper. They also add a compound called polyoxidonium. It appears to be an immunomodulator with a lot of bewildering claims. Hard to know if that would make a difference, but of course they're testing for that at the NIH.'

'If this is what you think it is, I pray it is Russia and not al-Qaeda,' said Majid. 'The world already thinks all Muslims are terrorists.'

Henry silently recalled the years he had worked to counter the Russian bioweapons program. Highly skilled Soviet scientists had crafted deadly and incurable diseases in their germ warfare centers – mainly, the Vektor Institute in western Siberia and the bioweapons research facility in Obolensk. The great scourges of history, such as plague and smallpox, were refined into aerosol form, manufactured by the ton, and resistant to any known treatment.

The chief scientist at Vektor in the Soviet era was Nikolai Ustinov. He was studying Marburg, a member of the poorly understood family of diseases called filoviruses. Marburg first erupted in the human population in the German city that would give it its name. In 1967, a lab worker died after culturing the virus in kidney cells from African green monkeys. Seven other researchers died in other German labs working with infected monkeys. Nine years later, a related virus erupted in Zaire, and it would be named after the Ebola River.

Nobody knew Marburg better than Ustinov. Like many disease researchers, even great ones, Ustinov was the victim of a fatal mistake. He was holding a guinea pig to be injected with the virus when his partner accidentally plunged the needle into Dr Ustinov's finger.

Henry once had the opportunity to attend a lecture by Kanatzhan Alibekov, who had been the first deputy director of Biopreparat, an arm of the secret Soviet biowarfare program. Alibekov defected to the U.S. in 1992 and changed his name to Ken Alibek. A heavyset man with large glasses and a round, fleshy face, reflecting his Kazakh origins, Alibek told the story, in a lightly inflected Russian accent, of what happened to Dr Ustinov. Immediately after his accidental injection, Ustinov had been given the antiserum, but the disease continued to progress. Over the next few days, for the purposes of science, Ustinov precisely described the course of his infection. He even joked with the nurses, until he was incapacitated by the disease's paralyzing headaches and nausea. 'He became passive and uncommunicative,' Alibek recalled. 'His features froze in toxic shock.' Small bruises covered his body and his eyes turned red; sometimes he would burst into tears. Then, on the tenth day, he suddenly seemed to get better. His mood improved, and he asked about his family, but inside his body the virus was finishing its work. The bruises on his skin enlarged and turned dark blue as the blood began pooling near the surface, and then it spilled out of his body, from his mouth, his nose, his genitals. He was in and out of consciousness. Two weeks after the infection, the genial Nikolai Ustinov was dead. During the autopsy his liver and spleen were removed, along with his blood. Ironically, the pathologist who conducted the autopsy suffered the same grim fate as Ustinov, having accidentally pricked himself with a needle while extracting a sample of Ustinov's bone marrow.

Before burial, Ustinov's body was covered in disinfectant and wrapped in plastic, then placed in a metal box that was welded shut. The virus that killed him, however, endured. It was extracted from Ustinov's organs. His colleagues labeled it Variant U, in Dr Ustinov's honor. The Ustinov strain was cultured and stockpiled and placed on ballistic missiles with multiple-entry warheads.

Trapped in Saudi Arabia by the quarantine, Henry spent his time in the field with Majid. The huge Health Ministry in Riyadh had a poorly used research facility. Majid confiscated whatever Henry needed to make it functional, but he couldn't provide knowledgeable lab assistants with experience in developing vaccines. Henry fought the disease with the only weapon he could muster: antiserum from the survivors.

He and Majid knew the risks. The program specified the regular bleeding of victims who were completely symptom free. Each was commanded (this was an absolute monarchy) to surrender five hundred milliliters of whole blood every week. Blood-filled tubes were placed in a centrifuge, which stripped away platelets and blood cells. An amber layer of serum floated on top of the red blood cells, containing all of a person's antibodies. The serum from one survivor was enough for a single injection of antiserum, so the quantity was far from adequate to deal with the hundreds of thousands who had been infected, and the purity was impossible to determine. The danger was that the serum might contain pathogens, including Kongoli itself, that hadn't been filtered out.

Marco and the team at the CDC were trying the same thing, hoping to find the correct dosage. 'So far we've had excellent success in vitro, and we're trying it in monkeys,' Marco said. 'What are you seeing with your human patients?'

Henry shook his head in puzzlement. 'For some reason, I can't get the records from the Health Ministry. I'm going to demand an answer tonight when I see Majid. There must be a reason for this. He knows as well as I how important this is.'

Majid had been visiting hospitals all day. When Henry came back to the palace and found him in his study, he was clearly exhausted and discouraged. 'There is no place to put all the patients,' he said. 'It feels as if half the country is ill. We've turned sports stadiums into additional wards, but we don't have the staff to support them. This is a challenge, Henry. I don't know how the kingdom can endure another month of this.'

'All the more reason to concentrate on the antiserum regime,' said Henry. 'We've expanded our pool of donors considerably, but without the data there's no way of measuring our success. You must tell me what's going on. Is it simply bureaucratic incompetence or is there something else at work?'

Majid looked away, unable to face Henry directly. 'I'm so ashamed to tell you this,' Majid said, his voice little more than a whisper. 'My family has commandeered the entire supply of antiserum we've secured so far.'

'Do they understand the danger?'

'What they see is people dying, and they are frightened. So, because they are princes, they assume they are entitled to save themselves first.'

'If I believed in an immortal soul, I would say it is the first organ to be contaminated by disease,' Henry said.

'We Muslims believe that illness is a test that God brings upon us.'

'That sounds like punishment.'

'Not at all. The Qur'an instructs us that if God were to punish humanity for what it deserved, there would be nobody left on earth! We are also instructed that, for every ailment, there is a cure. And so it is up to us to find it, my friend!'

Majid walked over to the bookshelf to find a passage in the hadith to support his argument. 'I forget the exact language, but I will—' As he was talking, a lamp suddenly flew across the room and Majid himself rose into the air in slow motion, his robe billowing around him, and was then hurled into a wall with shocking force, followed by shards of glass and masonry and a massive roar that ended when the lamp collided with Henry's head.

When Henry came to, the room was swirling with dust and smoke. He was alive. His breath was shallow. He was not in pain, but he was numb and confused, and for a moment he couldn't remember where he was. Someplace unfamiliar, black and ruined, dreamlike. He felt slow and strange, as if he were extremely old.

'Majid!'

As soon as he spotted his friend lying on the floor, Henry understood everything. Then the office door opened, and without thinking Henry threw himself over Majid's body.

He felt a pair of hands lifting him. It was Majid's bodyguard.

'Your Highness!' the bodyguard cried. 'Are you injured?'

The prince looked at the bodyguard in confusion and fumbled to sit up. When the bodyguard started to help him to his feet, Henry blocked him. 'Don't!' Henry cried. 'He may have broken bones.'

Henry carefully moved Majid's limbs to see that they were intact. 'You're bleeding,' he observed.

'You're shouting,' said Majid.

'Am I? I can hardly hear you.' His own voice sounded as if it were coming from another room.

Majid turned to his bodyguard and got a report. A suicide bomber had approached the gate. He was young, with an accent of the Eastern Province. He said that Prince Majid had promised him charity. When the palace gatekeepers refused to let him in, he blew himself up. Now the gatekeepers were dead. Seeing that Majid was alive and intact, the bodyguard rushed off to protect the palace until the police arrived.

Majid and Henry sat on the floor, staring at each other in the dazed amazement that only survivors know, where every detail is newly crisp and each fresh moment is like a crust of ice on a pond, a thin tangible layer between life and death.

'Where is your medical bag?' Henry asked. 'I need to attend to your wounds.'

'I must check on my staff,' the prince protested.

'First, we repair the damage to your face. You can't go around bleeding, you'll scare everyone to death.'

'Is it that bad?'

'It's not disfiguring,' Henry assured him. 'But I detect some puncture wounds near your eye. Let's make sure they're not near any nerves.'

Henry helped Majid to his feet. The prince looked at the damaged room in shock. The front of his palace was open to the city. He seemed paralyzed by the weird beauty of the scene. The night air invaded the room, the scent of explosives carried on the unfamiliar breeze singeing their nostrils. Both men jumped when the chandelier suddenly gave way. Majid was dazed and a little wobbly. Henry steered him to a more secure portion of the palace.

Fortunately the lights in the prince's bedchamber were working. They examined themselves in the bathroom mirror. They were both coated in white dust, making them look like corpses. Henry noticed blood on his left shoulder and an ugly contusion on the side of his head.

'So,' Majid said, 'we treat each other.'

While Majid cleaned himself, Henry sterilized a probe and tweezers, then examined the several small wounds around Majid's temple and nostril, extracting small bits of glass only millimeters from his eye. 'You were fortunate, *habibi*,' he said, using the Arab term of endearment.

It embarrassed Henry to remove his shirt. The signs of his childhood disease were obvious: the scoliosis that had left one shoulder higher than the other, the protruding breastplate, his swollen forearms. Henry never exposed himself in this way to anyone but Jill. Majid graciously pretended to focus only on the cut on his shoulder. 'Ah,' said Majid, 'you get to have stitches. And I haven't done this since medical school.'

It was a strange interlude full of unexpected intimacy. They had already been through so many fateful moments together, but the still undigested experience of surviving what was meant to be their final moment made them aware that they would always be bonded to one another as they would never be to anyone else.

Majid said, 'You saved my life.'

'I did nothing of the sort,' Henry protested.

'You attempted to do so. Maybe I would expect my body-guard to do such a thing had he been present. You are under no obligation to me, and yet you are willing to sacrifice yourself. You are a better man than I. And much, much braver.'

'You give me too much credit.' Henry winced. 'Although I don't think I'll want you to sew stitches in the future.'

'This is why I stay in the office and not in the hospital.'

As the shock wore off, both men began trembling. It was impossible to control. They laughed, giddily, still marveling at being alive. But it wasn't safe to stay in the palace.

The kingdom had been struggling with an insurgency even before the hajj. 'These are our own people, Shiites from the Eastern Province,' Majid confided. 'They are being supported by the Iranians to attack the royal family. And this is not their only attempt. One month ago, they bombed the National Guard headquarters. They are determined and reckless and it is obvious that we are going to respond.' His bandaged face suddenly contorted. 'How stupid this whole business is! We are facing such danger – the whole world! And yet these fanatics think only to take advantage of the chaos! And we are just as bad. We are blaming Iran for this disease, saying it is a Shiite plot, so the people will turn their attention to war and not revolution.'

Majid finally cast an appraising professional eye on Henry's distorted body. 'You know, we still have this disease in the Middle East,' he said. 'There is no reason for it. We have more sun than anyplace in the world, but people hide inside, and they don't get enough vitamin D. Seventy percent of girls in this country have low levels of this vitamin. It's not surprising, the way they bury themselves in those black robes. Nursing mothers refuse to take supplements, so it passes to the children.'

Henry said that, one day, he would tell Majid his story, but this was not the time. In any case, the police arrived, and the prince and his guest would be taken to a place of safety.

21

The Foaming

THE STEVENSON BARNS WERE ALREADY SURROUNDED BY trucks from the Minnesota Board of Animal Health, a local fire department, and a bus from the state correctional facility in Shakopee. There were nine other poultry farms to depopulate that day, and the state, undermanned for such a task, had enlisted volunteer prisoners for the statewide eradication. They were standing in the yard, suiting up, when Mary Lou Shaughnessy and Emily Lankau arrived. As the senior health official on the site, Emily had the unappealing job of dealing with Mr Stevenson, who was sitting in a rocking chair with a shotgun in his lap.

'Good morning, Mr Stevenson,' she said. 'I'm sorry about the test results.'

'I don't agree to this,' he said. 'I don't agree to this a'tall.'

'You know the rules. You'll be compensated.' She handed him a clipboard with some paperwork, which Stevenson scarcely glanced at. 'They did a count of 25,673 healthy turkeys this morning,' Emily said. 'Another seventy birds appear to be ill. Then I think you've got some eggs that would be covered as well.'

'There was twenty-seven thousand birds in there before you came,' Stevenson said defiantly.

'If you say so. In any case, that means you had more than a thousand deaths in a couple days. We don't pay for dead birds, and we pay less for sick birds, so what we're talking about is fair-market value for healthy birds and the standard amount for depopulation and cleanup.'

'This ain't gonna come anywhere near covering the losses,' Stevenson said.

'You're right. And it's not just you. We've got farms all over the state that are facing the same situation. But here's the deal. We're gonna kill your birds whether you like it or not. Then we'll clean it up and send you the bill. If you don't sign this paperwork, you won't get paid anything. That's pretty clear. Also, I wish you'd take that gun inside, it's making folks nervous.'

'You fill my yard with convicts and you worry about *their* mental state?'

'To be honest, I didn't know they were using prison labor, but I'm sure they'll be on good behavior.'

Stevenson's jaw set. Emily had the feeling he was going to say something he would regret. So she asked, 'Mr Stevenson, do you mind my asking your Christian name?'

He looked startled. 'Jerome,' he said.

'May I call you Jerome? You know this is something that has to be done. It's not the government singling you out. It's a terrible catastrophe. People everywhere are in danger. Your own family, I think, is in terrible danger. They'll need to be taken care of. You'll have to watch out for any fever or signs of illness and report it right away. Get to a doctor or a hospital as soon as you can.'

'They can't do shit.'

'What I hear is that fluids are essential. There can be a lot of pain, and doctors can help with that. People who are cared for have a better chance. I know you'd want that for your family, Jerome. I'm just saying, be on guard. I bet you're good at that.'

'I am,' he said.

'And the paperwork?' Emily said.

Jerome signed his name and handed her the clipboard.

Even with all her years in animal health, Mary Lou had never seen a mass slaughter. She was not looking forward to it. She had done many inspections that could lead to such an event, but it had never fallen to her to participate. The convicts had erected a fence of plastic panels that completely encircled the inside of the barn. The fence came up to Mary Lou's chin. Inside there were thousands of distressed turkeys, looking this way and that at the forbidding figures in their hooded white plastic suits who were dragging thick plastic hoses into the barn. The hoses were attached to a pair of tank trucks that had backed up to the doors on either end.

Mary Lou recognized Emily's eyes behind the goggles as she approached. 'Are you ready for this?' Emily asked.

'I guess.'

'Listen, it's a whole lot better than some other options. Sometimes they use these things like long-handled garden shears to break their necks, one by one. This goes a lot quicker, believe me.'

'Are they using gas?'

'Foam,' said Emily. 'Essentially, the same stuff fire

departments use. The little bubbles are just the right size to get inhaled and caught in the airways. They suffocate to death.' When Mary Lou shuddered, Emily said, 'They're all gonna die anyway. We're just giving them a better death.'

A man in a custom Tyvek suit with the company logo – Minnesota Foamers – on his chest approached Emily. She gave him permission to begin.

It took two men to manage each hose. They began on opposite sides of the pen, slowly moving down a parallel course. The pumps made a terrific racket, which had already upset the turkeys before the foam spewed out. It was slightly blue in color, and substantial, like the whipped cream that Mary Lou sprayed on her Thanksgiving pies. It mounded up unevenly. The healthier turkeys ran away from it, but as they were surrounded, some dipped their heads in the rising foam, or bathed in it. Their curiosity had gotten the better of them. Soon all you could see were the long, red, turkey throats sticking out of the rising blue-white foam, and all you could hear over the racket of the pumps was the gobbling, nervous and louder, and then the turkeys in the back where the foam was higher disappeared, and you could tell by the agitation under the foam that their wings were flapping. Finally, the foam curtain closed over the last of the turkeys. It looked to Mary Lou like an ocean wave in a stirring breeze, and then the breeze subsided, and that was that.

When Emily and Mary Lou turned away, they saw the Stevenson children standing in the barn door, Charlie and the girl in the pinafore and two others.

'Go back to your dad, Charlie,' Emily said.

Charlie walked back to the porch where Mr Stevenson was sitting in the rocker. It occurred to Emily that there was never a Mrs Stevenson around. He must be alone, with all these kids, and no one to talk to. She wanted to tell him that there would be another year, a better one coming. That he could start over again. That maybe he'd find someone to help him out, console him at times like this. But she couldn't make any such promise. Instead, she raised her hand in parting, and he nodded.

22

Queen Margaret

SINCE THE BIG OUTBREAK IN PHILADELPHIA, JILL HAD TAKEN the kids to her sister's farm. She did it to placate Henry. She was used to him going off to dangerous places, and she prided herself on managing without him. She was handy, she did the books, she kept the house running without disrupting her teaching. No one would fault her competence and independence. But now the dangerous place was everywhere, and Jill was scared. Henry would know how to deal with the anxiety that stalked her thoughts. He wasn't here to steady her and reassure the children. Both resenting his absence and desperately missing him, she tried to expel him from her thoughts and sink into another existence, her younger sister's life.

Helen and Teddy loved their Aunt Maggie and Uncle Tim. They farmed 240 acres in Williamson County, outside Nashville, one of the most beautiful parts of Tennessee. Their picturesque farmhouse had been a stop on a stagecoach line before the Civil War, a detail that put it on the National Register of Historic Places. It was a wreck when Maggie and Tim first drove across the covered bridge onto the graveled drive leading to the house. 'The repairs nearly broke us,'

Tim recalled, but now their home was such a showplace that it was featured on an episode of *This Old House*. There were azaleas and daylilies in the front beds, and dogwoods lined the drive.

Maggie and Tim's only child, Kendall, was two years older than Helen, although Helen was taller. They looked almost like twins, both lefthanded, both redheads, and both with blue eyes, a pair of genetic rarities with so many recessive traits. As soon as Helen arrived, the two of them disappeared, spending hours together in Kendall's room or in the barn. Kendall was in the Williamson County 4-H Club, and her room was full of trophies and ribbons and photographs of her prize animals.

One day, Tim took Kendall and Helen to a livestock auction in Franklin, where Kendall was shopping for a piglet to raise. 'I've had two Berkshires already,' she told Helen. 'This year, I'm going to get a Hampshire. They're really common, but the judges sorta favor them.'

Helen couldn't keep herself from cooing over the little black-and-white piglets with their floppy ears, sticking their snouts forward just begging to be petted. 'They are soooo cute!' she exclaimed. But Kendall was looking for other qualities. 'Shoulder angle, that's important,' she said. 'Size of the chest, the muscles of the loin. It's basically all about meat.' She finally picked out a fifty-pound gilt. The girls rode home in the back of Tim's pickup and Helen got to cradle the pig in her lap. All the way back she and her cousin talked about names, which Kendall said was important from a judging perspective. She finally settled on Queen Margaret, because that was her father's pet name for her mother. The girls laughed about that. When they got home, Tim made them change their clothes and shoes to keep from tracking any diseases from the auction tent onto their farm.

While the girls were at the auction, Maggie took Jill on a tractor ride around the property, towing Teddy behind them on a cart piled high with mulch, while Peepers raced behind, barking ecstatically. The sisters had a lot to catch up on. Maggie had had breast cancer the year before, and she was still recovering from the ordeal. Still, she insisted on going back to work on the farm. 'Every day, I think how fortunate I am to still be here,' Maggie said. 'To still be with Tim and Kendall, and to have all we have together. I'm so happy to be alive.'

Jill looked out at the rows of corn that were already two feet high. Maggie's life was so distant from her own. She reflected on the things that Maggie had that she never would – an intimacy with nature, for instance. Maggie didn't vote, she didn't even have a television, but she could recognize birds by their calls. Her kitchen garden was filled with herbs that Jill had never tasted before and varieties of tomatoes you couldn't find in a store.

On the other hand, Jill missed being home – their house, the neighborhood, running in Lullwater Park, listening to the voices of her students facing the quandaries that life posed for them. It seemed so isolated out here. Of course, that was what she and the kids had come for – refuge. And yet, the influenza still hadn't gotten to Atlanta, so it seemed pointless and indulgent to have left her job and taken the kids out of school as a precaution.

'Being sick had a weird upside,' Maggie was saying. 'We took a huge financial hit because of it. And I was in a lot of pain. What helped me through it was this . . .' She parked

202

the tractor in front of a drying shed. 'When we first bought the farm, they were using this place for tobacco,' she said, as they walked inside. Leafy bundles were suspended from racks.

'What is it?' Jill asked.

'You really don't know? Can't you smell it?'

Jill sniffed. 'Oh my God, is this legal?'

'Kinda.'

Jill stared a hole in her sister as Teddy and Peepers came into the shed. 'Ooh, what's that stinky smell?' Teddy asked.

'It's just the smell of these weeds,' Maggie said, giving Jill an ironic glance. Peepers ran around in confusion, jangled by the odor.

'Wait outside, honey,' Jill suggested to Teddy.

Maggie broke off the head of one of the drying stalks. 'When I was in so much pain, a friend of mine brought me some marijuana. It really helped. And then we found out you could grow it for the CBD oil, which is now legal in Tennessee. You just can't have any of the good stuff in it. So we do raise it for the oil, but also for, you know, humankind. It's the most profitable crop we've ever had. Primo weed, believe me.'

Jill was dumbfounded to realize that Maggie was a drug dealer. 'You always did have a green thumb,' she said gamely.

'I'll prove it to you when the kids go to bed.'

Maggie made a pork loin for dinner, which Helen avoided eating as soon as she found out what it was. She had made a private vow to become a vegetarian like her dad as soon as they got back to Atlanta. The idea of one day eating Queen Margaret was too awful to consider.

'It'd be like eating Peepers,' she told Kendall when they were in bed.

'Queen Margaret's not a pet.'

'But don't you love her? She's so cute.'

'She's not always going to be cute. She'll gain about two pounds a day, and pretty soon she'll be a huge old hog, and there's absolutely no point in keeping her unless you intend to breed her, which I guess is possible if she wins the grand championship. Also' – she paused – 'they're disgusting.'

'What do you mean?'

'They shit on everything. In their food, in their water. You have to clean it out every day. Anyway, they eat dogs in China.'

'They do not.'

'Yes, they do.'

'That's so totally gross.'

'I bet our moms are downstairs getting high,' said Kendall.

'You're kidding.'

'My mom's a pothead.'

Helen was scandalized. She had always thought that Aunt Maggie was so much cooler than her own parents, but imagining her mother on drugs was unsettling.

'I think I'll go to sleep now,' she said.

While Tim caught up on paperwork, Maggie offered Jill a brownie.

'I'm dieting,' Jill said.

'It's low cal and not that kind of brownie.'

'Oh.' She took a bite. A small one. 'It's even delicious.' Another bite.

'I've already patented the brand name for the day it's legal here: "Maggie's Magical Edibles".'

'You'll make a fortune, if you don't go to prison first,' Jill said.

'Let's go out and look at the stars.'

Jill followed her sister out to the field behind the house, where Maggie had planted peonies for the television show. The moon wasn't up yet, but the light from the stars was so intense that Jill could see her shadow. They lay in the grass in a clearing surrounded by sheltering sycamores, with spectral trunks that caught the starshine. It was perfect and marvelous.

'It's like the world would be if Martha Stewart were God,' Jill said.

Maggie laughed. 'That's the brownie talking.'

They stared into the sky. Jill felt the stars weighing down on her, physically pressing her body into the earth, the smells of nature wrapping around her like smoke from a campfire, and the ground melting away so she was just afloat in the universe. 'The Milky Way,' she said dreamily. 'It's been so long. Years, since I saw it. Camp DeSoto! Remember the stars when we'd sit out on the dock after dinner?'

Maggie pointed out the planets and the constellations she knew best. Jill only knew Orion and the Big Dipper, but Maggie had so many more in her head. 'The last time I saw stars like this was when Henry took us on that crazy trip out west,' said Jill. 'Oh! Is that a shooting star?'

'It's a satellite,' said Maggie. 'No, wait, I think it's the International Space Station.'

'Whoa!' said Jill.

'Whoa!' Maggie said, imitating her sister. 'You sound like a real stoner.'

Jill started laughing as well. She pretended to be even

more stoned than she was, which sent them both into gales of hilarity.

The spell was broken when Jill's phone rang. It was Henry.

'I'm all right,' he said, in a voice that seemed oddly slowed down.

'You're what?'

'All right,' he said.

'But I didn't ask,' said Jill, who was still caught in the delirious mood she had been in when Henry called. She cast a mischievous look at Maggie. 'I didn't ask, "How are you?"'

'You sound a little strange,' Henry said.

'I am strange,' she said. 'At this moment, I'm really strange.'

Maggie could scarcely keep herself from howling.

'I guess you haven't been listening to the news,' Henry said.

'God, the news, no. I'm sitting outside with Maggie looking at the stars, and we're both really stoned. She knows all the stars, it's so amazing. And Mars, you can really see, like, how red it is.'

In their entire married life, Jill had never expressed interest in drugs of any sort. Nor was she even much of a drinker. She was the last person Henry could imagine being intoxicated. 'I think I should call back tomorrow,' he said.

'No, I want to talk! I haven't heard from you in two days. I know you're really busy, but still. Tell me what's up.'

'There was a bombing,' Henry said carefully. 'I'm all right.'

In her unfamiliar state, it took a moment to take this in. 'There was a *bombing*? Jesus, Henry, are you all right?'

'Yes, that's what I wanted to tell you. I'm all right.'

'There's more to it than you're saying.'

'I got a bump on the head and a scratch, nothing serious. I'll tell you more tomorrow. I know it's confusing. It's late there.'

'Henry, I just want you to come home,' Jill said, now completely sobered by the news. 'I know you're busy, and what you're doing is important, but we all want you home. And safe.'

'Well, you know about the travel ban. And they really need me here. I feel somewhat responsible for the whole mess.'

'That again! Henry, I'm sure you did the right thing every step along the way. Nobody is more careful or responsible than you.'

When Henry said goodbye, Jill began to cry. Maggie tried to console her, but soon they were both sobbing. Henry had been gone more than a month, and in that time the world had gone crazy. Jill realized how vulnerable she suddenly felt without him.

'Mom?'

Jill was startled to see Teddy standing in the grass in his pajamas. 'What's wrong, sweetie?'

He looked at Jill and Maggie in confusion. 'It's okay, we were just having a sad conversation,' Maggie explained, wiping away her tears.

'Come here,' said Jill. Teddy came over and crawled into Jill's embrace. 'Look at the stars,' she said. 'Aren't they amazing? Don't you just feel like you could reach out and touch them?'

Teddy nodded. For such a bold little boy, he was strangely subdued. Maybe it's just that he caught me in that emotional moment, Jill thought. She rocked him in her arms, letting the warmth comfort them both.

'You smell funny,' he said.

'It's Maggie's perfume. Do you like it?'

'No, it's gross.'

'I won't wear it again, honey.'

Jill silently promised herself that she would never go off duty again until her children were grown and no longer needed a paragon for a mother.

'Mom, I think I saw a ghost.'

'Really? You know there aren't such things, right?'

Teddy ducked his head and didn't answer.

'What did he look like?' Maggie asked. 'Was he a soldier?'

Teddy nodded.

'People say there is a Civil War soldier who haunts this place, but I've never seen him,' said Maggie. 'Or Tim or Kendall either. He must have felt something extra special about you.'

Teddy took this in, then said, 'I just want to go home.'

23

Lambaréné

SOON AFTER HENRY WENT TO WORK AT FORT DETRICK, HIS BOSS, Jürgen Stark, came to him with a question. 'More than 40 percent of people infected with Ebola die of the disease, but many caregivers for Ebola patients who tested positive for the disease never showed symptoms,' he said. 'Why?'

Henry loved questions like that. It was where science began.

'Are you sure they didn't have the disease previously?' he asked. 'And if they didn't, how could they have developed resistance?'

'You go find out,' Jürgen responded.

So Henry flew to Gabon, in West Africa, and visited the hospital in Lambaréné that Albert Schweitzer had established in 1913. Few historical figures had had greater impact on Henry's childhood imagination than the Alsatian theologian and organ virtuoso, who decided to study medicine at the age of thirty and then dedicated the rest of his life to relieving the suffering of humanity. With his wife, Helene Bresslau, he established a hospital on the Ogooué River in what was then French Equatorial Africa. They treated leprosy, elephantiasis, sleeping sickness, malaria, yellow fever – all the afflictions of the jungle.

The rustic hospital Schweitzer built had been reconstructed several times, and when Henry visited, it was an accumulation of low-slung, red-roofed bungalows with overhanging porches to shield against the storms of the tropics. Schweitzer's vision was to create a native village, not an institution, and that original ideal remained. Dr Fanny Méyé, a vibrant Ebola specialist with the Centre International de Recherches Médicales de Franceville, took Henry through the research facility. She was overseeing a survey of the Gabonese population to determine the proportion with immunity to the disease. 'We found antibodies in more than 15 percent of people in our rural communities, and as high as 33 percent in some villages,' Dr Méyé said. 'These were people who never had any symptoms of Ebola! They never even lived in a place with an Ebola outbreak. So we ask ourselves, where did they get their exposure?'

'From the bats,' Henry ventured.

'Very likely, but why did they not become ill? How did they attain this immunity?' She explained that the antibodies of people who had been exposed reacted to specific proteins of the Ebola virus in the same way that some successful vaccines had done in test trials. 'We can only conclude that these people are naturally protected. We still don't know why.'

'It could be false positives,' Henry said. 'Or perhaps a virus epidemic similar to Ebola that is not pathogenic.'

'Yes, of course we thought of this, but so far such a disease has not been detected here.'

Every new pandemic raised a question that had confounded medicine since the earliest days: Why were some people immune to novel diseases that otherwise run rampant through populations? Twenty to 30 percent of people who were infected with influenza never manifested symptoms. Studies of sex workers in Nairobi showed that some prostitutes were naturally immune to HIV. There was also a small portion of people with northern European ancestry who were able to be infected with HIV but never developed symptoms. In both cases, it may have been a mutation of the CCR5 gene, which was required for the virus to invade the cell. These were interesting discoveries, but so far they had never led to a vaccine or a treatment for any of the diseases.

On the last night of Henry's visit, Dr Méyé took him to visit Albert Schweitzer's modest grave, and afterward they ate dinner under a thatched umbrella at a little fish café on the riverbank.

Henry looked out at something moving in the river.

'Is that a snake?' he asked.

'It's a bird. We call it a snakebird because it looks so much like a snake with its head out of the water.'

'I've always been afraid of the jungle,' Henry confessed.

'What is it that frightens you?' she asked.

'I think of the wilderness as being a place of death.'

'But it is actually so full of life!' she said. 'I think that is why Dr Schweitzer came here, the abundance of living creatures, the diversity, people say he bathed in it – is that correct English? That he took a bath in all this life, everywhere around him.'

'It's certainly a vivid way of describing it.'

Henry went on to talk about how affected he had been by Schweitzer's example and philosophy. Although Henry was an atheist and Schweitzer a highly unorthodox Lutheran missionary, his ideas took root in Henry's philosophy.

Schweitzer had been steaming up this very river, through a herd of hippopotamuses, searching in his mind for a universal basis for ethical behavior, one that stood above religious formulations. The answer came to him in a single phrase: 'There flashed upon my mind, unforeseen and unsought: Reverence for Life,' he wrote. Ethics, Schweitzer decided, was nothing more than that. 'Reverence for Life affords me my fundamental principle of morality, namely, that good consists in maintaining, assisting and enhancing life, and that to destroy, to harm or to hinder life is evil.' Those words lived in Henry's heart. The animal rights and environmental movements were born, in part, in Albert Schweitzer's writings. Henry said that his admiration for Schweitzer was something he shared with his boss, Jürgen Stark.

At the mention of Jürgen's name, Dr Méyé's face turned expressionless.

'Do you know him?' Henry asked.

'We have met,' she said. 'Like you, he came here.'

'Really? He didn't tell me that.'

'As a pilgrim. To see the grave. We get them every year. They are idealists, of course, or they wouldn't make such a long trip. Usually, we enjoy them.'

'But not Jürgen?'

'You know him better than I.' She turned her attention to the river, apparently not inclined to say anything else. Then she added, 'Some people carry this philosophy too far. They look at the damage mankind does to the natural world, and they forget that humans are animals as well, and also deserving of reverence.'

'He is a rather cold personality, I would say.'

'I thought he was frightening.'

212

'How so?'

But Dr Méyé would not go further. 'I scarcely know him,' she pleaded. 'I've said too much already.'

When Henry returned to Fort Detrick he brought along a bad case of norovirus, that gastrointestinal scourge of cruise ships. It was ferociously contagious, though less so for people with B and AB blood types. Unfortunately, Henry's blood type was O. So far nobody had figured out why blood type had anything to do with it.

As soon as he was well enough to go back to the lab, Jürgen asked for his findings. 'I find that immunity remains a mystery,' Henry reported.

He did not mention Dr Méyé or her observations about Jürgen, but after that, he studied his boss more carefully, searching for the qualities she had found unsettling. Perhaps the same qualities were also present in Henry, the ones that had enlisted him in this dangerous – some would say sinister – line of work.

24

Triple Play

'THERE'S A BUNCH OF FOLKS DEAD THEY'RE NOT TELLING US about,' Mildred, a fourth-grade teacher, said, as Jill and others ate lunch in the teachers' lounge. Up to now, they had been talking about how fortunate they were that Atlanta hadn't been badly hit. Schools around the country had reopened as the pandemic lost its grip. People were returning to work, filling up restaurants, and flocking to theaters and sporting events. They stopped wearing respirator masks, drinking in the air that had just recently been so treacherous. Jill had decided to return to the city.

'Like who?'

'I'm sure Anderson Cooper is dead. He's not on anymore.'

'I heard Brad Pitt is dead,' another teacher said.

'Oh, no!'

'You don't know that.'

'But it is true about Taylor Swift.'

Mildred seemed excited by the turn in the conversation. The indiscriminate nature of death excited her populist ire. Mildred would have been manning the guillotine in revolutionary France. 'They found a guy on the subway in New York who was fine when he left home and then he was dead like half an hour later,' Mildred continued. 'A Wall Street guy.'

'Do they know how many people have died?' one teacher asked.

'They say more than two million in the U.S. alone,' said Jill. 'But I don't think anybody really knows.'

'The pension fund is, like, destroyed,' Mildred said.

The nation had emerged from the first wave of the pandemic to find that the stock market was down 13,500 points and the economy was in the steepest recession in history. American Airlines declared bankruptcy, and the travel ban threatened to bring down other carriers as well, shaking the entire transportation industry. It had never been so clear what herd animals humans were. Almost overnight, they had disappeared from the subways and buses and trains. And almost overnight, they returned, though in smaller numbers. The worst was over, people told themselves. Time to pick up life where we left it.

The pandemic was still acute in Europe and the Middle East, but after Philadelphia no other American city had been hit as hard. Some experts on CNN were suggesting that the virus had mutated into a less harmful form. Commentators on Fox were applauding the forceful actions of the administration for stopping the disease, citing the much-criticized travel ban.

Mildred wouldn't stop. 'Did you hear about the teacher who died in her classroom?' she asked. 'Right in front of her students. Dropped dead.'

'Mildred, we're *alive*!' one of the teachers declared.

'And we have our jobs,' another chimed in.

When Jill returned to her classroom she sat at her desk

and watched the children returning from lunch. They faced a life of extra struggle, given the obstacles in front of them. The two Darrens, in addition to having the same name, both had fathers in prison. K'Neisha was the smartest in the class, and her mother, Vicky, did everything she could to protect her, but girls in her community were at a disadvantage no matter how smart and pretty they were. Jill believed that, despite the family problems and the absence of resources, these children would survive. Some of them would triumph. K'Neisha would.

Just don't let anything bad happen to them, Jill thought.

Later that afternoon, Jill went for a run in Lullwater Park. It was only a short walk from the CDC headquarters, and sometimes at lunch she and Henry would picnic by Candler Lake. She would feed Fritos to the mallards and the greedy resident swan who demanded the first serving. Loamy trails looped through the dense woods. Students were sunning themselves, surrounded by Canada geese munching on the grass. The students seemed a little too dazed by the splendid weather to be absorbed by their textbooks. Jill saw a couple kissing beside the lake. It was like a scene from another era.

She missed Henry more than ever. She knew that the world needed him. She wasn't naive about his importance, but sometimes she thought about what it would be like to be old and to finally have Henry all to herself, the long periods of separation over at last and the world no longer jealous for his attention. They had talked about having a cabin in the mountains of North Carolina or Santa Fe. There were so many possible moments she imagined for themselves, but she also knew it was a fantasy. Henry would never willingly stop or even slow down. She would never have him entirely to herself.

They met at a Braves game while she was getting her master's at Georgia State. Jill came with her then husband, Mark, who was doing his residency at Emory Hospital. Mark knew Henry by reputation, and talked to him over Jill, who sat between them. Henry was polite. It was clear that he preferred to watch the game, but Mark was intent on making an impression. Two things struck Jill at the time. One was that Mark was in awe. She had never seen him nakedly cultivate another intellect as he did with Henry. The conversation was quite technical – it had to do with an antibiotic-resistant pneumonia that was stalking Emory Hospital at the time – but, judging by Mark's reaction, Henry's responses were original and surprising. Among Mark's faults was a tendency to be garrulous and intellectually overbearing, but with Henry he seemed to be out of his depth.

The other thing that Jill noticed was Henry's interest in her. At first, she thought he was merely being solicitous. It is common in the South for gentlemen to court a lady's opinion even if he isn't interested in it, like holding the door open. Henry was no southerner, and not the type to surrender his integrity for the sake of custom or courtesy, yet throughout Mark's monologue he included Jill in his responses, even though the subject was beyond her grasp. There was one moment when the Phillies had the bases loaded with no outs. Mark was holding forth but Henry was staring intently at the game, expectantly, almost visibly signaling Mark to shut up for a moment. There was a sharp grounder to third, and both Henry and Jill leapt to their feet as the Braves' third baseman stepped on the bag and threw to second, who then fired to first. Impulsively, Jill hugged Henry.

'What happened?' Mark asked.

'Triple play!' Henry cried.

Jill had never seen one before. The play was exciting, but Jill found her reaction curious. Why had she embraced this little man she had just met?

Mark, who could be oblivious about social matters, noticed the hug. After the game, he invited Henry to come to dinner the following week, the first of several such occasions. Mark was angling for something. It wasn't a job – he was quite sought after and would soon be going into his own practice. He was destined to be one of those doctors who lives in a Tara-like mansion in Buckhead and serves on the board of a major pharmaceutical company. Jill had no objection to being a part of such a cosseted life, and, to be fair, maybe both of them needed something from Henry. Mark hungered to be elevated to the upper tier of scientific accomplishment, where people whispered about the competition for the Nobel. Mark himself would never be in that category – he wasn't fooled about his own limitations – but he could befriend someone who was, someone new and unattached, someone who might welcome the attention. Jill knew that Mark was exploiting the attraction she felt for Henry, and he for her. In a way, she felt sorry for Mark.

But what did Jill get out of it?

She puzzled over this. She was married. She was not discontented. Henry was a challenging figure. He was freighted with secrets, and that intrigued her. His mind was complex but also flexible enough to become thoroughly engaged by a baseball game. He was playful in conversation, which led Jill to wonder what he would be like in bed. Henry was certainly not a sexual object in any standard way. He was a little shorter than Jill, bowlegged and suffering from scoliosis, and he walked with a cane, but when Jill allowed herself to consider him physically, what immediately came to mind was his head, which was large and disproportionate to his body but also distinguished and, she thought, handsome. Dashing, actually. So when Mark left her for the heiress of a hedge fund fortune, Jill was shocked but not heartbroken. She knew that Henry would be there, believing that in some way he had always been waiting for her. As she had been for him.

Although Henry's intellect was rare, his brilliant mind was encapsulated by a flawed and diminished body. And yet he was never angry at those who underestimated him or gave him pitying looks. Jill despised them all. They didn't understand the one great quality Henry Parsons had, a trait that defined him in Jill's mind as no other did: his enormous capacity for love.

There was another quality that Jill wondered about endlessly. Henry had a guilty conscience. When they first met at the ballpark, Henry had been on temporary assignment to the CDC from Fort Detrick. He lived in a covert world and was never going to reveal what he did there. Shortly after they met, he took the permanent job at the CDC. That was sixteen years ago.

Henry gave Jill credit for bringing him into life, almost as if she had given birth to him. He always said that their wedding was the happiest moment he had ever known. It was for her as well. But happiness is a fickle quality, and Jill often feared that a tidal wave of despair was awaiting her, the reckoning for years of bliss.

Teddy was on the playground when the kid threw up on the jungle gym. A monitor helped the boy to the nurse's office, where there were three other children with nosebleeds and nausea. The principal, who had just heard the news, said over the PA that there was a Code 12 in effect, meaning that teachers were to keep the children in the classrooms and out of the hallways until parents arrived. Some of the parents had already heard, and they rushed over to pick up their children. Their eyes were full of fear.

Within the last twenty-four hours, another eighteen thousand Americans had perished of Kongoli, in seventeen cities – including Atlanta, where more than two hundred flu-related deaths had been recorded. The news was brimming with stories: the parents who died at the dinner table, leaving four orphans; twelve prisoners in a Detroit jail who succumbed and another thirteen who were ill, causing the county to simply open the gates because they were unable to protect them. These were parables of a society that was fractured by a disaster that everyone thought had run its course.

Most of those who died had been quickly struck down by their body's furious counterattack to the infection. Other victims would take as long as ten days to die, usually of acute respiratory disease syndrome, a virulent and overwhelming pneumonia. In the wake of the Kongoli pandemic, new, antibiotic-resistant strains were proliferating. The rate of death from flu and pneumonia combined was close to 50 percent.

Jill had to wait until the last of her students had been picked up before she could get Helen and Teddy home. Her pantry was practically empty, and she was frantic to get groceries before everything shut down. She rushed to the natural foods store near her house, where she figured there would be less panic, but she encountered a frantic crowd, women in yoga clothes (there was a studio next door) darting through the aisles, businessmen in suits pushing two or more carts, others walking out with their arms full of unpaid goods. Jill thought about doing the same. The two clerks were doing what they could to handle the sales, but they also were frightened and desperate to get away from possible exposure.

'Cash only,' said a slight Indian girl with a red tilaka mark on her forehead.

'Oh, come on, I don't have that much on me.'

'The credit card system is not responding,' she said. 'So cash, that's it.'

Jill noticed the businessman behind her with a handful of bills. Somehow everyone knew more than she. In her purse, she found forty-three dollars. The clerk simply took the money without counting up the groceries. Jill bagged them herself and left the store. She felt light-headed and was breathing shallowly.

When Jill got home, Henry called on FaceTime. He was in the Saudi Health Ministry, wearing a white lab coat with some Arabic writing on it. For some reason the sight of Henry comfortably at work inflamed Jill. 'Why are you still there?' she demanded. 'You don't belong there. You're supposed to be here, taking care of us. Running your lab. Instead, you're off in Saudi Arabia!'

Henry was caught off guard by Jill's vehemence. 'I'm doing everything I can to find a way to come home,' he said. 'The American ambassador here is pulling strings for me, but Saudi Arabia is still quarantined and all the flights are grounded. I don't know what else I can do.'

Jill burst into tears. For a long while, Henry just listened to her cry. She was afraid. She was going crazy trying to protect the children. Henry's own eyes were brimming, and when he spoke again, his voice quivered. 'It's not fair for you to have to take care of everything,' he said.

' "Fair",' Jill said, spitting the word out. 'You don't know what it's like here.'

'Tell me.'

'I never thought people would behave like this. Everybody is afraid to help each other, and nobody really knows what to do. Those who have hoarded food won't share it, or money, either. There were some community food banks, but they closed, I guess because nobody wanted to stand in line with other people, or else the food just ran out. It's everybody for themselves.'

'Listen, Jill, I'll be home soon, I promise. I do have contacts. Catherine is doing what she can, so is Maria. Everybody wants to get me home. It will happen, I promise.'

'People are escaping the quarantine, I hear about them. Can't you just drive across the desert and go to some other country?'

'The borders are sealed. There are air patrols along the Iraq border and probably others. I don't know that the situation is any better in Yemen. It can't last forever. The irony is that I'm the one who advocated for this. Now that it's too late to stop the spread of Kongoli, I'm trapped.'

'Oh God, I want you here so much,' Jill said. 'I know I'm being selfish. The only important thing is that you have to find a way to stop this disease. It's overwhelmingly terrifying. And I know you'll say it's not just you, but it is just you, Henry.'

25

Preserving the Leadership

THE VICE PRESIDENT WAS ON A TEAR. 'WHAT WENT WRONG? WE had this virus licked,' he said accusingly, looking directly at Lieutenant Commander Bartlett.

'Apparently not, sir,' she said. 'It went occult for a couple weeks, which isn't uncommon. As you may remember, we talked about this last week when you suggested that everyone go back to work.'

The vice president glared at her, but it was clear to Tildy by now that Bartlett never made insinuations or veiled threats. She was a pure scientist, and her allegiance to truth-telling set her in opposition to everyone else in the room. Tildy had come grudgingly to admire her implacable integrity.

'In a single day, this economy has lost – what is it, two trillion dollars? In a day! One fucking day! I don't know when we can open the markets again. And you tell me how many people have already died,' the vice president said, once again holding Bartlett responsible, but he wasn't pausing for her answer. 'We've got hospitals closing their doors, turning people away! We can't even bury people fast enough. How did we get to be so totally unprepared for this?' It was a rhetorical question. 'It's a goddamn mess,' he concluded, setting aside his evangelical piety. 'What's your name again?'

'Bartlett, sir. Lieutenant Commander Bartlett.'

'You have that antibody stuff that you talked about?'

'The monoclonal antibodies, yes, sir. We're testing them in ferrets.'

'Fuck that. From what you say, this is our best hope for creating some kind of immunity. Washington is infested with this crap. We need to preserve the leadership.'

What leadership? Tildy thought. The president had been almost entirely absent in the debate about how to deal with the contagion, except to blame the opposing party for ignoring public health needs before he took office.

'Okay, Bartlett, here's the deal,' the vice president continued. 'I want you to report to the White House tonight and bring a dose of that stuff for the president.' He thought for a moment. 'And his family members.'

'Should I bring an injection for you as well, sir?'

Tildy was amazed that Bartlett could ask that question with no inflection whatsoever. Everyone stared at the table while the vice president considered his response. It's the last life raft on the *Titanic*, Tildy thought. Do you save yourself or your humanity?

'How many shots of this stuff do we have?' he asked.

'About two hundred,' said Bartlett. 'We can't guarantee the safety or effectiveness of any of them right now. And every person is different, with different levels of immunity. The correct dosage is unknown.'

'Two hundred.' The vice president drummed his fingers on the cabinet table. 'Two hundred. Who to save. Hmm.'

Tildy decided to put him out of his misery. 'You should take it,' she offered. 'For continuity.'

'No,' he said, 'others are ahead of me. Military chiefs. Cabinet members. First responders. God, what a decision to have to make. I'm gonna have to pray on this.'

For the first time, Tildy felt a bit of sympathy for him. 'One other thing,' she said, as they were about to break up. 'I don't think we can chance meeting in person again until the contagion has passed. The White House will set up conference calls. Maybe Lieutenant Commander Bartlett can suggest how we should conduct ourselves until we're clear.'

Bartlett had little to offer except to shelter in place, wash your hands, don't go out in public unless vitally necessary, and, if you do, wear a mask and sanitary gloves. 'If you have symptoms, bear in mind that the hospitals are already full and may not be the best place for you anyway unless you need a ventilator. If you have no one at home to take care of you, make sure that you have at least two people who will call you twice a day. Drink fluids. Stay in bed.'

'Is aspirin okay?'

'Absolutely not!' Bartlett said, startling everyone. 'This is a hemorrhagic disease. You can't take anything that will thin your blood. No Aleve, Advil, Midol, Motrin, Percodan, Alka-Seltzer, Bufferin – a good rule of thumb is just don't take anything that makes you feel better.'

It was such a Bartlett thing to say. 'Tylenol is okay,' she conceded.

While they were packing up their briefcases, Joint Chiefs asked the agency man, 'Did you ever hear of this group called Earth's Guardians? My middle daughter is all caught up in it. Kinda cultish, you ask me.'

The agency man hadn't heard of it. Neither had Tildy.

'The reason I bring it up is they're anti-population growth, I mean in a big way. You see them at rallies. Down with humans sort of thing. They seem like the kind of folks who wouldn't mind shaving a few billion people off the planet. Not my daughter, exactly, but she's sympathetic.'

'The Bureau arrested some of them in Los Angeles,' said Justice. 'They broke into a sperm bank, of all places. Wrecked the place. Turned off the freezers and destroyed the whole inventory.'

Tildy observed that it sounded like a splinter group led by some crank.

'You'd think,' said Justice. 'But their leader used to be in the government. Led a lot of hush-hush stuff at Fort Detrick. Then he got canned and went off to do some dirty work with a private contractor.'

'A scientist?' Tildy asked.

'Yeah, a microbiologist. Named Jürgen Stark.'

26

The Human Trial

IT WAS AN OPPORTUNITY, JÜRGEN HAD TOLD HIM. PRICELESS. A
test of their theory. This was after Jürgen had become a liability and left Fort Detrick. Congress was investigating some
experiments that were hard to justify as defensive measures. It
was all done in secret session, but leaks were beginning to
spill. A decision was made to put distance between the CIA
and the dark operations that had been farmed out to Fort
Detrick. That meant cutting loose the talented impresario of
manufactured diseases.

In the shadow world that surrounds the intelligence community, Jürgen Stark was well known, and as soon as he
came on the market there were many competitive bids for
his employment. Private security firms had mushroomed
after 9/11 and the Iraq War. Trained by the best – the Navy
SEALS, CIA, Mossad, South African paramilitaries – their
operatives came from the worlds of intelligence and the military. Political consultants and academics were added to the
mix, along with computer hackers from the National Security Agency. In addition to supplying hired killers, such firms
could also function as turnkey interior or defense departments, fielding an actual army if the money was right.

Jürgen offered a competitive edge to the company that finally landed him, AGT Security Associates. The name gave nothing away. It was intentionally anodyne, although among those who moved in the shadows, AGT was known as the insider's choice. The next step for private contractors like AGT was microbiology. Hiring Jürgen was a masterstroke. He was immediately the golden boy, the future of the company. Jürgen had a vision, and he knew all the secrets. One of them was Henry Parsons's intriguing discovery.

At Fort Detrick, Henry had been working on polio derivatives. Poliomyelitis was one of the most dreaded pathogens of the early twentieth century. Like influenza, polio was an RNA virus, but it spread through food or water contaminated by human fecal matter – one of the reasons swimming pools were chlorinated. In the 1940s and 1950s, thousands of children were paralyzed each year. Hospitals had rows of iron lungs, the imprisoning mechanical respirator in which some victims were doomed to spend the rest of their lives. There was no cure for polio, but the near elimination of the disease caused by the introduction of the Salk and Sabin vaccines was one of medicine's great triumphs. As Jürgen knew, however, a population with almost no exposure to polio also created an opportunity: the virus's high rate of infectiousness and its unpredictable effects on the central nervous system made it an object of interest as a bioweapon.

Henry turned his attention to a common childhood infection called hand, foot, and mouth disease – also known as enterovirus 71 – which was closely related to polio. Symptoms were normally mild, although severe cases sometimes occurred, especially in Asia, causing permanent neurological damage. Although Henry's mandate was to explore the enteroviruses as a potential weapon, as a doctor he thought that if he could understand the mechanism that caused a harmless disease to become catastrophic he might unlock one of nature's jealously held secrets.

Henry found a way to marry EV 71 with poliovirus. The hybrid had the most peculiar effect on the mice first exposed to it: three days later, they collapsed and remained in a state of unconsciousness for several hours, then they recovered with no apparent ill effects. It was transient and benign. Mice in the same cages that had not been inoculated with the hybrid suffered a similar reaction, demonstrating that the virus could pass from mouse to mouse. Indeed, it was extremely contagious.

Jürgen immediately saw a use for the hybrid, and he enchanted Henry with praise for his genius, giving him credit for applications that Henry hadn't yet arrived at. We will change the ways wars are fought, Jürgen said. Not by conventional weapons or nuclear bombs, but by germs and viruses and toxins. Carefully targeted, scrupulously prepared, an aerosol version of Henry's – what should we call it? An incapacitant? A narcotic of some sort? – could render the enemy disabled long enough to be arrested or made harmless. It would be bloodless, to all appearances a natural event. Made possible by your discovery, Henry, your brilliant discovery.

An incapacitant. A narcotic. A kind of sleeping potion. It seemed so benign when Jürgen described it. Actually, no one knew exactly what it was; it hadn't been tested in humans. But Jürgen was in a rush, and in the private world, operating covertly in deserts and jungles and the unpoliced hinterlands, shortcuts could be taken. Here is a perfect opportunity, he told Henry, the human trial you've been asking for. Imagine this: in a rainforest on the border of Bolivia and Brazil, there is a group of narcoterrorists. Wicked sorts, a renegade spin-off from the Colombian FARC. They have evaded capture for years, raiding villages, burning crops, raping, plundering, imposing a regime of fear. The Brazilians have come to us for a solution, and you have created it!

Henry met the AGT team in São Paulo, where the operation was being staged from a military air base. The team was brisk, muscular, and efficient, and there could be no doubt of their success. They would load the 'agent,' as they called Henry's invention, into a crop duster and land on an airstrip in the Amazon forest near the village of Corumbá. They would wait until nightfall. The target was isolated, so there was little risk of spreading the infection beyond the objective. The lights of the cabins where the terrorists hid out would guide them, and darkness would confound any response. The crop duster would make several passes over the village. Unlike anthrax, which has to be inhaled directly, Henry's agent was contagious, so the infection would spread quickly. Three days later, the army would move in. Jürgen and Henry would follow as the medical team to document the effect. All would go well.

Henry did have misgivings. It wasn't scientific, not at all. On the other hand, there would have to have been a human test of volunteers anyway – the 'agent' was at that stage – and temporarily paralyzing a group of terrorists seemed a much better use of Henry's invention (if it worked at all). Moreover, the Brazilians were urgent in their need, and Jürgen was confident of success. These encouraging thoughts did not entirely set Henry's mind at ease.

Henry and Jürgen spent the third night in the rainforest. There was a welcome breeze that pushed the humidity aside and made the forest breathable. They drank corn wine and listened to the guttural cries of the howler monkeys. The howlers were being decimated by an epidemic of yellow fever, which Jürgen blamed on the unsanitary habits of the human population. The two men talked about the obstacles of treating animals in the wild. Henry could barely make out Jürgen's features except for the gleaming platinum hair that gathered the starlight. Then Jürgen made a remark that Henry never forgot: 'In the battle of man versus nature, I am not on our side,' Jürgen said. 'I am a traitor to my kind.'

It was a confession brought on by the wine and the dark, where intimacies are traded that in sober daylight would not have been said. Henry recalled Dr Méyé's statement at the fish restaurant on the Ogooué River. She had said Jürgen was dangerous. But there was no evidence in Jürgen's work that he was in any way subversive. It was only later that Henry would understand the truth of Jürgen's confession.

27

The Philadelphia Antiserum

AT SIX P.M., LIEUTENANT COMMANDER BARTLETT APPEARED AT the northwest gate of the White House, carrying a medical bag with seven doses of antiserum: five from Philadelphia, the other two from Minneapolis. There had been a furtive discussion at the NIH about which one the president should receive. The Philadelphia strain was more virulent, and the antibodies might protect against the most dangerous variant of the influenza. On the other hand, the Minneapolis serum was probably safer, although it was impossible to know. Bartlett might be either saving the president or killing him. A mild infection would be a relief.

She was shown into the family quarters upstairs, and taken to the Cosmetology Room, a place she had never heard of, white and brightly lit, with a shelf full of cosmetics and brushes and a professional hair dryer. A tanning bed was fitted against the wall. Waiting for her was the president's doctor, an Air Force general with a cleft chin and old-fashioned trifocals. Bartlett saluted. He wanly returned the gesture.

'Should I administer the injections, or you?' he asked. 'I'm not certain about the protocol for this.'

'There's nothing special about the technique,' she said.

'We recommend the ventrogluteal muscle, since there's too much material for the deltoid to absorb.'

'In that case, I'll do the president and you do the first lady. He's a little self-conscious about his girth. The others we'll split up.'

The adult children came first. They were solemn and cracking weak jokes about getting jungle fever. They weren't embarrassed by having to drop their pants so Bartlett could inject them just below the pelvic girdle in the side of their hip. She wondered if they considered the danger. She also wondered if they knew or cared whether they might be taking a chance for life away from someone more useful – a nurse, a cop, a pregnant mother. Or was this just the way it was going to be – the powerful, the rich, and the celebrated would be saved. She realized she was being naive. Of course this was how it was bound to be. This is the country we've become.

She did her job. The president's children pulled up their pants and walked out of the room, rubbing the sore spot on their hip.

The president came in. He really is heavy, Bartlett thought. She wondered what his triglycerides level was. He glanced at Bartlett and she turned away, busying herself by disposing of the syringes and packing her bag. She heard him say, 'She doesn't need to be here.'

'She's waiting for the first lady,' the general said.

'Well, she's not coming. I guess she doesn't trust you people. *Oof*,' he said, as the Philadelphia antiserum went into his body.

234

28

Ice Cream

DESPITE THE WARNINGS ABOUT GOING OUT IN PUBLIC, JILL decided she had to see her mother. She hadn't been to visit in more than a week, but it was Mother's Day and she wanted to make sure that Nora was being well cared for. She brought some snapdragons from her garden. There was a sign on the front entrance of the facility that she had never seen before: no visitors.

Jill was wearing a mask and gloves. She had not been able to reach her mother through the switchboard, and Nora didn't use a cell phone. Jill decided that 'no visitors' couldn't mean no family, so she went in. The front desk was unattended. She didn't see anybody at all. She took the elevator up to the third floor, where Nora had been moved after she broke her hip. The hallways were suspiciously empty, although Jill could see that the rooms were still occupied.

'Hey! Hey, you!' a man's voice called after her. 'Help me!'

Jill turned to look into the room where an old man was staring at her, his face in the grip of a powerful emotion, but what Jill noticed immediately was the stream of blood coming from his nose.

'Do you work here?' he asked. 'I need help.'

Jill took a step back. 'I'll get somebody,' she said.

'They won't come. Won't nobody come. You gotta help me. I'm not feeling so good and nobody has changed me.'

'I'm sorry, I'm here to visit my mother.'

'I really need a change. There's diapers over there,' he said, waving his bony finger toward the cabinet.

'I wish I could help, I really do,' Jill said, as she hurried away. His voice called after her pitifully, 'Help me! Won't somebody help me?'

Nora was watching TV when Jill came in. 'What took you so long,' she said sternly. 'I'm hungry.'

'Mom? It's me, Jill. Your daughter.'

Nora focused on her, shards of memory reorganizing themselves with this new information. She was usually better than this. Maybe she was thrown off by the mask. Jill could hear other voices crying out, joining the chorus of misery down the hall like baying dogs.

'How do you feel, Mom?'

'I told you. I'm hungry.'

'That's good, that's a good sign,' said Jill. 'Didn't they offer you anything?'

Nora made a dismissive sound.

'I'll tell you what,' Jill said, as she arranged the snaps in the vase Helen had decorated at camp. 'I'll run down to the kitchen and get you something. What do you feel like? You want cereal? Maybe some ice cream?'

'Ice cream,' Nora agreed.

'Okay! I'll be right back.'

Jill was now fully aware that the residents had been essentially abandoned. The executive offices of the facility also

236

appeared to be vacant, but she saw an open door to the president's office, and there sat Jack Sperling. There were dark circles under his eyes. It was a face of total despair.

'Jack, are you here by yourself?' Jill asked.

'We lost most of our staff when we got the first cases of flu,' he said. 'Some of them I think are actually sick, but most of them are just scared. They're not trained for this kind of medical emergency.'

'But who's taking care of everyone?'

'We've got a handful of folks. It takes a while to get around to everybody. Your mom, I'm sorry, she probably hasn't been fed yet.'

'Do you still have food?'

'We're getting some emergency assistance from the Department of Agriculture, but we're short on essentials, soft foods, like peanut butter, string cheese, chocolate milk – the stuff they like. Totally out of Ensure. But the real problem is medicine.' He gestured at a pile of documents on his desk. 'Most of our residents are on some kind of critical medication, but every pharmacy I've called is rationing supplies. I spend my entire day trying to round up diabetes and heart medications. We've got people who desperately need antidepressants, but that's got to wait till the critical cases get taken care of. There are other problems I don't want to burden you with.'

'Like Kongoli,' said Jill.

Sperling sighed. 'It's all over the third floor and the memory ward.'

'Why didn't you call me?'

'Tell me, Jill, would you really want me to? Do you want to take your mother home? If you do, please, help yourself.

237

We'd be happy to have one less mouth to feed, one less body to bathe, to take to the bathroom, to wake up in the night for their medicine. You'd be doing us a great favor, but maybe not your family, knowing she's been exposed. Think about it.'

Jill found the kitchen in the basement. There was one cook stirring oatmeal in several vats. She made a slight movement that Jill recognized as a cautionary don't-come-near-me motion.

'Ice cream?' Jill asked.

The woman shook her head. 'Long gone,' she said. 'Oatmeal's ready if you want.'

Jill carried a bowl up to Nora's room, along with a plastic spoon. Fortunately, Nora had forgotten about the ice cream. Jill sat on the edge of her mother's bed and fed her.

'Did I tell you about my trip to Maggie's?' Jill said, watching her mother's eyes search for the name. 'We talked a lot about you. You'd be so proud of her, what she and Tim have done with that farm. It's a showplace!' And so on, as if Nora were taking it all in. Jill knew that what was important was creating that feeling of familiarity, even if the names and details had long since scattered. But as she talked, another voice was speaking in the back of her mind, saying, 'Oh, Mama, what am I going to do with you?'

Once the kids were out of school and stuck at home, Henry began calling them every morning at ten from Riyadh, so Jill could get out of the house. It was a daily battle trying to assemble money or find groceries. Most businesses were closed down, but black markets popped up in different neighborhoods, where everything was for sale. Cash hoarding caused the ATMs to run low on money. The federal government had a large reserve of currency that it was trying to push into the economy, but the reserve was largely composed of spurned two-dollar bills, which cash machines couldn't accommodate.

The contagion had destroyed any sense of community. Jill recalled other natural disasters, such as hurricanes in North Carolina when she was a child. The city of Wilmington would snap into a well-organized humanitarian machine. Her father had a bass boat, and when the streets flooded, he rescued neighbors trapped in their houses. Nora made food baskets with her daughters. Jill and Maggie loved those purposeful and dramatic days when people pulled together and everyone seemed to care about each other.

Disease wasn't like that. Neighbors were afraid of each other. They hoarded food. It seemed like everyone was armed – gun shops were the last businesses to shut their doors. The boldest people were the rapacious black marketeers. Jill had no doubt that most of the available goods were stolen. The sellers had made a calculation: this was their chance to make a killing. When the plague passed, they would be kings. All they had to do was survive. Jill traded a string of pearls for a sack of tomatoes and a pound of rigatoni.

The government was constantly trying to reassure citizens that everything possible was being done, but the reassuring lies only gave credence to the most flagrant conspiracy theories. Fearing each other, people withdrew from the common social rituals that protected a society under siege. The absence of truth and the breakdown of trust opened the door to terror, and that was tearing society apart.

One morning, Jill grabbed the chance to go for her regular run around Lullwater Park. The trail was still slightly damp from a recent rain. She felt like she was in a zombie movie where the town was deserted and the people who remained were in a tremulous state between living and dying. But for now, I'm alive, she thought. Without any people around, she took off her mask.

As she rounded the first hill, she came upon a dead bird. She stopped for a moment to examine it. Olive and yellow with a black cap and a black throat. Beautiful. Some kind of warbler, she thought. Maggie would know. Maybe this bird was common in these woods, but Jill had never noticed it before. If I live through this, she thought, I'm going to pay more attention.

She remembered the previous winter when the lake had partly frozen over. It never really froze solid anymore. She had been for a walk with the kids, and Teddy was the first to spot the dog under the ice. 'Poor thing, he must have tried walking on it,' Jill had said, realizing it was Teddy's first real encounter with death. He was shaken by the scene. He found a stick and tried to break through the crust. 'Teddy, don't do that,' Jill had said. 'We have to wait till it thaws. The maintenance people will take care of him.' But Teddy continued to beat on the ice. 'Think about the people who own him,' he cried. 'Think about Peepers.'

'I know, sweetie. It's sad. But he's dead, and we can't bring him back.'

Teddy knew about death – abstractly, the way kids talk about sex – but now he *knew*, he really *knew*, his body trembled with understanding. Remembering this conversation now, Jill wondered what else she could say about death to

240

Teddy and Helen. They were frightened, but so was she. She longed now for her lost faith, for the near certainties that she used to feel about God and Heaven when she was her children's ages. They don't have that, she thought. We didn't give it to them. Maybe religion was all lies or myths constructed out of the fear of death that she was feeling now. There had been some pride in living without superstition, in the world of provable facts. Henry was so hostile to religion she would never think of broaching the subject of spiritual longing to him, but she felt it now, and she didn't know what to do about it.

When she came near the main drive in the park, she noticed several people in camouflage clothing feeding the ducks, standing in the same place she stood just a few days before, before the world changed. Something about them struck Jill as odd. She looked on the sloping hillside behind the lake and saw a flock of Canada geese, but they were all lying on the ground.

'What are y'all doing?' she shouted at one of the people feeding the ducks. She noticed a badge on his jacket.

'Ah, ma'am, you don't need to watch this, I'm sorry.'

'You're killing the birds?'

'It's an order. Nobody is happy about this.'

As Jill was talking to the bird exterminators, she saw the swan struggle out of the lake and walk onto the pavement. Jill knew this swan: he would nip at her shoes and flap his wings in a scornful display of majesty if she failed to offer Fritos or bread crumbs. Now he staggered drunkenly, his head drooping like a dead weight, and then collapsed in the grass across the road.

———

While Jill was out, Helen and Teddy told Henry on Face-Time about their projects and the books they were reading, and in turn he took a walk down the empty streets in the early Saudi evening, when the sun was not so blistering, and showed the children what that austere country looked like with all the people inside, just as they were in Atlanta.

Teddy was angry much of the time. It was so unlike him. 'You don't care,' he said when Henry asked about the crystal radio he was making.

'No, I'm very interested,' Henry said. 'I tried to make one when I was in junior high and it never worked.'

The idea that Henry had failed at something did intrigue Teddy, but that led him to ask, 'Why can't you cure this disease? Aren't you supposed to be the person who knows how to do that stuff?'

'I guess I am,' said Henry, 'and I'm doing what I can. But it's really hard.'

Helen had another concern when it was her turn. 'Mom's not okay. She's upset all the time,' she said. 'She pretends like she's got it all together, but she's, like, crying a lot. Not in front of us.'

'It's a horrible time,' said Henry. 'It's a time when people have to face things they never thought they would. I know that's true for you, too. But I also know that you're strong, Helen, maybe the strongest person in the family. Mom and Teddy can depend on you. You know that about yourself, don't you?'

Helen answered very quietly, 'I guess.'

'I wish I could treat you like my little girl, and maybe we'll have that chance again soon. But right now you'll have to be very grown up.'

Helen absorbed this, then said, 'Daddy, do you believe in Heaven?'

Henry could see her eyes glance away from the screen, maybe embarrassed for having asked the question so bluntly. Maybe fearful of the answer.

'I don't disbelieve in it,' Henry said.

'Tell me what you really think. Don't talk to me like a kid.'

Henry realized he was evading the question, one of the most important that Helen had ever asked him. 'I'm not religious, you know that,' he said. 'I'm a scientist. I look at the universe as a mystery I'd like to solve. But the more I know about life, the more mystified I am. Why do we exist? We don't know, we may never know. Is there a God? Often when I'm looking through a microscope at some infinitely tiny unit of life I'm so stunned by its beauty and by its function that I have to step back and catch my breath. How did we all come to be? Why is it that we can have a conversation like this, rather than be like Teddy's robot, just taking orders from its master? I'm trying to express thoughts to you that I've never fully worked out for myself. Let's say this: On the surface, I see life as being wonderfully simple. You can name the colors, for instance. When you taste something, you know the flavors. When you hear noise, you know immediately if it's music or not. When you look in the mirror, you see a person, and you know it's you.

'But if you look inside that person – if you look inside Helen – what you find is really complicated. Helen started as one single tiny cell, but now she is made up of trillions of cells that came out of that original Helen cell, and they all have different functions. And even though Helen is going to live to be a very old lady, every minute hundreds of millions of Helen cells die, and new ones are made – but she's still Helen.'

'Where do those cells go?' Helen asked.

'They're absorbed into the body, and their energy is used to create new cells. But they're all Helen cells. If you look inside those cells, things get even more complex. You remember the electron microscope I showed you in my lab?'

'Uh-huh.'

'I can magnify a cell ten million times. Can you imagine? The deeper I explore, the more amazed I am. And yet, there will always be a door I can't open. There's a secret inside I'll never unlock. If I could open that door, maybe I would find something like a soul.'

'What about Heaven?'

'I don't know. Nobody knows, honestly. I've heard of patients who have died on the operating table and been revived, and some of them have stories of seeing their dead friends and relatives. I take that as what we call a datum point, interesting but unprovable. I wish I could tell you there was a life after death, and that all the people you care about will be there, and we'll be together for eternity. I can't prove it one way or the other.'

Helen nodded. Henry worried that he had let her down. Then she said, 'I believe in Heaven. I think it's in our dreams.'

'What do you mean?'

'It's like we already have all these people and experiences in our lives, then in our dreams we rearrange everything, and have new experiences, and sometimes we meet new people, and we go on great adventures, and that's like Heaven, and sometimes bad things happen or nightmares, and that's like Hell. I mean, why do we have to think that Heaven is a place we can go only when we die? What if we have half our life awake on earth and then half in heaven, and then eventually it's all in heaven and that's when we're dead?'

'That's a very elegant theory,' Henry said admiringly.

29

Grandma's Biscuits

JILL WENT TO SEE HER MOTHER AGAIN AT THE ELDER-CARE facility. This time Nora recognized Jill as soon as she came in. 'Put on gloves' was the first thing Nora said. Jill took a pair of disposable gloves from a box on the windowsill, then put a pair on Nora. She held her mother's hand. 'I'm going to take you home,' Jill said.

'No, don't.'

'When was the last time you ate?'

'I'm not hungry.'

'Look, I brought you something.' Jill reached into a plastic bag and produced a pint of vanilla ice cream. It had cost her twenty-four dollars, as much cash as she had been able to muster.

'You shouldn't be here,' Nora said.

'Humor me, Mom, I'm in the mood to feed you.'

Nora smiled. It was the first time in months Jill had seen her do that. She spooned a small bite into her mother's mouth. 'Vanilla is your favorite, right?'

Nora nodded. After the first bite, she was ravenous.

'Your children . . .' Nora said vaguely.

'Helen and Teddy. They're fine. They're bored. They can't wait for you to come home with me.'

'I love them.'

'I know. And they know, too.'

'I can't go now.'

'Mom, I can't just leave you here.'

'I can't go. I'm sick.'

Jill tried to be calm, but her heart fluttered. 'Mom, I want to take care of you.'

'You shouldn't be here, either,' Nora said. Her chin trembled as she spoke. 'Somewhere I have the papers about the will and all that. You and your sister . . .' Nora looked furiously at the ceiling tiles.

'Maggie.'

'You and Maggie get everything.' She thought a moment. 'Do I still have a car?'

'Mom, let's not talk about that.'

'I don't want a big funeral.'

'Okay.'

'At Oakland, next to your dad. We have the plot, you know.' She remembered the most surprising things, or maybe these were the only important things for her now. She wanted her pastor – Jill knew whom she meant, at the Glenn Memorial United Methodist Church – to give the eulogy. Jill didn't tell her how impossible that would be, even if the church was still operating and the minister was alive.

'I love you, Mom,' she said, tearing up.

'I know you do.'

Jill spooned another bite of vanilla ice cream into her mother's mouth.

247

Three days later, Jill buried Nora at Oakland Cemetery, a beautiful old place on the south side. It wasn't in her plot. There were so many bodies to be buried that a trench had been prepared. Like most of the others, Nora was wrapped in a sheet. Mortuaries had shut down because of the fear of infection and the dearth of caskets. The bodies arrived in rental trucks. Few of the corpses had even been awarded a shroud. Some were in night clothes, others were naked. Attendants wearing Tyvek suits loaded the bodies onto pallets and a forklift lowered them into the trench. There were only a handful of mourners. This was a ceremony not meant to be seen.

For a moment, Jill's thoughts were carried away by a mockingbird's song. He was in a magnolia tree, trilling his various joyous tunes. Life, Jill thought, it's majestic, it's continuous, with or without us. And then she convulsed into sobs.

Suddenly she felt a hand on her elbow. It took a moment to recognize the face behind the mask: it was Vicky, the mother of K'Neisha, Jill's favorite student. No words were exchanged. Jill watched as one of the men in Tyvek took a small bundle from the trunk of Vicky's Nissan and placed it on top of the pallet with the other bodies.

Jill's fingers turned into sausages. She was dropping everything. She spilled lentils all over the stove. 'Mom, didn't we have this last night?' Helen asked. Jill stopped herself from snapping at her. 'Tonight it's different,' she said lightly. 'Tonight we have lentils and hot sauce.'

'Oh, great.'

Jill looked in the pantry. There must be something else she could put with the lentils. She worried that she wasn't feeding the children enough, but she also felt the need to ration their supplies until the plague exhausted itself, the stores reopened, the cash machines worked, and everyone went back to their ordinary lives. There were some extra canned goods in the pantry and a few items in the freezer – popsicles, a bag of frozen peas, a trout of undetermined vintage – but not enough to sustain them more than a few days.

In the back of the fridge Jill spotted a bag of flour. Her mother had always insisted on keeping flour in the refrigerator to avoid the boll weevils, an old southern habit. There was just enough Crisco to make biscuits. How many times, as little girls, had Jill and Maggie stood on stools to help Nora roll out dough for cookies and pies and especially biscuits – hot and flaky and filling the kitchen with a rich aroma that Jill could still smell vividly in her memory. Her knees went so weak that she had to grab the counter for support.

'There's no milk,' she said hollowly.

'Mom, are you okay?' asked Helen, constantly vigilant about her mother's moods.

'I was going to make biscuits, but we're out of milk.'

'Do you have to have milk?' Teddy asked guiltily. He had drunk the last of it.

'If you want Grandma's biscuits, you do.'

Helen made a dreaded suggestion. 'Maybe ask Mrs Hernández upstairs to see if she'll trade some milk for some biscuits.' Helen and Teddy privately regarded Mrs Hernández as a witch.

'Why do you think she's got milk?' Jill asked.

'She's got cats, so she's got milk.'

249

Jill handed a measuring cup to Helen. 'Take Teddy with you. See if she'll part with three-fourths of a cup.'

Helen hadn't counted on doing it herself, but Jill's distracted movements unsettled her. She was desperate to cheer her mother up. Something serious but unspoken was in the air.

As soon as the kids left the room, Jill sat at the kitchen table and wept.

Everyone called her Mrs Hernández, but no one in the family knew if she had ever been married. Jill supposed she lived off Social Security and a modest pension, which – judging by the bottles and tins in her recycle bin – went largely to alcohol and cat food. The television blared at all hours. Groceries and pizza were often delivered, or used to be. She drove a little Ford Focus that rarely left the garage. Jill suspected she was agoraphobic.

Teddy reached for Helen's hand as they walked up the dark stairway. Mrs Hernández wasn't good about replacing the bulbs. The children had only been upstairs twice, both times on Halloween, when Mrs Hernández gave them Mars bars. There was a glass-paneled door at the top of the stairway. Helen knocked. They could hear the floorboards creak as Mrs Hernández walked across the room and opened the door, a plump, white-haired woman in a blue bathrobe.

'Why hello, children,' she said. Then, 'Oh, Blackie!' as a large cat slipped by them into the stairwell. It stood there uncertainly. 'She'll come back in a minute,' said Mrs Hernández. 'She's just exploring.'

'We're making biscuits,' Helen said. 'Would you like some?'

'Oh, that's very thoughtful!'

'But we don't have any milk.'

A tabby cat brushed up against Teddy's leg. It seemed strange that Mrs Hernández had all the blinds closed on such a pretty day.

'Milk? Did you say you needed milk? But my kitties need their milk.' Mrs Hernández fixed Helen with a stern look. 'How many biscuits are you offering?'

'How many do you want?'

'Six,' said Mrs Hernández.

'Four.'

'You can't make biscuits without milk.'

'You can't make biscuits without flour and butter, either,' said Helen.

'Five,' said Mrs Hernández.

'Four,' Helen said stubbornly. In the pause that followed, she turned to leave, pulling Teddy after her.

'How much milk?'

'One cup, Mom says.'

Teddy started to say something, but Helen nudged him, so he kept his mouth shut.

Mrs Hernández opened her refrigerator. Helen could see that there were three bottles of milk there, and very little else. Mrs Hernández poured out exactly one cup. 'Four biscuits,' she said again before passing the cup to Helen. 'Now where's that black cat?'

Blackie was clawing the outside door, looking for an escape. Mrs Hernández scooped him up.

Now that dinner was over, and Helen had finished the dishes, Jill told her and Teddy to come into the living room. They needed to talk.

Jill realized her tone was ominous, but she couldn't help

herself. 'You know this terrible flu is really dangerous, don't you?' Jill said. Helen and Teddy nodded. 'Do you know anybody who's sick?'

'There's four boys in my class,' said Teddy. 'I think maybe more.'

'There's more,' said Helen. 'A lot.'

'I imagine there are,' said Jill. 'So many reports on television. People all over the world getting really sick.'

'Is Daddy okay?' Helen asked, picking up on the implications.

'Yes, honey, he's fine. He's doing what he can to keep people safe. We ought to be really proud of him, don't you think?'

Helen nodded gravely. Teddy said, 'I'm angry he's not here.'

'I know,' said Jill. 'I wish he were here, too. He'd know what to say. He's really wise.'

'What's wrong, Mommy?' Helen said insistently.

Jill had rehearsed this. 'You know that many people are really sick, and some of them don't get better. Some of them die. You understand what that means, don't you?' The children nodded. Jill could see the apprehension in their eyes. 'Aunt Maggie called me. Your cousin, Kendall. She got sick. She didn't get well.'

Helen turned white.

'It happened on Monday. She just got horribly sick, and there wasn't anything to do.'

'How did she get sick?' Teddy asked.

'Nobody knows, Teddy, but some people said that it was in the pigs.'

'Is Queen Margaret sick?' Helen asked.

'She died too,' said Jill, omitting the information that Maggie had herded all her livestock into a remote pasture and shot them. She didn't say that Uncle Tim was also sick, and that Jill had buried their grandmother that morning. One thing at a time.

30

What Would You Advise?

THE VIRUS HAD EVOLVED, MAGNIFIED, RETURNING WITH A vehemence that left the researchers deflated by their inability to contain it. 'We've missed every play,' Henry said to his team on a Skype conference. 'Have you looked at the NIH universal influenza vaccine?'

'It's for influenza A and B, and it's still in trials,' said Marco.

'Well, are the volunteers alive? That might indicate that it has some crossover potential to neutralize Kongoli.'

'We'll check.'

'What about the Pfizer vaccine?' Henry asked Susan, a young intern who had just stepped into the job of one of the best people on the team. That person had stopped coming to the lab. Nobody knew what had happened to her.

'The initial animal trials seem promising,' Susan replied.

'That's as far as you've gotten?' he said sharply. 'That was two days ago!'

'We don't have—'

'No baseline, no initial—'

'We don't know any of that!' Susan said, near tears.

'Henry, we're all working flat out,' Marco said. 'Nobody

has slept. We don't see our families, half of us are camped out in the lab. We're doing everything we can.'

'I know, I know you are. Sorry,' Henry said. 'I realize you're as frustrated as I am.' It was pointless to say that they needed more time. Everybody knew that. And everybody knew there wasn't more time.

Tildy settled on the couch with her elderly Pekingese, Baskin, to watch a historic moment in American history. She already knew what the president was going to say: Tomorrow there will be federal troops in American cities, protecting property and government offices. Health care will be nationalized. Tented infirmaries will be set up in shopping mall parking lots. The Red Cross will take charge of a massive volunteer program. And drug companies will be commandeered and made to focus exclusively on developing a vaccine – not just for Kongoli but for any strain of influenza, providing lifetime protection. The president will invoke the Allied victory in the Second World War and the elimination of smallpox as achievements that had also seemed impossible at the time. He will guarantee that the U.S. government will apply the full force of its mighty powers to protect its citizens and other peoples of the world against the greatest plague humanity has ever known.

All the channels were carrying the president's speech, which was to be broadcast from the Oval Office. On CNN, the panel of commentators were all wearing white masks and rubber gloves, which was bound to provoke a reaction, since those items were in short supply even in hospitals. The commentators spoke in somber tones, but it was also clear that they thrilled to the occasion. Years in the future, this scene of masked commentators would be part of the retro-spectives. The commentators would always be tied to this historic moment. It would be in their obituaries.

Finally, the president appeared at the Resolute Desk in the Oval Office. He appeared deeply tanned, either from extra sessions in the tanning bed or an extra-heavy layer of pan-cake. Still, Tildy thought, he looked nervous. Perhaps he was awed by the challenge. He was also aware of the furor caused by the *Post* story that Tildy had planted about his family getting inoculated.

'My fellow Americans,' he said, a half note higher than his usual register, 'once again we face an enormous chal-lenge. Once again, the world looks to America because only we can do it. And we will do it, we will conquer this disease, I guarantee you.' The president batted away a nettlesome fly.

'Tonight I am announcing major changes in how our coun-try will be run in the face of this terrible crisis,' he continued. 'First, let me say, our constitutional system will survive this test.' The president was now reciting the litany of actions that he was putting into effect, and his energy seemed to rise. 'Martial law,' he said, thumping the desk forcefully. 'I know, I know how it sounds, but a great man who once sat in this office said we've got nothing to fear but—'

As the president was speaking, what appeared to be a tear spilled down his cheek. The president furtively wiped it away, but another tear followed, and just at the same moment Tildy and the president and the American people realized that it wasn't tears, it was blood. The president's eyes were bleeding. Before he could finish the sentence, the transmis-sion cut off.

Twenty seconds later, Tildy's secure phone rang. 'We're

invoking COOP,' the voice said, referring to the Continuity of Operations Plan. The president was still alive, but deemed unable to govern, so the vice president assumed office. At that very moment, he and the senior cabinet members were being removed to Mount Weather. Buried in Virginia's Blue Ridge Mountains was a miniature city, with twenty underground office buildings, some three stories tall. In addition to its own sewage treatment and power plants, Mount Weather had a radio and television studio (part of the Emergency Alert System), a crematorium, and sleeping quarters for the president, cabinet members, and Supreme Court justices. They were airlifted the forty-eight miles from Washington. Several of them simply refused to leave their families, and one was already too sick to make the trip (no one with symptoms would be allowed in any case). The speaker of the House of Representatives, next in line for presidential succession, was relocated to Camp David, where there was another bunker – under Aspen, the presidential lodge – with access to a vast Defense Department installation carved out of the Catoctin Mountains of Maryland.

Tildy later learned that, because the vice president had been exposed to the president's illness, when he arrived at Mount Weather he was placed inside a large plastic ball, used in embassies to protect against biological attacks. The vice president, now the most powerful man in the world, was being fed through a tube, and inside that sanitized balloon he was running America.

From the window of her condo on the waterfront, Tildy could see the empty wharfs, the river moving along indifferently, nature turning its back on humanity.

III

In the Deep

31

Idaho

THE SUMMER BEFORE, IN A WILDLY UNCHARACTERISTIC MOVE, Henry had bought a fairly new Suburban the size of a small school bus and filled it with sleeping bags and tents and ice chests and fishing poles, then drove his family all across the country, staying in Holiday Inns and camping in national parks once they hit the mountains. Jill learned how to cook on a Coleman stove, making blueberry pancakes on the griddle for breakfast; in the evening, they'd roast potatoes in the campfire's coals and grill trout that Henry and Teddy caught in streams so lucid it was sometimes hard to determine where the water began. Helen was moody but enraptured by nature. She would go off by herself to read or listen to her music, which worried Jill, who didn't want her children out of sight. Then Helen would wander back into camp with blossoms in her hair.

Beauty was everywhere, but so was danger – danger of a kind that this very urban family had never fully experienced – although that was Henry's intention in taking them into ever more remote wilderness. He had a theory that manageable doses of hardship would build immunity to the greater challenges that life would pose. Roughing it in the Mountain

261

West – away from Netflix and wifi and refrigerators and toilets and the props of civilization – revealed one's inner resources. How else would you know what you were made of unless you set aside your devices and slept under the stars, 'like sleeping under a Christmas tree,' Teddy had said the first night they tried it, in a little campground at the base of Uncompahgre Peak in Colorado. Helen woke up screaming when a fawn licked the salt off her face. A herd of startled deer disappeared into the woods like apparitions from another world.

Civilization can take us so far away from our true natures that we never know who we really are. At least, this was Henry's belief. And so he spent time teaching Teddy and Helen how to whittle and tie knots and build a fire. Teddy was in Cub Scouts and already knew the basics, but Helen, four years older, caught on pretty quickly. Henry had his own fears. It was not so much the danger of a snake bite or falling from a ledge that worried him, but of leading his family to the edge of danger and then failing to protect them.

Still, he insisted on going ever deeper into the places on the map where the roads came to an end. After Yellowstone and the Grand Tetons, he steered away from national parks with their nice showers and toilets and campsites that you had to reserve. Instead, he roved the logging roads in the national forests that covered so much of the West. The green patches on the map indicated public lands, which were endless and theirs to explore. Because of his disability, Henry couldn't hike long distances, but he had a knack for discovering unmarked jeep trails that were just within the capacity of the massive Suburban to navigate. Jill fretted constantly that Henry was going to tear out the transmission or some vital piece of the undercarriage, leaving them stranded in nowheresville, but as long as there was gas in the tank Henry was unconcerned. He didn't care about getting lost; in fact, that seemed to be his aim. Jill might be muttering in the front seat about slowing down or turning around, but suddenly they would land upon a giddying field of fireweed and golden asters. It was maddening, in a way, that Henry had such luck in discovering one spectacular spot after another, each different in its majesty, whether it was the flowers or the mountains or a glacial lake that seemed to have been just created. Everyone was exhilarated and exhausted and sleep deprived and desperately needing a bath.

It was in Idaho that Henry hit upon the idea of renting horses and packing into the Nez Perce forest. He had been studying a highway map and saw that the road ended in a place enticingly called Elk City. It was the remnant of an old mining town, with a saloon and a café and not much more – exactly what Henry had hoped. There was a Native American outfitter who agreed to guide them over a pass and drop them off in a remote spot on Meadow Creek, 'the prettiest place you'll ever see,' he promised. 'Some say it's sacred.' He was missing a front incisor and a couple of fingers, but somehow his name was Lucky.

They set out before dawn, but even in the dark the horses knew the way to the trail. There were five horses for the riders and two mules to carry the tent and sleeping bags and food for a week. Neither Teddy nor Helen had ever been on a horse before, and Teddy's feet couldn't reach the stirrups, but that was all the more reason, in Henry's opinion, that they should undergo this experience. He was heedless of Lucky's cautions about the bears and moose and poisonous weeds and timber wolves, a catalog of perils that had drawn Henry here in the first place. Jill, however, was paying attention, and the prospect of being left alone in the mountains, completely cut off from civilization, surrounded by unfamiliar perils, filled her with foreboding. She could not fathom Henry's obsession, and as the horses lurched up the steep trail through forests of spruce and fir and lodgepole pine, her anxiety mounted, along with her anger at Henry for placing their children in danger. The fact that Lucky carried a pistol also made her nervous, both because she didn't like being around guns and because they wouldn't have one themselves, if it were actually needed. After several hours she was saddle sore and had to dismount and walk beside her horse. Henry knew Jill well enough not to try to placate her.

Henry studied Lucky and his easy way of sitting in the saddle, his familiarity with nature, his pleasant absorption in every moment. By contrast, Henry was still on the run from his duties. He longed to fully escape his distraction and give himself over entirely to the joy of the adventure and the love of his family. Surely that was also part of his drive to plunge deeper and deeper into the wilderness.

They stopped for lunch beside an artesian spring spilling out of a rock. Lucky showed Teddy how to cradle his head in the moss and drink from it. Teddy wanted to do everything the way Lucky did it, so he let the water cascade over his face and came out giggling, then Helen had to try it, and soon everyone had been refreshed by the frigid spring, and the wilderness did not seem quite so menacing. The pure cold water was like a baptism into another life.

When they remounted, Lucky put Jill in the lead, followed

by her children, and then he followed behind Henry so that he could have a quiet word with him.

'Even I get a little spooked out here by myself,' Lucky said. 'A week is a mighty long time.' Henry recognized that Lucky was giving him good advice, but he had an arbitrary marker in his mind that a week in the wild was the exact dose of adventure required to save his family from . . . whatever.

'I could pick you up in three days and give you a discount,' Lucky offered.

Henry thought about it, then said, 'Five days, I think.'

'Yessir, that'd be a good amount. All you'd need.'

Henry hoped Jill would be mollified by his willingness to compromise.

When the kids turned restive, Lucky began to sing. He had a low, pleasant voice, and the song was vaguely familiar to Henry.

> *Over hill, over dale*
> *As we hit the dusty trail,*
> *And the caissons go rolling along.*
> *In and out, here them shout,*
> *Counter march and right about*
> *And the caissons go rolling along.*

'What's a caisson?' Teddy asked.

'I don't rightly know,' Lucky admitted. 'It's just a song we used to sing when I was in the Army.'

'I think it's an ammunition wagon,' said Henry.

'Yessir, you're likely right,' said Lucky. He sang it again a couple times, and then Teddy joined in, imitating Lucky, and in a bit they were all singing, making the time pass, shooing away the apprehension that threatened to defeat Henry's great experiment.

Henry never knew his father's parents and, frankly, he didn't care to know any more about them. They had never supported him in any manner. He had grown up in the home of his maternal grandparents, Ilona and Franz Bozsik, Hungarian refugees from the 1956 revolution that the Soviets had so savagely crushed. Franz had carried Henry's mother, Agnes, who was two, on his shoulders through a minefield into Austria. He believed the definite loss of freedom was worse than the possible loss of life.

Everything Ilona and Franz had, except Agnes, was lost. They learned other languages, moved through different cultures, and through the vagaries of opportunity wound up in Indianapolis. Franz, who had been a professor of economics at the Technical University of Budapest, where the revolution began, became a cabinetmaker. Ilona taught piano. They were quiet, perhaps because their English never became proficient. When Henry came into their lives they were already in their early sixties, and both in fragile health. Henry was four. They weren't ready for another child in their lives.

Ilona was kind but passive, traumatized by having the life she had planned for torn apart. She didn't know where to fit in, or how. Her strategy was to encourage others. Henry grew up listening to her praise her students, rewarding them with walnut cookies or kolaches, even when they hadn't practiced. And she did the same with him; she was a fountain of encouragement with little life of her own. She had her pleasures, however, in the garden and the kitchen, but mainly in music. The house was always full of it, whether it was the students muddling through sonatinas from the Schirmer catalog or Ilona herself playing the Hungarians – Liszt or Bartók – with a passion that was nowhere else evident in her life. Her favorite composer was the melancholy Austrian, Schubert. She would listen to Vladimir Horowitz play a grave Schubert impromptu and weep. Her kindness was in some way a noble expression of grief.

Franz, on the other hand, used to frighten Henry with his ferocity and bitterness. Perhaps he regretted the life he had forced on his family. He must have resented the loss of the status he had enjoyed in Budapest as an esteemed professor with a secure position. It wasn't until the end of his life that he talked with Henry about the old days, and then it was as if he were remembering a lost love. Loss, indeed, was the defining element of the Bozsik household. They had all lost Henry's mother.

Franz imparted two things to Henry that would mark him for the rest of his life. One was his hatred of religion, which he blamed for seizing his daughter's mind and leading her to catastrophe. 'They stole her! Like robbers, they take her away,' Franz said in his accented English. He spoke of it in the same way he talked about the loss of Hungary to communism – with a puzzled fury about how a dangerous belief system could take over the minds of reasonable people.

The other thing that Franz taught Henry was to prepare himself. Franz recognized that Henry was small and sickly and full of fears, but he also saw strength in him. He saw intelligence and curiosity. Henry later supposed that these were qualities his mother also had. 'She was smart, she was talented, your mother,' Franz told Henry. He wouldn't say her name. He devoted himself to making sure that Henry was armored against the assaults that life would present. Henry would need to make himself physically strong. He would have to be skeptical and intellectually rigorous. He must make a career that would always provide support.

Most of all, Henry would have to confront his fears. He was easily startled and shied away from confrontation. Even when Henry was really young, Franz would taunt him, he would shout 'Boo!' or toss him in the air; later, he would attack Henry's ideas and force him to stand up to ridicule. Franz was dying of heart disease, and his lessons were sometimes cruel and too urgent. He knew time was running out. He passed away while Henry was in his second year of high school.

All of his life, Henry had been losing the people closest to him. The lesson that he drew is that others cannot protect us. This was what Franz had sought to impart. Like him, Henry had a need to repair the past, which was unfixable. His grandfather's death steered him into medicine. Without money, he had to be the best, and so he excelled in his studies and received scholarships all the way through Purdue University and medical school at Johns Hopkins. Henry would not have been the man he became if his own parents had lived. It was Franz and Ilona who showed him how to live.

As abbreviated as his time with the Bozsiks was, they at least gave him the idea of a family. Henry knew that he was not by nature a particularly caring person. He was happiest in the lab or in his reading chair. Like many persons of extraordinary intellect, he could become so absorbed in his thoughts that he subtracted himself from the current of life around him. He could sit in a noisy coffee shop and be totally unaware of conversations right over his shoulder as he performed mental calculations. He could easily have lived alone. Indeed, he thought this would be his destiny. But then he found Jill and they began a life together, and children came, and love called Henry into the world.

The pass was still snowy in early July. As Lucky pointed out animal tracks, Henry realized how little he knew about the natural world outside of the laboratory. He lived in miniature, in so many respects, seeing life through a microscope. Now he felt microscopic himself, dwarfed by the trees and the mountains and the risky task he had set himself, which was beginning to feel like a trap.

The forest thinned out, and the trail switched back and forth in wide swings. The horses picked their way through a boulder field as pikas played hide-and-seek on the rocks. 'If you're especially fortunate, you might see a wolf,' said Lucky. 'If you do, you can think of me.'

'Why is that?' Jill asked.

'That's my Indian name, Yellow Wolf. Many people in my tribe are named Wolf-something. We regard Mister Wolf as very wise and cunning.'

Finally the trees fell away and the land opened into a vast meadow with high grass and flowers. The Bitterroot range lay across the horizon, jagged, snow-capped, splendid. Jill drew a breath. 'It's glorious,' she said.

'This was the way it was before they found gold and everything changed,' Lucky said. He hitched the horses to a post under a stand of fir and led them to the place where the creek spread into a broad pool, which was percolating with brook trout feeding on the hatch. He helped Henry put up the tent and then tied a rope around the food chest and hoisted it over a limb about fifteen feet off the ground. 'Just out of reach in case a grizzly passes through,' he said.

'Are there grizzlies?' Jill asked. This was not something she had reckoned with.

'Not really. Black bears, yes. Maybe there was a report or two about grizzlies, but we never see them. They're pretty shy. Still, best to keep your food out of reach. Don't encourage them.'

Lucky had to get back over the mountain before dark, so he rounded up the horses and left Henry, Jill, Helen, and Teddy alone. It was just what Henry had longed for, although without horses they were essentially marooned in this paradise; at least, Henry was.

That first evening they sat in camp chairs watching the animals come to the creek. A herd of elk tore the grass on the opposite bank, and then a huge male moose with a rack six feet wide stomped into the pool. Henry had never appreciated how lethal such antlers could be, shaped like great opened hands with sharpened fingers, some of them a foot long. The moose announced his presence with a trumpeting bellow that caused the children, on that first night, to dart into the tent. He came every evening near dusk with the same bold cry. Teddy began calling him Bullwinkle. A bald eagle perched on a nearby boulder, preening itself, unfazed by their presence. All of the animals displayed a kind of regal indifference, as if they were only tolerating the presence of the Parsons family. They returned the human gaze with equal curiosity. We are all animals here, they seemed to be saying.

The third night it rained hard, with lightning strikes

bursting right overhead, so bright that they lit up the tent like flashbulbs. Helen buried herself in her sleeping bag, but Teddy enjoyed the show, until one strike came so close they all jumped. Jill pressed her body into Henry's, and the children inched their bags closer to his. Henry lay awake like a sentry until the storm passed and the thunder grumbled in the distant mountains. As he finally fell asleep, he thought that this was exactly what he was aiming for, an experience that brought them closer and showed them that what is frightening is not necessarily fatal.

Teddy asked him, 'I'm like Lucky, aren't I?'

Henry and his son were collecting firewood after the rain. Henry showed Teddy how to whittle the bark off the wet sticks, which were dry inside. 'You mean, because you're both Indians?' he said.

Teddy nodded.

'Well, yes, you are the same ethnic group, but pretty different in other ways. The Nez Perce are thousands of miles away from your tribe in Brazil.'

'But they're still alive, right? Lucky's tribe.'

'Yes, they are. Many of them still live in this region, I'm sure.'

'What's my tribe again?'

'The Cinta Larga. It means "broad belt".'

Teddy made a face. 'It's a weird name.'

'Well, I guess that's what they liked to wear. But I doubt they had a choice in the matter of what outsiders called them. I don't really know what they called themselves. Like Nez Perce means "pierced nose". Don't you think that's because they liked to decorate their faces with jewelry?'

'Are my people still alive?'

'There are still some scattered around the jungles of Brazil. I don't know how many there are. Would you like to go back someday and meet them?'

'I don't think so,' Teddy said. 'I think they're all actually dead.'

'Why do you say that?'

'That's what you told Mom, right? You said they all died, and I was the only one left.'

'She told you that?'

Teddy nodded.

'I think she meant that the people in your little village died. Not the whole tribe. It was a disease they had.'

'And you couldn't save them.'

Henry started to speak, but his voice failed him. He began to whittle another stick.

He jerked awake as if he had picked up a burning coal.

'What's wrong?' Jill whispered urgently.

'Nothing,' he said. 'Bad dream.'

'You're soaking in sweat.'

'Go back to sleep,' he said. 'It's okay.'

She knew it wasn't okay. In the early years of their marriage, Henry had trouble sleeping, often shaken by powerful nightmares, but they had succumbed to the gravity of normal life. Now he rolled over and pretended to fall asleep, and eventually Jill drifted off.

As Henry lay there, listening to his family breathing, which settled into unison, he realized that something else had driven him into the wilderness, something that had nothing to do with his wife or children. He still fought against the unwanted

272

memories that threatened to drag him back into the moments of his greatest fears. He refused to be incapacitated by the traumas of his past – and yet, why had he dragged his family into a journey that was really about facing his own fears and failures? Jill had cautioned him from the start. How many conversations had they had about why he was doing this? He had said that adventure would toughen up the children and strengthen family bonds. He had told himself that it was about preparing Jill and the children to face the unexpected tribulations that awaited them – eventually, without him – just as his grandfather had taught him. They didn't have the skills or instincts to protect themselves from unanticipated dangers. In their nice brick home in Atlanta, they were safe and coddled. But Henry hadn't been honest with Jill, or with himself. He was here for his own reasons. Returning to the wilderness was bound to trigger memories that were full of horror.

Jill lay in the tent until the smell of coffee brought her around. As much as she had dreaded being cut off from civilization so completely, she had to credit Henry for making it happen. She felt somehow new. The family had never been closer. Each had grown in confidence. As she lingered in the sleeping bag, she had to admit that Henry's plan had achieved its goal. In the mornings, they went on hikes or fished, and each afternoon everyone took a book and sat alone for a couple of hours. Teddy, a precocious reader, was on the second volume of the Harry Potter series, Helen was deep into *The Hunger Games*, and Henry had brought along a new biography of Marie and Pierre Curie. As for Jill, she had already gulped down the two Iris Murdoch novels she had thought would last the trip, so she spent delicious hours sketching wildflowers. She thought about how the Nez Perce Indians would go on vision quests in these mountains, alone, seeking a guardian in the form of an animal or bird that would protect them for the rest of their lives. She wondered if that still happened. She wondered if Lucky had brought them here for a reason.

Finally she emerged from the tent, appealingly bedraggled in Henry's eyes, with a towel over her shoulder. She was insistent on staying clean, so each morning before the children arose she braved the chill and plunged into the creek, washing her hair with eco-friendly shampoo and brushing it out beside the fire.

'You were up last night,' he said. It was their fourth morning. Lucky would be coming for them the next day.

'I started my period,' she said. 'And do you know what else? Helen did, too.'

'Helen? Already?'

'She's eleven. That's not unusual.'

'Weird that you would both—'

'I know.'

'Is she okay?'

'She's mortified. I think she's also proud, in a way, but you know how she hates to go to the bathroom outdoors, and now she's got this to deal with. Tomorrow night we sleep in a motel.' It was an order.

Henry lit the Coleman while Jill mixed the pancake dough, then he roused the children. It was their last full day, and immediately after breakfast they set out on an ambitious hike. Henry replaced his cane with a walking staff he had carved from a birch branch, which gave him the look of an Old Testament prophet. It was still early enough that the birds were chittering madly. The ponderosas smelled sharply of resin after the storm. Henry walked haltingly, but the route they had chosen, along Meadow Creek, gently sloped downward as it rolled north toward its terminus in the Selway River. They hiked in the valley between the peaks of the Bitterroot range and the Clearwater Mountains. When Henry had to rest, he and Jill sat on the bank as the kids picked huckleberries and waded in the creek. There was nowhere else in the world but here in this moment.

The creek stirred and widened as the slope became more acute. Henry picked his way down using his staff to brace himself on the steep parts. They began to hear the falls ahead, a dim but constant roar, like highway traffic, growing in intensity until finally they came to where the waters merged and gushed ferociously through the ancient channel sawn through the black granite hills. The river raced through the debris of rockslides and downed trees, through eddying pools and long stretches of whitewater, frantic, like a great mob fleeing some untold disaster.

The family made their way down a rough path to a point where they could see the falls clearly, and then Teddy spotted the salmon leaping, waving their tails in the air for propulsion. The fish were huge, some as large as three or four feet long, but they seemed overmatched by the torrent.

'They're already beginning to spawn,' Henry said.

'What does that mean?' asked Teddy.

'They lay their eggs in the fall, but first they return to where they were born. They come all the way from the Pacific Ocean, swimming a thousand miles upstream. Then they have their babies, and then they die. This is their final journey.'

'Wow!' Helen cried, as one of the mighty fish leaped high into the air and seemed to hang there, defying gravity, before falling back into the torrent.

'You may be the last generation to see this,' Henry said. 'The dams along the river and the warming oceans have taken a toll on the salmon population. It's heartbreaking, isn't it, when you see how heroic they are.' As Henry spoke, an osprey shot through the canyon walls and scooped up a salmon that had just made it into the upper river. The squirming fish appeared larger than the bird, but the osprey's powerful wings lifted them over the canyon walls and into the forest.

The children were quiet on the hike back to camp. Helen was a little teary. That night they ate the last hot dogs, and when the children crawled into their sleeping bags, Henry and Jill sat for an hour sipping bourbon and watching the stars populate the universe. Perhaps if Henry had been more clearheaded he would have hoisted the food chest back into the tree, but there was so little left it seemed pointless.

He never slept soundly in the tent, so the rustling awakened him instantly. There was no question that it was a bear. It was throwing the food chest around, trying to break it open, grunting with frustration and what sounded to Henry like rage.

'Dad!' Teddy whispered urgently.

'Shhh!'

They were all awake now. The bear was close enough that they could hear every footstep. They heard it claw the tree, then bat the food chest around some more. There was nothing in there now but cereal and powdered milk. Henry just hoped that the bear would be able to break into it, despite the secure latch, and then it happened – the sound of the rigid plastic being torn apart by mighty claws, a sound of shocking violence. The panting and grunting were answered by a grunt on the other side of the tent, followed by a roar that froze them all in terror. Henry realized there were two of them out there, maddened by hunger, fighting over the remains of the powdered milk.

Then the bears became quiet. The family could hear their movements as they circled the tent. Henry decided on a course of action. He would unzip the portal of the tent, then run into the creek, drawing the bears as far from his family as he could. He grabbed the flashlight he would use as a club, until the end.

One of the bears loomed right outside the tent, pressing its nose against the fabric, his hot breath passing right through the sheer nylon, and then he roared, the loudest noise anyone had ever heard. His roar was answered on the other side of the tent.

Suddenly Teddy began to sing:

> *Over hill, over dale*
> *As we hit the dusty trail,*
> *And the caissons go rolling along.*

One of the bears roared again, but Teddy kept singing, and then the rest of the family did as well, loudly and defiantly:

> *Then it's hi, hi, hee!*
> *In the field artillery,*
> *Shout out your numbers loud and strong!*

277

For where'er you go
You will always know
That the caissons go rolling along.

They kept singing until they heard no more sounds outside.

Lucky arrived around noon. He walked around the camp, reading the tracks and shaking his head in amazement. The food chest had been shredded. The paw prints showed a male and a female grizzly, Lucky said. It was the end of mating season. The male paw prints measured more than two feet from toe to heel, not counting the claws. He just couldn't get over it.

'What did you do?' he asked.

'Teddy started it,' Helen said proudly. 'He sang.'

'He sang?' Lucky asked.

'Yeah, that song you taught us,' said Teddy.

As they rode away from the camp and back to civilization, they were all solemn. They were alive, but everything had changed. It wasn't clear yet who they were. When they finally got back to Elk City, Lucky refused to be paid. 'It wasn't your fault,' Henry said. 'I insist.' He held the money out, trying to press it into Lucky's three-fingered hand.

'That's not it,' said Lucky. 'What you experienced is something that we think is holy.' Then he added, 'We will talk about it many times. We will call you the Bear People.'

32

Something to Remember Me By

MY PEOPLE HAVE ALWAYS LOOKED TO THE HEAVENS FOR POR-
tents,' Majid said when Henry found him on the roof of his
cousin's palace in Taif, where they had taken refuge, peering
through a telescope. The stars were dizzyingly brilliant.

'Are you learning anything?'

'For me, the messages are usually about my personal failings. The stars are my mothers-in-law.'

The war had only been waiting for some fresh insult, and
the Saudis had provided it with a missile attack on an Iranian oil depot on Kharg Island. It was in retaliation for the
suicide bombing at Prince Majid's palace and the attack on
the Saudi National Guard headquarters. Iranian destroyers
moved to block the Strait of Hormuz, shutting off the passage of oil from the Persian Gulf. The war had begun.

'You've been very kind to me,' Henry said. 'Now I have
another favor to ask. I must find a way to go home. I've tried
everything. I know you've done what you can, but I cannot
wait any longer. I need to go home. At once.'

Majid looked at him, his face full of sadness. 'I agree, you
must go, it is too dangerous here. This war is going to be
very cruel. We have looked to this day for many hundreds of

years, and now the fanatics want to finish it, even if it destroys Islam. As for getting you home, I would offer you my personal aircraft, but the ban is still in effect. Also, my pilot, he is dead already of the Kongoli. I would fly you myself, but this foolish war.'

'There must be some way,' Henry said despairingly.

'There is no guarantee, but if you could make it to Bahrain, an American naval base is there. Maybe they can help you. I hesitate to mention this because it is in the war zone. The Russians have heavily reinforced Iran. It is even more dangerous in the Gulf than here.'

Danger meant little to Henry now. 'How do I get there?'

'I was going to tell you goodbye at dinner. I must take a battalion to the Eastern Province. From there it is a short distance. If you really wish to take this risk, prepare your things and we will leave before sunrise. I am sorry I cannot be more helpful, but at least we will have some more hours together before we part.'

Henry tried to sleep in the brief time before dawn, but images of his family assaulted him. The guilt he felt at being absent for so long in their time of need was sharp and ceaseless. He should never have come to Saudi Arabia. What good had he done, after all? The infection would have spread its inevitable course in any case. It was like trying to stop a tsunami. There was nothing to be done but to huddle with loved ones and pray.

He was shocked that the thought of praying had leapt into his mind – a sign of his helplessness. Everyone he deeply cared about was in danger. They were suffering. They needed him. And he was so far away.

Majid knocked on his door a little after four in the morning.

Henry's few belongings were packed in the suitcase that Jill had sent – was it only six weeks ago? Majid wore a military uniform. Once again, he seemed like a different man entirely from the doctor in Western clothes Henry had first met years ago or the prince in his robes with whom Henry had worked day and night in the kingdom. Now he was a soldier. 'I do not go to fight in the war, I go to fight against war itself,' Majid said, as he drove an open jeep to the National Guard base, where a small battalion, in Humvees and armored personnel carriers, was already formed up. 'I will do what I can to stop this great folly. But in the end, this is my family.'

By the time the sun appeared on the eastern horizon, the convoy that Majid led was deep into the voluptuous desert. Danger lay ahead of them, and they were rushing toward it, each man for his own reasons. Hours of anxiety drew stories out of the two friends that had been held back until now.

'My mother was a slave,' Majid confided. 'A better word is "concubine," but because my father was pious, he married her when she became pregnant. She was the fourth of my father's wives, and despised by the other three. He soon lost interest in her, but by then I had been born, so he provided, even after the divorce. When I speak of him now, it sounds as if I resent him, but in truth, I loved my father. He was a man of our culture, no more nor less. I might have become like him except for my education. Those years at Cambridge and Swansea not only taught me medicine. I learned other ways of seeing life, and I saw what the world outside of the kingdom thought of us.

'I tell you, Henry, many times I considered that I would never return to Arabia. To live again on the sand with nothing but a flat horizon between you and eternity – why go back to that when I had finally escaped? I could live in May-fair and practice internal medicine, with amusing and sophisticated friends who knew more about the world than I could ever have conceived. Whereas here' – he gestured to the empty sands – 'minds are as barren as the desert, and yet we believe that we are uniquely favored by God. Why is this? We educate ourselves in religion, rumors, and folklore, and despite our ignorance God rewards us with the greatest prize in all the world! Three hundred billion barrels of oil! What did we do to deserve this wonderful gift? Only one answer: We have been rewarded for our piety. And so we become even more pious. The Qur'an instructs us that true piety is believing in God, caring for those in need, freeing those in bondage, and being patient in the face of misfortune, but for the fanatics piety becomes a contest. It's not enough to take care of others, to work for freedom. No. We must annihilate those who believe differently or less than we. Those we call heretics must be punished. And so we squander this great gift, using our wealth to cleanse the world and make it as empty as the minds of these fanatics.'

After this outburst, Prince Majid fell silent. Bitterness had taken over his mood, an aspect of his friend that Henry had never seen. 'Why, then, did you return?' he asked.

'I often ask this question of myself,' Majid said. 'I dream of being back in London, but it's impossible, given who I am.'

'I suppose being a member of the royal family comes with many obligations.'

'We say that every blessing carries a curse. So yes. I am a prince. I have ten thousand cousins just like me. We are rich, yes. We have power. But we live with the knowledge that one day our tribe will be overthrown. This will happen; we

know this. Two things we don't know: when this will happen and what will come after us. We close our eyes to that.
We are like thieves who hear the police sirens, but there is no
place to run.'

'Why did you never marry?' Henry asked boldly.

'I had an exceedingly common fantasy that I would marry
a blond Western girl with blue eyes and excellent taste and a
fine education. And, in fact, I did this.'

'You never told me you are married!'

'I am divorced. Her name was Marian. She was a part of
the whole picture, the townhouse in Mayfair, the rewarding
medical practice, tea and crumpets in the afternoons, a civ-
ilized life with shade trees and foggy streets and elevated
friends. The complete expat dream! But as I say, every blessing comes with its own curse. For me, the curse was the
realization that I would never be a part of that life, I would
always stand outside, peering in the window like a spy. I
loved my wife, but there was a divide between Marian's
world and mine. I looked at who I was in their eyes and saw
an Arab. A Muslim. That was the main thing. Not a prince.
Not a doctor. After 9/11, that was constantly on my mind.

'And then came the bombs of 7/7. You remember the suicide bombings in the London Underground? More than fifty
people killed. Seven hundred injured, including my beautiful
blond, blue-eyed, well-educated wife. They took off her right
arm above the elbow. I loved her, I swear. I love her now. But
she could no longer live with me. It wasn't my being an Arab
and a Muslim. Marian couldn't live with my shame.'

'What happened to her?'

'Oh, she married again, another doctor, one of those Brits
with a hyphenated name, a very fine man. I am always

283

grateful that he cares for her so well. They have two lovely children. I see pictures of them on Facebook.'

'Your story makes me realize how fortunate I am,' said Henry. 'I have been given more than I deserve. My family is my greatest happiness, but I've always been afraid that they would be taken away from me, and this would be somehow my fault – and this is exactly what is happening.'

'The odds are in your favor, Henry. Most people survive this contagion.'

'I am helpless. It's killing me that I can't save them.'

'Do you ever pray, my friend?' Majid asked.

'Never.'

'Does it occur to you, the yearning to do so?'

'Just last night, as I tried to sleep, the idea of prayer did come into my mind, but only as a measure of my total defeat.'

'Perhaps it is a message, a knock on the door from the Great Unknowable.'

'I hope you won't take offense, but I've renounced all forms of superstition, including religion. I have nothing against Islam that I don't hold against all beliefs.'

'You are such a Muslim, Henry.'

'Nothing of the sort. I'm a hard-boiled atheist.'

'On the one hand, you suggest that the blessings you receive you did not earn, and on the other you believe that you are responsible for everything bad that happens. This is a very Islamic attitude.'

'Don't get your hopes up,' said Henry.

The sun was in their eyes like a searchlight. Majid handed Henry a headscarf to shield himself from the merciless rays.

'See? You even look like a real Saudi now,' Majid said with satisfaction.

'I feel more like a boiled lobster.'

Majid laughed. 'I have met atheists before, many of them. In London, everyone is a pagan! They never think about the things I worry about all the time. We believers say that we are good because we believe, but the nonbelievers I meet are good people, most of them, just like Muslims and Christians and Jews. So I wonder what difference it makes to believe or not to believe.'

'A friend of mine once said that when good people do good, and evil people do evil, it is not surprising. But when good people do evil, it takes religion to do that.'

'I think he saw a wound in you that cannot heal.'

The sun was now directly overhead, turning the sky white with heat. The shadows disappeared and the desert became a single flat plain, a skillet of sand. Behind them, the military convoy stretched out along the highway for many miles. Ahead, a war was under way, one that would not end soon. Henry wondered if his friend would survive it. He could not imagine that a personality as vivid and valuable as Majid's could be extinguished by a foolish military adventure, but amid so much arbitrary death the horizon of one's own existence seemed alarmingly near. They were both mindful that this might be their last conversation.

'I promised some days ago that I would tell you my story,' Henry said. 'What I am about to say I have told only a few people ever. They were so alarmed that I decided I would never talk about this again. I despise having people judge me or pity me, so I pretend to forget the details of my childhood, or I make up an alternative history that people accept without question. Even those who are closest to me don't know the full story. Who would lie about his parents and the

285

disease that has marked himself all his life? But I have lied, over and over, as if the lie would chase away the truth.

'The evidence of my parents' neglect is obvious. I was starved. Not intentionally. They did not mean to be cruel – the very opposite. They were idealists who got caught up in a movement. Social justice, racial equality, nonviolence, these were the tenets of their group, a mixture of Marxism and evangelism. They were going to make a paradise on earth, or so their leader told them. He was grandiose, paranoid, always fleeing imaginary enemies. He relocated his movement to San Francisco, and then to a small country in South America. In the jungle where I was born.

'My parents were true believers. To them, their leader was a prophet, like Jesus or Muhammad. They were good people, I'm sure – kind and considerate – but they didn't have time to take care of an infant, they were too busy saving the world. I was often placed in the colony's nursery, but occasionally they simply forgot about me – at least, this is my supposition. I only remember the loneliness, the hunger, the fear that no one would come for me.

'Looking back now, as a doctor, I can diagnose the physical problem. Just imagine, we were in the tropics, but I was kept inside a hut most of my early years, fed on bananas and porridge. I didn't grow. My legs bowed, my bones broke easily and often. No one in the camp was capable of diagnosing or treating a disease as outmoded as rickets. Once, I was taken to the leader to be healed. I remember only his terrifying black eyes staring at me, while he invoked some language that was supposed to straighten my limbs and make me grow. But, of course, that didn't happen, and I became an embarrassment, a rebuke to the leader's healing powers. Finally, when I was four, it was decided that I should be sent back to Indianapolis where my grandparents lived. And that was the only thing that saved me – my disease turned out to be my salvation. I suppose you could call it a curse that carried a blessing inside it. Two months later, everyone in the camp died. My parents would have been among the first.'

'How did this happen?'

'Cyanide. They all drank it. More than nine hundred people.'

'This was Jonestown!'

'Yes,' said Henry. 'This was Jonestown.'

'Oh, Henry.' Majid's eyes were full of tears. He didn't know what else to say.

'I beg you, don't feel sorry for me. I have hidden this story for so many years because I know it changes how people see me. It's like saying your parents were Nazis or lepers or worse. I am who I am despite my background. I don't want to be judged as some helpless victim. I've learned that it is better just to keep that part of my life in the dark.'

Majid was still too stunned to reply. He wanted to be consoling, but he was overwhelmed with grief for his friend. Finally he said, 'I can't help being furious at your parents. I'm sorry, Henry, I'm just too angry at them for what they did to you.'

'It's my struggle, not yours. One day, maybe, I'll be able to forgive them, but the older I become, the more I see their failings in myself. That's the hardest part, seeing how I'm like them. I know what it is to surrender to a powerful idea or personality. We all may imagine that we have strong moral bearings, but those same instincts that lead us to do good in the world may be bent toward the vilest actions.'

———

Henry and Majid continued to exchange intimate philosophies across the whole span of the Arabian Peninsula. Finally, the convoy came over a rise of red sand hills, and before them, gleaming in the slanting rays of sunset, was the vast Ghawar oil field, the largest in the world. Pumping jacks stretched endlessly across the desert floor, and gas flares like street lamps illuminated the storage tanks. Henry noticed another piercing light in the sky, just above the horizon, like a low-flying comet, which was hard to account for. At first, Henry accepted it as another feature of this exotic landscape.

Suddenly, Majid braked hard, holding up a stopping hand to the convoy behind. 'Missile!' he cried.

As Henry watched, a series of antimissiles were launched from the Saudi defenses against the incoming Iranian rocket, leaving smoky trails as they bent to meet their target. A huge orange fireball ignited like a sun, followed seconds later by the thunderous sound of the explosion. Another missile appeared from a different spot on the horizon, and another, eliciting dozens of antimissiles. Smoke from the first explosion drifted toward the convoy, enveloping them in an acrid cloud.

Majid radioed the commander in the Humvee behind him. 'Spread out!' he demanded. 'We're slow-moving targets on this road.' One of the Iranian missiles broke through the oil field defenses and struck a storage tank, setting off an enormous conflagration.

Henry was transfixed by the tableau before him, splendid and forbidden, and he understood at once the lure of combat. Then he noticed another missile skimming just above the desert coming directly at them, maneuvering, searching for them through the fumes. The instrument of death was fast and intelligent and would not be denied, and yet Majid kept his foot on the accelerator, as if he were rushing to meet it. A sound was coming out of Henry's mouth, but he couldn't hear his own voice. Suddenly Majid swerved into the sand and the missile exploded in the roadside just behind them. The shock rocked the jeep, but Majid immediately turned back onto the highway. 'We'll be safer when we get past the oil field,' he said. 'That must be protected at all costs. But we are expendable.'

It was dark now, and the lights of Dammam flickered in the distance. As Majid barked orders on the radio, Henry could see the refinery at Ras Tanura glowing on the eastern horizon, a city made for machines, absent of beauty or comfort. The missiles found their targets or exploded in the sky. Storage tanks and wellheads burned with vivid intensity, the blaze changing from red to orange to yellow to white as it got closer to the fuel source, until finally, at the bottom, the fire was as blue as a glacial lake. The horizon in the south was blackened by the fires at Abqaiq processing facilities.

'Henry, I have bad news,' Majid reported. 'The causeway to Bahrain has been destroyed. I can get you to the seaport at Dammam. That is as much as I can do.'

Henry nodded. The idea of getting home, or even living another day, seemed increasingly moot.

The military convoy continued toward the garrison at Ras Tanura, while Majid and Henry broke off and drove alone into the empty streets of the freshly destroyed industrial city of Dammam. They passed an apartment building that had been sliced apart as cleanly as if a knife had gone through it, exposing kitchens and bedrooms and closets with clothes still on hangers, reminding Henry of a dollhouse he had made for Helen years before. Majid pointed to a pile of rubble. 'That was our main desalination plant on this side of the peninsula,' he said, then fell silent as the implications sank in.

When they arrived at the seaport, the wharves were deserted, the massive supertankers having retreated to open waters. There was no one in the guardhouse to raise the gate, and no ships in evidence. 'I cannot leave you here,' Majid said, his mouth set in a hard line. 'And I cannot take you with me.'

'I'll find a way,' said Henry. 'Bahrain is not far, is it?'

'From here it's no more than fifty miles. There must be something!' Majid ducked under the guardrail. Henry followed him down one of the piers, past the giant moorings. Two boys were fishing in the dark water, which glistened with oil stains. Majid spoke sharply to them about the danger they were in, but they laughed at him. Henry could see the shock in Majid's eyes at being so carelessly disregarded. The war had thrown off any sense of authority or obligation or respect. Saudi Arabia would never again be what it had been.

At the end of the darkened pier there was a little two-masted dhow, nearly invisible until the men came upon it. Majid called out three times, but no one responded. 'Henry, can you sail?' he asked.

Instantly a small man in a turban appeared on the deck, brandishing a pistol. Majid and Henry stepped back in alarm. Majid spoke to the man in Arabic, but he responded in English. 'You try to steal my boat!' he cried.

'Please, my friend, we will pay,' said Majid.

'Now you say so, but you intend to steal.' From his accent, Henry thought he was Indian or Bangladeshi. His eyes darted about in fear, making the pistol in his hand all the more menacing.

'It's true, I am desperate,' Henry admitted. 'I have to get home to America. I would do anything to see my family again.'

'You think this boat can go to America?'

'I just need to get to Bahrain, to the American base there.'

Majid took his watch off his wrist and held it up. 'Sir, this watch is worth as much as your dhow. I offer it to you if you will take my friend.'

The owner of the boat lowered his pistol and examined the watch. He nodded at Henry. 'But you know it is dropping off only,' he said. 'No round trip.'

Henry agreed, then turned to Majid. 'Thank you, my friend,' he said. 'I don't know if we'll meet again.'

'Our fate is already written,' Majid replied. 'Every Muslim knows this.' He reached into the pocket of his uniform. 'I have this for you to remember me by. It's an English Qur'an. You don't have to read it, but if you do, you might find some wisdom and perhaps some solace. Anyway, you may remember our friendship, and that would be enough.'

They embraced, and then Henry climbed aboard.

33

The War Zone

THE RUSSIAN FOREIGN MINISTER WAS TALL AND ELEGANT, A PER-
fectly carved diplomat, made of obdurate material like one of
those great stone heads on Easter Island facing the typhoons
of the Pacific, content in the knowledge that every storm
passes and that lies are rarely held to account. 'We are not in
Iran in any meaningful way,' he insisted in his interview with
Chris Wallace on Fox News. 'We sold them military equipment, which we also service, so this is our only obligation.'

'If America supports the Saudis in their war against Iran,
what will the Russian response be?' Wallace asked.

The foreign minister shook his head dismissively. 'No, no,
this discussion presumes we are choosing sides in this conflict. We do not make this choice.'

'U.S. intelligence says otherwise,' Wallace said. 'There's a
report in *The Wall Street Journal* this morning that Su-57s
have been stationed in Tabriz and Mehrabad, Iran. Your
most advanced stealth fighter jets, is that correct?'

'It is correct that it is our most advanced jet, but all that
you say except for that is false. We do not deploy this aircraft outside Russian borders.'

'You see this image on the screen?' Wallace said, gesturing

292

to a grainy picture of an airfield taken from a satellite. 'The report says those are your jets on the ground in Tabriz.'

The foreign minister stared at Wallace as if he were a small dog that had hold of his pants cuff. 'You accuse us of misinformation, of deception,' he said. 'We also accuse you, the United States, of lying to the world about the greatest plague we have ever seen, this Kongoli virus.'

'What exactly is your charge, sir?'

The foreign minister's eyes narrowed. 'We have information. Our scientists have analyzed this virus. It is not natural. It comes from the laboratory. There is only one place that has the capacity for making such an evil disease. Your Fort Detrick.'

'Are you claiming that the U.S. manufactured this disease? More than ten million Americans are dead. Hundreds of millions worldwide. Why would we do this?'

'The cause, we can only speculate. Perhaps it is released by mistake. Such things happen. But we can say for sure this is an American product.'

'Back in the 1990s, the Soviet government was behind a disinformation campaign called Operation Infektion,' Wallace recalled. 'Phony scientific papers accused America of creating HIV/AIDS as a part of our biological weapons program at Fort Detrick. Your own director of the KGB later admitted it was a propaganda campaign. Where is your evidence for this new charge?'

'The proof is obvious,' the foreign minister said, crossing his arms indignantly. 'This virus is man-made. We did not create it. Who else has the capacity for making such a pathogen? Only you, you Americans, in your death labs at Fort Detrick.'

'Those were shut down years ago,' Wallace pointed out.

'So you say.'

'Americans are dying at a far higher rate than Russians,' Wallace observed. 'Many on our side of the fence suggest that it was the Russians who created Kongoli. Otherwise, how could you have engineered a vaccine that provides some degree of immunity for yourselves?'

'This is no surprise,' the foreign minister said. 'Russian medicine is far more advanced than in the West.'

'And yet, American and European scientists who have examined your vaccine find it ineffective. They say all pandemics vary in their virulence across continents.'

'They must say something to explain their failure to produce an effective vaccine,' the foreign minister said. 'Total lie. Fake news.'

As soon as Prince Majid entered the naval headquarters command center in Al Jubail, north of Ras Tanura, he recognized the dangerous dynamic in the room. His uncle, Prince Khalid, the elderly minister of defense overseeing the plans was among the most pious members of the royal family, appointed to his position largely to appease the clerics. The generals in the bunker were trying to skirt his influence, but Khalid was a foolish old man bent on making a reputation. Like many senior princes, he harbored dreams of becoming king before he died.

Majid looked around to see if there was anyone who could restrain his impulsive uncle. There was no one. The officers were deferential, and they looked to Majid with silent pleas in their eyes. Majid did not pretend to know anything about the conduct of war – he was there to advise on the health of the troops – but he was the only other member of the royal family present. General al-Homayed of the National Guard took Majid aside and whispered urgently in his ear. 'He intends to strike Tehran and Isfahan immediately,' he said.

'Why the cities?'

'They are less defended than the bases, and he hopes to destroy the population.'

'Does the king know?'

'Prince Khalid says so, but we wonder.'

'The crown prince?'

'Unfortunately, he agrees with this decision.'

Majid reeled. There was no one to appeal to, except his uncle, who was standing over a topographical map of the Gulf, wrapped in self-importance, with the Iranian and Saudi forces arrayed in their battle order before him. Republican Guard fast-attack boats, armed with missiles, were swarming the Saudi fleet and had already sunk a frigate and two corvettes. The Ghawar field was in flames. The latest Hawk antimissiles had been ineffective against swarms of Iranian drones. Meantime, the Saudi thrust into Iran had been swiftly repelled by Russian anti-aircraft defenses. 'Our F-15s have succeeded in reaching Arak and bombing the reactor and heavy-water plant, but at a very great cost,' the air force general who was conducting the briefing said. 'We also see landing craft forming up at Bandar Abbas.'

'But where are the Americans?' Majid asked.

'They are coming!' Prince Khalid exclaimed. 'We must first provoke the Russians into the field. We have the promise of the American president that Iran will be destroyed. Russia cannot save her.'

'This action should not be taken before the king gives his

consent,' Majid said in alarm. 'It is not only a war crime to attack the population, it is a crime against Islam. It means there will be no end to this war until both nations are extinguished.'

'I have been entrusted with the decision,' Prince Khalid said imperiously. 'The king has given me full authority to defend our sacred land. The choice has been made, the outcome is already written. God has given us this power and we must use it.' The old prince turned to the air force general and said, 'You have my command.'

Majid stood for a moment, frozen in shock. Then he walked out of the bunker.

The night had turned cold. He found his jeep and stripped off his uniform, replacing it with a simple Saudi thobe. He put on his slippers and walked past the frantic crowd of sailors to the main gate and on through the empty town. A breeze pushed sand through the dusty streets.

On the edge of the settlement there was an officers' club with a camel track. As Majid walked through the barn, the smell of the oats and the camels was familiar and consoling. They were beautiful animals; they didn't deserve to die. He opened the barn door and prodded them out into the night. The camels were apprehensive. He was a stranger to them, and freedom was unfamiliar, but they grunted and reluctantly accepted their fate.

One of the animals looked questioningly at Majid. She was the most curious of the beasts. She bent her head so that Majid could stroke the spot between her immense eyes. '*Marhaba, habibti,*' Majid said. 'Will you take me from this place?'

Majid found a blanket and a saddle, then mounted the

camel. She was tall and powerful. Together they found one of the ancient trails into the desert.

The sounds of war kept Henry from sleeping. As the dhow sliced through the phosphorescent Gulf, military aircraft screamed overhead, sonic booms chasing their passage. Henry had the feeling of watching the war from another element, under water, as distant explosions lit the horizon on both sides of the Gulf, some of them modest and others – an arms depot or a refinery – immense, gigantic, filling the sky like sunrise. So much could be destroyed so quickly, years of labor and unimaginable wealth instantly lost, and what would follow but decades of misery? The cost of war was never honestly tallied against the price of ordinary, strife-ridden peace. Even the victors were ruined in ways that could never be fully calculated. It occurred to Henry that he was witnessing the death of the Age of Petroleum.

As the sky lightened, Henry perceived the island emirate off the bow. Skyscrapers loomed on the tiny spit of land like passengers standing in a canoe. Henry wondered how much longer those proud buildings would stand when the war inevitably spilled over into the neighboring countries. The region had already chosen sides. Neutrality was completely absent, and in any case the nature of war is to expand and consume everything it can reach.

The dhow steered toward a large harbor, enclosed by refineries and ports. The captain, who went by the name Ramesh, indicated what looked like a large industrial complex dead ahead. 'Americans,' he said.

Just then, Henry noticed two patrol boats racing toward him at top speed. He waved at them, but it was soon obvious that they were not a welcoming party. 'Turn about! Turn about!' a voice cried over an address system. 'You are entering prohibited waters. You will be fired upon if you come closer!' The same warning was given in Arabic.

'I'm an American!' Henry shouted, but he wasn't heard, and if he had been, it wouldn't have made a difference.

Ramesh was slow to act, but when a burst of gunfire raked the water in front of him, he abruptly brought the dhow around, the sails shifting sharply.

'No, wait!' Henry yelled at him. But Ramesh was not inclined to be shot at again.

Henry thought for a single instant, then jumped overboard.

He was not a strong swimmer. He watched the wind billowing the sails and the dhow leaving him behind, in the middle of the channel. Ramesh cast him a brief and unrepentant glance. Henry was impossibly far from land. After a moment, one of the patrol boats roared back to the base, leaving him bobbing on the swells of its wake. The other boat sat idling in the water. Two young naval officers wearing wraparound sunglasses stared at him, expressionless. When Henry began swimming toward them, the pilot put the boat into reverse and slowly backed away, keeping a measured distance. They're just going to watch me drown, Henry thought, his shoes and his clothes weighing him down. He kept dog-paddling – what else could he do? Finally, the pilot put his boat in neutral, allowing Henry to swim within talking distance.

'Sir, what the fuck are you doing?' the pilot asked.

'I'm trying to get home.'

'All due respect, sir, you're lucky you didn't get your ass

shot off already. You swim that way' – he pointed to a landing that looked to be about two miles away – 'you'll be in
Emirati territory, and they can deal with you.'

'You know I'll never make that.'

'You made the choice, we didn't. This is a war zone. We
got our rules, sir. We're under strict quarantine. No one in
or out. It's for your own safety.'

Henry didn't bother to respond to that absurd advisory.
'Please, I'm an American,' he said. 'A doctor. I'm just trying
to get home to—'

'You're a doctor?' The pilot's tone suddenly changed.

'I am.'

'A medical doctor?'

'Yes.'

The pilot cast a look at his companion, then back at Henry.
'Come aboard, sir. We got some folks that really need a
doctor.'

Henry swam to the ladder in the stern. As soon as he got
out of the water, he began to shiver, whether from the cold
or from the fear that he had held at bay until now. The other
officer handed him a life vest as the pilot gunned the boat
and sped toward the base, faster than any boat Henry had
ever been in. His teeth chattered uncontrollably.

'Sir, see that submarine?' the pilot said. The sub was large,
gray, sleek, and whale-like, with a fin improbably rising
from its head like a metal cross. 'It's headed to Kings Bay.
They've been requesting medical assistance, but they are forbidden to enter the base.'

'Kings Bay, Georgia?' Henry said. It seemed like a
miracle.

'There's Kongoli on board.'

'I'll take that risk.'

'Your choice, sir. But it's deadly.'

All Henry could think was that he was finally going home.

34

Snapdragons

JILL HAD BEEN DEAD FOR A WEEK BEFORE HELEN FINALLY SUM-
moned the nerve to bury her. She waited until Teddy was
asleep, then went to the backyard to dig the grave. She couldn't
believe how hard it was. The deeper she dug, the more unyield-
ing the soil became. Then she ran into a huge tree root that
stopped everything. She sat in the grass and wept. The hole
was so shallow. When she stood in it, the surface was not even
level with her knee.

It was really dark outside. The neighbors' lights were off.
Helen hadn't seen anyone other than Teddy in days. She
wanted help, but she didn't know whom to ask. Maybe no
one will ever help me again, she thought. Maybe everybody's
dead. I'll just have to be the grown-up that I'm not ready to
be. She was furious with her parents – Henry for being absent
and Jill for being dead, leaving her to tend to Teddy and now
this.

Her father was surely dead, too. He had betrayed her,
tricked her into thinking that he would never fail her, but then
he had vanished. 'We never heard from him again.' That's
what she would tell people one day. The phrase went through
her head like a song she couldn't shake.

There was a time when Helen was embarrassed by her father. She became conscious of how other people looked at him. Helen was beautiful – this was a defining fact of her life. Henry was not. Helen wanted to stand apart, to be seen as wholly beautiful and well made, not attached to someone pitiable. Henry understood. He gave her room in public to be separate from him, and his nobility is what finally broke her heart. She cried, thinking how much she loved him, ashamed that she ever had felt embarrassed by him. Now he was gone, and she wouldn't have the chance to make it up to him. She hated herself for despising his infirmities. She couldn't imagine what it would be like to be alive and not be perfect. And yet on the inside, she was ugly. Inside, she was small and deformed and her father was tall and beautiful. The smartest man in the world.

But he hadn't saved Jill.

Digging her mother's grave became the most important thing Helen had ever done. If she could do that, she might be able to survive. She would be the kind of person who could do adult things like digging a real grave, a grave that animals could not easily unearth. That thought gave her the creeps.

She found an ax in the garage and began hacking at the tree root with a fury and determination that seemed to come from someplace she had never known about. She was vaguely aware that she was sobbing. The root was the diameter of her head. At first she just struck it again and again in the same place, but then she recalled Henry chopping firewood. He had showed her how to tilt the ax head slightly to the right and then to the left, so that the ax made a V in the wood. Chips flew until she collapsed in exhaustion.

She looked at the root with hatred. It was standing in the way of what she needed to do. It was unfair. It was too big a challenge. She would have to chop through each end. And when that was finished, she would have to go back to digging into the soil that she also hated and that hated her back.

Her eyes were adjusted to the dark, but it was even darker in the hole, so she went into the house to turn on the kitchen light, which shone into the backyard. Inside, the smell of her mother's death embraced her. There was a flashlight in a drawer, which she carried outside and set on the edge of the grave.

The light from the kitchen and the flashlight projected her shadow onto the neighbor's garage, giant and cartoonish. She imagined Teddy laughing at her. But then she wondered when anybody would ever laugh again. She was ashamed even thinking it was funny. And then she felt rebellious and dark and wicked, and that gave her energy to chop until one end of the root broke free.

She lay in the grass for a while, filthy and covered in sweat. Everything about her life that had been so wonderful was strange and awful. At least I'm alive, she thought. But Kendall is dead. Mom is dead. Dad is probably dead. And life just keeps going on as if our existence means nothing at all. The only thing that matters is digging this hole to put my mother in. She stared at the little playhouse that Henry had built for her when she was three years old. So many hours she had played in there. So long ago. So unknowing.

It was stupid to think she was ever perfect. She was tall, the tallest girl in her class, taller than most of the boys. Doomed to be a giant. One time she had asked Henry why she was so tall. He was short, and Jill was average. Helen was taller than either of them when she was eleven years old. 'You get your height from my side of the family,' Henry said. Helen had never really considered Henry's side of the family. He had no pictures, except of his grandparents, and he never spoke of his actual parents.

'But you're not tall,' Helen said.

'My genes are tall,' Henry said. 'It was the disease that made me short. I don't really remember how tall my parents were, but people remarked that my mother was almost six feet. My father was several inches taller than that. So you shouldn't be surprised that you have the wonderful advantage of being visible for all to see.'

'Was your mother beautiful?' Helen asked.

'I think so. My grandmother had pictures of her as a child. She was certainly attractive. The only photo I ever saw of her as an adult her face was shadowed by a kind of sombrero, so I couldn't really see. My dad was striking. He had strong features, and red hair like you. Anyway, there's no gene for beauty. It's not like height.'

'It's so sad that they had to die.'

'Yes, it is.'

'Was it like an airplane crash or something like that?'

'Something like that.'

Secrets. Henry had walked out of the room. Now she would never know.

She chopped. She dug. The sky began to lighten. She chopped. She dug. She wept.

Henry didn't believe in God, but Helen did, her secret rebellion. God was her real father, perfect, caring, present. But that was before. Not anymore. The fact that the sunrise was still beautiful was like God saying, *So what, I don't*

304

need people in my world. My new religion, thought Helen: There is a God, and he hates us.

She was so tired. The root was even thicker on this end. Of course. That's what God would want. To make it impossible. Every stroke of the ax was to prove God wrong. There was a bird singing that hadn't been exterminated yet. If she had a gun she would shoot it. They were the carriers. They even infected the pets. Peepers was gone. She wished she could cuddle him and believe that love was something that still mattered.

She wanted to get this done before Teddy woke up. She allowed herself to think: Why couldn't it have been Teddy who died and not Mom? Why do I have to be the one in charge? Teddy is useless and a burden. But she didn't want to be alone.

When the root finally broke in two, Helen dropped to the ground. She didn't know how long she was asleep, but when she woke up the sun was in her eyes and she was lying in her mother's grave.

She dug with renewed fury. Her stomach was cramping, but she couldn't stop. When the soil got too hard she chopped it with the ax and then scooped out the dirt. She knew that graves were supposed to be six feet deep. That was impossible. She wouldn't even be able to get herself out of something that deep. She began to bargain with her conscience. How deep could a twelve-year-old girl be expected to dig? She was up to her waist now. She wanted the shape of the hole to be perfect, and it wasn't.

'What are you doing?'

Teddy, on the porch steps, in his pajamas.

'Are you feeling okay?' she asked. He nodded. 'Hungry?' He nodded. 'There's a little cereal left. I'll be finished soon.'

Teddy went back inside, his question unanswered. But he knew.

Helen began digging again. It was really hot, but the soil under her bare feet was cool. Sweat ran into her eyes. Suddenly she sat down, totally spent. She needed to eat. She needed water. Jill would have told her these things. Now she could almost hear her mother's voice. She would come in from playing and lunch would be on the table. And that would never happen again. Because of God.

Her feet dangled into the grave. It was deep enough.

Helen went into the kitchen. 'Is there any cereal left?'

Teddy shook his head guiltily. Helen thought about her mother's mayonnaise and tomato sandwiches, with the crusts cut off. Chocolate yoghurt. Pringles. Chicken noodle soup. None of that. There was nothing in the pantry except lentils, and even those would be gone in a few days. There was a piece of ham in the fridge and one of those Laughing Cow cheeses wrapped in foil and shaped like a tiny piece of pie. Everything Helen ate would be taking it away from Teddy, but she didn't care. Or maybe she did. She wasn't sure where her relationship with Teddy stood anymore, now that there was nobody else.

Teddy was looking at her with an expression she recognized as awe, or something like that. Amazement. Because she was so dirty, probably. Then he looked away, into his empty cereal bowl. 'Thanks for burying Mom,' he said.

'I haven't buried her yet.'

'I know.'

When Helen had finished the cheese, she and Teddy went back outside and stood over the grave. 'It's not very deep,' Helen said.

'I think it is.'

'You do?'

Teddy nodded.

Helen went back into the house. Once again the smell greeted her. She took a dishtowel from the stove handle and wrapped it around her face like a bandit. 'Go to your room for a while,' she told Teddy.

Helen walked down the hall and opened the door to her parents' bedroom. Her mother's mouth was open. She was blue like the porcelain lamp on her bedside table. There was a trail of blood all over the sheets and in little dried rivulets from her eyes and ears and nose. This is what God did to my mother, Helen thought.

Jill's hand was so cold, like it had been in the freezer. How could a body be so cold all by itself? Everything about Jill was hard and rigid and cold, and her body seemed to be bolted onto the bed. Helen pulled the sheets back and her mother's nightgown was all in disarray. Helen started to cover her, but then she told herself, This is not my mother anymore. This is a big clumsy object. Stinky. Dead.

Helen grabbed Jill's heels and turned her body toward her. The entire body moved like a plank of wood. The arms were in some odd familiar gesture, as if Jill were about to receive a present or she was offering an embrace. Helen pulled her mother toward her, turning her eyes away as the nightgown rode up Jill's body. Suddenly the entire body came off the bed and slammed to the floor, Jill's head hitting the bed frame so hard on the way down that Helen heard the skull crack. Helen wanted to scream, but then she told herself again, This is not my mother. This is not my mother.

When she got to the hallway she turned the body around

and pulled it through the kitchen and onto the back porch. She rested for a moment, then she went into the hall closet and got Teddy's football helmet. She put it on her mother's head. Then she pulled the body down the steps, the helmet bouncing on each one.

She paused on the edge of the grave. She was afraid to roll her mother in, because she might land face down, and that was wrong. She stood inside the grave and heaved her mother toward her. Jill's body came slowly down from the mountain of excavated dirt, then leapt at Helen, as if it were springing back to life, knocking her backward so that she was half buried under the corpse, pinned in the narrow grave by her mother's rigid blue legs. Helen writhed and shoved her mother aside, slipping out from under her weight. Before she climbed out of the grave she arranged her mother's nightgown. Then she took the shovel and tossed in the first load on her mother's face, which she didn't want to see anymore.

It was nearly dark when the grave was full and the dirt mounded over Jill's body like a loaf of bread just out of the oven. As Helen stood there, Teddy came to her, carrying a bunch of snapdragons that he had cut from the front bed. They placed them on Jill's grave.

35

All Life is Precious

UNDER THE ASSAULT OF KONGOLI, GOVERNMENTS EVERY-where were dying. It wasn't surprising when vulnerable governments fell, initially in Lebanon, Iraq, and Afghanistan, one after another, anarchy tracking the course of contagion, killing the strongest and pushing the weak aside. When Italy and Greece both collapsed on the same day, June 30, the fragility of Western society revealed itself. Civilization was like the polar ice caps, thinned out by decades of global warming, and it was melting away. France was next.

But as the Deputies Committee reconvened over secure videoconferencing, the main subject was war in the Middle East. A dogfight between a Russian Su-57 and an American F-22 Raptor over the Zagros Mountains resulted in both being shot down by highly advanced radar-guided missiles. The technology had evolved to the point that targets were hard to miss. The dogfight became a flashpoint for a larger war between the U.S. and Russia and their proxies. The Saudi oil fields were still blazing. In Iran, much of the ancient city of Isfahan was demolished. The casualties in Tehran were in the tens of thousands. Both sides had entered the war already weakened by disease, and just as in 1918, armies propagated the contagion. Hospitals, already overfilled by flu victims, were unable to treat more than a fraction of the wounded. And yet the war raged on, pulling both countries and their neighbors back into a pre-industrial world. Little was left of modernity except for weapons.

The first shock of war was, as always, how little control there was over the outcome.

'We destroyed the Iranian naval base in Bandar Abbas, but we lost four more aircraft to Russian defenses,' Joint Chiefs reported.

Defense reviewed the balance of forces in the region. 'Very much in our favor, but shifting,' he said. 'The Navy's Fifth Fleet is stationed in Bahrain, and the Air Force operates in Qatar, out of the largest U.S. facility in the Middle East, with B-52 bombers at hand, ready to annihilate Iran and easily within range of Russia itself. The Russian Pacific Fleet is steaming toward the Gulf, and additional highly advanced Russian aircraft are in Iran, with more coming. Russia has the advantage of defending a far more powerful and resilient ally. The Saudi plan, as we know, has always been to let us do the fighting.'

'The environmental consequences are also extensive,' State reported. 'Thousands dead of smoke inhalation in the Eastern Province. Prevailing winds are carrying toxic smoke westward. Skies are black all the way to southern Spain.'

Commerce spoke up with a heretical thought. 'Is it even worth defending the kingdom?' he asked. 'It will be years before either of these countries becomes important again to the world economy.'

State agreed. 'Iran is one thing, but do we really want outright war with Russia?'

'They must be making the same calculation,' said Defense.

Both the U.S. and Russia were in a fever of paranoia and hatred, lusting for some kind of orgasmic finale that was somehow short of all-out nuclear war. Still, Tildy saw this as a key moment to put the Russians back in their cage. 'What do we get out of waiting?' she asked. 'Strike now before their fleet reaches the Arabian Sea. Run them out of the Gulf. With Putin, you don't get many moments where you have a clear advantage.'

At the end of the meeting, a recommendation was sent to the principals: Put the B-52s in the air, destroy the Russian defenses, and block their Pacific Fleet. If Russia still wanted to prosecute the war, it was going to pay a terrible price.

That night, Tildy sat down with her microwave dinner and her dog, Baskin, at her side and watched the news. At the peak of the pandemic in the U.S., government services were shut down and Congress had stopped meeting. The new president, still sheltering in the vast Mount Weather bunker with other senior officials, issued a reassuring statement on the Emergency Alert System that a cure was on the horizon, stores would soon be open again, the baseball season would resume – all lies, as everyone knew, but respectfully reported.

'Tonight we have a special report on the sabotage of the biomedical research laboratories at MIT's Whitehead Institute,' Wolf Blitzer reported. There were shots of the Whitehead, which Blitzer described as one of the leading animal research facilities in the world. Like every significant biomedical facility, the Whitehead had been enlisted in the effort to develop a vaccine for Kongoli. It had gotten samples from the CDC and was growing the virus in monkeys, ferrets, and humanized mice. Many of the researchers were living in their labs, sleeping in hallways on bedrolls, as they puzzled out the secrets of the new pathogen. Because of the pandemic, security around the facilities was notional at best. It had never had the layered levels of fencing, cameras, and scanners that Fort Detrick enjoyed. Then one morning a number of people – the security cameras recorded fifty-two – wearing respirator masks, lab coats, and gloves arrived on a bus. 'We thought they might have been a relief crew, or new security,' one of the scientists remarked. They said nothing as they marched down the hall and into the elevators. 'They knew the codes,' the scientist said. 'No one questioned them. People just don't get in without clearance. But here they were.'

They went directly down to the animal suites. Inside were four chambers, two with ferrets and one with green monkeys and mice. The fourth was empty. They entered without space suits, which was crazily dangerous. Each of the masked intruders carried away two cages, concentrating on the primates. The remaining animals were simply set free to roam the halls, contaminating everything. Ferrets were everywhere, many of them lying listlessly on the tile of the lab floor, too ill to move, and mice just disappeared, as they do, into offices, behind bookshelves, and under desks. There was video of the abducted primates that had been let loose in Harvard Square. Blitzer interviewed the chief of police in Cambridge, who said that his force and members of the National Guard had hunted down the monkeys all night, shooting them on sight. The last two were finally tracked down in the subway tunnel on the Red Line.

'Police suspect that the leaders of this raid were members of an animal-rights organization called Earth's Guardians,'

Blitzer said. The leader of the group, Jürgen Stark, was in the studio. He denied that he or members of his organization had anything to do with the insider attack on the White-head, although members had infiltrated the institute in the past. Blitzer clearly didn't believe Stark's denials. 'They had the security codes,' he said. 'They knew exactly where to go.'

'Yes, it's puzzling,' said Stark, noncommittally.

'You don't consider this a crime against humanity?'

'Let us be clear about this,' Stark said. 'What people are doing to animals, not only at the Whitehead and Fort Detrick but at many other facilities around the country, is a crime against nature. Those laboratory animals have done us no harm. They are tortured and murdered in the name of science. I know. I used to do it myself, to my great shame. Is the benefit to humanity worth the sacrifice of so many animal lives? I say no.'

'Most scientists say yes,' Blitzer remarked. 'Millions of people around the world are already dead from the Kongoli flu. It's impossible to know how many, but we have been tabulating the responses we've gotten, and so far they suggest a death toll in excess of three hundred million people.'

'Out of a population of eight billion, that's a manageable portion,' Stark said coolly. He examined his glasses and wiped off a speck. 'Consider the birds. How many have been slaughtered? Do you know? Have you "tabulated the responses"? And what good has it done? I'll tell you what will happen when you tip the balance of nature. You prepare a catastrophe, one that is certainly greater than what has presently befallen us. You would think by now that we would have learned this lesson.'

'Is it your opinion that every life is equal?' Blitzer asked.

'All life is precious,' Stark said. 'Why do you even ask?'

'I'm just wondering – if you had to choose between saving the life of a baby human or a chimpanzee, which you would choose.'

'It's an interesting question, but I no longer make such choices. That is part of my past.'

'Do you believe that the life of a virus is as precious as that of a human?'

'Viruses are not "alive".'

'But they are a part of nature.'

'Yes, they are essential.'

'But humans are not?'

Stark stared at Blitzer, hesitating, weighing his response. 'Humans have become a problem,' he finally said. 'Speaking as a human, selfishly, I hope that our species endures. But there is little doubt that the planet would be better off without us.'

36

Captain Dixon

THE MOMENT HE CAME ON BOARD, HENRY SENSED THE UNEASI-ness. The crew of the USS *Georgia* was not enthusiastic about having a new doctor aboard. The last one had brought Kongoli with him, and because of that, the submarine was under quarantine. Now five members of the crew of 165 were ill and the doctor lay dead in the chill box, as the massive refrigerator was called. The submarine was filled with brave young sailors, but they were surrounded by an enemy they couldn't fight.

Ordinarily, the medical needs of the crew were handled by a medical corpsman trained in first aid and minor emergencies. There was a small pharmacy with a horizontal door, which would allow a patient to be transferred directly onto the examining table on a stretcher, since there was no room to navigate through the hallway. In the pharmaceutical closet Henry discovered cartons of bendamustine and ibrutinib, which explained why the doctor had been aboard.

A submarine is an ideal breeding ground for disease. The air continually circulates and everyone breathes it. 'If somebody has a cold, we all get it,' the medical corpsman, Petty

Officer Second Class Sarah Murphy, told him, as she gave him the tour. 'There is no escaping the contact.'

Everyone called her 'Murphy'. Shipmates were typically on a last-name basis. She was prim and businesslike, but that seemed to be the norm. Only ten women were on the boat, and each wore her hair in a tight bun, making their faces as prominent as those of the close-cropped men. Murphy was a farm girl from Duluth, Minnesota, and she had the accent to go with it. 'Minnesooota', she called it. The sailors teased her for being a milkmaid. Thin and lithe, she moved down the ladders with gymnastic ease, slowing to let Henry catch up, then passing through a circular hatch, resembling the door to a large safe. Inside was a long chamber filled with twenty-four missile tubes painted lipstick red, each tube originally equipped to hold a forty-foot Trident intercontinental missile. 'We're rigged a little different, sir,' Murphy said. 'We have Tomahawk cruise missiles instead, non-nuclear.' In between each of the missile tubes was a nine-person dormitory with bunks stacked three on a side. Henry couldn't imagine a worse environment for containing a respiratory illness.

Infected submariners simply had to remain in crew's quarters. If they became terminally ill, they would be removed to the canteen below the control room so their companions wouldn't have to watch them die. The metallic smell of blood suffused the room.

'How are you treating them?'

'Saline drip,' Murphy said.

'Antivirals?'

'No effect.'

In the canteen were three terminally ill patients, two men

and a woman. Murphy raised the sheet on one of them. His feet were black. 'Same with the doctor,' she said. 'Black feet, blue face.'

One of the patients was conscious enough to notice. 'Are you a doctor?' he asked. Henry nodded. 'Am I going to die?' He was a teenager. His lips were blue. Henry could read his destiny clearly.

'I think you'll be fine,' Henry said. Sometimes hope was all he could offer, even if it was false, but he reproved himself for lying.

The young sailor began to weep. Murphy stroked his feverish head with a baby wipe.

'I was so scared,' he said.

When they were out of hearing, Henry asked Murphy, 'What do you do with the bodies?'

'Protocol now is to return them to our home port. We've got room in the chill box, but honestly, it's a problem.'

Henry was given the dead doctor's quarters – a mattress on the floor at the end of the missile chamber, next to the nuclear reactor that powered the sub. A sheet served as a curtain. At least it was private. Henry coated the space with Lysol. The dead doctor's few belongings were in a plastic bag taped to the wall, and his clothes were laid out under the mattress. A pair of sneakers made it obvious that his clothes would never fit Henry, who was still wearing the garments that had gotten soaked when he jumped overboard. Murphy scavenged the wardrobes of the dying sailors and laundered a sack full of underwear and socks.

The sub had put into port to repair a damaged piston. The missing part to make the repair was not available, so the sub was going to have to make the long trek across the Atlantic with a damaged, noisy piston, the last thing a stealthy submarine needs.

There was no sense of motion on the submarine, but Henry's ears popped as they submerged, and he found himself standing at a weird angle whenever the boat adjusted its bearings. The sailors didn't seem to notice when they were no longer perpendicular. Henry expected that he would gradually grow accustomed to this narrowed, interior world, with its subtle gyrations, but he had to fight off moments of alarm. He slept fitfully, tossed about by disturbing dreams that left no trace in his memory.

He awakened on his first morning to the smell of breakfast. He hadn't realized until then how famished he was. The mess had the feeling of a clubhouse, with souvenirs from various ports and Navy pennants and a photo of Jimmy Carter, former governor of Georgia and the only submariner ever elected president. The sailors were loading up their plates with scrambled eggs, sausage, and biscuits with gravy. They were all so young, Henry thought. He took three pieces of toast and a bowl of dry granola.

Murphy was just finishing her meal when Henry sat down. 'Hello, sir. I would think you'd be eating in the ward room with the officers,' she said.

'Is the food better?'

'Not a chance.'

'I think the commander regards me as an uninvited guest, which I suppose I am,' said Henry. 'I've never been on a naval ship before, much less a submarine. I feel totally lost.'

'Boat, sir. A submarine is the only vessel in the navy we call a boat. And the commander, that's his rank, but his billet is captain, so that's how we address him, although skipper also works. You have to understand him. He treats everybody equally, which means he can be a tough SOB. But he's the best officer I've ever served with.' Murphy flushed a bit when she said this.

'He looks a little too tall for this job.'

Murphy laughed. 'Even me, I'm always bumping into those dang pipes and such, and I'm no giant. We get a lot of head injuries. But, yeah. I wouldn't want to be up where he is.'

'So who are all these people?' Henry asked, indicating the twenty or so other people eating breakfast.

'Enlisted people, like me, sir. We actually run the boat, although nothing against the officers. Those guys' – she pointed to a knot of young men at a booth – 'they're the missile control operators. We like to think they're the sane ones. But honestly, I see them all. They're just as human as anyone else. If one of them receives a bad family-gram, like death or divorce, they get just as depressed as anybody else.'

'So what do you do?'

'My mom is a child psychologist, and she has these little furry balls with googly-eyes on them to give to the kids when they're feeling blue. Maybe you saw the jar in the pharmacy that looks like a bunch of jawbreakers. They're called warm fuzzies. I know it's not real medicine, but I've been giving out a lot of them these days.'

'Always good practice to offer something. And who are those beefy gentlemen over there?'

'They're SEALs. We have a contingent on board for reconnaissance or sometimes we drop off a landing party. They don't do much except eat and work out. They're sweethearts, but you know – don't piss them off.' She cast a pitying look at them. 'They came on the boat acting like Superman, like nothing could scare them. But this flu has them back on their heels. See how subdued they are? They seem more vulnerable than everyone else.'

'Aren't you scared as well?'

'Hell, yes, I'm scared! Everybody's calling this a death boat. And it is. We're trapped. I feel totally useless. Reduced to my warm fuzzies. I just hope you can help us.'

After breakfast, Henry visited three more symptomatic crewmembers. And that didn't count the one who had died in the night.

The submarine had felt surprisingly commodious when he first boarded, but the sense of confinement quickly pressed upon him. He was not claustrophobic by nature, but the close quarters, combined with the eerie experience of being deep under water, charged him with apprehension, amplified by the fear that stalked the haunted crew. Henry quickly found a rhythm, working with Murphy in the pharmacy, doing what he could to allay the terror, parceling out the supply of Xanax and Valium to treat the most worrisome panic disorders, but there was no way to lift the pall of anxiety that shrouded the boat. The crew seemed drugged by despair. They all knew the odds. So far there was only a handful of symptomatic patients, but everyone was exposed. Most of those who fell ill would die.

On the second day, Henry was summoned to the captain's stateroom. Captain Vernon Dixon was improbably large for a submariner, tall and muscular even in middle age. His voice was resonant and musical.

'We don't normally have actual medical doctors aboard,'

the captain was saying. 'Sub crews are healthy crews. You can't ship out if you have any underlying illness. And we try to be careful in port, as well. Not always possible.' While the captain talked, he fed a cage of colorful little birds nestled on the small desk next to the computer, using seed and broccoli florets. 'Before we had this damned flu, we had to leave behind a couple knuckleheads who got themselves tattooed in Djibouti and picked up hepatitis. So we were already shorthanded when your predecessor came aboard with the flu. Man, you're a hungry little sucker,' he said to one of the birds.

While Dixon refilled the water tray in the bird cage, Henry took in some of the photos pasted on the captain's locker – a young black man and woman in graduation gowns, whom Henry took to be his grown children, but no wife evident; group shots of crews he had served with; and a picture of a young Vernon Dixon in his football uniform for the University of Southern California. 'Oh, you're *that* Vernon Dixon!' Henry interjected.

Dixon turned from his birds and stared at him evenly, seemingly annoyed at being interrupted, then burst into a deep laugh. 'Man, you got a long memory on you,' he said.

'I certainly remember that run in the Rose Bowl.'

Dixon beamed in pleasure. 'That was quite a day,' he said. 'Of course, we nearly got our ass kicked by Ohio State anyway.'

The birds were exquisite, various and garish in their coloring, with green backs and either red or black heads, blue tail feathers, yellow bellies, and purple chests – as if they had been assembled from parts of other birds that didn't match. 'They're Gouldian finches,' Dixon explained. 'Picked 'em up in the souk in Doha. Brightens the place up, don't you think?' He grasped one of the birds in his giant hand and tenderly trimmed its nails with a tiny pair of scissors. 'This one is Chuckie. He's the leader of the pack, I reckon.'

'They're extravagantly beautiful.'

'Endangered, too, they tell me. I guess all birds are these days. I figure I'm doing them a favor. Like Noah's ark.'

They watched as the chittering finches jumped from one perch to another or keened their beaks on a corn cob.

'Look, man. I got a sick crew. A scared crew,' Dixon said. 'My head navigator died. We need a full complement to run this boat, and we're already at reduced capacity. Our safety is at risk. I know you don't have much to work with, but is there something – anything – you can do? I can't afford to lose anyone else.'

'Nor can the crew afford to lose you,' Henry said.

'Every submariner aboard is indispensable,' Dixon said sternly.

'But nobody is at greater risk than you. I've seen the ibrutinib in the pharmaceuticals cabinet. I've read your charts. How long have you been on chemo?'

The shoulders of this mighty figure slumped a bit. 'About a month,' he replied. 'They tell me it's leukemia.'

'Chronic lymphocytic leukemia,' Henry said. 'As you must know, it's slow to grow, but it comes with its own set of problems. Since it's a disease of the white blood cells, it makes you much more vulnerable to contagion and less able to fight this disease.'

'Yeah, they told me all that. Normally, they wouldn't let a sick man on a submarine, but it's not contagious. They didn't have an officer of rank to take the slot, so I gave 'em the old forearm shiver and bullied my way back on board. After this one, I guess they'll put me out to pasture.'

'I'm not an oncologist,' Henry said, 'but we can talk about treatment options. Meantime, I want you to wear these.' He handed the commander a mask and plastic gloves.

Dixon looked at them suspiciously. 'Have you got this stuff for the rest of the crew?'

'Ten masks and a box of gloves. But they can be useful. Maybe they won't stop an epidemic, but they might give you some layer of protection.'

Dixon handed them back to Henry. 'Every person on board this boat is at risk for infection, not just me. Any one of them could die. I'll take my chances, same as the rest.'

'I admire your spirit, but not your logic. You're at greater risk than any person aboard. And you're more important.'

'A ship is like an orchestra,' the commander said. 'Every instrument is needed. I'm just the conductor – arguably the *least* important figure, as long as everyone plays the score. You just figure out how to help my crew and then you can worry all you want about me.'

37

Dolly Parton and John Wayne

HENRY WAS BECOMING ADJUSTED TO THE STRANGE RHYTHMS of a submarine. Lighting imposed an artificial sense of day-time. The public areas were dim during the 'night' and bright during the 'day'. Some submarines operated on Greenwich Mean Time – 'Zulu Time' in military parlance – but Captain Dixon preferred to observe the local time as the boat crossed the Atlantic, meaning the clocks would be set back nine times by the time they reached the eastern shore of the U.S. Henry's diurnal rhythms were always a bit off kilter. There was so much idle time on the boat, interspersed with periods of intense and inscrutable activity. The dead doctor had left an e-reader, and Henry was grateful to discover a long list of classics to indulge in. He picked up *War and Peace* where his predecessor left off, with Pierre on the battlefield in his swal-lowtail coat.

One day, Murphy presented him with a pair of blue Navy overalls that she had tailored to fit. 'It just needed a few adjustments in the hem and such,' she said, downplaying the thoughtfulness of her gift. Henry was immensely touched. When he put on the overalls it finally occurred to him, now that he was visibly folded into the crew, that he really needed a haircut. The barber was an assistant chef who cut hair on extra duty. His name was Thistlethwaite, but everyone called him Cookie. 'What do you want, doc? Just a trim?' he asked.

'Give me the full Marine cut,' Henry told him.

'Lose the beard?'

'No, I want the beard,' Henry said. 'But you could trim it a bit.'

Afterward, in his berth, Henry studied himself in the mirror. He looked like a different man. His scalp was prickly and nearly bare, and his face appeared enlarged, as if he were being seen through a magnifying glass. His beard was short and nicely shaped. He thought, I will look this way for the rest of my life.

When Henry returned to the pharmacy, he found Murphy waiting with a submariner wincing in pain. He must have been about nineteen years old, with a rash of red pimples.

'Fever?' Henry asked Murphy.

'Wisdom teeth.'

Henry pulled Murphy aside in the hallway. 'I'm not a dentist,' he told her.

'No, sir, I know that.'

'Does he know that?'

'We've never had a dentist on board, so yes, sir, he understands.'

Henry went back into the pharmacy. The young man was looking at Henry with dread in his eyes. His nametag said mcallister.

'What's your given name, son?'

'Jesse.'

'How much pain are you in, Jesse?'

'A lot, sir, or I sure wouldn't be here.'

'Open up and let's take a look.'

Henry took a tongue depressor and stared into McAllister's mouth. He could see the swollen, infected gums behind the lower molars, which were being shoved forward by the buried wisdom teeth coming in aslant. It was clear that the teeth needed to come out. Probably the upper ones, too, but they weren't infected, so Henry could leave them alone. Henry touched the swollen gums with a probe, and McAllister jumped.

'Murphy, have we got Xylocaine in supply?'

'Yes, sir. And, sir, if you're going to operate, we should move to the wardroom. There's better light.'

Henry looked through the surgical tools. There was an elemental selection suitable for minor operations: two scalpels of different sizes, a cannula, curettes, a pincette for grasping and holding tissue, clamps, forceps, a needle holder for stitches, and various retractors sufficient for what Henry needed. But it had been a long time since he had performed any operation at all.

The captain and a chief petty officer were enjoying a game of cribbage in the wardroom when Henry and Murphy arrived with their morose patient. Without a word, the officers put away their game and Murphy cleared off the table and turned on the overhead surgical lamp. Henry was continually impressed by the elegant economy of space.

Fortunately Murphy was adept with the injection, and soon McAllister's gums were numb. But his eyes followed Henry as he picked up the scalpel.

'Jesse, if we're lucky, you won't feel anything,' Henry

said. 'I'll be as careful as I can be. Just don't bite my hand, okay?'

McAllister made a little sound that might have been a laugh.

Henry made an incision behind and then in front of the bulging gum, revealing the intruding tooth. He pulled the tissue away as Murphy vacuumed the blood and pus. Henry could smell the infection as he cut deeper, searching for the root of the molar. McAllister's body trembled with anxiety. Long ago, Henry had steered away from surgery because he hated to inflict pain.

He tugged the tooth out without much problem, but the jaw below was infected. Without a dental drill or other implements, Henry had to chisel the abscess out of the bone. McAllister grunted in appalled astonishment as Henry relentlessly forced the implement deeper into his jaw, again and again, until the bloody hole was finally clean and pure again.

'That wasn't so bad, was it?' Henry said proudly, as he began to stitch up the vacancy and Murphy stuffed cotton around the wound.

McAllister nodded apprehensively, knowing what was coming.

'Now let's do the other side,' Henry said.

That evening one of the most embarrassing episodes in Henry's life occurred: he walked into the women's shower. He was wearing the dead doctor's oversized bathrobe and flip-flops, with a towel around his neck, as he had seen the submariners do, and he went directly into the room where three women, including Murphy, were showering or drying off. For a second, Henry stood absolutely frozen. 'Get the fuck out,' one of the women advised, and he quickly retreated to his berth, totally mortified.

Half an hour later there was a light tap on his door. It was Murphy.

'Oh my God,' Henry said. 'I can't apologize enough.'

'It's okay, sir. We know it's not your fault. Nobody explained the code to you. We've got men's hours and women's hours for the shower, and the only way you'd know that is by the picture on the door.'

'I didn't notice.'

'Dolly Parton for the gals and John Wayne for the guys. Nobody thinks you did it on purpose. Our fault, we should have told you.'

When he went to the mess hall, where the crew was watching *Black Panther*, Henry realized that everyone on board already knew about his experience in the women's shower. They were nudging each other and making wisecracks under their breath about the 'rider' – meaning him, the stranger. In no time at all, he had become a legendary buffoon. Or pervert. He had no idea what else they were saying about him, nor did he care to hear.

'Hey, Doc!' one of the SEALs said. His companions tried to shush him, but he shrugged them off. 'My buddy died this morning.'

'Which one was he?' Henry asked.

'Petty Officer Second Class Jack Curtis. You told him he was going to be fine.'

Henry could see the rage and grief in the young man's face. 'I'm sorry, there was nothing I could do,' he said.

'Then what the fuck are you doing here? While this fucking disease picks us off one by one?'

'We don't have a cure for this—' Henry began, but the young man wasn't finished. 'I'm here because I know how to do my job,' the SEAL said. 'But you're just occupying space.'

There was nothing Henry could say in return.

38

Mrs Hernández

'WOULD YOU LIKE SOME MORE KETCHUP SOUP?' HELEN ASKED
Teddy. She was sick of waiting on him, but there was really no
one else to talk to. She could call friends on her mother's cell
phone, and occasionally someone would drop off some food
on the porch, but it wasn't sufficient. They were out of lentils.
The cupboard is bare, Helen thought, like in a fairy tale.

Teddy didn't answer. His head was buried in Jill's
computer.

'What are you doing?' Helen asked.

'I'm trying to find Mom's passwords.'

'For what?'

'The ATM.'

'They wouldn't be on the computer.'

'I think I already know it.'

'What is it?'

'Your birthday. 0325.'

'Why do you think that?'

'She uses birthdays for all her passwords. Sometimes she
writes them out, like here.' He showed her the webpage for
Jill's Target card. 'The password is March25 and the PIN
is 0325.'

Helen looked at Teddy. He's such a weird little guy, she thought. Maybe a genius, or close. How could he figure out things like that? They were so unalike. He was small and brown and she was tall and fair. He was smart and self-contained and she was pretty and popular. Helen used to categorize their differences to underscore how little they had in common. Now that they only had each other, they had everything in common.

Although the disease had crested in Atlanta, people were still hesitant to go out. Some businesses had reopened, but restaurants mostly stayed closed and the shelves in grocery stores were practically empty. Helen had been making a list just in case they found a way to buy supplies. On the list were peanut butter, cookie dough ice cream, macaroni and cheese, Honey Nut Cheerios, Froot Loops, and toilet paper.

The children ransacked the house looking for cash. Jill's wallet was empty. There were credit cards in her purse but they probably didn't work, and the children wouldn't be authorized to use them anyway. Jill had been too confused in the last days of her life to prepare for the consequences of her death.

They rode their bikes to Little Five Points, where there was a Bank of America ATM. It was strange outside, reminding Helen of a big snowstorm when all the streets were empty and enchanted and there was no school. It was exactly like that but without the snow.

The ATM was out of money. And so was the one on Ponce de León.

'We could steal stuff,' Teddy said. 'Everybody's doing it.'

'I'm scared of getting caught.'

'But if we get caught, they'll take care of us, right?'

That seemed logical. There was a Kroger on Caroline Street, but Helen got scared when she saw the armed guards. Teddy wanted to go in, but Helen got back on her bike and headed home.

'What are we going to do now?' Teddy asked.

Helen went through the cabinets again. About the only thing remaining was their dad's bourbon in the liquor cabinet. Helen stared at it. 'We're going to make a trade,' she told Teddy, brandishing the bottle. 'Mrs Hernández is an alcoholic, like something terrible. She'll give anything for this.'

Teddy made a face.

'I don't want to do it, either,' said Helen, 'but we have to do something!'

The two of them stood at the bottom of the stairwell. 'Mrs Hernández?' Helen called, a little too quietly. There was no response.

'Maybe she's not up there,' Teddy whispered.

'Her car is here. And she never goes anywhere anyways.'

The bulb in the stairwell had still not been changed, and the stairs creaked spookily. Helen knocked on the door at the top of the stairs, but there was no answer, no sound of footsteps. Helen waited a moment, then pounded on the door. 'Mrs Hernández!' Then Teddy joined in, both of them shouting, *Mrs Hernández! Mrs Hernández!*

The door was locked. Helen looked apprehensively at Teddy, then broke a glass pane with the bourbon bottle. She reached inside and unlocked the door.

There was a dead cat stinking up the living room.

The children stood uncertainly, their hearts pounding.

'Mrs Hernández?' Helen said in little more than a whisper. She was beginning to lose her nerve, but then Teddy walked ahead of her. At the end of the hall was Mrs Hernández's bedroom. The door was partially open. A powerful now-familiar odor drifted out of it.

'Mrs Hernández?'

Teddy pushed the door open. It was hard to make out exactly what was happening at first, then Helen screamed. The black cat that was eating Mrs Hernández's face wheeled around and hissed. Teddy pulled the door shut, and the children ran toward the stairs.

Suddenly, Helen stopped. Something inside her that was deeper than fear took control. She insisted on surviving. She insisted that Teddy would live. She didn't care what it took. She would not give up.

She forced herself to return to Mrs Hernández's kitchen and examine the pantry. There was some grown-up cereal, jelly, stale bread, and about twenty cans of cat food. In the refrigerator were several bottles of wine, milk, three Dr Peppers, carrots, and half a carton of eggs that were probably bad. Helen got a grocery sack and began packing up everything. 'Find her purse,' she told Teddy. 'Maybe she's got some money.'

They went through the apartment, stealing everything they thought they might be able to eat or trade, but the purse was nowhere in evidence. Finally, they went back into the bedroom. This time the black cat bolted out of the room. They didn't look at what was left of Mrs Hernández. Teddy found her purse on the bureau. Her wallet was inside, along with a hairbrush and a small gun. Teddy didn't say anything. He gave the wallet to Helen and put the gun in his pocket.

39

Satan is Loose in the World

THE PRESIDENT WAS QUICK TO DECLARE VICTORY IN THE MIDdle East showdown with Russia. A surprise cruise missile strike on the airbases where Russian aircraft were stationed took out at least half of the Su-57s and destroyed the runways, eliminating their airpower as a factor in the conflict. The Russian Pacific Fleet was blocked as it rounded the Maldives by an armada of U.S. and British warships. For Putin, it was a humiliating retreat. Inside the Kremlin, there were whispers about the end of his rule.

For Tildy Nichinsky, it was as sweet a moment as she had ever known. The president had trusted her advice, and look how it paid off. He informed her that he was appointing her his new national security adviser – a signal to insiders that the days of placating the Russian leader were over.

It was finally deemed safe for the president to emerge from Mount Weather and move back into the White House, having survived the contagion along with most of his cabinet. The secretary of commerce was dead, as were two Supreme Court justices. At least forty members of Congress had died. It would be weeks before basic transportation could be back in service and people felt safe enough to emerge from their shelters. And, of course, there were so many funerals to attend.

Just at this moment, when the number of reported cases of influenza began to decline in most countries and recovery seemed imminent, the lights went out. Tildy awakened late because her alarm failed to go off. When she went to brush her teeth, the water didn't come on. The gas was off on the stove. She tried to call the White House switchboard, but there was no signal, nothing, on either her landline or her cell. Her secure phone had not yet been installed after the president's announcement.

Unwashed, with her hair tucked beneath an Astros cap, Tildy set out to walk to the White House. It was raining, just her luck. She walked up 7th Street toward the National Mall, the wind shoving her umbrella about. Dogs ran loose. She noted the looted stores and the absence of police. The only people on the street were dangerous-looking teenagers, perhaps members of one of the orphan gangs she had read about. She often heard gunshots. That very night, there had been several explosions. Tildy reminded herself that she was now one of the most powerful people in the country, but in her condo, alone, she felt like a scared old lady.

The rain was coming down hard, making puddles in the potholes. There were no lights anywhere, no traffic signals. Three fire trucks blocked the intersection of D Street. Several townhouses that once stood on the corner were now a pile of rubble. 'Gas main explosion,' one of the firemen explained, the rain spilling off his helmet. 'We got 'em all over town.' They were digging out the bodies.

At least there were still firemen, so there was still

government, so there was still civilization. It felt crazy to be thinking such things.

The White House was on its backup generator, which gave the place a feeling of normalcy, but everything inside was in transition. Most of the former president's cabinet were still in office – those who were alive and functioning – but the new president wanted his own people close to him, so a new chief of staff greeted Tildy.

'I know he's going to want to see you,' the chief said. 'We can't get hold of people. You did the right thing just to come directly here.'

She handed Tildy a shawl to put around her wet shoulders. The new chief had made history by being the first woman to occupy that office – if history was still being made, Tildy thought darkly. Practically no one outside of a small circle in Washington knew what was happening. The internet was down. There was no television or radio. Only a few newspapers were able to print. Piece by piece, the bricks of modernity were being substracted.

Tildy waited, wrapped in the shawl and looking at the family photos of the former chief of staff still on the shelf behind the desk. She knew that one of the children in the pictures had died. She supposed that all group photos would be looked at that way in the future: who lived through it, who did not.

The chief returned and motioned Tildy into the Oval Office.

The president was staring out the window, a legal pad in hand. The office was bare. The presence of the previous occupant had been wiped clean; even the desk had been swapped out. This one was the Theodore Roosevelt. 'Tildy,' the president said softly, indicating the gold couches. They sat down, facing each other. 'So?'

'Russians.'

The president nodded. 'They've got the capability.'

'How many systems are down?'

'It's spotty, but maybe half the country is without electricity. Texas is okay, they're on their own grid. Water systems, gas, here and there, are real problems. Viruses took out most of the internet. Data in the Cloud wiped out. Private industry wrecked. Stock market closed. We were already in the worst depression since the thirties. I don't know when or how we're going to get everybody back to work. It's a comprehensive mess.'

'What's your top concern?' she asked.

'I'm really worried about our nuclear utilities. I've got a report that the safety mechanisms have been defeated at the Bellefonte plant in Alabama. We haven't heard yet from other facilities. Grand Coulee Dam is fully open, flooding everything downstream. Could be other dams as well. People will drown. Houses are blowing up because of overcapacity in the gas lines. Hospitals are without power. They sure picked a helluva time to pull the switch.'

'What are we going to do about it, Mr President?'

'We'll have to respond. But it's going to take us days to get it sorted out, get some kind of secure communication going so I can speak to my commanders.'

'What if they launch before that?'

'Our emergency systems are in good enough shape that we can easily counterattack. We can take Russia off the map. But is that what we want to do? And to be honest, we can't do anything till we get the GPS back online. We're in great peril.' Tildy saw that he had started making a list on the legal pad. Nuclear strike was at the top.

She had learned enough about dealing with powerful men that she waited to be asked. The president was agonizing and looking for answers. She had never really respected him, but she saw him now as an intensely moral man with an awesome responsibility he had never hoped to shoulder – to take revenge and possibly kill more people with a single decision than any individual in human history. His first presidential act.

Finally: 'What do you think I should do?'

'Do you have the capacity to shut down Russia's utilities?' she asked.

'Not as totally as they've done to us. I'm afraid it would make us look weak. Putin has the advantage of having a system that is not as dependent on high tech as ours.'

'Then there's the flu.'

'You think he's behind that, too?'

'There seems to be more immunity to Kongoli in Russia than elsewhere. It suggests that they may have had a vaccine prepared for this virus before they released it upon the world.'

The president stared at Tildy, his jaw slightly open. Then he shook his head. 'I do believe in evil. But could they stoop to this? Is Satan loose in the world?'

'I don't know, sir.'

'We also have to think of the future. I don't know how long it will be before societies get back to where we were. Estimate I'm hearing is that the world population is down maybe 7 percent. It's impossible to measure the economic impact, but let's say in our own country we're at maybe

40 percent of our GNP. We've entered a new era already. Do we dare take the next step?'

Tildy knew Putin. He was always testing the limits, expanding the boundaries, setting traps. The takedown of the grid had been years in the planning. This was his chance to catch America on its heels, and he wasn't going to let that go to waste. This was payback for humiliating him in Iran. The game that the stone-faced Russian leader was playing was built on many levels of deception and deniability, but an American response was required.

'For a starter, you should have him killed,' she said. 'It's the most economical reaction in the short run.'

The president thought for a moment, then wrote another item on his list.

40
Suez

HENRY WAS IN THE PHARMACY WHEN HE HEARD A SCREAM. He rushed to the dormitory where the sound was coming from. The other crewmen in the dorm were trying to restrain a panicked sailor, who was fighting them off. 'Lemme go! I'm sick, I'm sick!' he yelled. The other men immediately backed away.

His name was Jackson. Henry persuaded him to come to the pharmacy for an examination. He had no fever, no swollen lymph nodes, no symptoms at all except for the elevated blood pressure caused by his distress. 'I'm not sick?' Jackson asked in disbelief. 'I felt strange. I couldn't catch my breath. I thought I was going to suffocate.'

'At the moment, your vital signs are fine.'

'Are you telling me I'm just scared?'

'Everybody is.'

Jackson shook his head and stared at the floor. 'I'm a fucking coward,' he said. 'I guess I always knew that. Now everybody knows. I don't think I can face the other guys.'

'What scares people the most is having no control,' Henry said. 'It scares me, too. Maybe me more than you because

I'm trained to fight this particular enemy, and I just don't know how.'

Once again, Henry slept restlessly, kept awake by the muffled clunk of the damaged piston. He thought about Captain Dixon's plea to do something to save his panicked crew, the grief-stricken SEAL in the mess hall, poor frightened Jackson. Each day the roll of infected sailors grew, and more bodies were stored in the chill box. These were vigorous young people who should have been the most resistant to the infection, but their powerful immune response was killing them, just as in 1918, by filling the lungs with fluids to fight the infection but drowning the body in the process.

Henry ransacked his memory, going through everything he knew or thought he knew about treating influenza. He considered taking nasal secretions from contagious patients, microwaving them to kill the virus, then swabbing the inactivated virus into the noses of the uninfected submariners. But at best, there would be one to ten million virion particles per microliter – nowhere near enough to engender an immune response even if it were injected.

He recalled the example of smallpox, one of the most infectious diseases that ever afflicted humanity, and also one of the most merciless. Once inhaled, the virus moved from the lungs and lymph nodes into the bloodstream and the bone marrow. It felt like influenza at first: cough, fever, muscle pain, followed by nausea and vomiting. Two weeks after the infection, red spots appeared on the tongue, throat, and mucus membranes. As those lesions grew and erupted, new lesions appeared on the forehead, then began their march across the body's entire surface, forming swollen and dimpled pustules that gave the appearance of a body densely covered by bees. When the pustules dried up, they turned into scabs. In survivors, these lesions finally resolved as characteristic disfiguring smallpox scars.

In 1796, an English physician named Edward Jenner realized that one group of people enjoyed a curious immunity from smallpox: milkmaids. Jenner knew nothing about viruses at the time – no one did. But he fervently believed that the key to immunity could be found among the young women previously infected with cowpox, a similar but milder disease primarily found in animals. The disease was detected in humans who had touched the udders of infected cows. So persuaded was Jenner of his theory that he extracted some tissue from the hand of a cowpox-infected milkmaid named Sarah Nelmes and injected it into James Phipps, the eight-year-old son of his gardener. Jenner called the procedure a 'vaccination'. The word itself comes from *vacca,* Latin for 'cow'. Six weeks later, to prove his point, Jenner injected young Phipps with smallpox pus. Phipps did not get ill. It was a reckless and unethical but legendary moment in the history of medicine. Jenner's decision to risk the boy's life must be weighed against the fact that the toll extracted by smallpox in Europe alone was about 400,000 people a year. At one point, roughly 10 percent of the world's population died of the disease. Of the survivors, a third became blind.

Cowpox was a European disease, uncommonly found in the Americas. Responding to a widespread outbreak of smallpox in the Spanish colonies, King Charles IV ordered a corvette to ferry the vaccine to the New World. At the time, there was no feasible way of transporting live cowpox virus across the ocean. The king's court physician proposed that an infected person be accompanied by uninfected companions, who subsequently would be exposed to the virus, passing pus from one victim to the next, so that the cowpox was constantly refreshed and still viable upon arrival in the Americas. The court physician recommended a Spanish doctor, Francisco Javier de Balmis, to lead the expedition, and the king provided the recruits Dr Balmis needed for the mission: twenty-two orphan boys, aged eight to ten. After delivering the vaccine to the Americas, the Balmis expedition went on to the Philippines, Macau, and Canton, still carrying infected orphans as their sole cargo.

Henry felt very much like that long-ago seafaring physician, on a boat with an infectious disease. But Dr Balmis was also carrying a cure.

Henry drifted off to sleep and then awakened hours later to an aching erection. He had been dreaming of the women in the shower. He had a photographic image of them in his mind; it was indelible, three young women, beautiful in their nakedness, especially Murphy, whom he hadn't really noticed as a sexual creature until that moment, when he saw how magnificent she was, how well formed were her limbs, her breasts, the small of her back. He fought the image and tried to push it away. But then he realized it was not Murphy's body he was imagining but Jill's.

Was she lost to him now? She must be, she must be gone, along with any kind of intimacy that he – ugly, ill-made – could ever hope to have with another woman. And his children, were they alive? The thought of them, of losing them, was an icicle in his heart. Everything meaningful to him was gone. He was desolate and useless. For the first time he considered death as a way out.

––––

'Good day, sir.'

Henry blushed when Murphy sat down at breakfast.

'It's a big day,' she said. 'We're going through the Suez Canal.'

'Sounds exciting,' Henry said wanly.

'That means we get to surface. News. Sports scores, that kind of thing. Fresh air.'

Henry brightened immediately. 'Can I make a call? Send an email?'

'Crew only receives brief emails, but we can't respond. It's a security thing. Sure keeps you guessing, but after a couple months you just block those thoughts. Unproductive, they tell us.'

After breakfast, Henry spent the next several hours doing everything he could imagine to slow the transmission of the disease. He recalled an experiment that had been conducted at Mount Sinai's medical school using guinea pigs. Cages with sick pigs were placed near cages with uninfected animals, with air blowing from the former to the latter. By varying both the temperature and environmental moisture, researchers learned that the rate of disease transmission dropped as heat and humidity increased. When the temperature reached 86 degrees Fahrenheit, there was no transmission at all. Could that work on a submarine? Henry cranked up the heat and had the humidifiers running at full blast. Everyone was pouring sweat. 'It's a fucking steam bath!' one of the officers snapped at him. But Henry had the captain's blessing, as everyone knew, and they prayed that their perspiration might stall the remorseless advance of the disease.

Henry reflected on his own childhood disease. Without the sun's ultraviolet rays, the body doesn't produce vitamin D, which in turn limits the number of white blood cells available to fight infection. And yet absence of sunlight defined the submariners' existence. They were all as pale as paper. Although Henry hated to encourage increased animal consumption, he persuaded the chef to create dishes that included dietary sources of vitamin D, featuring egg yolks, tuna, fortified soy milk, and beef liver. Cod liver oil was artfully blended into the hot sauce and salad dressing.

While he was instituting these new protocols, Henry felt an unfamiliar lurching motion in the boat. The captain ordered the hatches open, and Henry realized that the submarine had surfaced. Air, real fresh air, came aboard.

Henry climbed onto the missile deck, where other members of the crew were gathered, the healing Egyptian sun bearing down on them. Henry felt a little nauseated – probably seasickness, caused by the unfamiliar rocking of the vessel.

'Doctor!'

Henry turned to see Captain Dixon on the bridge above him. 'Come up!'

Henry climbed the narrow stairs and edged through the hatchway, wondering how the gigantic Dixon managed to slip through. 'You got the boat smelling really sweet,' the captain said. 'Like a goddamn locker room.'

'You asked me to do what I can to stop the infection.'

'Well, you won't find it in the ladies' shower.' Dixon chuckled, but seeing Henry's obvious discomfort he turned to another subject. 'Given your civilian status, I shouldn't be telling you this, but you're a part of the crew now, so you may as well know. There's bad news all round. The internet is down everywhere. We don't know for how long. Part of a broad cyberattack on the infrastructure in the U.S. and Western Europe. This boat might be put into play if things really go south and some muckety-mucks start thinking about pulling the trigger.'

'And do you think they will?'

'It's possible. I could let you off in Port Said if you could find your way home in some other fashion,' Dixon said.

'Is there another way?'

'God only knows.'

'I think I'll stay aboard, if you'll have me.'

Henry gazed out at the flat Egyptian landscape. The canal sliced through the desert like a blue highway, unnatural in its linearity. Ahead in the canal was what Captain Dixon identified as a Russian destroyer, part of a convoy.

'What would that be like for you?' Henry asked Dixon. 'To actually launch nuclear warheads?'

'I try not to think about it.'

'But you do.'

'As a religious man, or at least a wannabe believer . . .' He trailed off. Henry waited him out. Finally, the captain said, 'I do wonder if I'd go to Hell.'

'You'd be following orders.'

'I seriously doubt St Peter is gonna take that into account. I'm glad it's out of my hands now. These Tomahawks are marvelous weapons, but they're not the end of the world. I was XO on a boomer. That's what we call the nuclear-armed Trident subs. Every single one of them can wipe out half of civilization all by themselves. You're trained and trained, but there's no way to know for sure what you're going to think if you ever get that order.'

'I'm not religious myself,' Henry said, 'but I often think

that if God made us the way we are, he made an animal that threatens to destroy his entire creation. On the other hand, if nature made us, as I believe, we've evolved into a species that is almost godlike in every respect. All the power we have, all the creativity, all the wisdom! But there's a piece of genetic code inside us that wants to blow it all to pieces.'

As the submarine entered the Mediterranean Sea and submerged once again, Henry studied tissue samples of the patients who had survived the virus. Five submariners had died in the last twenty-four hours. The chill box was full of corpses wrapped in sheets. At this rate, most of the crew would die before they reached the Georgia coast.

Henry had to do something.

He went through the pharmacy's supplies once again. Murphy had already tried Tamiflu, which had been totally ineffective. He noticed some leftover FluMist, a nasal spray vaccine containing attenuated live viruses for two influenza A viruses: H1N1, the descendant of the Spanish flu, and H3N2, as well as two influenza B viruses. If Kongoli had been any of those influenza types, Henry might have hoped that the viruses in FluMist would swap genes with Kongoli, creating a competitive and – he would hope – less lethal virus. But Kongoli defied ordinary categories.

Cut off from the array of sophisticated laboratory devices available to twenty-first-century medicine, Henry had to take himself back in time, hundreds of years, to a period before the great vaccines of the twentieth century countered the scourges of the past – typhoid, chicken pox, tetanus, rubella, diphtheria, measles, polio – an era when doctors had to work instinctually, with few resources and none of the science that later untangled the secrets of so many pathogens. They learned how to turn the disease against itself.

Henry thought back to the nineteenth century, when Louis Pasteur, the father of microbiology, who lost three of his own children to typhoid, provided proof of the germ theory of disease. While studying cholera in chickens, Pasteur's lab assistant had forgotten to inject the birds with fresh bacteria before going off on a month-long holiday. When he returned, the virulence of the bacteria had diminished in the summer heat, but the assistant injected the chickens anyway. Several days later, Pasteur noticed that the birds developed only a mild version of the usually lethal disease. When the chickens were completely recovered, he inoculated them with fresh bacteria, but they did not become ill. Pasteur reasoned that the weakened form of the live disease had awakened the immune system and given it time to learn how to fight the infection. Pasteur later developed the first vaccines for anthrax, and then for rabies, which made him an international hero. And yet Pasteur had far more resources at the École Normale Supérieure in nineteenth-century Paris than Henry did on a twenty-first-century submarine a thousand feet deep in the middle of the Atlantic Ocean. Even Edward Jenner had cowpox available to create the smallpox vaccine. All Henry had to work with was the disease and his intuition.

Physicians from various traditions had observed that smallpox survivors enjoyed a lifelong immunity to a second infection. A technique known to have been practiced in China in the fifteenth century involved making a powder of smallpox scabs and blowing it into the noses of uninfected individuals, who typically contracted a milder case of the disease. During the American Revolution, George Washington, a smallpox survivor himself (and, later, an anthrax survivor as well), ordered that all of his troops, and also his wife, be inoculated. The procedure at the time required making a cut in the arm, inserting a pustule scab from an infected victim, and sealing the infection with a bandage – a process called 'variolation'. Typically, people who received the inoculation got a less virulent form of the disease, but it still could take more than a month to recover. John Adams got inoculated by way of variolation prior to his marriage, but his recovery was marked by 'headaches, backaches, knee aches, gagging fever, and eruption of pock marks'. About 3 percent of those who subjected themselves to variolation died. Still, while John was away helping to draft the Declaration of Independence, his wife, Abigail, took their four children to Boston to have them inoculated. One of the sons had to be inoculated three times, apparently to overcome his innate immunity to the disease.

Henry reasoned that influenza normally entered the body through the mouth or nose – the superhighways to the lungs, where the damage was done. What if the infection took another route? Instead of being inhaled, what if it were injected intravenously, where it would pass through the heart, activating the immune system? By the time the virus reached the lungs, the body's defenses might be strong enough to repel the invading pathogen. It was, of course, only a hypothesis, and a dangerous one to prove.

Henry saw the risks, but could see no alternative. Once he decided on his course of action, he knew there was no time to waste. He found Captain Dixon in his quarters, sound asleep. The crew rotated hours among different shifts, so every other week Dixon changed his sleeping schedule to be available to another shift. Like all submariners, he was trained to snap awake at the slightest tap on the door.

'Henry?' he said groggily.

'I need a favor,' Henry said. 'One I truly hate to ask.'

'What is it?'

'I'm running an experiment, but it's a risky one, and it's going to require a terrible sacrifice on your part.'

'What is that?'

'I'm going to have to kill your birds.'

41

The Finches

HENRY AND MURPHY VISITED THE MOST RECENTLY INFECTED crewmen. They were all extremely ill, running fevers of 103 or higher. Clearly, the virus had not abated. One of the crew was Jesse McAllister.

'How are your teeth?' Henry asked.

'They're okay,' McAllister said warily.

'Don't worry, I'm not going to do any more surgery. I'm only here to take a nasal swab.'

Murphy handed Henry Q-tips, which he used to root out copious amounts of snot from McAllister's nostrils. Then he returned to the clinic, where the captain's Gouldian finches were fluttering from perch to perch, vividly alive, a kaleidoscope of color. They were named after the great ornithologist John Gould, who categorized the five hundred bird specimens that Charles Darwin brought back from the voyage of the HMS *Beagle*. Captain Dixon's birds were about to be the latest animals to suffer and die in the name of science. Given the limited number of birds, Henry decided to inject them subcutaneously, in a process similar to variolation.

If he had been in a laboratory, Henry would have filtered the snot suspension to clean out the bacteria, but there was nothing available on the sub for that. One of the reasons he chose McAllister was that he was still on antibiotics from the dental surgery, which might provide some protection. Henry diluted the suspension tenfold with saline solution and injected the first bird. The next finch received a dose that was diluted an additional tenfold, and so on, until each of the six birds had received an injection of diminishing viral potency. The colors of the finches were so various that Henry simply called out to Murphy, 'Red head, purple chest,' or 'Blue back, black head,' and noted the diminishing doses the birds received. In an ideal experiment, the birds injected with the greatest amount of virus would die; those with the least would not be infected; and in the middle there would be birds that became ill but recovered.

But twenty-four hours later, five of the six birds were dead. They lay in the bottom of the cage, their brilliant plumage splayed in a wanton pile. One bird, Chuckie, was still standing – listless and rheumy-eyed, and definitely ill, but not dead. Chuckie took some water Murphy administered from an eyedropper. Once again, Henry was struck by the raw virulence of Kongoli, even in such a dilute form. That made his next decision even more difficult.

Captain Dixon was subdued when Henry returned his one surviving bird. 'What does this mean?' he asked.

'I think it could mean that Chuckie's immune system had just enough time to keep this disease from being fatal.'

'You "think"?'

'There's no way to confirm the findings. If we had more birds and more time, I would infect them with the surviving bird's virus to see if it has modified. But we don't have either.'

'So what now, doc?'

'I've selected a human volunteer as a guinea pig to receive the virus. If he survives, we'll work on the theory that we have found a way to reduce the mortality. That's the best we can hope for, I'm afraid.'

'I want to be that volunteer,' Dixon said.

'You're ineligible. Your immune system is too compromised to provide a baseline.'

'What's the name of the sailor who volunteered?'

'Actually, he's not a sailor.'

'Are you insane, Henry?'

'Desperate. I injected the solution half an hour ago.'

'Is it safe?'

'There's no way for me to know the right dose without testing it. If I survive, we'll give it to other members of the crew. It's not something I would ever do in another environment. I could wind up killing people who might otherwise have survived. I just couldn't think of any alternative.'

The fever came on quickly, along with the chills. The rapid contraction and relaxation of muscles was the body's way of generating heat to fight the infection, but the shaking was unlike anything he had experienced before. Whether it saved him or killed him, there was nothing he could do about the cytokine storm that was waging war on his behalf.

For Henry, time was always formless and confounding in the submarine, and now he was totally lost, not knowing if hours or days were passing. He remembered seeing Murphy's face in his moments of consciousness when she came to take nasal swabs.

Once again, Henry felt the urge to pray. This sensation was happening more frequently now, and Henry dreaded its appeal. There had been times when he was so brimming with joy that he wanted to express his gratitude, to say thank you to the universe or some divine power or a familiar spirit for the unmerited happiness he had known in his life. He wished that some supernatural force could give him instruction about the way ahead. And he also yearned for forgiveness.

He did not believe in mercy. Religious terms such as sin and evil and damnation were theological constructs that had no meaning for him. Nor did he accept the idea that mere belief in God wiped the moral slate clean. In Henry's mind, there was a ledger of actions, good and bad, but the line between them was not always easy to find. He wondered how Majid was able to balance science with his religion, which he wore as lightly as his sheer ceremonial robe, even though the prince was as demanding of proof as Henry, and every bit as suspicious of supernatural explanations when science supplied a plausible answer.

The thought of Prince Majid made Henry think of his gift, the waterlogged Qur'an that had survived Henry's plunge into the Persian Gulf, the only personal item that remained in Henry's possession – a beautiful edition, tipped in gold leaf. In his fever, he tried reading it, looking for guidance in a book he did not trust. The pages were warped and brittle, but only a few of them were stuck together. The first chapter was seven sentences long. 'In the name of Allah, the Compassionate, the Merciful,' it began. That was repeated in the third sentence. Then, 'Thee do we serve and Thee do we beseech for help.'

'I beseech you,' Henry said. 'I beseech you.' He didn't know how to pray, but he had no other ideas, no other place to turn. His heart was full of guilt and reproach and despair.

Why had this plague happened? He had always known that other catastrophic diseases would come, and he had trained himself to be a warrior against them, and he had failed: influenza had swept the globe before humanity even had a chance. Huddled in his bunk, unaware of events, Henry could only imagine what must be happening in the world above the waves, not knowing that his darkest fears were more than matched by the devastation that had befallen humanity. Someone did this, Henry thought. Nature can be cruel in its way, but his own experience had shown that the hand of man was also capable of ingenious and fatal destruction. We truly are godlike, he thought. Our curse.

His attempt at prayer left him feeling hollow and hypocritical. The Qur'an was full of warnings about the end of days, and despite his skepticism Henry continued to read, looking for . . . something. He didn't know what. He carried a burden, imposed by his country, in the name of science. He wanted to atone; he wanted a clear conscience. That seemed as unobtainable as flying to Mars.

Although Henry steered away from religious language and concepts because they arose from superstition and wishful thinking, there was one maxim that he had drawn from Albert Schweitzer's philosophy: All life is sacred. 'Sacred' was a word that never came to Henry's lips, but it expressed his stance in the world. Life itself was a miracle – another word that Henry would never use, but a truth he inwardly acknowledged.

'Surely good deeds take away evil deeds,' the holy book said. Henry had tried to live an exemplary life, and these words registered with him. He still felt guilty for entering Mecca and pretending to be a believer of the faith. In bouts of delirium, he argued with Prince Majid: 'This is what I believe. Is that what being a Muslim means? This is as much of a Muslim as I can become.' He wondered how Majid would have replied.

Cornered by thoughts that he had trained himself to avoid, Henry remembered all the animals he had subjected to scientific torture. The monkeys, the mice, the guinea pigs, the ferrets. The Gouldian finches. He had always told himself that he did this for a higher cause. A noble cause. But then his memory confronted him with the face of a monkey he had infected with Ebola. Henry was wearing his space suit at the time. He was a huge puffed apparition, looking like the Michelin Man. He pushed a button and the back wall of the cage moved forward, mashing the animal against the front of the cage so that it had no chance to struggle. Henry remembered the look – a look of beseeching, just like Henry, beseeching some cruel deity. But the deity the macaque prayed to believed he was working for a higher purpose and killed him most awfully. Eventually, Henry stopped eating meat and began wearing canvas shoes – just like Jürgen. He finally concluded that having slain so many animals in the name of science, he didn't need to eat them as well.

He prayed. He asked whatever power there was to reunite him with his family. That is all I will ever ask, he pleaded. He had not been the father and husband he should have been. Faced with death, he realized his selfishness, his inadequacy. He only wanted to make it up, to be redeemed in the eyes of the people who loved him. He had come to the end of his resistance, or even his reason. He had only one goal: to embrace his family once again.

Henry curled up protectively, withered by the chills and the fever and the pummeling memories. He descended into a very dark place. He felt something moist on his cheek, and wiped it away. Then it happened again, and he thought that the bleeding had begun. But he was not bleeding. He was weeping.

42

Into the Jungle

IN THE MORNING THEY WERE FERRIED DOWN THE JURUENA River in a shallow-bottom fishing boat. The river was broad and wildly beautiful, with lilies growing near the banks and the air brimming with mosquitos and gnats and unknown insects of dazzling variety. Even in this wilderness there were marks of civilization: small tin huts built on piers in the water with satellite dishes on the roof. A native boy waved at them. He had a bright green snake wrapped around his shoulders. The march of modernity stopped here.

Henry had always feared going into the jungle. The fear had different levels to it, like an apartment building. On the high floors, he was fine, actually blithe, rarely thinking of the dark and damp and matted and can't-get-your-breath sensations that jungles held for him. It was safe to say that Henry spent most of his life on the upper floors of his phobia. He was like a person who was afraid of flying but never actually flew. The few times he had been in the wilderness had been clarifying. When he visited Lambaréné, for instance, he clung to the village, fearful of getting lost. At those times Henry was no longer on the upper floor, but he was not out of control. He steeled himself. He felt better for having confronted an irrational dread. Jungles were really nothing more than forests; forests were nothing more than trees.

It was in his dreams that he descended to the basement, where the stark fear raged and he shivered in terror. Then Henry felt like a child trapped in a horror movie and unable to break the spell. He longed to awaken, to have the sun chase away the darkness and reality disperse the fantasies so he could breathe again.

They heard gunshots. Their guide halted the boat and talked on the radio to the AGT team leader on the ground, who was supervising the Brazilian commandos at the terrorist encampment. Yes, he said, the agent Henry had created had been applied as directed, but it was only partially effective. Some of the terrorists had survived.

'What was that?' Henry said. 'What did he say?'

'He says many were killed, but the wind caused the agent to drift.'

Henry looked at Jürgen in alarm. 'It was not supposed to kill anyone,' he said.

'But it is a success,' the guide said, smiling. 'The resistance is minimal.' His eyes congratulated Henry – marveled at him, really, the great genius Jürgen had spoken of.

In a few moments the shots ceased, and the guide resumed the journey to the encampment. The commandos were masked and gloved, looking like doctors as they went through the huts and tents making sure that everyone was dead. There was no pretense of capturing and disarming anyone. Some of the corpses were bloodied by the shootout, but most were lying in contorted positions, eyes open and tongues bulging out, having died in the middle of a scream. One or two were still alive but convulsing, until they were finished off by the commandos.

I did this, Henry thought.

Jürgen appeared indifferent – or, rather, simply curious. He set about examining the bodies and drawing samples. He was not frightened of the jungle.

'You said the wind carried the agent,' Henry asked the guide. 'In what direction?'

The guide asked the team leader, who impatiently pointed east, toward the sun, which was just cresting the treetops.

'Are there any people in that direction?' Henry asked.

One of the Brazilian commandos acknowledged that there was a village of Cinta Larga Indians nearby. The way he said it meant that it was a matter of no consequence.

'Take me there,' Henry demanded.

The guide turned to Jürgen, but Henry said again, insistently, 'Take me there, now!'

Jürgen nodded.

The guide took Henry farther up the Juruena to the point where the Arinos River flowed into it. The outboard motor left a trail of blue smoke. Henry forced his thoughts into focus. Again and again one has to learn the lesson that animal models don't always predict the outcome in humans. Thalidomide was safe in animals but in humans caused frightful birth defects. Fialuridine was a promising antiviral designed to counter hepatitis B. It was tested in mice, rats, dogs, monkeys, and woodchucks, at doses hundreds of times higher than would ever be tested on humans. Not a single animal showed a toxic reaction. But even minimal amounts of the drug were fatal to human volunteers, killing five of them; two others survived only after having liver transplants. Nothing in Henry's experiments had suggested that his own agent would be lethal to humans – but that's what human trials were for.

At the juncture of the rivers, Henry spotted a dozen slender wooden canoes tied up along the bank. The guide maneuvered the boat to the makeshift landing, then dropped Henry off, along with his medical bag, and swung around without a word, leaving him on the bank, alone in the jungle.

A narrow footpath wound through the overgrowth, dense and still and quiet except for the hectoring cry of a macaw. Henry remembered the sound like a dream. He heard his muffled footfalls as the undergrowth thinned out below the towering trees, and he shrank into the landscape like a child. It was all too familiar. When he coughed, the sound resonated in the hushed forest sanctuary. The silence was also known to him. Henry's breathing grew shallow but audible, almost the only sound except for the mosquitos that welcomed the great blood feast that was offering itself to them. He could almost hear the sweat boiling out of his skin.

He came upon an abandoned fire pit. A hatchet. Drying fish hanging from a rope line strung between two trees. Then Henry saw that he was in a village of mud-brick huts and thatched roofs, so much a part of the land that the place was almost invisible until he was upon it. Some of the huts were open on the sides. Then he heard the flies.

It was as he pictured it in his dreams – dozens of people lying in contorted positions. Everyone dead. Just like Jonestown.

He saw women with brilliant feathers in their hair. Men with blue tattoos. A teenage boy wearing a Hard Rock Cafe T-shirt, his arm sticking upright in the air.

'Hello?' Henry said into the emptiness, then louder, '*Hello?*'
Flies. There was a cage of chickens, all dead.

His heart drumming, he went from hut to hut, searching
for human life, knowing it was pointless except as a form of
mortification. The image he had been holding at bay his entire
life forced itself into his mind: his own parents, sprawled on
the jungle floor. Just like this. Killed because of some mad-
man's fantasy. Bodies massed together or scattered, solitary
or in pairs or threes. Exactly like this. Families piled on top of
each other, clawing at their faces in agony. A dead child lay
under his father's arm, staring blankly into space. I could
have been you, Henry thought. I should have been you.

A dead mouse lay under a chair.

In one hut there was a powerful-looking man with facial
tattoos, lying on his side and reaching toward his wife. His
last gesture. For love, for protection. Toward her naked, very
pregnant belly. Two dead children lay beside them. Henry
silently begged their forgiveness, feeling unworthy of even
asking. Then he saw the woman blink.

Henry almost jumped out of his shoes. She was alive, staring at him. Did she know he was responsible? Was that
blame in her eyes – face-to-face with her killer – an expression of such intense focus that it felt physical, burning,
lacerating, a look that would stay with him until Henry took
his own final breaths? There was nothing he could do to
save her.

Then he saw movement in the woman's abdomen, rippling
like the surface of a pond when a fish has stirred, and he
realized what her eyes were asking.

Not thinking – no time for that – he took a scalpel from
his bag and sliced into her abdominal wall, rudely pulling

aside the liver and reaching into the body cavity. The mother made a deep guttural cry. He could feel movement inside her, as if the baby were reaching for him, for life. His fingers found the ropy umbilical cord and he tugged on it, but the mother's body still clung to her baby, so Henry cut deeper through the uterus into her womb and severed the cartilage that held the pubic bone together. Her body opened like a book. She had nothing left to grasp her child. And then it came out of her, like an offering.

The baby was still inside the amniotic sac, a bloody stocking that covered its body. He was tiny, but he already had thick, dark hair; his arms were crossed in front of his chest, and as Henry looked at him, the baby yawned. Henry made a light incision through the membrane and the baby flailed, pulling himself free and screaming into life. He showed him to the dead mother, wondering what he would ever tell Jill.

43

$34.27

SINCE JILL'S DEATH, HELEN HAD BEEN SLEEPING WITH A MONKEY-like stuffed animal that she had named Joe Banana. She used to sleep with him as a little girl. Night was the only time she allowed herself to sink back into the irresponsibility of childhood and imagine that her parents were still there, still taking care of her, and that she was only waiting for them to come and tuck her in and kiss her goodnight. But she knew that they would never do that again, and so she hugged Joe Banana and whispered secrets to him as she did when she was little. Teddy slept beside her on a mattress on the floor.

Helen startled when she heard glass break. She shushed Teddy as he started to say something. They heard the foot-steps and the voices of men who weren't bothering to be quiet. Helen pulled Teddy into the closet and quietly shut the door. They hid behind her dresses.

The men broke things. They cursed. They didn't care if people heard them. Then they came into her bedroom.

A flashlight swept across the floor, illuminating the crack under the closet door. Helen stopped breathing. Teddy pressed into her, hugging his knees to his chest. Then the light went

away. Helen heard her bureau drawers being opened. Someone laughed, high and strange. 'Less go usstairs,' a slurred
voice said.

'Not yet.'

'Fuckin' stinks.'

'No shit.'

Helen heard her Miss Piggy bank being shaken. The men
laughed. She had $13.20 in there. Then the glass bank shat-
tered and the men cursed. She could hear them picking the
coins out of the glass, all the money she had in the world.
Helen started counting the coins in her head, distracting
herself from the fear. She stacked them up in her mind,
quarters, nickels, dimes, pennies. There was a Sacagawea
dollar that Henry had given her on her twelfth birthday,
last October. Quarters with commemorative images on the
back: Illinois, Land of Lincoln; Cumberland Gap, First
Doorway to the West; Ellis Island. She had examined them
many times.

'Cut my fuckin' finger,' one of the men said.

Helen imagined his blood on her coins. She hoped he bled
to death.

'C'mon, let's go.'

Footsteps. Leaving. Then they stopped. The light flashed
again under the closet door.

'C'mon!'

Footsteps. Coming toward them. The closet door opened.
The light probed the shelves above, then made a quick pass
across the dresses. Then stopped on Teddy's feet.

'Fuck, look at this.'

The dresses were pushed aside, and the children stared
into the blinding beam.

'Goddamn. It's a girl.'

Helen was blinded by the light, but she could hear the men breathing; they sounded as if they were panting. One of the men grabbed her arm and yanked her out of the closet. She tried to scream, but she couldn't find her voice. Instead, she heard Teddy yelling and then a horrible noise that she knew was a grown man's fist hitting him, again and again. And while she heard this she realized that her nightgown was being ripped off her. She was thrown onto the mattress on the floor. A corner of the flashlight beam caught the brown-red fringe of a man's beard as he fell on top of her, emptying her of breath. His hands ran across her. She tried to push him away, but he was so big. He forced her legs apart, and she finally found her voice.

She screamed so loud that she wasn't sure she even heard a gunshot, but the man on top of her made a sound in her ear and then went slack. It felt like a refrigerator was lying on top of her. She heard someone running away and a door slamming. She thought she would die, squashed by this monster she couldn't move off her. Then he began to move again, although he wasn't moving himself.

'Get off! Get off!' It was Teddy's voice.

Helen pushed the man and found a way to squeeze out.

'Teddy!'

'Are you okay?'

Helen couldn't speak. She was heaving sobs of fear and anger. And then she realized she was naked and felt so ashamed. She grabbed a pillow and hugged it to her as she moved away from the mattress.

'Are you okay?' Teddy repeated, urgently.

She had to tell him she was. He had to feel safe, even

366

though there was no safety anywhere. 'I'm okay,' she said in someone else's voice. The flashlight lay on the floor. Helen picked it up and shined it on the man lying on the mattress. There was blood all around his head. Helen thought it must be the flu. But then she spotted the gun in Teddy's hand and remembered hearing a gunshot.

'Teddy! What did you do?'

'I'm sorry!' he said. She could hear the confusion in his voice.

'No, it's okay! It's good!'

'I killed him.'

'Yes, you killed him. It's okay. There was another one . . .?'

'He ran away,' said Teddy.

Everything was so strange. Teddy had a gun. There was a dead man on the mattress. Something had happened to her that she didn't want to think about. And then she remembered: 'They hurt you. I heard them hitting you.'

'I'm okay,' he insisted.

She shined the light on Teddy's face, then sank onto the floor and cried and cried. She couldn't be strong. She couldn't be who Teddy needed her to be.

While Teddy slept on the couch, Helen sat in Henry's chair, staring at the television that might never come on again. The gun was on the coffee table just in case. By dawn, she had a plan.

They had to leave. That was her plan.

Mrs Hernández's corpse was still upstairs. Maybe the cats had eaten it down to the bones. Who knew. Who cared. Helen would never go back up there, but Mrs Hernández certainly made her presence felt. One day the smell would drift away, but Helen knew they couldn't wait any longer. Anyway, the dead man in her bedroom was going to start stinking soon enough.

There were crickets all over the house making a horrible racket, which eventually melded into a single droning tune pulsing in Helen's head. When the sky was finally bright enough that she could see in the kitchen, she opened a drawer and took out a butcher knife. Then she went back into her bedroom.

She knew he was dead, but she was taking no chances. He wasn't as huge as she thought. Part of his ass was exposed. He looked so stupid. She stabbed him. She heard a great exhalation and jumped back in terror, then she realized it was her own breath she had heard, not the dead man's.

She took his wallet. There was some money in it. She dug in his front pockets and got her coins and some bills. The Sacagawea dollar was there. She counted all the money. It came to $34.27. One of her quarters was still missing.

A few hours later, the dawn sun hit Teddy's eyes, and he stirred and saw Helen sitting at the dining room table with the money laid out in stacks of denominations. He looked at her questioningly. 'You need to pack,' she told him.

'Where are we going?'

'We're going to Aunt Maggie and Uncle Tim's place. They'll take us in.'

'But we gotta wait for Dad,' Teddy said.

'Daddy's dead,' Helen said evenly.

'You don't know.'

'If he were alive he'd be here.'

Teddy began to cry, but Helen was insistent. 'Teddy, we have to go!'

'I don't want to!'

'Teddy, we need parents!' Helen said impatiently, adopting a tone she had heard her mother use when Henry was being impractical. She would have to be Jill now.

'How will we get there?'

Helen had been thinking about this most of the night.

'I am going to drive us,' she said.

44

Let Her Talk

ON AUGUST 2, TILDY HAD A SERIES OF MEETINGS IN HER CORNER office in the West Wing. Unlike in her little Homeland Security cubby in the basement, she now enjoyed stately windows that filled the room with sunshine. She was steps away from the Oval Office. Her close relationship with the president awarded her power that her title, national security adviser, only hinted at.

There hadn't been much time to redecorate her new quarters, but she did have a bust of Henry Kissinger brought up from the storeroom. As soon as things settled down, she was going to change out the carpet, maybe go back to the cheerful Condi Rice yellow. Tildy believed in claiming her space as rapidly as possible, and if people were offended by her aggressiveness, that only added to the aura of power that she – after all these years – had earned.

In the morning, Tildy had a brief conversation with the new agency woman. The meeting was off the schedule and unrecorded. The agency man had been buried at Arlington, replaced by this tight-faced older woman whose hair had gone strikingly white on one side while remaining dark on the other. Tildy wondered if it was a deliberate fashion statement to make her resemble Cruella de Vil. But fashion was never in fashion at the agency.

'There's going to be trouble getting to Putin,' the agency woman said. The CIA hit squad had arrived in Moscow, finding the place a total mess. 'Conspiracy theories competing with actual conspiracies, coupled with disinformation to provide cover for Putin's cyberattack on us. The level of paranoia is out of control.' Putin's schedule was rarely posted, so he was hard to track down. The kill team was provided with Novichok, the toxin developed by Russian chemists that had become the favored means of assassination by security services. The Americans got a sample of the toxin from German intelligence and manipulated it to make sure it was impervious to possible antidotes. Tildy thought it entirely suitable that Putin be given a dose of his own medicine.

Defense and State joined the meeting later. They had not been read into the assassination plan, although they would not likely object. The new president had been diligently eliminating the soft-on-Russia leftovers. Everyone knew the program now. Russian troops were massed on the border of Ukraine. No one understood Putin's game better than Tildy: his goal since the dissolution of the Soviet Union had been to restore the empire. 'The gambit in Iran was a misdirection play,' she said.

State concurred. 'Now that we're overcommitted in the Persian Gulf, his path to recapturing eastern Europe has been made easier.' The question was how to respond.

'An unfortunate accident has taken place in a plant in Kursk,' Defense said, admitting nothing, but allowing the ironic tone in his voice to convey the message. There were eleven older Russian nuclear reactors of the RBMK-1000 type, the same as the one in Chernobyl that suffered the cata-strophic meltdown in 1986. Although the reactor was shut down within thirty-six hours, Defense reported, 'a cloud of radioactive gas is drifting indolently northward toward Mos-cow. The capital is in a frenzy.' Similar plants near population centers were compromised throughout the country. The ter-ror caused by radiation fallout was more advantageous than using actual bombs. It was a way of making Russia nuke itself. Even better, much of the world was blaming Moscow for its failure, once again, to safely contain its nuclear materi-als. Tildy thought the whole operation was handsomely done.

But it's never just one thing.

That afternoon, Lieutenant Commander Bartlett arrived for her daily briefing. 'Good news, I expect,' Tildy said dryly.

'The influenza season peaked in early July, and reported cases have dropped to their lowest point since early spring,' Bartlett said.

'Well, that actually *is* good news.'

'Yes, ma'am. And we are in trials with three different vac-cines. We hope to have one of them ready and in production before the virus returns this fall.'

'You keep saying that. Why must it return?'

'That's what influenza does. We don't know why exactly. So far, this pandemic has resembled the pattern of the 1918 Spanish flu, and if that continues, we predict the second wave to be much worse than the first. It's now been seeded everywhere on earth. You can expect it by October.'

Two months away.

'Will it be the same flu?'

'Or some variant. That's what worries us in the vaccine

372

department. We're trying to anticipate how the virus may change, but it's only educated guesswork. We've sequenced the virus thousands of times, but there's no guarantee it will be the same virus when the vaccine is ready. Some years the formula we develop for seasonal flu is totally ineffective.'

'What about this Russian vaccine?'

'It's for seasonal flu, not for Kongoli.'

'But I keep hearing that it has some magic ingredient.'

'Polyoxidonium.'

'If you say so.'

'As far as we can tell, it induces interferon production, which should cause significant side effects. We've been unable to validate its efficacy. We don't know why the incidence of Kongoli is lower in Russia than in neighboring countries. It could be accounted for by ordinary variance in the virus.'

'What date will you actually have a real vaccine for Kongoli?' Tildy asked.

'If we do develop an effective vaccine, it won't be in full production until mid-October.'

Tildy had always avoided hating the messenger for bringing hateful news, but Lieutenant Commander Bartlett tested her patience. Tildy had to keep her priorities straight. The idea that the Kongoli influenza would return in a couple months, in an even more virulent form, was nothing more than a theory – a worst-case scenario aired by people who thought of nothing else. Whereas this new kind of war with Russia was happening now and had to be dealt with.

Bartlett seemed to be reading her mind. 'You still don't understand, do you?' she asked.

Tildy bridled at the impertinence. 'Understand what?

That we're possibly, in theory, facing another round of disease? We lived through it, most of us. We'll march on. We always have.'

'I'm not talking about a setback,' said Bartlett. 'If you paid any attention to the role of disease in human affairs, you'd know the danger we're in. We got smug after all the victories over infection in the twentieth century. But nature is not a stable force. It evolves, it changes, and it never becomes complacent. We don't have the time or resources now to do anything other than fight this disease. Every nation on earth has to be involved, whether you think of them as friends or enemies. If we're going to save civilization, we have to fight together and not against each other.'

Tildy let her talk. Just let her unburden herself so she could say that she had done what she could. People saw the world through their own narrow lenses, whereas Tildy had to see it whole. Another pandemic, perhaps even worse than this one, was appalling to consider, but there were bigger things – war – on the table.

After the meeting, Tildy went back to the Oval Office for a private talk with the president. As soon as she walked into the office, she noticed that he too had done some redecorating: a Bible on the desk, family photos on the credenza, a portrait of Abraham Lincoln, and a bust of Churchill.

'Wartime leaders,' the president explained. 'I never wanted to be one of them. But I find that they are in my mind constantly now.'

45

Driving Lesson

JILL'S CAR WAS IN THE GARAGE, A 2009 TOYOTA CAMRY WITH less than half a tank of gas. Thieves had not yet siphoned it dry. Helen didn't know how far she could go on that, but she figured she could get close to Aunt Maggie's. She had the $34.27. Teddy still had his gun.

Knowing that they would never return to their house, the children packed two suitcases each, filled with clothes and toys and schoolbooks. Helen also took Jill's jewel case and a watch of Henry's that she would give Teddy one day. She hid the items in the well where the spare tire was stored. There was so much they left behind, but in the rush to leave it was impossible to think clearly.

'Maybe we should bring our bikes,' Teddy said.

'I don't think we have room.'

Helen climbed into the driver's seat. She had only ever done that once, when she sat in Henry's lap and pretended to drive. She was five years old then and the pedals were far away. Now they were too close for her long legs. Helen realized that she didn't even know how to move the seat. She pushed a likely button on the door, but a window lowered.

Teddy found the owner's manual in the glove compartment and figured out where the seat controls were.

'You gotta adjust the mirrors,' Teddy advised her.

'I know that. Put on your seatbelt.'

But finding the controls for the side-view mirrors was too frustrating, so she just turned the rear-view mirror to the point that she could see the long driveway stretching out behind her for miles.

There were only two things she had to do: learn to drive, and find their way to Aunt Maggie's.

'You do the navigation,' she told Teddy.

'That's easy,' he said. 'I-75 north.'

'Which way is that?'

'Just head toward downtown and we'll see it.'

Helen turned the key in the ignition, but nothing happened. She looked more closely and saw where it said start. She turned the key farther and held it until it made a horrible screaming noise. As soon as she took her hands off the key the noise stopped, but her confidence was shaken. She took a deep breath and tried to put the car into reverse, but the shift lever simply wouldn't move no matter how hard she pulled it. Meanwhile, the car was running, wasting gas.

She turned the car off while Teddy read the manual. Maybe the Toyota was broken. Mrs Hernández had her little Ford in the garage as well, but that would require going back to her room and finding her keys, and Helen would never go back there. Her whole plan depended on escaping the house and getting to Aunt Maggie's, and now she couldn't even put the car in gear to get out of the garage. Her face burned with frustration.

'You're supposed to push the brake at the same time,' Teddy announced.

'Well, that's stupid.'

She turned the car back on and pushed the brake. She also pushed the accelerator just a little. When she put the car into gear it leapt out of the garage like a wild animal. Helen pressed the brake harder, but she also pressed the accelerator.

'Brake! Brake!' Teddy shouted.

'I am braking!'

She finally took her foot off the gas, but by then she had crashed into the brick wall of the raised flowerbed along the driveway.

Helen's hands were trembling when she got out to assess the damage. There had never been a single scratch on Jill's car, ever. Helen had always been impatient with her mother's driving, so careful and needlessly slow. Now look what I've done, she thought. It was an awful scrape and there was big dent and the taillight was busted. The car was wedged at an odd angle in the drive. Helen looked at the rest of the driveway and saw how terribly far it was to the street. She would have to pass through the porte cochere where Jill always parked when it was raining, but now it loomed like a guardhouse gate she would have to squeeze through.

'Let me drive,' Teddy said.

'Are you kidding? You can't even see over the steering wheel. And I need you to navigate, remember?'

Helen got back in the car. The tires squealed as she turned the steering wheel, and then she put the car into drive. She put her foot ever so slightly on the gas and almost immediately braked again. She repeated that action several times, lurching and stopping, lurching and stopping, and for the first time she thought maybe it wasn't so hard. Finally she got the car straight and back in the garage.

Now she had to try reversing again.

She must have watched Jill do this a zillion times, but she couldn't remember how her mother did it. Did she turn around? Look in one of the mirrors? 'Teddy, you get out and direct me,' she said.

'Okay, but don't run over me.'

'Don't be stupid.'

Teddy stood between the Toyota and Henry's workbench. There was no room for error. Teddy looked directly in Helen's eyes, then held up his hands as if he were holding a steering wheel.

There had never been such an intimate moment between them as this.

Helen put the Toyota in reverse. It started moving as soon as she let up on the brake. She looked down at the pedals to make sure her feet were in the right place and somehow the car got a little crooked again. When she looked up, Teddy was shaking his head and turning his hands, and Helen turned the wheel in response. Then he turned his hands back and she did the same, braking and releasing and moving ever so slowly and never taking her eyes off Teddy. A shadow came over the car and she realized that she was all the way under the porte cochere, but she couldn't allow herself to think about that. Teddy was guiding her. And then he suddenly held his hands up and she stopped because she was at the end of the driveway.

Teddy got back in the Toyota. They stared for a long while at the house they had grown up in, which once had contained such wonderful memories. Now it was full of death and they would never, never return to it. 'Okay,' said Helen, and she backed into the street, then headed toward Nashville.

46

Schubert

HENRY AWAKENED TO THE SOUND OF A SAXOPHONE. MURPHY was standing over him. 'Well, hello,' she said. 'Sir.'

Henry responded, but his voice was cracked and dry. He felt woozy, not sure if he was dizzy or the sub was swaying. Murphy held out a spoon with something that smelled wonderful. 'Chicken soup,' she said. 'Still number one.'

'I'm a vegetarian,' he said.

'I know, but at the moment you're also my patient, so eat.'

There was no bargaining. Henry quietly thanked the chicken for its sacrifice. He felt like a child as he let Murphy feed him.

'I didn't bleed, did I?' he asked.

'No, sir.'

Henry let this sink in. 'We should begin infecting the crew,' he said.

'I've already done that, sir. I hope that's okay.'

'Thank goodness for you, Murphy.'

'We lost two more men, and we came real close with you, sir, if you don't mind my saying so. There are some pretty sick folks and your name has been invoked more than once, and not so favorably. But we've only got seven sick enough to be in the canteen, and I'll bet they're mostly out in a few days.'

'Where are we?' Henry asked.

'Thirty-four degrees seventeen minutes north, forty-five degrees fourteen minutes west,' she said. 'Dead center Atlantic Ocean, sir.'

'How deep are we?'

'We're on the surface. You feel strong enough to get some air?'

The idea of actually going outside was so tantalizing it seemed like a fantasy. 'If I could just take a shower first?'

'You'd have to be able to stand on your own.'

Murphy helped Henry sit up and then gave him a boost to standing. He wobbled. 'Are you sure?' Murphy asked.

'It's a matter of some urgency.'

Murphy handed him a towel and helped him down the hallway. The Dolly Parton sign was on the shower door. They both laughed. 'Let me just check,' Murphy said. She returned in a moment. 'Coast is clear,' she said, turning the sign to John Wayne.

So many questions he hadn't thought to ask. How long had he been out of it? Bits of memory floated into his mind. Were they real or imagined? He had no sense of time at all. As he thought about these things he let the steaming water cleanse him. Submariners are taught to be frugal about water usage, but Henry indulged himself in the luxury of the hot suds on his skin and in his hair and beard. He could feel the sickness washing away. But the weakness remained.

After he toweled off, he noticed his pallid reflection in the mirror, gaunt and old. His beard was the color of tarnished silver. He accepted the evidence in the mirror that his

381

lingering youthfulness was behind him. But he was alive, and a feeling that he had not known for such a long time spread through him like an infusion. It was joy.

'Are you all right in there?' Murphy asked.

'I'm fine!' Henry said. He wrapped the towel around his waist and hobbled into the hallway. Murphy took his bare arm and guided him back to his berth. She had changed his sheets and put out fresh clothes for him. He had to brush back a tear. He was not strong enough to withstand the emotional assaults of human kindness.

When he was dressed and groomed he joined Murphy on the missile deck. The breeze greeted him with a warm embrace, and the sun nearly blinded him. He looked through slit eyes. There were dozens of submariners jumping into the ocean, whooping and laughing in the delicious air. Henry had not heard such exuberant sounds for weeks.

'We call it "steel beach,"' Murphy said.

Henry lay on the rubberized tiles on the missile deck with submariners who were drying off from their plunge in the Atlantic. Murphy indicated an officer standing on the conning tower holding an automatic weapon. 'For the sharks,' she said casually.

'Did I hear a saxophone or was that a fever dream of mine?' Henry asked.

'Yes, sir, that was the captain. He's recovering very well.'

His experiment had worked. He immediately began thinking of how it might be scaled up, but he had to consider the potential liabilities of giving an entire country – or maybe the whole world – an injection of the deadliest strain of influenza ever known, however attenuated it might be. Thousands could die to save millions. Millions could die to save billions. Who could allow such a gamble? On the other hand, if it was attenuated to an extreme and shown to still provide protection, it might serve as a stopgap until a better vaccine emerged from the trials. Henry stared out at the ocean, its vastness imposing a sense of eternity and calm.

'Some ships,' he said casually, pointing east. 'Way over there.'

'Yes, sir. They've been tailing us since Suez.'

'Tailing us? Why would they do that?'

'So, doctor, you've come back to life!' The booming voice belonged to Captain Dixon. He loomed over Henry and Murphy, brimming with health, his giant shadow encompassing both of them.

'You as well, I see,' Henry croaked. 'Sorry, my voice is still weak.'

'If you're feeling up to it, maybe you could join my table at seventeen hundred.'

Henry dozed awhile in the sun. He had a marvelous dream. Jill was in it. The kids were really young. They were going on vacation somewhere. Mountains. Maybe his grandmother appeared, he wasn't sure, in any case there was some other benign presence. His parents were there, and his mother spoke to him. She was wearing the sombrero that shadowed her face. She said, 'Beautiful'. He didn't know what she meant by that. His father called him by name. In the dream, Henry felt very small and other times he was not. It was an imaginary world where dead people were alive. He woke up when he felt a burn coming on.

The vision of his lost family drained his emotions. He knew that mood swings were a sign of recovery, but still he wondered how to contain the extremes – his grief at the loss of the people he loved, his exhilaration at saving the lives of the submariners. So many emotions were colliding inside him, leaving him confused and morose.

Glorious sounds washed over him as he entered the ward-room and saw an actual string quartet. Young McAllister was among them, playing viola.

'Mind a little music?' Dixon asked. 'Helps the digestion, I believe.'

'It's Schubert!' Henry exclaimed.

'I figured you for a man of some refinement,' said Dixon. 'Jazz is more my thing. Ellington. Monk. Miles Davis, when Herbie was on the keys and Wayne Shorter on sax. That's my man, Wayne.'

'Yes, I heard you. You could say your music brought me back to life.'

'That's a really nice thought.' Dixon indicated the quartet. 'Took me years to assemble this group. I'm still on the look-out for a clarinetist. There's some Benny Goodman tunes I'd love to play.'

Henry laughed. 'I played clarinet in high school. "Moon-glow". "Body and Soul".'

'Oh, man!' Dixon said, looking genuinely pained. 'Why didn't you join the Navy? Maybe not too late!'

'I think I've still got it stuck in a closet somewhere,' Henry said.

They both grew contemplative as the mood that Schubert cast took hold – deep, melancholy, profound. 'I guess you're not up on the news,' Dixon said.

'Hardly.'

'Picture we get is pretty bad. Government broken. Mobs

in the street. This is America we're talking about, can you believe it? Land of opportunity.' He paused a moment as he chewed a piece of T-bone. 'Who did this to us, Henry? You don't believe it's just chance, do you?'

'It could be,' Henry said cautiously.

'Way I see it, it's a part of a pattern. I can't tell you what I've been picking up in our communications – not everything, anyway – but there's a very strong indication that there's a foreign hand in all this.'

'You mean Russia?'

'They've been poking holes in our society. Attacking our infrastructure. So, yes, Russia. But they're not alone. We've been under attack for years. Iran. China. North Korea. And, yeah, a lot of it is our fault, picking fights we didn't need to get in. Now they're ganging up. They sense the weakness. Like a wolf pack. It's all coming to a head.' Dixon went quiet again, leaving the implications hanging in the air. Then he said, 'You're welcome to stay aboard for as long as you like. It's a dangerous world out there.'

'I've got to find my family,' Henry said. 'See if they're still alive.'

'Of course you do. I don't know why I said that.' Dixon seemed embarrassed by the personal appeal implied by his invitation. 'In any case, we gotta stop in Kings Bay to fix the damn piston,' he said in his usual gruff manner. 'Speaking of which, those three ships you may have seen? Russian. They picked up our piston clatter in Suez and have been bird-dogging us ever since. I decided to surface to ascertain their intention. Pretty clear now. They're just hovering. Gonna encircle us and move in. They've been waiting, and now they know they've got a wounded duck. I bet they wouldn't mind getting hold of our nuclear fuel rods, either. Most valuable substance in the world, now that oil's done. Travel forever . . . Dig in, you haven't touched your chow. If you want one last breath of fresh air, hike up top after your meal. We'll be taking her down shortly.'

47

The Party Begins

BONG! BONG!

Henry jerked awake. The noise seemed to be banging on the inside of his skull. Then came the voice: *'Battle stations! Battle stations! Now man your battle stations!'* He dressed hurriedly, but realized he didn't know where his battle station was, or even if he had one.

He waited until the rushing about had subsided – the last thing he needed was to be run over by a well-fed six-footer and become a liability himself – and then he ventured down the hall and into the submarine control room, uncertain whether he should be present. He spotted Dixon with other officers. Henry stood attentively and, he hoped, inconspicuously in the back of the room.

'I've got two additional targets, Sierra Four bearing 270, range 60,000 yards, Sierra Five bearing 185 at 75,000 yards,' the sonar operator said.

'So that's what they've been waiting for,' Dixon said. 'The party's about to start.'

The crew was frozen at their posts. No one took the time to explain what was happening, nor would Henry dare to ask, but the extreme peril was like a suffocating odor suffusing the command center. The only noise was the beeping of the sonar as the dial swept past the Russian warships maneuvering into their search formation. An hour passed. Despite the tension, Henry's stomach growled.

'Sir! Torpedo in the water!'

'Change course! Thirty degrees north!' Dixon said.

'Thirty degrees north! Aye!'

'Ahead flank speed.'

There was a swiftly moving blip headed exactly toward the center of the dial, pinging as it homed in on the submarine. The pinging became louder and more rapid, like Henry's heartbeat as he watched death approaching. Then the pinging slowed and the blip paused.

'Sir, correction, it's a UUV,' the sonar operator reported, meaning an underwater drone.

'They want to get a read on us,' Dixon said. He turned to his navigator. 'Open torpedo tubes one and two. Let's be ready.'

'Aye, sir, torpedo tubes one and two open.'

'Dive officer, bring us to periscope depth.'

As soon as the sub reached a depth of sixty-eight feet, Dixon sent an urgent message via the UHF mast to Submarine Force Atlantic headquarters in Norfolk, Virginia: *Georgia* is at Defense Condition Two, one step below war. He quickly scanned the horizon through the periscope. Radar picked up a Russian antisubmarine helicopter, probably dropping motion sensors in the water. Was this a game? The Russians were always challenging American ships and planes, then backing off at the last possible second. But everything the convoy had done indicated that they were prepared for war.

There had to be some response to the American bombing

388

of the Russian warplanes in Iran and the blockade of their Pacific Fleet. Perhaps the Russian planners calculated that a single American submarine was a proportionate response. Or maybe the larger war had already begun.

There were five ships in the Russian convoy. The *Georgia* carried fourteen torpedoes, but could only fire four at a time; no doubt that was why the Russian commander was waiting for reinforcements. Dixon's best chance was to put as much distance as possible between his submarine and the Russians. The surface was turbulent, which could complicate the Russian attempts to track the *Georgia*'s acoustic signal, but the damaged piston made silent evasion almost impossible.

'Open main ballast vents,' Dixon told the dive officer.

Immediately came the blasting *OOGA OOGA!* The sudden clamor was jarring. *'Dive! Dive Dive!'* was the command.

'Diving officer, make the depth eight hundred feet.'

'Eight hundred feet, aye.'

Henry grabbed a handhold as the submarine lurched nose-downward. Seawater noisily filled the ballast tanks. His ears popped. Everyone leaned backward at a steep slant, as if they were being blown to the ground by a hurricane wind.

Down, down, they went.

'Give us a report on eddies and currents. We'd like to find a thermocline to hide behind,' the captain said to the navigation officer. Dixon figured that by now F-18s from the American carrier group in the Mediterranean were in the air. If he could escape the drone and come to a dead stop in the deep, he might have a chance. Otherwise, the *Georgia* was doomed.

'Sir, the Russians are closing to weapons distance, forty thousand yards,' the sonar operator said. The ships were moving slowly in order to keep track of the submarine. The faster they traveled, the less they would be able to hear over their own engine noise. That was why they had planted a drone on the *Georgia*'s tail. Dixon ordered his executive officer to generate target solutions for the Russian ships.

'Launch countermeasures,' Dixon ordered.

The evasion devices – noisemakers and bubbles – were meant to throw off the drone, but it wasn't fooled. Russian technology had gotten so much better in the last few years. Torpedo tubes three and four were opened.

'Sir, the UUV is surfacing,' the sonar operator reported.

The drone was rising to communications range to report the GPS coordinates of the *Georgia*. Whatever the intention of the Russian commander, it would be made clear momentarily. The Russian officer certainly knew what Dixon was up to, racing to deep water to hide behind a thermal gradient. They were both running out of time.

'Sir, we have firing solutions,' the executive officer reported.

Captain Dixon had a momentary advantage. As soon as the drone broadcast his location, the Russians could launch their torpedoes. It would be an onslaught. On the other hand, Dixon could fire first. A surface ship had no chance against *Georgia*'s Mark 48 torpedoes. They were wire-guided and had their own sensors as well. They were almost undetectable until they blew up the keel of the ship they were programmed to attack. But he wouldn't be able to destroy all five ships at once.

A loud clatter suddenly came on the sonar. The screen clouded over with particles like champagne bubbles.

'Sir, something strange!' the sonar operator said.

'Source?' Dixon asked.

'It's all over the place, sir!'

'Frequency?'

'Two hundred decibels, sir!' It was slightly louder than a gunshot; on the sonar it sounded like bacon grease popping in the pan. The noise created an acoustic fog that would confound the *Georgia*'s torpedo targeting. Of course, it would also do the same for the Russians.

Dixon suddenly began to laugh. Everyone on the sub came to the same realization at once – everyone except Henry, who had no idea what was going on. 'Make 270 west, flank speed,' Dixon ordered. Then he noticed Henry's puzzled expression. 'Shrimp, Henry!' he said. 'We've been rescued by the snapping shrimp.'

Later, Dixon ordered a ration of beer for the crew, which he stored for extraordinary occasions. Henry heard them singing:

> *Submarines once!*
> *Submarines twice!*
> *Holy jumping Jesus Christ!*
> *We go up*
> *We go down*
> *We don't even fuck around!*
> *Oooga! Oooga!*

In the wardroom, Dixon brought out a bottle of Gunpowder Irish Gin and mixed up martinis for the officers. Henry had never seen this crew so merry. The relief on their faces made even clearer to him how much danger they had been in.

'I still don't understand what happened,' Henry said. 'Shrimp made all that noise?'

'The snapping shrimp, such an amazing creature,' said Dixon. 'We think humanity has the best weapons, but the snapping shrimp has a claw that closes so fast it creates a shock wave that kills its prey. The noise you hear is the air bubble popping when the claw snaps. They create a microburst of heat that is about the temperature of the sun. And they sure light up the sonar. We were looking for an acoustic pocket to hide in, and along comes a heavy metal band!'

The officers began to sing the submarine song, which became even more inventively profane. Soon they would be home.

IV
October

48

Dolphins

WHEN THE COMMANDER OF THE KINGS BAY SUBMARINE BASE learned of Henry's part in saving the *Georgia*'s crew he swore that, by God, he was going to nominate him for the Navy Medal of Honor, the highest accolade the Navy awards, although Henry was rather certain he wouldn't qualify. 'There's only one request I have,' he told the admiral. 'I must return to Atlanta as quickly as possible.'

'There's damn little transport, I'm afraid,' the admiral responded. He was one of those savvy country boys that Henry had once distrusted but had come to admire for their solidity. 'Roads aren't safe. Even for us. We travel in convoys when we go out. We're all pretty much confined to base, under the current threat level. Goddamn,' the admiral said ruminatively. 'I'll tell you what. They got a naval air station in Marietta, right outside Atlanta. I'm gonna have 'em fly down here and pick you up. I'll come up with some fabulous excuse. This is strictly out of bounds in every respect. Meantime, come to dinner tonight at the Dolphin House, soon as you get cleaned up.'

The cleaning up was an order. Submariners stank when they came ashore. Solid waste on the boat was compacted before it was discharged into the ocean, to prevent any bubbles from giving away the location of the vessel, but the gas stayed on the boat. It was partially neutralized by a disinfectant that had its own powerful imprint. Eventually the boat came to smell like a giant perfumed fart, but so gradually the crew didn't notice. But their spouses certainly did when they greeted them, pale and stinking like rotting fish.

Henry was dropped off at the Navy Lodge just outside the gates of the base. It was a modest cinder-block government building set in a forest of pines and run by a delightful woman named Theresa who immediately directed him to the washing machines. Outside of the military, nearly everything electrical was shut down, but the Navy Lodge was on a generator for four hours a day.

He felt the strangeness of being back on land mainly in his vision. For weeks there was nothing in the range of his sight that wasn't a few feet away. But when the van picked him up to take him to the admiral's quarters, Henry had a hard time focusing. Everything was so far apart. It was disorienting and headache inducing to look down the endless highway. The sky that he had longed to see again was forbiddingly bright and distant. He found himself staring at the dashboard.

Dolphin House – the admiral's quarters – was a redbrick home banked by azaleas in a palm-lined cul-de-sac. Henry was a little abashed that all the other officers were wearing their dress whites, while the best he had to offer were the blue overalls that Murphy had tailored for him. Liquor was served in abundance, and the room was soon full of laughter, but as much as Henry enjoyed the company of the officers, he was conscious of being outside their circle. This was a community of men who had pledged their entire careers to military service, as he had done in the name of a different calling. Their fraternity made him all the more eager to return to his own life, to his lab and his colleagues, and most of all to his family, if he still had one.

He knew he was racing against the clock. October was coming, and it would bring another round of Kongoli. Henry understood the disease better now, but he had been working at a terrible disadvantage away from his lab. He didn't know what Marco and other researchers around the world might have discovered while he was under the sea for six weeks.

The admiral did have a final surprise for Henry. 'We only give this to submariners who have earned their stripes,' he said, as he pinned the insignia of the submarine corps on Henry's overalls: a pair of dolphins. 'You're a true bubble-head now, sir,' the admiral said. Then everyone saluted him.

Afterward, Henry went for a stroll around the base with Captain Dixon. It was a beautiful night, moonlit, warm and swampy but clear. Lightning bugs danced around the path in front of them, leading the way to a dark pond. The only sound was the hum of generators providing energy for the base. Henry had a little trouble walking. It had been so much easier on the sub, with the narrow hallways and handholds everywhere. At times he had to take the captain's arm.

'It's hard, sometimes, getting your land legs back,' said Dixon.

'I never really had good legs to start with. Not like you!'

'Yeah, well, I was blessed, blessed, indeed. Watch out for the alligator.'

Henry thought Dixon was joking, but then he noticed an

397

alligator on the edge of the pond. It seemed to be dozing, so the men walked on.

'Looks like my retirement party has been postponed,' Dixon confided. 'The officer ranks have been so thinned out that they want me to stick around for another deployment. So I'll be stuck in Kings Bay while we refit.'

'It's beautiful here,' Henry said.

'Mmm.'

Something was tugging at the captain, but he was having trouble giving voice to it. Henry waited; Vernon Dixon was not a man who could be prodded. Finally, he said, 'I want to show you something.' They walked around the pond to a display of missiles of various sizes. 'Standing before you is the history of the submarine ballistic missile program.' The captain pointed to a short missile with stubby wings. 'This one is the TLAM – the Tomahawk Land Attack Missile, or cruise missile, which is what we've got aboard the *Georgia*. I know it looks pretty tame, but it's been decisive in projecting American power in the conflicts we've been engaged in since the first Gulf War. Our Tomahawks are conventional, but we have the option of deploying a nuclear-tipped version. These others' – he gestured to the larger missiles behind the Tomahawk – 'are all ICBMs carrying thermonuclear devices.' Three white missiles comprised the first generations of the Polaris. 'That first one came into service in 1956. Think about that. More than half a century ago, before I was even born.' Then there was the Poseidon, somewhat larger, squat, ringed with copper-colored bands, which Dixon described as the first submarine-launched missile with multiple warheads. 'Still before my enlistment, though. I came in with these babies, the Tridents.' The newest and largest was the Trident D5, brick red and more than four stories tall, overshadowing its predecessors. It was amazing to think it could even fit on a submarine. 'I served on the *Tennessee* when we had a full rack of twenty-four Tridents,' Dixon said. 'Each of them with eight warheads, a total destructive power equaling more than eleven thousand kilotons. Compare that to Hiroshima, just fifteen kilotons. Multiply that one boat times a fleet of fourteen boomers, and you get more than 150,000 Hiroshimas! Can you imagine? Our boomers are the most powerful war-fighting machine ever created. They don't even have to sail out of port to hit most any target of interest. But the same is true for our adversaries. This place will be the first to go when the shit starts flying.' Dixon stopped and stared at the sky. When he spoke again it was in a low, uncertain voice. 'Thing is, and I can't be totally candid about this, there may come a time very soon when being underwater is the only safe place on the planet.'

'We're that close?' Henry asked.

'If it happens, a lot of us think there won't be much point in going home,' Dixon said, letting the implications speak for him. Dixon was offering to save Henry's life. 'Let's just say some people thought about exploring,' Dixon continued, almost apologetically. 'Looking for a safe harbor. They point out we've got provisions for a year, considering reductions in the crew. We've got chow, warm bunks, plus a full complement of Tomahawks saying "Keep your hands to yourself". But here's the thing. We need a doctor on board. I do, anyway.'

'That's certainly true.'

'People might misunderstand what I'm suggesting,' Dixon said, so softly Henry could scarcely hear him. 'They take

mutiny pretty seriously in this outfit. If you have to say anything to anybody, it's all idle chatter. That's what it is. Idle
chatter.'

'I would never say anything to anybody. I swear.'

'We'll be laid up here for a couple weeks. Supposing you
don't find what you're after. We could always use a clarinet
player.'

Murphy had a berth in the base hospital. 'They're shorthanded, and I thought I'd help them out,' she explained,
when Henry came to bid farewell. 'You're going back to
Atlanta?' she asked.

'Tomorrow.'

'So I won't see you again?'

'We don't know what life has in store for us. Didn't they
teach you that in Wisconsin?'

'Minnesooota.'

Murphy stuck out her hand to say goodbye, but Henry
held on to it. Her thumb rubbed across his knuckles. 'I hope
they're waiting for you when you get there,' she said. 'I hope
there's a big welcome home, and everybody's safe and happy.'

Henry kissed her hand, the most natural thing in the
world.

When he returned to the Navy Lodge, he fell into bed, his
emotions still all jumbled. He really was finally going home.
What would he find there? He dreaded learning the truth,
but he couldn't stand not knowing. He was safe but in danger. Overjoyed but apprehensive. And surprised when there
was a knock on the door and it was dawn and he had been
deep asleep. There stood Vernon Dixon.

'They got a car to take you to the airfield,' Dixon said,

looking a little scandalized that Henry wasn't dressed and ready at this hour.

'Can I brush my teeth?'

Henry hurried through his ablutions, still in a state of disbelief. That a car was waiting. That he was going to fly to Atlanta. Home.

As Henry was about to get into the car, Dixon handed him a business card. 'If the internet ever comes back on or the cell phones work again, you'll have my contacts.'

In exchange, Henry found a waterlogged card in his wallet. He wrote a number on the back. 'This is Jill's mobile number, just in case.' His own cell phone had drowned in his plunge into the Persian Gulf.

'Oh, here's something else,' said Dixon. 'I saw you had a little trouble getting around last night.'

Dixon handed him a beautifully wrought cane.

Henry was speechless. 'Where . . .?' he sputtered, unable to finish.

'Guys in the shop here can make anything. It's a Georgia hickory stick. Makes a good billy club if you ever have need of it. Might even work as a putter.'

The handle was a bronze submarine.

49

The Graves

A SINGLE-ENGINE PROPELLER-DRIVEN BEECHCRAFT, A TWO-seater, about as powerful as a lawnmower, taxied onto the runway. Henry sat in the rear, in the trainee's seat, staring at his reflection on the back of the pilot's helmet. The pilot didn't say much except to remark, 'You must be pretty important.'

'Not at all,' Henry replied.

The little plane slowly gained speed, then hopped into the air. The bubble canopy was clear glass, so the Georgia landscape unfolded below, vast and green. There was no traffic on the roads, and the fields were fallow. Henry thought this is how Georgia must have looked when the Creek Indians lived there.

Was that long-ago past now the future? Henry was flying in a plane, itself a near antique, that was taking him backward in time. He had read enough history to know that civilization moves unevenly through millennia of progress only to undergo cycles of great destruction. He had always been intrigued by the collapse of great civilizations. A team of scientists from the Max Planck Society had uncovered the pathogen thought responsible for killing 80 percent of the native population of Mexico in the mid-sixteenth century – a form of salmonella, probably brought by the conquistadors, that destroyed the Aztec empire. With Jill, Henry had toured the ruins of Luxor and Mycenae, and spent days exploring the glorious Alhambra in Spain. Great civilizations, now dead. Twice they had visited Pompeii, an entire city that had been entombed in an instant. If there was a lesson in these ruins, Henry thought, it was that civilizations were built on the arrogance of progress. We believe that nature is no match for human ingenuity and that nature can be tamed. Pompeii reminds us that the incomparable ferocity of nature will never be fully tamed.

So Henry shouldn't have been surprised by what he saw unfolding below him – nature already reclaiming the marks of civilization on the land. Although the contagion had subsided, it had left behind a society that was broken and distrustful and flooded by despair. Kudzu was enveloping abandoned farmhouses and roadside gas stations. The slow and perhaps inexorable process of consuming human history was under way.

And yet there remained scattered signs of life. Smoke rose from brushfires where some determined farmer was clearing land. A few cars were visible when the plane flew over the interstate highway and banked toward Atlanta. The great city itself looked unmarred but also vacant, despite the spider web of highways feeding into it. Defenseless, Henry thought. Another round of Kongoli could render Atlanta extinct.

At least the military was still operating. The admiral had been thoughtful enough to issue Henry a week's worth of provisions in a backpack – mainly crackers, peanut butter, fruit, nuts, and cereal, out of consideration for Henry's vegetarian diet, although he included several packages of buffalo jerky in case of desperation. He also provided fresh underwear, socks, and T-shirts. Henry still had his wallet with about a hundred Saudi riyals, along with a MasterCard and a debit card of uncertain usefulness. Aside from that, Henry had his Qur'an and his new cane.

The little plane dropped like a mosquito onto the runway, then taxied past a fleet of giant C-130 transport planes, coming to a halt on an apron of pavement beside a giant hangar.

'Where do you go from here?' the pilot asked.

'Atlanta.'

'Well, good luck, sir.'

'Wait,' said Henry, 'how do I get to Atlanta?'

'It's a pretty long hike, I'd say. Tell you what,' the pilot said, pointing east, 'if you walk a couple miles in that direction, you'll come to the interstate. From there, it's about twenty miles to the city. Folks are pretty cautious, and there's not a lot of traffic, but you may luck out and catch a ride. You don't look all that threatening.'

It took Henry an hour under the swampy September sun just to get to the interstate cloverleaf. Fortunately, he had three bottles of water in the backpack, which weighed heavily on his shoulders. Sweat poured down his back and soaked his shirt. He stuck out his thumb whenever a car passed, but there were so few and they all went by as if they were fleeing justice.

Still, he was alive. He had never felt more intensely the privilege of existence than he did walking along the shoulder of the bright interstate. What a beautiful highway, Henry thought, a marvel, really, the mark of a once formidable civilization. What will people of the future think – if there are people of the future – when they come upon this magnificent road, buried perhaps under vines or layers of sediment.

He set the pack down and ate almonds in the shade of an overpass. There was a single flip-flop nearby and an empty bag of chips caught in a crevice that fluttered when cars drove past. He considered his conversation with Captain Dixon the night before. Doomsday. Could it really happen? Henry had vivid childhood memories of the Cold War and the threat of a nuclear exchange. It was always there but not really there, the possibility of universal extinction, a fantasy that he used to entertain sometimes at night when his grandmother put him to bed. How often he had fretted over what would happen to him if she too passed away. These sober thoughts were interrupted by a giant cloud of gnats that swarmed around him. He waved at them fecklessly, unable to breathe without inhaling them. He pulled the neck of his T-shirt over his nose and pressed on.

Another car zoomed by.

To avoid speculating about his family, Henry contemplated his return to his old lab at the CDC to learn what progress they had made on Kongoli. Marco and the team must have developed a vaccine by now. He longed to hear their thoughts, to be in the familiar and exciting confines of the lab, where the battle could be fairly joined. There was so little time.

He saw a big semi headed his direction, the first all day. Henry reached into his backpack and took out two packages of jerky, which he waved in the air. Like every other vehicle the truck sped up, but then the airbrakes squealed and the truck came to a halt fifty yards down the interstate. Henry negotiated a ride as far as downtown Atlanta for three packages of jerky – one of the few occasions that being a vegetarian turned out to be an economic advantage.

The driver was an older Hispanic man with a white goatee and a pronounced accent. He was listening to a scratchy radio show in Spanish. 'It's from Mexico,' the driver explained, pronouncing it *May-hee-ko*.

'What are they saying?'

The driver laughed. 'The Mexicans they say get out! Come to May-hee-ko, our brothers! The gringos are loco!'

'Any American stations?'

'Sometimes I hear WWL in New Orleans. I think they have electricity there. Not like here.'

The driver turned the dial, which was mostly empty, except for a station in Tallahassee, which was broadcasting Alex Jones. 'We've all been expecting this, haven't we?' Jones was saying. 'Big Brother has been looking for a way to exercise total control. It's a plot to eliminate Christians. Look at who lived through this plague. That's right, the Jewish mafia. Jews and the communists – a global, corporate combine. They tell you it's a disease, this Kongoli stuff. Don't buy it! It's a lie! They put chemicals in the water. They targeted good Christian Americans . . .'

The driver looked for other stations, but Alex Jones was the only voice in English.

The truck was carrying emergency radiation detection devices. The driver didn't know why they were needed. He let Henry off at the North Avenue exit.

The city was still gleaming and splendid, but pedestrians were scarce. The skyscrapers appeared to be vacant. Henry could see through their windows to the city behind. Despite the strangeness, he was struck by the splendor, the majestic architecture amid the natural beauty that Atlanta was built on. In the scope of the world, it was a mere bijou, a small brilliant monument of civilization. Behind the cityscape, the sun was sinking into a ravishing persimmon gloaming. The sunset made him think of the Thelonious Monk tune 'Crepuscule with Nellie'. Vernon Dixon must love that song. Maybe one day they would play it together, if there were more days. In the absence of traffic, the air was super pure and too rich. Henry felt like he was breathing straight oxygen.

By the time he crossed over the parkway leading to the Jimmy Carter Presidential Library, the moon was up, shaped like a cup into which Venus was about to drop – the star and crescent, symbol of Islam, still destroying itself in a pointless war. The night was dark and the sidewalk was uncertain, with fallen tree limbs occasionally blocking his path. Henry's eyes adjusted to the dim glow of starlight. He was close to home now. He cut through the park, passing the playground where he had taken Helen and Teddy when they were young and the community garden where Jill had always intended to get a plot. He was so close. His heart began to pound.

Then he heard the dogs.

At first he couldn't see them, hidden in the shadows of the trees, but suddenly there they were, a pack of eight or nine, not barking, but growling in a low, almost inaudible tone. One of the smaller dogs began yipping and dancing around in excitement, but the largest dog advanced slowly, head down, stalking. Henry held his cane up as a warning, which caused the alpha, a German shepherd, to hesitate. But there was another intelligence at work, the mind of the pack. The dogs spread out, flanking Henry on either side. Henry would have to take out the alpha with the first blow.

As the shepherd came within leaping distance, Henry slammed his cane on the ground and yelled, 'Sit!'

The dog immediately sat. Most of the other dogs followed his lead. They were abandoned pets that had not yet forgotten their training. Henry slowly bent down, avoiding eye contact and making sure that he appeared unthreatening. He picked up a stick and waved in front of the shepherd's nose. Then he tossed it into the trees. The dogs all rushed to retrieve it.

Henry started to hurry away, but the dogs returned too quickly, the stick in the shepherd's mouth, ready to play. Henry threw the stick again, and then again, hoping to wear them down, but the dogs were now in a kind of ecstasy. Perhaps they too were remembering another life. They wouldn't let him get away. Finally, he unwrapped the last package of jerky and threw it as far as he could. That began a brawl that allowed him to hurry on, crossing Linwood Avenue and arriving at his block on Ralph McGill Boulevard.

All the houses were dark, the windows black and full of secrets. He was frightened. He thought about calling out the names of his neighbors, but he could not. He didn't know why. The silence seemed too great to be broken.

He stood on the long brick veranda where his children had spent so many hours playing. There were marigolds blooming in the flower boxes. He peeked in a window into his study. Despite the dark, everything looked in order. He could make out his desk, the photo of his grandparents on the wall. On the arm of his chair was the novel he had been reading before he had gone to Geneva. It's not so bad, he thought. I've been scaring myself.

The glass was broken on his front door.

Henry went inside. There was more glass underfoot. He stood quietly, listening, hearing nothing but the drone of crickets, smelling nothing but death. No one is here, he was sure, but still he called out, 'Jill?' His voice cracked. 'Jill?'

He couldn't bring himself to say his children's names.

He walked through the living room and dining room to the breakfast nook, where he kept a flashlight in the utility drawer. It wasn't there. He now saw that there were pie pans and broken dishes on the floor of the kitchen. The pantry doors were open, and it was dark and bare inside. Henry remembered where the matches were and lit one. He spotted the candle on the window ledge behind the breakfast nook. Sometimes, when the kids were asleep, Jill would light the candle and they'd have a very domesticated romantic dinner together. He lit the candle.

Cupping the small cone of light, he moved through the hall to their bedroom. It was in disarray. Bloody sheets were pulled halfway off the empty bed, signifying something ominous. His clothes were still in the closet, but so were Jill's. Could there be a note, at least? If not a letter, some clue that would tell him where his family was. But why would they have believed that Henry was alive all this time? Why should they assume that one day he would return to save them?

Teddy's room was empty. Henry went through his drawers. No underwear or socks. His backpack was gone. Surely he's safe, Henry thought, he must be somewhere safe.

Teddy's robot was on the desk. I wish he could tell me where his master is, Henry thought.

In the candlelight Henry saw a man on the floor of Helen's room. Henry stopped cold, then crept closer until he could see the man was dead, lying facedown on a mattress in a pool of crusted blood, his pants partly off, with a knife in his back. Maggots crawled in and out of a head wound, which Henry determined had been caused by a gunshot. There was more glass on the floor: Helen's Miss Piggy bank. A robbery, Henry concluded. But nothing made sense. There was a coin under the dresser. A quarter.

Maybe they're upstairs, he thought.

When he opened the door to the stairwell, several cats darted out. Henry was so startled he just stood there catching his breath. There was cat shit all over the place, along with the smell of urine so sharp that it made his eyes water. He was not surprised by what he found.

He walked back downstairs through the kitchen onto the screen porch. In the dim moonlight, Henry saw the graves in the backyard.

He went to the garage to get his shovel. Jill's car was gone. Mrs Hernández's Ford Focus was still in its spot. Jill must have left. She'd fled with the children. Something had happened, an intruder was killed, so Jill had taken the children and sought safety. Maybe to her sister's.

But that didn't explain the graves.

Henry began to excavate the smaller of the two graves. It had been thoughtfully done, with stones and bricks on top to keep the animals out. He set the rocks aside and began digging, his heart pounding, not wanting to find what he had to find.

Something felt different. He dropped the shovel and dug with his hands, carefully, tenderly. He reached into the dirt, groping, finally touching the body. He brushed the dirt away. It was Peepers.

Henry knelt beside the dog's grave and wept, exhausted with sadness and shivering with relief. But the other grave waited for him. He covered Peepers and replaced the stones atop his grave and began to dig again.

It took hours to excavate. Who could have dug this, he wondered. Not a child. It must have been Jill. Her car was gone. She must be alive. But so much was unexplained. The dead man in Helen's room. The graves. He puzzled on these things as he dug. Bits of stone and a large root were piled into the hole. It had been chopped in two. Could Jill have managed that?

Somewhere in the middle of the night a chorus of frogs began croaking. His back strained from the effort, but he couldn't slow down; he couldn't allow himself to break the furious rhythm of motion, pressing the spade into the soil with his right foot and heaving it over his left shoulder, again and again without pause. And then he felt the outline of a hardened form beneath the soil. He brought the candle to the lip of the grave. Once again, he used his hands to dig. He could feel a body just inches below the dirt. As he was scooping, he felt something hard, something metal or plastic. He pushed the dirt away furiously. It was Teddy's football helmet.

A cry escaped his lips. Teddy was gone. Teddy, his miracle child.

Henry sat back against the wall of the grave. He had thought Teddy was safe. His clothes were gone. His backpack was gone. Helen was gone. Jill's car was gone.

He forced himself to brush the dirt away from the face inside the helmet. And there was Jill, her dead eyes staring at him.

What had happened here?

Jill was dead. Not Teddy. Henry was totally numb.

After he reburied his wife, Henry sat on the porch of the playhouse he had crafted for his children. He had placed the candle on top of Jill's grave. Awful things had happened to his family and he had not been here to take care of them. He tried to keep his grief at bay but it was banging relentlessly on the door of his consciousness. Jill was dead. She was wearing a helmet. Her car was gone. The children were gone. He would have to find them. Somehow. The pieces didn't fit together. But Jill was dead.

Drowning in shame and sorrow, reeling in confusion, he crawled into the playhouse and slept for hours.

50

The Cosmos Club

STREETS WERE DARK, TRAFFIC SIGNALS DIDN'T FUNCTION, BANKS had stopped making loans, grocery stores were practically bare, the internet was still down, D.C. was sweltering, but high-end hotels and restaurants found a way to reopen. The Mandarin Oriental, Trump International, the Palm, Cafe Milano – one by one, the oases of influence came back to life. The rich and powerful had a ledge of safety that couldn't be reached by ordinary people, such as reporters for *The Washington Post*.

Influenza had taken a toll on Tony Garcia. He had lost his sister and his wife, and he had nearly perished as well. He lived above a Wok and Roll in Adams Morgan, alone now except for a chihuahua, with no utilities, in the middle of another record-setting autumnal heat wave. Survivors were still recovering from the contagion. Some were physically broken; nearly everyone was crumpled by grief.

Cyberattacks had sabotaged the news business. A few television stations were getting back on the air, but newspapers were publishing only sporadically. The *Post*, thanks to its billionaire owner, fared better than others, but it also struggled to get answers from a government that had suddenly gone silent. Rumors and imagined conspiracies shoved real news aside. As a result the country was a cauldron of emotions – paranoia chief among them.

There was still no clear evidence that the cyberattacks originated in Moscow, although everybody knew that they had. The genius of the new kind of hybrid war that Russia was waging was not only in its deniability. There was also its near-magical ability to stir up insurrection – such as the Army of American Patriots, fomented by Russian bots and manifested in the actual recruitment of hundreds of armed American citizens subverting their own government, unaware that they were acting as a fifth column for the Russians. Putin had created the American Patriot movement and then blamed it for the cyberattacks. Meantime, he was also charging the U.S. with the sabotage of Russian nuclear plants. In that, at least, he was telling the truth. He was able to produce the only surviving member of the CIA hit team, who laid out Tildy's assassination plot very persuasively.

It was a war of viruses, biological and virtual, and in both the U.S. was at a disadvantage. Its biological weapons program had been dismantled, whereas in Russia it simply went underground. If Kongoli was the product of many years of inspired biological engineering, who knew what else the Russians had stored in their secret laboratories? Smallpox, Marburg, Ebola, all waiting in line to be put in play. These were the harvest months for Fancy Bear, as the viral seeds planted on Western computers were finally ripening.

Garcia had been summoned to the Cosmos Club, where presidents and Nobel Prize winners and Supreme Court justices came together to celebrate their importance. He was immediately struck not by the grandeur of the place, but by

414

the air conditioning, which seemed lavish in a way that he had never appreciated before. He was shaken by nostalgia for a life he had once had and never properly appreciated. He moved around in a cloud of loss.

The maître d' in the club's capacious dining hall immediately sized up Garcia with a disdainful glance. He might as well have been carrying a bedroll and a backpack, as were so many citizens these days. But when Garcia mentioned the name Richard Clarke, the supercilious eyebrows rose higher in acknowledgment. 'Table fifty-two,' the maître d' said to the hostess.

Even here, in the lair of the mighty, Garcia observed the aftereffects of the influenza. The highly ornamented room was scarcely populated. The chandeliers were lit, but dimly. The carpet was stained and full of lint, like an artifact of the French empire, long past its glory days. Even the hostess's blouse was rumpled and probably hadn't been washed in some time. She opened a frosted-glass sliding door, which led to a small dining room with a table for two.

'You do like your privacy,' Garcia observed.

'Privacy is the most valuable commodity in this town,' Clarke said. 'What do you want to drink? Something in a bottle, you can't trust the ice.'

Garcia could tell that Clarke was looking him over, evaluating the damage. He knew how he looked, emaciated, the pallor of Kongoli still clinging to him. Clarke, on the other hand, appeared more than fit; he was rejuvenated and battle-ready. He ordered the crab cakes. Garcia had the scallops.

'Tomorrow morning, Russian troops will enter Estonia,' Clarke said. 'It's Putin's next step in his grand design. First there was Crimea. Then Ukraine. Now come the Baltics.'

'How do you know this?'

Clarke shrugged. 'Check the wires in the morning. AFP will have it. Too bad the *Post* will be behind the curve. Again.'

'And what will the president do?'

'What he *should* do is sink their fleets. Bomb their refineries. Mine their ports. Send cruise missiles through every window in the Kremlin. We all know what they're up to. We've been at war for years, only we wouldn't admit it. We didn't label cyberattacks as real war. We didn't think of Kongoli as a weapon of mass destruction.'

'You're sure it was them?'

'How do you explain a novel disease that devastates the West and leaves Russia . . . not untouched, but not destroyed? You think it's coincidental that our grid is taken down, our communications disrupted, our economy in ruins, and just at this moment Russian troops march into the Baltics?'

'Several million people died in Russia. You honestly think Putin would do that to his own people, not to mention to the hundreds of millions who've died around the world?'

'Would you be asking this question if Stalin were alive?'

'No.'

'Well, he is.'

416

51

A Farewell Kiss

HENRY KNOCKED ON HIS NEIGHBOR'S DOOR. THE HOUSE belonged to Marjorie Cook, who had lived there long before Henry and Jill moved onto the block. No one answered. He had yet to see any of his neighbors; the whole street appeared to be vacant. The house across the street had been burned.

As he turned away, the door suddenly opened. 'Henry,' a voice said.

'Hello, Marjorie.'

'I didn't expect to see you again.' Marjorie stood behind the screen door, wearing a faded housecoat and holding the handle as if it were a barricade protecting her against disaster. 'I thought you were all gone. Well, I didn't know what to think, to be honest. Tell me you aren't the only one.'

'I don't know,' Henry said. 'Jill is dead. Somebody buried her in the backyard, I have no idea who. The kids are gone, and I don't know where. I was hoping you could tell me something. Did they ever come to you? Did you see them? Do you have any idea what happened to them?'

'I can't help you,' Marjorie said tersely.

Henry had known her for fifteen years, but she seemed a stranger to him.

'Marjorie, the car's gone. Did somebody steal it? Did some friend take the children?'

'I wouldn't know.' Distress was written all over her. 'It was awful, Henry,' she blurted out. 'I just hid. I'm sorry, I should have been a better person. I was scared. I'm not forgiving myself, it's just the God's truth.'

Henry stared at her for a moment, then turned to go.

'There was a gunshot,' she called after him. 'I don't know any more than that.'

There were other families in the neighborhood, some with children, but none of those who answered Henry's knock had seen Helen and Teddy. He drew up posters with their names and asked for information, giving his address, and he stapled them to the telephone poles among similar posters. They were everywhere.

He walked over to the fire station on DeKalb Avenue and examined a list of people from the neighborhood who had died or were missing. His own name was entered in the dead column. He scratched that out and wrote in Jill's name. His children were not on the list.

Someone had taken them, he was certain. He hoped that someone was a friend. Where would they have gone?

'They're probably at the stadium,' one of the firemen said. 'They got a temporary shelter for the orphans. The families are at the convention center.'

Henry's Suburban was still parked at the Atlanta airport for what was supposed to have been a brief trip to Geneva, so he found the keys to Mrs Hernández's Ford and drove to the Braves stadium. On one of the columns there was a hand-lettered sign that said registry, with an arrow pointing to the First Base Gate. Henry paused a moment as he entered

418

the stands, remembering: This is where I met Jill. The triple play. She embraced me and my life changed.

The stadium was transformed into a refugee camp for children, with orderly rows of white tents in the outfield and masses of children confined behind hurricane fences. A heavy middle-aged woman was peering at them through binoculars. She looked up when she heard Henry approach.

'I'm looking for my kids,' he said.

'Well, we've got 312 of them,' she said. 'How many do you want?'

'Two.'

'Just pick out a couple and sign the waiver.'

'You don't understand, I'm looking for my own children.'

The woman sighed. 'Names?' she asked.

'Helen and Theodore Parsons. Might be Teddy instead of Theodore.'

She looked at her list. 'Well, the names aren't alphabetized, we had to do all this by hand.' She wetted a finger and turned a page, and then another, making a show of how much trouble he was causing.

'Can I go down there and see for myself?'

'You'd need an escort,' the woman said grudgingly. Then, 'Oh, well.' She pushed herself up and slowly made her way down the steps to the gate beside the home team dugout. They walked onto the field, across the pitcher's mound and into the outfield grass. The fence holding the children was about twelve-feet high.

'We have them separated by gender and age, to keep the problems down, so if they're here they won't be together.'

'It's a prison,' Henry observed.

'Well, in case you haven't heard, we got a tremendous

problem with orphan gangs. Not saying these kids are a problem. But desperation leads to bad actions. Here at least they get fed, they are in a healthful environment, they got a shelter, and if there's trouble we can take care of it. Just don't be so quick to judge, is what I'm saying.'

Henry walked beside the fence of the boys' encampment, calling Teddy's name, then did the same for Helen. The children stared at him hopefully, as if he might also call their name. One girl did answer to Helen, but she was not Henry's Helen. She burst into tears when he walked on. I am also an orphan, Henry wanted to say. I am one of you.

The story was the same at the convention center. Desolate families living on meager charity, their curiosity was barely stirred by Henry's passage through the enormous dormitories, past boxes of donated food and clothing. A magician was doing card tricks for the children as actors in Disney costumes paraded by. Someone working for FEMA sat at a card table facing a long line of exhausted applicants looking for housing. But Helen and Teddy were not there. They were nowhere to be found.

Helen and Teddy's school had been ransacked. The door was open, and Henry walked through the halls, peering in the empty classrooms. It looked like a tornado had gone through the building, scattering papers and books and overturning desks. Someone had taken a shit in the middle of Teddy's second-grade classroom.

Henry heard a rhythmic sound that he suddenly recognized as a basketball. He followed it to the gym. It was full of children. He didn't see Helen and Teddy, but perhaps some of the two dozen or so children gathered here would know where they were. Several were teenagers; most of them were younger, Teddy and Helen's ages. They had made a dormitory for themselves out of blankets and bedrolls. The older boys were shooting baskets.

The children now finally realized he was there. The gym became quiet. Henry looked around for an adult but saw none. He did notice a familiar face, one of Helen's class-mates. 'Laura?' he said.

The girl came over to Henry. She had been on the soccer team with Helen. She stood for a moment in front of him, then suddenly embraced him. Several other children sur-rounded them.

'What happened to your parents?' Henry asked Laura. She began to weep.

'Everybody's dead,' an older boy said in a disgusted tone.

'Why aren't you down at the stadium with the other orphans?' Henry asked.

'It's a jail,' one of the other kids said.

'And we hear things about what happens there,' Laura said.

'We get by all right, on our own,' the older boy said. He gestured toward a knife sticking out of his belt.

None of them knew where Teddy or Helen were. As Henry was leaving, the older boy boldly demanded money. Henry handed him all he had. 'What's this, play money?' the boy said.

'No, it's Saudi money. It's all I've got.'

The boy threw it on the floor. 'That's fucked up,' he said.

Henry spent the afternoon disposing of the bodies in his house. He buried Mrs Hernández along with her cats. The dead man in Helen's room he buried behind the playhouse so he'd never be reminded of him again. His backyard had become a cemetery. He spent the rest of the day putting his house back together. He couldn't think beyond that. He went from room to room like a dervish, cleaning and straightening, trying to restore order, the one thing his life would never have again.

As he swept up the debris, he searched for clues. He found Jill's iPhone in her purse. There was still some battery left, but it was in the red. Her last call was to her sister, Maggie, two weeks before. Henry tried calling Maggie, but there was no response. He didn't allow himself to read too much into that.

He was standing in the bedroom changing the sheets when the house groaned back to life and he realized that the electricity was back on. The radio began to play, but only static, no broadcast. WABE, Jill's station. She must have been listening to it when she died. Henry wondered if life was now going to bend back toward normality – or was this merely a temporary reprieve? He felt absurdly grateful just to have the lights on.

In the evening, he put on freshly laundered clothes and walked to Little Five Points. A few shops were open, as well as the Mexican restaurant where he and Jill used to take the children. It was astonishing how quickly life came back once the power was on. He was even able to get some cash out of the ATM. He sat at a table on the sidewalk and watched people drifting by, walking in the street because there were still so few cars. Their faces were blissful. He could read their thoughts: The worst is over. We're back. We've suffered, but everything is going to be okay now. We survived.

Henry would have liked to believe that, but he knew what they were dealing with. Influenza never made just a single visit. This peaceful moment, while he was eating a tomato and mozzarella salad with a glass of Mexican beer, was a momentary, cruel intermission.

Tomorrow he would return to his lab at the CDC. He had had no contact with it for weeks, and who knew what state it was in? He had to find his children, but where else could he turn? Where would they go? Were they in good hands? Were they in trouble?

So many unanswered questions awaited, but in this moment, he had to say goodbye. He asked the waiter for a glass of pinot grigio – what Jill had ordered the last time they were here. He set it across the table, where she would have been. Before he left, he took a single sip of the wine, like a farewell kiss. When he got home, the house was still empty. And haunted.

52

Now It's in Us

THE HISTORIES OF THE 1918 PANDEMIC ALL OBSERVED THAT survivors rarely talked about it afterward. You could almost believe that it hadn't happened, except for the gravestones with similar dates. *We lived through it:* that was the attitude. It wasn't like the Great Depression or the world wars or terrorist attacks; survivors of those events lived their lives with one eye on the past even as they moved on. They wrote books, they joined societies, they had reunions. They brought their grandchildren to view the battlefields. They got therapy. But survivors of the 1918 flu did their best to purge the episode from their memories – and, therefore, from history. It was the nature of the era. At the beginning of the twentieth century, the epidemics of cholera, diphtheria, yellow fever, and typhoid were either still happening or resided in recent memory. Death by disease was so commonplace it was scarely remarked by history. The 1918 flu killed twice as many people as died in combat during the entire four years of the First World War, and yet the customary horror of another pandemic was overshadowed by the drama of combat.

Now Henry wondered if humanity was once again sleep-walking toward a pointless, civilization-annihilating conflict,

424

astride another great pandemic that was randomly mowing down populations with industrial efficiency. The question that still haunted him was whether Kongoli was an engineered virus – an act of war – or a natural occurrence? He knew, as very few people did, how close the U.S. and Russia were to opening their arsenals and letting fly the instruments of apocalypse.

Henry rode his bike to the CDC, as he had done for years. It was a heavy red mountain bike, ponderous, many generations past the latest refinements, but Henry valued its solidity. He took the side streets into the Emory University campus. There were no students, but some of the maintenance crew were hauling furniture and personal effects out of abandoned dormitory rooms. Life almost seemed normal.

He had never seen soldiers guarding the gate to the CDC before, but now they were patrolling behind the fence in full combat gear. As Henry approached, two of them blocked his path. He showed his ID, but a stern young soldier told him that it was no longer operative.

'But I work here!' Henry said in amazement. 'I run the infectious diseases section.'

'Sir, that may be true, but new identification has been issued, and your name is not on the list.'

Henry sputtered, demanding that they call the director. The impassive response of the soldiers infuriated him. He was still arguing when a voice commanded, 'Let him in.'

'Catherine!' Henry said.

'Henry, we thought you were dead,' Catherine Lord responded when the gate opened. 'We hadn't heard from you for the longest time. God, we need you.'

The facilities were secure and intact, but Catherine explained that much had changed. 'I'm the new director. We lost Tom. Your team, well, it's reduced, I'm afraid. Marco is still with us. We've moved people around to fill in the gaps. You'll have to take the stairs, the elevators are down. I'll have new credentials prepared for you by the end of the day.'

When Henry entered his old lab, every face turned toward him. There was a world of explaining to be done, but that would have to wait. Marco approached him, and without a word they embraced. Then Marco guided him through the lab, reporting on the various strains that Kongoli had manifested, some more virulent than others, but all of them evading the prospect of an immediate cure or vaccine. 'What we have is a mutant swarm,' said Marco. 'Meantime, NIH has created an RNA replicon vaccine.' The replicon masqueraded as a virus-infected cell, fooling the body into believing that it had been infected. If successful, it would prompt the cells to make antibodies. 'We're running it through the ferrets. The assays suggest it might work, but we're still trying to pin the tail on that donkey. We don't have anything to offer right now.'

Henry explained his experiment on the submarine, using the variolation procedure. Marco looked at him with unbridled astonishment. 'You figured this out on a *submarine*?' he asked.

'Well, I had to do something.'

'You must make your variolation technique public right away,' Marco said.

Henry nodded in a distracted manner.

426

'Henry! You did it! You've effectively created a vaccine! Don't you realize what you've done?'

But he hadn't found his children. Over the next week he spent mornings and evenings searching the city and afternoons in the lab. The city was odd, broken, diminished. Others were wandering through the hospitals and cemeteries, like him searching for records or familiar faces. In Centennial Park there were hundreds of Missing posters pasted on a wall. They told a story of shattered families and lost loves. Some had photographs taped onto them. So many happy faces.

The absence of any formal order was the city's most noticeable quality. No cops, no soldiers, just people. This is what anarchy looks like, Henry thought. There wasn't as much chaos as he had expected, although gangs and beggars filled the streets and public places. They seemed more insolent than threatening. Henry realized that everyone was in shock.

There was a woman in Centennial Park who approached him as he was putting up his poster. 'Your children?' she said.

'Yes.'

She smiled and said how sweet they looked. Then she said, 'My children are dead.'

Henry looked at her. She was in her thirties, he supposed, although like with many survivors her face was ravaged by the disease. Her hands were red and raw. He said how sorry he was for her loss.

'I hope you find yours,' she said.

'Thank you. I will.'

'I hope you do.' Then she leaned toward him and whispered, 'Do you want to kiss me?'

Henry quickly drew away, then realized his unconscious reaction had been a dart in her heart. 'I'm sorry,' he said. 'I'm in mourning. It's just not the right time.'

The woman was crying now. 'I just wanted someone to talk to me,' she blurted out.

'I can talk to you,' Henry said. 'What do you want me to say?'

'Tell me I'm beautiful.'

Henry looked at her blotched and pitted face. 'You're beautiful to me,' he said.

Henry was bothered by the fact that the first human case of Kongoli had not been firmly fixed. It could explain whether the virus had passed from an animal host or was genetically engineered. While he was journeying home, the lab had tracked the previous infections in China, which were confined and likely passed from birds to individuals. The path of infection suggested that Kongoli originated in Manchuria or Siberia. He asked Marco to track any animal die-offs in that region preceding the Chinese infections. That might offer a clue to the origin of the virus.

'Anything new on the phylogeny?' he asked.

'We can't find a direct evolutionary path,' said Nandi, a lab technician who had worked on Ebola with Henry. She had a dendrogram of Kongoli on her computer screen. It resembled a family tree, tracking backward to show how the influenza viruses had evolved. On it, the outbreak in Indonesia seemed to have come out of nowhere.

'Either it's from outer space or it's an engineered virus,' Marco said.

'Right,' said Henry. 'Or . . .'

Everyone stopped what they were doing. Henry was famous for his off-the-wall ideas. 'Suppose it's not new. Suppose it's old – really old.'

'Some kind of protovirus?' Marco asked.

'It would still be on the graph,' Nandi insisted. 'It covers more than a hundred years of influenza mutations, all the way back to the 1918 pandemic.'

'Can you extend the temporal markers by checking against archaic viruses?'

'I'd have to get into a different database,' said Nandi. 'There was a phylogenetic tree I saw somewhere on PubMed that postulated the early origins of influenza.' Five minutes later she asked, 'How far back?'

'Try a thousand years.'

Nandi entered the parameters. Here she found the common branch of the A and B viruses, but nothing that resembled Kongoli.

'Five thousand,' said Henry.

Here influenza C appeared and was connected to the stem of A and B viruses.

'We're close,' said Henry. 'Let's try ten thousand years.'

Nandi suddenly drew back from her screen. 'Oh, wow. I got something.'

Everyone in the lab gathered around her computer, blocking Henry's view. 'What is it?' he demanded. The team parted enough for Henry to see. There was a sequence that looked very similar to Kongoli. 'What's the history of this agent?' Henry asked.

'It came out of Iceland,' said Nandi. 'According to the documentation, it was unearthed by a paleontology expedition in 1964, from tissue extracted from a frozen mammoth found in the glacial ice. It's never been classified.'

The team stared in wonder at an electron micrograph image of the ancient virus as the implications sank in. 'What we're looking at is the ancestor of the entire influenza family,' Henry said. 'It must have found a home in the mammoths, maybe lasting for a million years before dying with them. Somehow it's back in circulation.'

'How?' Nandi asked.

'Somebody dug it up and propagated it in a lab,' Marco suggested.

'The Soviets did that with the 1918 flu as part of their bioweapons arsenal,' Henry said. 'You'd have to take the various sequences that you find and try to reconstruct the entire influenza genome. It could be done experimentally in the lab. Or nature could do it by itself, reaching into its genetic arsenal to make something very old new again.'

'Could it have been responsible for the mammoth extinction?' Nandi asked.

'Certainly possible.'

'And what about the Neanderthals? They were contemporary with the mammoths.'

The researchers looked at each other, and then Nandi said what was on everybody's mind. 'Now it's in us.'

53

The Ustinov Strain

HENRY'S BIOHAZARD SPACE SUIT WITH HIS NAME SCRAWLED on it hung on the peg in the decontamination room where he had left it months before. Once he was back in the familiar plastic garment, he attached a yellow hose to the socket in his chest, and the air filled the suit like a balloon, deafening outside sounds. He had never gotten used to how cumbersome it was to gird himself before entering the most dangerous place in the world, the Level 4 biocontainment facility.

He walked through the staging room, then unhooked his air hose as he entered an air lock. The door clapped firmly behind him, as his suit collapsed from the lack of air. Through another steel door was Level 4. He opened the door and attached another air hose.

Researchers were working at different stations, operating centrifuges or incubators or transferring virus samples to slides with pipettes, focusing on the perilous tasks they were engaged in. No one paid attention as he walked through the lab into a small room, where two massive freezers stood next to the liquid nitrogen tank. Henry entered a code on

431

the keypad of one of the freezers and a green light appeared. He opened the door.

Inside were the most lethal pathogens ever known. Ebola. Marburg. Lassa fever. Each disease carefully filed away, on icy racks in Eppendorf tubes, a library of woe. Henry knew it was pointless to ascribe consciousness or intentionality to a disease. It was not remorseless or cunning. It simply was. Its purpose was to be. But he also knew that diseases were constantly reinventing themselves, and there would never be a freezer large enough to contain the manifold weapons nature employs to attack its own creatures. And here in its own tube was the newcomer, Kongoli, with so much death on its hands already, and so much more to come.

Henry felt he had done what he could to counter the disease. His variolation technique would be recognized as a potent stopgap measure and quickly put into effect around the globe. Promising Kongoli vaccines were finally about to go into human trials. It was a race to save as many people as possible. But there were so many other viruses in the freezer. He had a foreboding that the ongoing war against disease would inevitably be lost. Humanity had enlisted the microbe as a weapon. He could imagine the day when all the diseases in the freezer were set loose.

Including his own.

The viral suspension of Henry's disease looked like a pink ice cube. He had puzzled over it for years. Why had it killed so many people in the jungle when it had been harmless in the lab? He had studied it, trying to unlock its secrets, trying to find a reason to excuse himself. How inadequate we are in our attempts to bring nature under our control, Henry thought. How careless of us to believe that we can manipulate diseases to kill, rather than to cure. We're like schoolchildren playing with matches. One day we'll burn the house down.

Nandi had something. 'Remember the Siberian cranes?' she said when Henry came back into the lab. 'Practically extinct now. They migrate from their breeding grounds in Siberia to Poyang Lake, in eastern China, near where we had one of the early human cases of Kongoli. About twenty of the remaining cranes were fitted with satellite transmitters to track their migration patterns. We know they carried the disease. Anyway, I was able to determine that five of those tagged birds perished during the course of migration. I don't know if that's unusual, you'll have to ask an ornithologist. But that got me thinking about other endangered animal populations, because so many of them are actually tracked by the World Wildlife Fund and other organizations.

'So, it turns out that in 2019 there was an invasion of polar bears in this little archipelago in the Russian Arctic. There's a settlement called Novaya Zemlya. Apparently the bears drifted in on ice floes and discovered the city dump. They wandered through the streets and into apartment buildings – a huge nuisance. Anyway, the bears were sedated and collared and shipped off to this atoll called October Revolution Island. It's just north of Siberia in the Arctic Circle. The thing is, they all died. Their GPS collars showed that they stopped moving, one by one, about a week after they were transported.'

'Maybe they were traumatized by the relocation,' Marco suggested.

'Could be. Or the tranquilizer that was used to capture

them was contaminated. All I'm saying is we've got a mass die-off of polar bears and no clear reason for it.'

'Did the transmitter send any information, heart rate, respiration, anything that might give us a clue about their symptoms?' Henry asked.

'Sorry, guys, it's just what I said. They used GPS trackers. It only shows you where they move around – or stop moving.'

Marco looked at Henry. 'What is it?' he asked. 'I can tell you're thinking of something.'

'Something from the old days,' Henry said. 'October Revolution Island was an outpost of the Soviet biochemical warfare program. I'm thinking that if they did engineer this virus, that would have been a logical spot for it – remote, a place where biological experiments can take place in relative safety. It was totally uninhabited, until the bears came along.'

In the morning, Henry drove to the house of one of Teddy's playmates, Jerry Barnwell. If Teddy wanted to go someplace safe, he might have found a way to get to the Barnwells'. They lived in Decatur, just east of Atlanta. It would have been quite a hike for the kids, which is why Henry hadn't gone already.

As he drove, he tried to remember the parents' names. He had dropped off Jerry several times after practices, and had chatted with the parents more than once, but the names eluded him. He recalled that Jerry had two older sisters, one maybe a year older than Helen. The Barnwells lived in a blue Victorian bungalow with white trim. One look and Henry decided it was deserted. The Barnwells had been so fastidious,

434

but now the yard was overgrown and the kudzu was advancing, even here in the suburbs. There was mail in the box from months before. Thomas and Jeannette, those were the names on the bills. Henry knocked just because he was there.

In a moment he heard footsteps, and the door opened. It was Jerry.

'Hello, Doctor Parsons,' Jerry said. A little blond boy with neat manners and a precise manner of speech, smaller than Henry remembered. He didn't seem surprised.

'Jerry, are you here alone?'

Jerry nodded. 'I am alone now, but my sister Marcia is here sometimes,' he said.

Henry didn't ask about his parents.

'Is Teddy okay?' Jerry asked.

'I don't know where he is,' Henry said. 'I was hoping you might have seen him.'

Jerry shook his head. 'Nobody ever comes to see me now,' he said.

'Who's taking care of you?'

'Marcia makes some money.' He paused. 'Sometimes men come to get her and then bring her back the next day. I thought you might be one of them.'

'No, I'm just looking for my own children.'

'I sure miss Teddy.'

'I do, too.'

When Catherine Lord heard about October Revolution Island, she immediately called Homeland Security, and despite Henry's protests he was shunted into a government car and driven at high speed back to Dobbins Air Reserve Base. Henry understood that this was an emergency and he was badly needed, but he was frantic about his children and resented being pulled away.

He was flown to Washington in an Air Force Gulfstream, the only passenger in an era when air traffic was at a standstill. By four in the afternoon, he was in a small, windowless conference room inside CIA headquarters at Langley meeting with Matilda Nichinsky and a woman who looked like some evil character in a Disney movie. They were very interested in what he had to say.

'It could be that there was some durable toxin lying around and the bears stumbled onto it,' Henry said. 'I can think of a dozen that would qualify, especially in the Arctic, where the cold acts as a preservative.'

'Maybe the Russians repurposed the old biochem plant and cooked up something new,' Tildy suggested. 'In a place only a handful of people know exists.'

'*We* didn't know,' the agency woman confessed.

'We're in this spot,' said Tildy. 'NATO is pawing the ground over Estonia. What's the appropriate response? Take out the Russian fleet, for starters. Move the 173rd Airborne into Latvia. But that's just to block further aggression. It would be nice to know for certain that Putin is behind Kongoli. The whole world would turn against him and his thuggish regime. They'd drag him to the docket in The Hague and hang him. This is my dream. But things are escalating too fast. Damn. I wish we could put you on that island. Get samples. Prove to the world what we all know.'

The door opened, and a man entered, a man with black glasses and silver hair. Henry drew a breath. Nobody bothered to introduce them.

'The president needs options,' Tildy continued. 'Something we can deny. Something that doesn't have our signature on it.'

'Something chemical or biological, in other words,' the agency woman added, looking directly at the man with the silver hair.

'But I am out of this business now,' Jürgen Stark said.

'The U.S. has been out of this business ever since Nixon, supposedly,' said Tildy. 'But we know you kept alive a classified program at Fort Detrick after 9/11.'

Jürgen cast an appraising glance at Henry, who could not meet his eyes.

'They say you were the best,' the agency woman added. 'Now all our biological stock has been destroyed. Nobody left who knows the recipes. The techniques. The institutional memory you two represent. Your country needs you now. Both of you.'

'Is the president really willing to kill hundreds of millions of people?' Jürgen asked.

'That's already happened with Kongoli,' said Tildy.

Jürgen took a sip of the cold brew he had purchased from the Starbucks in the basement of the CIA. 'How do you know Russia is responsible?'

'We can't divulge our sources,' the agency woman said.

'Let me rephrase,' said Jürgen. 'At what level of confidence do you rate this information?'

'Medium to high.'

'There's a lot of uncertainty in that assessment.'

The agency woman acknowledged that the intelligence was short of perfect, but what could you do? Unsaid, but understood: Putin killed our assets and we're blind.

Henry watched the conversation as if he were dreaming. Old emotions of loyalty and inadequacy roiled his mind. As he studied the older man now in front of him, he saw for the first time how alike they had become, each having recoiled from the work that had brought them together in the first place. As usual, Jürgen had gone to an extreme, using his idiosyncratic genius to resurrect endangered and extinct animals. He had publicly stated that all life forms were equal, so he was as happy to replicate polio as he was to bring the dodo back to life. He was still the most dangerous man Henry had ever known.

'We have to go back to the president with a recommendation,' Tildy was saying. 'He cannot stand aside from this attack on America – not just America, the whole world! Putin created this virus—'

'Speculation,' Jürgen interjected.

'– and unleashed this plague on humanity. Then he took down the grid. Not speculation. Fact. Hit us at our weakest moment. Millions of people have been killed, incidentally or by design. The economy is essentially dead. We must retaliate. The president will act. He has no choice. He cannot let this attack go unanswered.'

'How governments choose to fight each other is outside my realm of interest,' Jürgen said. 'And what you've done to the avian population is unforgivable. You are already at war, but not with Russia. There is a far greater enemy. That is nature. You will not win this war.'

'We deserve that, yes, we do,' Tildy said. 'Awful things we've done, not just with the chickens and such. Some poor decisions were made, yes. But that's how it's done. People get in a room, like we are now, the four of us. Options are put on the table. Politics makes a great noise in the outside world, but in this room we have only a few choices among terrible alternatives. What will it be? Let us say we go with option one.' She turned to the agency woman. 'What's the status of the Russian nuclear forces as of this moment?'

'Highest alert.'

'Typical of Putin,' Tildy said. 'He escalates quickly to freeze our response. Then he can deescalate a bit to make us think we've won something. He's been cheating on every arms control agreement we've ever had with him. And in the agency's judgment, how likely is he to fire the first nuke?'

'He will do so at the slightest indication that Russian security may be compromised.'

'We're talking about the end of civilization, not just for Russia and the United States, but for who knows. And that's not your concern, I realize,' Tildy said to Jürgen. 'Maybe Mother Earth would be better off without us. But you tell me what the world would look like after an all-out nuclear exchange. Your animals, for instance.'

Jürgen refused to be drawn in. He just stared at Tildy.

'Option two. Endless cyberwar. A continual attack on progress. Inadequate, no clear end to it. Fewer people die, I'll give you that. But we fight at a disadvantage. Russia has been waging cyberwar on us for years. We've survived, they've survived. But Putin went too far, he made an all-out strike on our infrastructure. This is something he's had in his bag for years and years. And yes, we can punish him in the same way. But it doesn't hurt him as much, you see. He doesn't have enough to lose. Not like us. So we have to find another response. And that's where you come in, Dr Stark. Option three.'

'You want me to create a pathogen?'

'There's no time for that. We need something now. Off the shelf. Something that looks like it might have walked out of a Russian lab. But with minimal blowback for us.'

'That doesn't exist. Look at Kongoli, it spread around the world in three weeks, a universal pandemic. You could choose a noncontagious agent, such as anthrax. But then you have to distribute it. Same with toxins. Spray it from crop dusters, package it in warheads, but there's nothing accidental about it. They don't "walk out of the lab" the way diseases do – the way Kongoli may have. It's too obvious.'

Tildy was struck by Jürgen's indifference to the contingencies that were being placed before him. He was unimpressed by the confidences that were being shared – secrets of the very highest level. A cool customer. Thin. Spidery. Handsome, or certainly striking, with that chiseled face and long silvery hair. And frightening. He would have made a wonderful Nazi, she thought. She noted how quiet Dr Parsons had become. They used to work together, her briefing notes said.

'And how would you have done it, Dr Stark?' Tildy inquired.

'I would have chosen a different agent.'

'What would you have chosen?'

'I know of only one ideal candidate. So far as we know, it is only deadly in humans, where it shows an extreme level of lethality. It was developed, of course, by Dr Parsons here.'

It had happened. Henry had always dreaded that his secret would be disclosed. He had imagined being arrested, put on trial. He had thought about what his family would think of him. He had seen himself in prison. But he had

440

never expected that Jürgen would betray him publicly, or that his own government would turn to him because of his invention's singular capacity to kill.

'You assured me that all the stock of my virus was destroyed,' Henry said in a voice gone dry.

'It was. We used up your batch in our little experiment in Brazil,' said Jürgen. 'And we don't have your lab notes to re-create it.'

'This agent that you speak of, could it be released in Moscow and Saint Petersburg, surreptitiously, so that there is no evidence of the source?' Tildy asked.

'If it is as infectious as we think it is, it will decimate the Russian population in a short period of time,' Jürgen said. 'There is nothing they can do to control it. But then, neither can we.'

'What was the level of mortality in your experiment?' Tildy asked. Her clinical tone suggested that they had already gone far past moral considerations.

'Near total,' Jürgen said. 'Some subjects were disposed of by other means, but it is likely they would have died anyway.' He looked at Henry. 'We know of only one survivor, but that was an unborn child.'

'This sounds perfect,' said the agency woman.

'I can't stress enough, you have no idea what you're unleashing,' said Henry.

'We must choose from terrible alternatives,' said Tildy.

'Perhaps Dr Parsons has not been brought up to date on the Chicago outbreak,' the agency woman said.

Henry looked around the room. Everyone else seemed to know.

'Putin has been blaming us for Kongoli,' Tildy said.

'Imagine the gall. In any case, he's taken the next step. We've gotten a report that there have been five deaths in the last two days in Chicago from Marburg hemorrhagic fever. There's a likely case in Seattle. It's a Category A bioterrorism agent.'

'The Ustinov strain,' Jürgen added.

Henry felt his resistance crumble. The lines were all pointing in the same direction. For the first time, he allowed himself to focus the rage and blame that were boiling inside him but which had no way of escaping. It was clear now: they had killed Jill. The image of her sightless eyes in the grave flashed into his mind. This is the world we labored to prevent, he thought, Jürgen and I. All along we have known this might happen. We prepared for it. So did they. We bear the moral cost. Yes, there was a part of us that longed to see our work go out in the world, just to observe the spectacle of destruction that we had stored in our biological warehouses. And now it was done.

But what was the right response? More death?

'By the way, what do you call the agent?' Tildy asked Henry.

Jürgen answered for him. 'We named it *Enterovirus parsons*, after its creator.'

54

Eden

HELEN AND TEDDY HAD BEEN AT AUNT MAGGIE'S FARM FOR A week before Helen discovered the body. They were harvesting the corn that Uncle Tim had planted in the spring. Maggie's pantry had been raided and the marijuana in the drying barn had been picked clean, but the burglars missed a root cellar stocked with seed potatoes and turnips. Electricity hadn't been turned on again in this part of Tennessee, but the gas stove worked. 'We can live here forever,' Helen said.

That same day she stumbled over a boot in the cornfield and realized it was connected to a leg bone. She wanted to scream, but all the screams inside her were wrung out. A kind of animal indifference to anything except survival had taken hold.

The leg was there by itself. It had been partially eaten. Helen recognized the boot, so she knew the leg was Maggie's. She set down the basket with the ripened ears and searched through the towering corn stalks. She didn't want Teddy to see this. She could hear him rustling nearby.

The rest of Maggie's remains were scattered about. Helen found a shotgun, which answered her question about where the head was. She picked up the weapon because it could be useful. There were pieces of Maggie's dress caught up in the corn like calico flags. The torso had been torn open and eviscerated by coyotes or wild pigs. Maggie and Jill, sisters, both gone. Uncle Tim's grave was in back of the house by the arbor. Kendall was there, too. The flowers and shrubs they had planted for that television show were in bloom. It was beautiful back there. Helen really didn't want to leave Aunt Maggie out there for the vultures to finish.

She noticed the bulge in the pocket of what was left of Maggie's dress. Her cell phone.

Helen walked out of the cornfield and stood by the gate, yelling Teddy's name. He came toward her voice and emerged with a full basket. His eyes widened at the sight of the shotgun. 'I found it,' Helen said. 'And this.' She held up Maggie's phone.

'She's out there?'

Helen nodded.

'Any battery in the phone?'

'Totally dead.'

They went back inside. They were living in Maggie and Tim's bedroom because Teddy didn't want to sleep alone. He had seen the Confederate ghost again. He wasn't as afraid of the ghost as he had been before, but it reminded him of when he had crawled into Jill's lap and she had cuddled him and made him feel safe.

In a desk drawer in the bedroom, Teddy found a charging cord.

'What are you doing that for?' Helen asked.

'I got an idea.'

They went to the garage where Uncle Tim's pickup was

parked. The keys were in the ignition. Teddy got into the driver's seat.

'No you can't,' said Helen.

'I'm not going to drive, I'm going to charge the phone.'

He started the truck and plugged the charger into the USB port in the dashboard. After a moment or two, the screen-saver lit up with a photo of Maggie, Tim, and Kendall at a stock show with one of Kendall's prize pigs. They all looked happy and beautiful and alive.

'I'm checking to see if the internet is up,' Teddy said. The browser flickered back to life. There were several unopened emails that had been sent in August, and dozens more began downloading. Then Teddy touched the phone app. He stared at it and held the phone away from him, as if it contained something frightening or incomprehensible.

'What?' Helen demanded.

'Mom called. Like two days ago.'

Jürgen Stark's laboratory was in a remote section of central Pennsylvania, in Amish country. An occasional buggy clopped by the gates. The only billboards were stark passages of scripture. The air was clean and the fields were carefully tended and cornflowers lined the fences. It was a vision of a preindustrial world in which humanity had played a smaller role, serving as stewards of the land. Except for the religion, it was a vision of society that Jürgen fiercely endorsed.

The government car turned off the state road and pulled up to an iron gate. The steel barrier surrounding the acreage had been artfully planted so that it didn't look like a prison or some federal fortification. The gate opened into a disin-fectant chamber, where the car and its undercarriage were sprayed. They went through a second gate, where Henry and the driver were made to stand aside as guards vacuumed the trunk and the interior and power-washed the engine block – all of this, Henry realized, to keep out pathogens that might destroy the unique life forms that Jürgen was re-creating inside this compound.

Henry was met by a weathered middle-aged woman with cropped hair, wearing an Earth's Guardians hat. Her name, Heidi, was embroidered on her shirt. 'It's an honor,' she told Henry. 'Dr Stark has often spoken of you. What great friends you are.'

Jürgen's minimalist aesthetic was evident in the low-lying stone buildings that surrounded the campus. Gardens spilled over with unfamiliar flowers and vegetables. Hyacinths and lilies and tulips of novel colors were laid out in mulched beds. 'This section alone represents nearly a hundred varieties of squash that have been brought back to life,' Heidi said. 'Look at them, aren't they amazing? You'll have some in the soup tonight.' They walked through an apple orchard bearing fruit of unusual colors and sizes. 'So much was lost to mindless civilization,' said Heidi.

A portion of the campus was a kind of zoo, although Heidi cautioned that the word should not be applied. 'We only hold the animals until they have developed a sufficient population to be released into the wild. We settle them in the habitat where they once flourished and hope that they'll make a go of it again. And here's one of our greatest triumphs.' Heidi pointed to a wire cage the size of a boxcar containing about fifty red-eyed gray doves. 'They're passenger pigeons,' she said. 'Once, the most common bird in America, then extinct for a hundred years. Jürgen brought them back. Just think about that. God made these creatures and we made them again. It's truly the Lord's work.'

Henry studied Heidi's awed expression and thought how he must have looked like that once as well. It was the face of a true believer.

Jürgen was waiting in his office. 'Tell Craig to make something wonderful,' he said to Heidi, as Henry came into the room. A glass wall jutted into a forest of red oak on the rocky banks of a creek. There were no pictures on the walls; nature itself was the art, sere and impersonal, like Jürgen.

'Did Heidi show you your lab?' Jürgen asked when they were alone.

'Not yet.'

'It's not up to Fort Detrick standards, but we have the essentials.' Jürgen rarely smiled but he did so now, with an unfamiliar fond look in his eyes. 'You know, Henry, I've often dreamed of this, that we would work together again.' Henry didn't respond, so Jürgen continued: 'We managed to obtain the same strains of poliovirus and EV 71 that you used in your hybrid. It shouldn't be hard for you to bring it back to life. That's what we do around here, as you've probably gathered.'

' "It may be within my power to take a life. This awesome responsibility must be faced with great humility and awareness of my own frailty",' Henry said. ' "Above all, I must not play at God." '

'Are you quoting something?' Jürgen asked.

'It's the oath I took when I became a physician.'

Jürgen gave him a quizzical look. 'I make no apology for our work here. Playing at God is the only choice we have if we want to save the earth. Consider what humanity has done to the planet. Your brilliant discovery will help restore the balance.'

This is how the great crimes of history begin, Henry thought, with the perpetrators congratulating themselves. 'There's something I've wondered about,' he said. 'That hybrid virus I created was never fatal in the laboratory.'

'Not in mice,' said Jürgen.

'No, not in mice. Which is what still confuses me. I've often thought about that day in the Indian camp. In addition to the humans, there was a dead mouse in one of the huts.'

'A different species, no doubt.'

'Of course, and yet. Was there something different about the "field test," as you called it? So many variables. It troubled me for years. So I decided to see if I could replicate the results of that original experiment. I re-created the same hybrid and gave it to mice. They lost consciousness but fully recovered, exactly as they had done before. There was nothing surprising about this. I tested it in ferrets and guinea pigs with the same result. I had always suspected and hoped to find that the hybrid I created did not kill anyone.'

Jürgen said nothing.

'It took some time for me to figure out how you did it,' Henry continued. 'Only someone with your talent could have imagined the alteration that would take an apparently harmless – what did you call it? An incapacitant? – and engineer it into a massively fatal disease. Only you would have had the skill to modify the virus's genetic control elements to alter the virulence. It took me many trials to achieve the same result in laboratory animals. So I know how you did it, but I still don't understand why. Again and again you told me that the subjects would not be harmed, that this was the humane way of removing an evil from the world.'

Jürgen stared out at the oaks, aflame with color and just beginning to carpet the earth with fallen leaves. 'That's not what the client wanted,' he said quietly.

Henry thought for a moment and said, 'It's not what *you* wanted.'

'Perhaps, yes, I agree,' said Jürgen. 'It was also a test for me. To see if there was a perfect way of annihilating much of humanity. I know what you think when I say those words. But we face a choice, Henry. To save the earth or to allow humanity to continue to wreck it. I have made my choice. If you were totally objective about the situation, you would agree that it is the correct one. I realize that for a man like you, with family, friends, you cannot see the situation clearly. To do so would be inhuman, this is what you think. Of course it is. But this is only because you *are* human. If you had an infestation of termites that was destroying your house, you would think nothing of exterminating them. Because you don't see the situation as a termite does. This is how we are different, then, you and I. For me, the termite and the human, they are equal. They each deserve life. I speak for the other creatures. I defend them. Many people say they do as well, but no one else is willing to impose the only solution that will work, which is to reduce the human population to the point that precious life forms other than our own are preserved.'

'There are better ways of preserving life,' said Henry. 'Even right here – they showed me – you are bringing extinct forms back into existence.'

'Insufficient,' said Jürgen. 'The earth is ransacked by

extinctions every hour. We cannot hope to make a real difference.'

'You don't really expect me to help you in this insane endeavor, do you?' Henry asked. 'I don't know why you sent for me.'

Jürgen smiled awkwardly. 'I can't hide the truth from you. That's always been a problem. You're correct. To make the virus again, this is not impossible. I have done it already. But I need you, because there is no one else in the world who can stand in my way. No one else who knows the virus so well, no one else who could possibly create a vaccine or a cure. And so you must stay until we are finished.'

Henry went to the door. It was locked.

'Henry, you can't just walk out of here. The compound is totally secure.'

'There's no point in holding me,' Henry said.

'I seem cruel, I know. If there were a god, I would be damned, I am sure of it. But we have no gods, do we, Henry? We, who have the ultimate power to create and destroy, must act in their place.'

'What we created was a mistake,' Henry said. 'It should never have been brought back to life.'

Jürgen shook his head dismissively. 'As I said, you will remain here until the contagion has done its job. I'm doing you a favor, Henry. As a prisoner, you don't have to take on the moral guilt. It is all on me. I doubt you understand, but I've agonized over this. I'm not mad, you know. The world will be better because of what we do.'

'When I discovered how you manipulated the virus, I realized you would probably use it again,' Henry said. 'And so I spent many precious hours studying its secrets. And I succeeded, Jürgen, I've cured *Enterovirus parsons*. Now my name will not be associated with the genocide you intend to inflict.'

'Unlikely,' Jürgen said. 'This virus is very complex.'

'I've published the details on the internet already. By now, you should have an email from Maria Savona at WHO describing the virus and its treatment.'

Jürgen looked at him uncertainly, then checked his email. The letter from Maria was part of a worldwide health advisory. Jürgen was quiet as he read through the technical details. After a moment, he looked up. 'It's beautiful work, Henry. I wish you hadn't done it.'

Jürgen walked to the glass wall and stood silently for a moment. 'I suppose I should have you killed,' he said, almost as if he were asking permission.

'You can do with me what you will. But I will not go back into the laboratory.'

'They'll carry on without us anyway,' Jürgen said. His expression was oddly serene. 'You should accept this, Henry. Our participation is of no consequence. The diseases are being liberated even as we talk. This is humanity's chosen means of suicide.'

Jürgen picked up his phone and called for Heidi. 'Dr Parsons is leaving now,' he said. 'Let him go.'

55

October Revolution Island

THE MESSAGE WAS BRIEF: 35.101390, -77.047523, 10/31, 0630.

Just before dawn on Halloween, Henry sat with Helen and Teddy at a picnic table in a public park on a spit of land at the juncture of the Trent and Neuse rivers, near New Bern, North Carolina, where the GPS coordinates indicated they should wait. It promised to be a crisp and beautiful day, the last they would see for quite a while. Henry did not want to unsettle his children with that news, even though they were not the people he remembered. They were harder. He thought: The children of the future will be like this.

The second wave of Kongoli was sweeping across the globe. Doctors were frantically learning Henry's variolation technique to stem the contagion. Meantime, viruses that had been engineered in laboratories were making their debut, attacking weakened and vulnerable populations. The first great biowar was under way, and, unlike all other wars, no one could stop it.

The sky lightened. Just across the barrier islands the Atlantic awaited, vast and indifferent. The tide was in and water spilled over a retaining wall that had been built long before global warming raised the seas. Coastal communities like this one were in retreat. Henry imagined the great cities of the world sinking into the ocean like Atlantis, one after another.

Teddy walked down to the edge of the water and began skipping stones.

'See those clouds?' Henry asked Helen as the sun came up. 'They're called stratocumulus. They usually mean a great storm is coming.'

Helen took in the clouds, which were streaked in vermillion. 'They're beautiful,' she said.

'Remember this day,' Henry said. Helen nodded. She didn't ask why.

As Teddy was about to throw another rock, something shifted in the river. He took a step back. Suddenly an immense form rose to the surface. It seemed to fill up the whole river. It was the USS *Georgia*.

As Captain Dixon appeared on the bridge, a group of SEALs paddled a rubber launch to the shore. Henry had told his children they could bring only a few changes of clothes that could fit in their backpacks. He had brought a weathered leather case that held his high school clarinet.

'Extra crew?' Dixon said.

'They're pretty competent,' Henry said.

'Well, they may come in handy. We're shorthanded. This is an all-volunteer mission.'

Dixon let the children stand on the bridge as the submarine navigated through the tidal river into the Atlantic. By the time they reached the continental shelf the sun was high and it was time to dive.

Murphy was waiting in the pharmacy. Henry introduced her to his children as Murphy, but she told them, 'You can call me Sarah.'

The *Georgia* navigated north, rounding Labrador, threading a path through the shallow waters of Baffin Bay into the Arctic, where it lurked under the ice, two hundred miles off the coast of Siberia. Captain Dixon was shocked by how fractured the Arctic had become in the two years since he last had gone under the polar cap. There were now large stretches of open water called polynyas, where the submarine could rise to periscope depth and receive messages in brief coded bursts. The messages now came from the National Airborne Operations Centers, which meant that the president and other key members of government were operating from Doomsday airborne command posts while the biowar raged.

The *Georgia* was one of the two Ohio-class submarines equipped with SEAL Delivery Vehicles, submersible pods that allowed a team of commandos to carry out clandestine operations at some distance from the boat. The battery-powered SDVs were small and quiet and nearly undetectable.

Henry met with the SEAL team that would accompany him. 'We are not acting as warriors but as historians,' he told them. 'One day, people will ask, "Who did this to us?" And we will have the evidence. History will make its judgments based on what we find.'

The burly leader of the SEAL team, Lieutenant Cooksey, openly worried about Henry's ability to accompany them. 'We train for this,' he said. He didn't have to mention that they all looked like they could play in the NFL.

'I'm the only one who knows what we're looking for,' Henry said curtly. No one was going to keep him from this mission.

Before the team entered the SDV, Henry went to talk to his children. Teddy's leg was jiggling as it did when he was really worried. 'It's cold in the water,' Teddy said. 'I'm worried you'll freeze.'

'They have special suits,' Henry said. 'I'll be back in time for dinner. And then we'll stay underwater until the war is over. We'll be safe.'

Helen didn't say anything, but her eyes were brimming. She embraced Henry and then took Teddy's hand.

Murphy whispered, 'I'll take care of them.'

Henry went into the lock-out chamber with eleven members of the SEAL team. It had been a long time since he had put on scuba gear. The last occasion had been in the tropical Bahamas, when he hadn't even needed a wetsuit. In these frigid waters, divers required a dry suit – a far more complicated apparatus. Henry followed the steps that Lieutenant Cooksey modeled for him. The divers were already wearing quilted jumpsuits and thick woolen socks. Cooksey showed him how to open the double-zippered top, which ran from one shoulder to the navel and back to the other shoulder, exactly like an autopsy incision. Henry crawled inside and reached into each arm of the suit, pushing until his fingers were deep inside the neoprene gloves of the suit itself. It was a struggle to get his large head through the neck seal. Cooksey helped him with the tanks and regulators, then Henry put on the mask and pulled the edge of the hood over the lip of the mask so that water didn't leak through. He felt as if he were inside a balloon. He gave a thumbs-up to Cooksey.

The men carried their fins and climbed into the two dry-deck shelters containing the submersibles. The pilot and copilot took their places at the front of the vehicle, and then the ports opened and Arctic water flooded the open pods – frigid even with all the insulation inside the dry suit. After about forty-five minutes, when the chambers were fully flooded, the hangar doors opened and the two SDVs were manually guided out into the sea. They hung in the water like a pair of baby whales. The *Georgia* lay beneath them, like a sunken galleon. And then they began to move.

There was life down here: fanning beds of kelp, algae hanging like moss from the underside of ice floes, and tiny fish with residual fins slithering snakelike through the water. A walrus took a look, then scurried away. Henry thought of nature's abundance and wondered what mankind was doing to it at this very moment.

It took an hour to get to the designated insertion area. The pilot signaled to the other submersible and they came to a halt. One by one the SEALs swam out of the pods. Henry was the last to emerge. He swam through a cloud of cod. When his head emerged from the water, two SEALs grabbed him under the arms and lifted him onto the narrow rocky shore.

Removing his mask, he saw low-lying glacial mountains in the distance. Between the coast and the mountains a retreating ice field exposed a barren tundra. The most remote place in the world, Henry thought; no wonder the Soviets had chosen it. His map indicated that the biological warfare plant was half a mile inland, behind an icy hillock. The SEALs took a moment to prepare their weapons, then began their approach.

Although it was midafternoon, the polar sun was low, and their footsteps made a sucking noise as they trudged through the slushy tundra in the autumnal twilight. Henry was slowing everybody down. Cooksey motioned to his team, which spread out in formation to approach the factory from different angles. When they got to the hillock, Henry and Cooksey climbed a ways up and knelt behind the crest. Cooksey looked through his field glasses, then passed them to Henry.

The factory was half buried in a snowdrift. Nothing emerged from the three towering smokestacks. Nearby was an old railroad track with telephone poles running beside it, but no lines on the poles.

Cooksey waved the team forward.

They came to the entrance, a barn-like door, wide open. Inside, remnants of the lab were still in place, warming ovens and vats that may have held anthrax or smallpox. Perhaps they still did. What was clear was that they had not made Kongoli in this place. The lab had been abandoned for decades, probably since the Soviet Union had dissolved.

Cooksey looked at Henry. 'Are we done here, doc?'

Henry walked out of the decrepit building into the dim Arctic light. Cooksey gestured for the team to retrace their steps. 'You go on,' said Henry. 'There's something else I have to see. You can wait for me.'

'You're not going anywhere alone, doc,' said Cooksey. 'How far are we talking about?'

'It's another mile, I'm afraid.'

'What are we looking for?'

'Dead polar bears.'

In the soggy tundra, the hike took more than an hour of

precious twilight. Henry followed the coordinates on his GPS device, indicating where the bears had stopped moving. They would be in a rather tight circle, and they should be fairly well preserved in this climate, even with the melting permafrost. There were few predators here, other than the bears themselves.

At first, Henry didn't see them. The white of their fur looked like patches of snow, but once he saw one, the entire group came into view, about ten of them. They lay on the ground, deflated by death.

'Jeez, what the hell is that?' one of the SEALs said, pointing at what looked like a log.

Under an apron of snow, Henry saw something large that had emerged from the melting ice. It wasn't a log. It was a tusk.

Henry used his map to brush the snow away, exposing a giant face. The furry torso had been ripped apart by the polar bears.

'It's a mammoth,' said Henry. 'Don't touch it. It's contaminated with Kongoli.'

The SEALs backed away. They were the only people in the world who knew what had happened.

'Well, doc, what are we going to tell history?' Cooksey asked.

Henry looked up. The last flock of Siberian cranes had taken flight, headed for China.

'We're going to say that we did this to ourselves.'

Acknowledgments

I could not have written this book without the assistance of some of the most knowledgeable figures in the field of public health. In the early days of my research, I was aided by the distinguished microbe hunter Ian Lipkin, the director of the Center for Infection and Immunity at Columbia University. Professor Lipkin did me the favor of lending me his research assistant Lan Quan, now a senior scientist at Stony Brook University. Lan patiently explained many of the laboratory procedures used in these pages. Others who gave so generously of their time and expertise include Jamie Lee Barnabei, a veterinary medical officer at National Veterinary Services Laboratories in Ames, Iowa; Guy L. Clifton, MD; Sally Ann Iverson, a veterinary epidemiologist; Larry Minnix, retired CEO of LeadingAge; and Curtis Suttle, professor in the Faculty of Science at the University of British Columbia.

I have to single out a very patient group of sources who not only sat for lengthy interviews but also read all or large portions of the manuscript for accuracy. I owe them a debt that I can only acknowledge here but never actually repay. They include: Philip Bobbitt, professor of law at Columbia University; Richard A. Clarke (who also loaned out his persona), chairman of Good Harbor Consulting and Good Harbour International; Dr Philip R. Dormitzer, chief scientific officer of viral vaccines at Pfizer; Dr Barney Graham, a viral immunologist and vaccine expert from Bethesda, Maryland; Kendall Hoyt, assistant professor at the Geisel School of Medicine at Dartmouth College; Sally Ann Iverson, a veterinary epidemiologist; Jens Kuhn at NIH/NIAID/ Integrated Research Facility at Fort Detrick, Maryland; Emily Lankau, a veterinary epidemiologist at the Ronin Institute (who also makes a real-life appearance herein); Admiral (Ret.) William H. McRaven; and Dr Seema Yasmin, professor of science journalism and global health storytelling at Stanford University.

I owe a special thanks to Lieutenant Katherine A. Diener, the public affairs officer for Submarine Group 10 at Kings Bay, Georgia. Thanks to her kindness, I was able to take a tour of the USS *Tennessee* (SSBN-734), overseen by Commander Paul Seitz, and got to meet the boat's very capable and welcoming Blue Crew. Lieutenant Tyler Whitmore and Executive Officer Lieutenant Commander James Kepper showed me around this formidable instrument of war. I was also able to talk to a number of submarine officers who spoke very candidly about their underwater lives: Assistant Operations Officer Lieutenant Steve Hucks, Culinary Specialist 2nd Class Santos Alarcón, Information Systems Technician (Sub) Chief Ryan Doyle, Senior Chief Hospital Corpsman Ricardo Parr, Operations Officer Commander Justin Kaper, and Deputy Chief of Staff Commander Chris Horgan. Captain Mike Riegel at the Submarine Force Museum in Groton, Connecticut, and Vice Admiral (Ret.)

Acknowledgments

Albert H. Konetzni Jr also gave me the benefit of their considerable expertise.

As always, Stephen Harrigan read the first draft and provided useful guidance on the writing. The germ of this story was originally proposed by filmmaker Ridley Scott. Thanks to him and to Michael Ellenberg for their creative input.

I've been lucky to have the best people to work with in my professional career, and that certainly includes my agent, Andrew Wylie, and my editor, Ann Close, along with all my talented colleagues at Knopf, and to Edward Kastenmeier and Caitlin Landuyt at Vintage.